TERRA AND IMPERIUM

BOOK THREE
OF THE DUCHY OF TERRA TRILOGY

TERRA AND IMPERIUM

BOOK THREE
OF THE DUCHY OF TERRA TRILOGY

GLYNN STEWART

FAOLAN'S PEN
PUBLISHING
faolanspen.com

This edition published in 2018 by:

Faolan's Pen Publishing Inc.

22 King St. S, Suite 300

Waterloo, Ontario

N2J 1N8 Canada

ISBN-13: 978-1-988035-47-5 (print)

A record of this book is available from Library and Archives Canada.

Printed in the United States of America

1 2 3 4 5 6 7 8 9 10

First edition

First printing: August 2017

Illustration © 2017 Tom Edwards

TomEdwardsDesign.com

Read more books from Glynn Stewart at faolanspen.com

CHAPTER ONE

THE WOMAN IN THE VIDEO HAD BEEN DEAD FOR THREE YEARS. Captain Elizabeth Sade had been killed with her command, *Queen of England*, in the desperate battle to defend Earth from the Kanzi assault.

Three years to the day. Captain Harold Rolfson was *usually* better about not torturing himself with could-have-beens and would-have-beens than this, but on the anniversary of his lover's death, he'd dug out the old videos they'd made when they'd returned to Earth and before everything had gone to hell again.

It was extremely early in the morning by the ship's clock aboard *Liberty*, and few of the heavy cruiser's sounds filtered into the Captain's cabin. She floated in hyperspace, roughly one light-year away from the Alpha Centauri system—real-world distances didn't map neatly to the strangely fluid dimension the species of the galaxy used for faster-than-light travel—and *Liberty* was always a quiet ship at any point.

The video frame that hung on Harold's wall normally held a slowing rotating image of *Liberty* herself, recorded at her commissioning six months before. She'd been the first of the Duchy of Terra's new heavy cruisers, a combination of native technology and the skill and knowledge of their Imperial overlords.

It could be switched to show anything, however, and right now it showed the ethereal blonde Harold hadn't realized how much he'd loved until it had been too late, allowing the Captain his allocated time of self-pitying moping where no one could see him.

The alert chime rang through his quarters with its carefully calibrated attention-gathering song.

A tapped command restored the video frame to its default, and Harold rose to face the intercom, letting the cabin's system recognize that he was responding to the call and link it through.

"Captain Rolfson," he greeted. "What's going on?"

"Sorry to wake you, sir," his tactical officer, Nida Lyon, greeted him from the small video screen. "We have something odd on the anomaly scanner and I wanted to get your take on it."

The officer on duty's job was to inform the Captain if she thought he was needed, so Harold simply nodded.

"What have we got, Lieutenant Commander?" he asked.

"It looks like several anomalies moving in convoy toward Centauri, but their approach vector doesn't line up with any known currents or Imperial star systems," she replied. "I make it four ships, moving at point six cee."

Harold whistled silently. *Liberty* was a *Thunderstorm*-class cruiser, built, like the Duchess's old cruiser *Tornado*, to do everything as well as possible regardless of cost—and her reactionless interface drive could pull point six cee for only limited "sprint" maneuvers.

"That's not a colonist convoy," he noted. Any of those would be coming from Sol along the carefully mapped currents. "Or Imperial, either."

There were two hundred thousand people at the colony in Centauri. Technically, their protection was the responsibility of the Imperial Navy...but since Sol was nearby and the colonists were human, *Liberty* was there.

"Any identifiers?" he asked.

"Nothing," Lyon replied. The anomaly scanner didn't give them much to work with—all it really told them was that someone's drive existed and how fast it was moving.

"I'll be on the bridge momentarily," Harold told her, then paused to consider.

"Take us to Condition Two. This doesn't feel right."

THE DIMMED HALLWAY lighting of a night-shift watch had returned to the bright of full operations by the time Harold left his cabin. Condition Two had alerts going off all over the ship, but they were quieter things than the full battle-stations alert, targeted by the ship's computer systems to the crew members who needed to join the night shift.

Liberty had been designed by Terrans based on Imperial technology and a few things Harold wasn't supposed to talk about. Less modular than *Tornado*, the first hyperspace ship Harold had served on, it had also been designed by a Militia that had earned its spurs in battle.

The most immediate consequence of that was that the Captain's cabin was less than twelve steps from the bridge, and Harold entered the massive two-tiered horseshoe that ran his warship mere moments after telling Lyon he'd be there.

The Captain wasn't an immense man, but he'd long since cultivated his long red hair and bushy beard into an image far larger than he was. Technically, his hair was a violation of the uniform regulations the Militia had inherited from the pre-Annexation United Earth Space Force, but *Tornado*'s original crew were given more slack than others.

"Report, Lyon," he ordered, dropping into the command chair on the raised dais at the center of the bridge. Repeater screens, carefully designed to allow the Captain to understand just what all of his senior officers were looking at, folded in around him, the computer easily remembering his usual preference for their positions.

"We've solidified our scans," the bleached-blonde tactical officer told him briskly. "We've confirmed four targets moving in a formation approximately one hundred thousand kilometers across. They're definitely en route to Alpha Centauri, and we make it over ninety percent likely they're heading directly for Hope."

Hope was a chilly world, only semi-habitable by human standards, but its proximity had made it humanity's first colony under the auspices of their new alien overlords.

"Commander Popovitch." Harold turned to his communications officer. "Per the last update when we left Sol, what's the Centauri picket's strength?"

"Two of our *Capital*-class destroyers, two Imperial *Sunlight*-class light cruisers and four Imperial *Descendant*-class destroyers," Nazar Popovitch reeled off instantly. "Only the *Capital*s and one of the *Sunlight*s have been upgraded to the full new defensive specifications."

Three years of work by the rapidly expanding yards in Sol, and the Imperial Navy still lacked non-shield passive and active defenses on many of their non-capital ships. The Duchy of Terra Militia, however, had *designed* the new specifications.

The three fully upgraded ships would be a problem, but *Liberty* could probably have taken the entire Centauri picket herself.

"Lieutenant Malie, do you have an intercept worked up?" Harold asked the junior officer currently in charge of his cruiser's navigation. The young Hawaiian woman was the third-ranking member of the department, but with neither of her superiors on the bridge yet...

"Yes, sir," she replied crisply, her braids swinging gently as she turned to face him. Only her eyes showed her nervousness at being on the spot. "If we go to flank speed in the next sixty seconds, we can intercept them ten minutes short of the gravity limit. If this is their full speed, we can stay with them in sprint mode the rest of the way."

"That gets us inside the visibility zone?" he checked. There was no point catching up to the strangers without getting inside the one-light-second range where *Liberty* could actually see anything beyond their drives.

"If they don't adjust course, intercept will be at seventy thousand kilometers," Malie confirmed, and Harold made a mental checkmark next to her name. Her quiet night watch had turned into a potential combat situation and she'd manage to get everything right.

Not bad for being two months out of the new Academy.

"Execute at your discretion, Lieutenant," he ordered. "Lyon: I want all of our launchers loaded and the proton beams charged before we enter the visibility zone.

"These guys aren't supposed to be here. They might be lost, but *nobody* should have four warships swanning around this close to Sol that we don't know about."

———

THE STRANGE SHIPS didn't appear to react to *Liberty*'s approach, continuing on their course for Alpha Centauri like the big cruiser wasn't even there. If the Terrans could see them, however, Harold was quite certain the unknowns could see his ship.

"Time to visibility zone is just over five minutes, Captain," Malie told him.

"We are in missile range," Lyon added. "I have them dialed in as best as I can, but..."

"But that barely qualifies as a lock," Harold acknowledged. "Stand by all launchers anyway. Spin up Sword and Buckler, too—they might not be as conservative."

His repeater screens showed the response to his order, as the cruiser's anti-missile laser turrets rotated slowly, checking all of their bearings were working, and four of her defensive drones dropped free of their docking points.

He was far more likely to lose the drones in hyperspace, but the whole situation was making him nervous. He couldn't even talk to the ships until he reached the visibility zone, but their sustained speed was unusual.

They might be Core Power ships, which...shouldn't be out this far. Terra was the far end of the A!Tol Imperium from the Core, easily a thousand light-years away from where any ship that could pull that speed should be.

"Vampire!" Lyon suddenly snapped. "I have anomaly separation, multiple missiles inbound."

"Battle stations!" Harold replied. "Full active defenses; give me numbers and speed."

His tactical officer inhaled loudly enough that the Captain could hear it, and flipped the data to his repeater screens rather than giving it aloud.

Four ships had launched sixty missiles—all of them closing on his command at point eight five light. Ten percent of lightspeed faster than his own missiles could reach, and he was supposed to have the best in the sector.

His anti-missile lasers were only going to have fractions of a second to engage either way, but fractions of a second could make all of the difference. This was going to hurt.

"Understood," he told Lyon loudly. "You are clear to return fire, Commander Lyon. Focus on one target and give them a full salvo."

"Yes, sir," she replied, her voice steadying as she spoke. "Launchers one through thirty online, targeting Bandit One. Fire."

Harold laced his fingers together and studied the screens around him. The number of launchers meant he was facing destroyers or light cruisers, but the speed of the missiles strongly implied he *was* facing Core ships, which...was bad.

They'd have stronger shields, better maneuverability, and more effective active defenses. *Liberty* probably outmassed all four ships combined, but if they were Core warships, his command was badly outgunned.

And they'd opened fire first.

"NAVIGATION, bring us parallel to their course and activate the sprint systems," Harold ordered after the immediate shock had faded. Even at eighty-five percent of lightspeed, they had some time to respond.

"Lyon, push the Buckler platforms out to a quarter-million kilometers," he continued. "We're more likely to simply lose them out there, but we need the extra depth against birds this fast."

The drone platforms moved out, almost doubling *Liberty*'s visibility zone in the direction of the missiles before they engaged. Rapid-cycling lasers, unimaginably powerful to men and women who'd served in Earth's Pre-Annexation military, opened up from the remote platforms.

It was over in seconds, faster than any human could process what was going on. Once the missiles arrived, it was all down to computers and the semi-sentient artificial intelligences managing them. Even moving the drones out gave the computers less than two seconds with the missiles in the visibility zone.

The Sword and Buckler system was designed for exactly that problem. The four drones opened fire first, their lasers cutting through the missiles the moment they emerged from the strange "fog" of hyperspace, and their sensors relaying their data back to *Liberty* herself.

Then the turrets opened fire, the invisible lasers drawn into the main holographic plots as clean white lines as missile after missile died.

It wasn't enough. Harold had known it wouldn't be enough from the moment the strangers had opened fire, and warnings flashed on his screen as missiles hammered home into his cruiser's shields.

"Shields are holding," Lyon reported. "Detecting no active defenses; all of our birds hit home."

"Who the hell has point eight five missiles and no active defenses?" Harold demanded. "ETA to Centauri?"

"Twelve minutes," Malie reported quietly before her freshly arrived boss could answer.

"Bogies launching a second salvo," Lyon added. "I make it a fifty-second cycle time."

That, too, didn't add up. *Liberty* had launched two salvos while the bogies had launched one, but the bogies were packing missiles the Terran ship couldn't match.

"Hold the range," Harold ordered. "Keep pounding them and get the second layer of Bucklers out."

"They're clearing the boat bay in sixty seconds," his executive officer told him, the younger man finally linking in from secondary control. Mohammed Saab was a competent officer, one of the few Militia officers of his rank who wasn't a veteran of the UESF, but he slept more heavily than Harold preferred for a naval officer.

"Running all of the data we're getting into the warbook," Saab continued. "It's not lining up with anything we know of the Core Powers—all of them have equivalent missiles, but they *all* have active defenses of some kind."

"Their shields are damn tough too," Lyon added. "My birds are smart, they'll all have hit the same target, so we've pumped sixty point-seven-five missiles into something that looks destroyer-sized."

"And they haven't even flickered," Harold acknowledged grimly as another set of warnings flashed across his screen. He couldn't say the same for *Liberty*'s shields. She'd taken fewer hits, but an extra ten percent of lightspeed *doubled* the energy of the impacts.

"Second layer of Bucklers deploying."

Another four of the drones spilled out into hyperspace, their own interface drives lighting up as they maneuvered out to protect their mothership—just barely in time to get in the way of the third salvo.

Not in time *enough*. The big cruiser's shields flickered longer this time, a localized failure in the iridescent energy field that protect Harold's command, and three of the missiles made it through.

Liberty rang like a gong, vibration tearing through the ship and sending unsecured objects flying as her armor held.

"Engineering, damage report!" Harold snapped.

"Still here," Lieutenant Commander Min-Ji Moon replied crisply. "But diagnostics show armor plates are *dented*. That...is not supposed to happen. Support structure intact, some vibration damage. Sending drones to shore up."

Harold's ship's armor was hyper-compressed matter, not to the level of a neutron star but certainly sufficient to withstand almost any force without breaking. For it to have *dented*...he'd underestimated how dangerous the incoming missiles were.

"Keep me advised," he ordered Moon. "Lyon! I need you to kill one of these bastards for me!"

"I can't *see* them well enough to know if I'm doing anything," the tactical officer replied. "All I can say for sure is that it looks like my missiles are hitting them, but the anomaly scanner just tells me they're still there!"

"How long until they enter Centauri now?" Harold asked.

"Eight minutes," Lieutenant Commander Tristan Cuesta responded with a sharp glance at Malie. It looked like Harold was going to have to have a word with his senior navigator—if they lived.

"Third layer of Bucklers is out; shields held against the last salvo," Saab replied. "That's all of our Bucklers deployed, Captain. If they can't take down enough to keep the shields intact..."

"Whoever these bastards are, they're not going to let us run at this point," *Liberty*'s Captain pointed out. "Moon: start feeding the plasma capacitors for the lance."

His XO and tactical officer were silent for several seconds.

"Sir, I thought we weren't—"

"—supposed to use the plasma lance except in critical situations," Harold agreed with Saab. "Commander, if *we* can't stop these bastards, the Centauri picket definitely won't be able to!"

"Cuesta, Malie, cut the angle, I want to drop out of hyperspace two light-seconds from the bastards. Lyon, keep pounding them with missiles. Saab, set up a proton-beam and plasma-lance alpha strike for the moment we come through the portal."

Neither the A!Tol Imperium nor the Duchy of Terra was supposed to have plasma lances, an obsolete weapon by Core Power standards that was still almost a century ahead of the Imperium's technology. The Duchy, however, had acquired some unusual immigrants who had been *very* helpful in designing their new generation of warships.

"We're holding against the missiles now, mostly," Saab told him after the next salvo came in. "That won't last once we're in normal space; hyper screws the missiles up almost as badly as it screws up our defenses."

"That, Commander, is why I want you to *kill the bastards* once we're in Centauri," Harold ordered calmly.

CHAPTER TWO

LIBERTY'S SENSORS HAD A MOMENTARY, BADLY DISTORTED glimpse of the Alpha Centauri system as the strangers ripped open the hyper portal and dove through. It wasn't enough to give them any data at all, not with them several million kilometers away in hyperspace, but it was enough to allow them to localize the strangers' emergence point.

That, in turn, allowed Cuesta and Malie to mark the distance for their own hyper portal. Four and a half seconds after their quarry entered normal space, *Liberty* followed them, tearing a hole back into reality that should have brought them out barely four hundred thousand kilometers from the unknowns.

Cuesta, however, had guessed wrong. They'd emerged "ahead" of the strange ship's origin point, along the course toward Hope, but the hostile had instead swung "around", orbiting around the nearest of Centauri's suns on a course that brought them nearer to the colony but indirectly.

"Range?" Harold asked after watching the plot take shape.

"Unknowns are at two million kilometers and the range is growing," Lyon reported. "Targeting with missiles, but they are well out of range for beams or the lance."

"Understood," he accepted. "Popovitch, hail the picket," he continued. "Dump our data and advise them that the unknowns have fired on a Ducal vessel. We are formally requesting the assistance of the Imperial Navy."

Despite the Duchy of Terra's heavy involvement with the system, even the Terran-built ships orbiting the colony were units of the Imperial Navy. The Duchy of Terra was the majority shareholder of the Centauri Colonization Corporation but, and the Imperium was quite clear on this, Centauri was *not* part of the Duchy of Terra.

Hope was an Imperial world and the Imperial Navy would defend her—not that those rules had prevented three quarters of the Imperial personnel in orbit of Hope from being human, or from the Navy making sure that the picket was under the command of one of the exactly two human flag officers in the Imperial Navy.

"Sir, warbook has a tentative ID on the hostiles," Saab informed Harold. "They can't identify the class, but they're definitely destroyers and..."

"I'm not liking the sound of this, Commander," *Liberty*'s Captain said into the silence his XO had left.

"Sir. Computers make it sixty percent likely we're looking at Kanzi warships of an unknown design," the XO concluded.

"The Kanzi don't have missiles or shields like those," Harold said, watching as Lyon's latest salvo slammed home amongst the destroyers. *Now* he could see their shields flickering under the pounding, but if they'd managed to keep even half of their fire focused on a single target, that meant those destroyers had tougher shields than his cruiser.

"That's why it's tentative," Saab replied, an alert blaring behind him as *Liberty*'s shields flickered again. "Basics metrics on the drive and design structures are definitely Kanzi, but weapons, shields, engine power...all of those are way off from what we expect from the smurfs."

The Kanzi looked a *lot* like humans built on a three-quarters scale with blue fur. Their slave-taking theocracy was also the second most powerful empire in this region of space, and they'd tried to conquer Sol for themselves.

"The Kanzi don't want another war right now," Harold muttered, half to himself. "Intel says they've barely begun deploying active defenses and don't have CM armor, let alone shields ten times stronger than ours and point eight five missiles!"

"I don't know, sir," Saab told him. "I'm studying the scans and the imaging, and I don't think the computer's wrong, but... The tech is wrong, but the design...the design is Kanzi to the bone."

"Well, it's not going to matter today," Harold concluded. "Get me Division Lord Harrison. I don't care who these bastards are at this point, they are *not* reaching Hope!"

DIVISION LORD ALEXANDER HARRISON of the A!Tol Imperial Navy was an older man with steel-gray hair cropped short in the style that had been common among senior United Earth Space Force officers—designed to go under the tighter vac-suit helmets of forty years earlier.

"We received your report, Captain Rolfson," his recorded image told *Liberty*'s commander. "Our own scans have come up blank as well; we have no idea who these ships are.

"Nonetheless, they have attacked a Ducal vessel without provocation. I am deploying my ships to intercept and summoning them to surrender in the name of the Empress."

Harrison didn't seem to find his own words particularly strange, though Harold certainly found it incongruous. Harrison might have signed on with Earth's conquerors after they'd proven their bona fides by losing half a fleet defending Sol, but he'd once been a Rear Admiral in the UESF.

"I recommend that you fall back and stay at extreme range until we've intercepted the strangers," Harrison continued. "While this system is Imperial responsibility, I'm not going to turn down your help dealing with an unknown threat.

"We will coordinate as best we can. I make it twelve minutes from your receipt of this message until we reach our own missile range of the intruders. Do me the favor of staying alive, Captain Rolfson."

Harold chuckled.

"I fully intend to, people," he told his crew. "Cuesta, pull us back to nine million kilometers. Let's see if their computers are good enough to compensate for thirty seconds of lightspeed lag."

The interface drive meant his ship didn't noticeably suffer from relativistic dilation, but his sensors and his communications were still limited to speed of light. *Liberty*'s missiles could travel nine million kilometers, but she couldn't reliably hit an evading target with modern drives at that range.

Hopefully, neither could the strange Kanzi ships.

"We got one!" Lyon suddenly announced as they fell back. "Shields are failing on Bogey One, multiple hits clean through— damn! She's still intact."

Harold focused one of his repeater screens on Bogey One, studying the recording of the hits. The shields had gone down, flickering and coming back up after a few moments but allowing four of Lyon's missiles to strike home.

"We got a piece of her but she's still flying," he said softly. "CM armor, no question about it."

"But no active defenses," Saab replied from the secondary control. "That doesn't line up with intel about the Kanzi at all."

"Whatever these people are, we're going to have to ask questions of anyone we take alive," Harold said grimly. "For now, keep pounding Bogey One and make sure Harrison's people know we hit her."

As he spoke, *Liberty* lurched again, her own shields flickering and allowing two more of the terrifyingly fast missiles through.

"Plates holding," Moon reported instantly. "Support structure badly fracturing. Next hits will break plates off."

That was not good at all.

"Cuesta, pull us back out of range until Harrison moves in," Harold ordered. "I can't believe I'm running from four goddamn destroyers, but I am *not* losing this ship when I have reinforcements close to hand.

"Keep us dancing," he continued. "I don't trust their range to be our range, not when they've got a tenth-of-lightspeed advantage on their missile drives."

ALMOST AS SOON AS *Liberty* had fallen back out of range, the intruders turned inward, heading toward Harrison's picket force—and for Hope itself.

"Bogey One is leaking atmosphere," Lyon reported as the Terran cruiser swung around in the enemy's wake. "We hit her pretty hard, but she's keeping up with the rest of their force."

Harold nodded silently. *Liberty* was currently running at flank speed, falling even farther out of range every second as the attacker's speed advantage pulled them forward.

"No sprint for at least five minutes," Moon told him. "Then only ninety seconds. All you'll get today."

"We've already run at sprint for longer than we're supposed to," he confirmed. "Thank you, Lieutenant Commander."

"What's the plan, sir?" Saab asked. "Harrison is six minutes from range, but if we couldn't take these bastards..."

"Harrison has eight ships, not one, and three of them are modern," Harold reminded Saab. "But you're right, XO. I'm not leaving half a dozen destroyers and light cruisers to face off with a fleet that gave us a run for our money.

"Cuesta: thirty seconds before Harrison hits range, I want full sprint mode right up their tailpipes," he ordered. "If they think point six is the best we can do, let's give them a shock. If all we can do is push them further into Harrison's grasp, fine, but I want lance range if you can give it to me."

"We'll only have six thousand KPS on them even at full sprint," the navigator said. "Cutting the angle means we'll pull into missile range a few seconds after Harrison, but unless they run back at us, there is no way I can give you lance range, sir."

"Fair," Harold acknowledged. "Get us in range for the missiles and then keep an eye on their course for me. If they turn, I want us to cut the vector. They're between us and Hope now; they shouldn't be able to get out of this system without coming within our beam range."

"Yes, sir."

"Harrison has hailed them three times, sir," Popovitch reported. "Imperial frequencies, Kanzi frequencies and general multinational emergency frequencies." The dark-haired Ukrainian man shook his head.

"Dead silence on all frequencies. They don't want to talk to us."

"Then this discussion continues in the only language they appear willing to try," Harold told him. "Until they either talk or we've blown them to hell."

Or, somehow, four apparently Kanzi destroyers took out over four times their tonnage in Imperial warships, with all the horror that implied for the current balance of power. It was the Captain's job to portray confidence, though, which meant that was a thought he couldn't share.

THE FOUR DESTROYERS continued on a head-on course for Hope, giving the eight ships coming to meet them about the same attention as they were giving *Liberty* trailing in their wake. The lead *Sunlight*-class ship was Division Lord Harrison's flagship, *Gleaming Dawn*—an A!Tol-built, Terran-upgraded, light cruiser with the same style of defensive suite as *Liberty*.

The two *Capital*-class destroyers also equipped with the modern defenses flanked *Dawn*, while the five ships without followed in a second echelon behind Harrison's flagship. The *Descendant*-class ships carried more modern beam weapons than the *Capitals* but lacked the updated defenses of the Terran-modified destroyers.

"Harrison is in range in thirty seconds," Cuesta reported. "Going to full sprint."

Despite Moon's assurances that the cruiser could do it, Harold found himself holding his breath as *Liberty* lurched to her full power.

"Stabilizing at sixty-two point six percent of lightspeed," the navigator concluded. "Our missile range in forty-five seconds from...now."

"Launchers armed. I have the bastards dialed in as cleanly as possible and the Bucklers deployed," Lyon confirmed. "Harrison is firing, focusing on Bogey One."

"He's the anvil. Let's play hammer. Time our salvos to arrive simultaneously with his," Harold ordered. "Let's see if Bogey One's shields can take *that*."

The answer was rapidly proven to be no.

Between the three cruisers and six destroyers, Bogey One was the target of over a hundred missiles, and her shields had clearly been damaged by the earlier hits. A single missile—one of *Liberty*'s—punched through from the first salvo and sent the destroyer tumbling, her drive momentarily disabled.

It never came back up, as the second hundred-plus-missile salvo slammed home. Bogey One's shields collapsed completely, and at least fifty missiles moving at three-quarters of the speed of light struck home.

"One down," Harold said calmly. "Well done, Lyon. Coordinate with Task Group Centauri and let's send the rest to join them!"

"Sprint is done," Cuesta warned. "We're losing ground; we're only going to have missile range for two more salvos."

Harold nodded, watching the range suddenly start increasing

even faster than it had been dropping—and the range between Harrison and the attackers was coming down even faster.

"In just over a minute, they're going to hit beam range of Harrison's fleet and punch right through him," Saab said quietly in his ear. "What the hell are they playing at?"

"I'm not even certain they're trying to fight us so much as get past us," Harold concluded aloud. "Whatever's going on, they're trying to get to Hope, not kill us. Harrison can stay with them the whole way, and we can intercept them if or when they break for hyperspace, but I'm not sure we're going to *stop* them."

The Imperial detachment had seen the same thing Harold and Saab had, their courses reversing as Harrison continued to keep his better-defended ships—ships that had so far wiped out every missile the strangers had sent at them—in front of the others and all of his ships on a vector that would keep them in range of the attackers.

"We're out until they run," Lyon announced. "Our last missiles will hit home as they reach beam range of the Imperials. After that, we're out of range unless they hold in orbit or make a break outward."

"Watch for breakaways," Harold ordered. "Harrison's people are closer, but they're about to be in the middle of it—which is exactly when I'd expect them to try to hide landing-craft launches."

His bridge was silent.

"That would be insane," Saab replied. "They'd lose half at least!"

"Only if Harrison realized it was happening. The computers will spot it, but in a beam duel, no one is going to pay attention," Harold concluded. "So, let's watch for Harrison's people and make sure Hope knows if they're going to have guests."

The first thing Harold realized, watching the three remaining destroyers plunge toward the defending fleet, was that they weren't evading. Harrison's ships were dodging back and forth in three dimensions around their base course, the maneuverability afforded by the interface drive allowing them to render long-range targeting for direct fire almost impossible.

The attackers simply charged forward, allowing a clean line of fire that the Imperials finally gave into the temptation of. *Liberty*'s computers drew the swarm of proton beams in as clean white lines that connected the firing ship and its victim—and none of the attackers dodged.

The major weakness of the shield used by most powers of the galaxy was sustained beam fire, and the Imperial beams tore through the attackers' shields in a matter of moments, and for about half a second, Harold thought this extended nightmare was over.

Then the beams disappeared. Somewhere between the outer shield and the hull of the strange alien ships, there were brilliant bursts of light and the proton beams simply stopped.

"What the *hell*?" Lyon demanded aloud.

"They have some kind of secondary shield that's stopping the proton beams cold," Saab concluded as his secondary control team tore into the data. "I've never heard of anything like it, but it's either a hundred percent efficient or close enough that the beams aren't even scratching the armor!"

That was impossible...but it was exactly what Harold was seeing. Three ships sailed through the massed beams of eight without even noticing, approaching calmly until they were exactly one light-second away from Harrison's ships—and then fired their own weapons.

Gleaming Dawn simply...disappeared. One moment, the light cruiser was running ahead of her enemies to keep the range open, flinging missiles and coherent energy back at the attackers. The next, she was an expanding ball of fire.

The second *Sunlight*-class cruiser followed, but she didn't die alone. The Imperial ships' beams might not have been doing much, but they'd kept up the missile bombardment and they were firing at close range. A second destroyer came apart, followed by two of the *Descendant*s among the defenders.

Then both fleets were breaking apart, vectoring away from each other at over half the speed of light apiece. The two remaining strange destroyers appeared undamaged but out of missiles, and the

Imperial detachment had clearly lost their nerve with half of their number destroyed.

"Cuesta, can we cut them off?" Harold said grimly.

"Yes, sir," the navigator confirmed. "I don't care how they vector; we have the angle advantage now. I can get you lance range."

"Good, because apparently our proton beams are useless," the Captain replied. "Lyon, did they do anything before they broke off?"

"Exactly what you expected, sir," she said grimly. "I've got what looks like eighteen heavy assault shuttles heading toward the planet."

"Let Hope know," Harold ordered. "I don't know what the Imperials have here for ground troops, but I doubt it's something these guys want to tangle with.

"Sadly, I don't think our twenty-man security team is going to make any difference," he continued, "so we're going to make sure these people don't get to go home. Let's get these bastards out of the Empress's skies, shall we?"

TWO THINGS rapidly became very clear as *Liberty* moved to cut off the destroyers' retreat: firstly, that after firing off over fifteen hundred missiles apiece, the destroyers appeared to have finally run out of their scarily fast weaponry; and, secondly, they had no intention of avoiding action with the Terran cruiser.

"We're not much better off than they are for missiles, sir," Lyon warned. "Maybe five more salvos."

"If they want to come to us, Commander Lyon, I suggest we let them," Harold told her. "The lance capacitors are charged?"

"They are," she confirmed.

"Then hold your missiles for the moment," he concluded. "Let them close the range, then launch everything we've got at the lead ship at two million kilometers."

"Yes, sir."

An eerie silence fell over *Liberty*'s bridge as the three ships rushed toward each other. Harold and his people knew this was a side show now—the real point of today was the shuttles charging toward Hope—but that didn't make the next few minutes any less potentially deadly.

"Any idea what they hit our people with?" he asked Saab, almost sub-vocalizing to make sure only the executive officer in the secondary bridge heard him.

"Not a clue," the other man replied. "Our sensors aren't even sure they detected a beam. It was like a chunk of the Imperials' armor just...exploded.

"It appears to be a lot shorter-ranged than our beams, however."

"And they seem to be counting on their ability to no-sell our proton beams," Harold agreed. "Let's...see what happens."

There were eight hundred people aboard *Liberty,* and if he'd calculated wrong, he might be ordering them all to their deaths.

"Two million klicks," Lyon announced. "Missiles away, targeting Bogey Three."

There was barely enough time for the first salvo to hit home, sending light and energy cascading over Bogey Three's shields, before they crossed the three-light-second mark.

"Cuesta, break up," Harold snapped. "Lyon: fire!"

Liberty suddenly flipped ninety degrees in space, cutting away from the strangers at fifty-five percent of light speed. They were still gaining on her, but now Harold had almost forty seconds before they reached the apparent range of whatever they'd killed Division Lord Harrison with.

Powerful electromagnets along the length of *Liberty*'s core flashed to life, creating a focused magnetic field that flashed out into space and latched itself onto the closest metal object: Bogey Three.

Then six kilograms of hyper-compressed superheated plasma blazed along the channel at ninety-nine point seven five percent of lightspeed. Bogey Three didn't know enough to try and break the connection, and the plasma packet slammed into her hull, heat and kinetic energy alike slicing through shield and hull with pathetic ease.

To Harold's surprise, Bogey Three survived—but her shields went down and their missile salvos were still in space. Thirty one-ton missiles arrived moments after the destroyer's shield collapsed and tore the strange ship to pieces.

"Bogey Four is breaking away," Lyon reported. "I don't think they were expecting the lance."

"After him, Cuesta," Harold ordered. "Charge time on the lance?"

"Thirty-two seconds and counting. Can we keep them in range that long?"

Everyone looked at Lieutenant Commander Cuesta, who smiled, baring perfectly white teeth. "You're going to have a two-second window, Commander Lyon," he told her. "Make it count."

Seconds ticked down and *Liberty*'s Captain had to stop himself from holding his breath. His repeater screens happily showed him both the charging status of the plasma lance's capacitors, refilling from the cruiser's hyper-dense fusion-core secondary power plants, and the distance to the fleeing destroyer.

"And...now," Lyon murmured, barely loud enough for her Captain to hear her—and Tactical was right next to the Captain's dais.

Liberty shivered as the electromagnets flared to life again, reaching out to touch the enemy ship for a deadly few moments. This time, the destroyer tried to dodge—but all she achieved was to give Lyon a fraction of a second longer to make sure the plasma packet arrived.

This time, the pulse hit the rear of the destroyer and continued clean through the entire ship, ripping a hole several meters wide through the vessel.

For a moment, the intruder simply drifted in space, her engines, drives and power plants down.

Then she imploded, her armor and hull crumpling inward as

something crushed the entire ship into a tiny ball that then collapsed into a burst of stunningly white light.

Harold studied the screen for a few long seconds.

"What the hell was that?" he asked calmly.

"I have no idea, sir," Lyon admitted. "We've got full sensor records; we'll forward them to the Imperials."

"Good." Harold turned to Popovitch. "What news from Hope?"

"The shuttles have broken atmosphere; they seem to be landing well away from the colony. The Marines and Ducal Guard are going after them. General Wellesley is on the ground and the Imperial Battalion Commander has deferred authority to him."

"James is here?" Harold asked. "Oh, those poor alien bastards."

CHAPTER THREE

James Arthur Valerian Wellesley, younger brother to the Duke of Wellington after his father's death, had done everything in his power to prevent Duchess Annette Bond from hanging a General's stars on him.

At the point that the Ducal Guard under his command finished assembling its continental security forces, air division and suborbital division, as well as the security details aboard the Duchy of Terra Militia's spaceships, he'd commanded just over seven hundred thousand people.

Having the top of that rank structure be a Colonel had started to cause problems, so he'd caved and allowed Annette Bond to hang three stars on his collar and finally given up on being his old Captain's personal bodyguard.

Generals, though, had to make inspection tours, which had landed James on Hope when everything went to hell in a handbasket.

Technically, he had no authority to be in the Imperial Planetary Command Center. His Ducal Guard were basically corporate security here on Hope, protecting the ownership interest of the Duchy of Terra in an Imperial-protected colony.

In practice, the Command Center was a glorified precinct office with authority over two companies of Marines, one Yin and one Human. There wasn't enough security to keep him out, and given that he had an entire battalion of troops to the Imperium's three-hundred-odd troopers...

"General Wellesley, sir!" the Yin Battalion Commander greeted him as he charged into the office. The Yin were a tall humanoid race with multicolored feathers over mostly blue skin and hard black beaks. They got along quite well with humans, enough so to be an occasional problem, given that Yin females like the Battalion Commander shared certain secondary sexual characteristics with human women.

Battalion Commander Indus might be six and a half feet tall, with a black beak and dark green feathers, but she was also curvaceous enough to qualify as attractive to at least some humans.

Which was part of why James was here, since he'd just had to send the Major commanding the Hope detachment home in disgrace for *cross-species sexual harassment*.

"Battalion Commander," he greeted the Imperial officer. "I hope you don't mind the intrusion, but I was hoping for an update."

Indus gestured the dark-haired General, who was tall enough to just barely be able to look over her shoulder, over to the display she was standing next to.

"Division Lord Harrison is dead," she said flatly, the translator in James's ear easily carrying her harsh, grim tone after years of practice with both humans and Yin. "*Gleaming Dawn* was destroyed, as were half her escorts. The enemy ships have broken off, but they have launched a major landing effort."

"Damn." James studied the screen. Hope was scheduled to receive an orbital defense constellation, but the singular focus of the Duchy's industrial efforts since Annexation hadn't left them with a particularly diverse manufacturing base. They could upgrade and build warships, but defensive satellites weren't inside Terra's capacity.

With the Imperial picket scattered, there was nothing to stop the fifteen assault shuttles the scans were showing him.

"Any details on what we're facing?" he asked.

"None," Indus told him. "Like the ships, the shuttles appear to be of Kanzi design, but they're not a class we're familiar with. We're still localizing their approach vector, but I'm assuming they're coming for the colony."

James nodded slowly.

"The Guard has eight hundred troops on the surface," he told her. "We have power armor for two of those companies and Marine-grade plasma weaponry for all four. I would be delighted to place those soldiers at your disposal."

Indus shook her head, a gesture humans and Yin shared.

"That would make no sense, General," she admitted. "I have two companies, though both are fully equipped with power armor and plasma weapons. You have far more experience in command—especially in commanding human troops!—than I do, and this Colony is owned by the Duchy of Terra.

"I will gladly defer to your command, General Wellesley, as I think we can both agree that is the best way to protect this world."

James blinked in surprise. In his experience, the soldiers and spacers of the Imperial armed forces were loath to surrender any authority to the forces belonging to the homeworld Duchies. Neither he nor Indus knew Hope well, though—nobody did; the colony was barely a year and a half old—and she was right that he had more troops and knew how to lead humans better than the Yin officer did.

"The Guard doesn't have any heavy anti-aircraft or anti-space weapons," he pointed out after a moment's thought. "Do your Marines?"

"We have two mobile surface-to-orbit missile launchers," Indus told him. "That's all we have for heavy equipment, though."

"Move them to the perimeter of New Hope City," James instructed. "We'll move the ground troops out to protect them—our priority has to be protecting New Hope, but if we can cover the external settlements as well, we have to."

"The launchers have horizon-to-horizon capability," she replied. "With the satellite net intact, we can even fire over the horizon. They can't avoid our launchers, but..."

"I'm sensing another shoe here, Battalion Commander," the General pointed out dryly.

"Another shoe, sir?" Indus asked.

"Never mind," James said, shaking his head. "An unpleasant aspect I'm not expecting."

"We only have five missiles per launcher," she admitted. "Unless those shuttles are inferior to ours, which wouldn't be consistent with today's insanity, we're only going to take out three, maybe four of them."

"Damn." He returned his attention to the screen. "Get me a close-up of those shuttles," he ordered the tech next to him, then studied the resulting data.

"Roughly the size and mass of a Kanzi heavy assault shuttle," James concluded. "Depending on gear and if they're carrying slave cages, anywhere from thirty to a hundred ground troops."

He shook his head.

"Get me a map of the area round New Hope and a com link to all of the Guard and Marine company commanders," he told the man who'd grabbed him the visual. "We're going to need to place people carefully; the numbers are going to be more even than I'd like."

"GENERAL, BATTALION COMMANDER," a Yin tech, his feathers ruffling with distress, interrupted the radio conference.

James and Indus were about halfway through ordering the deployment of the Guard troops and Marine sub-companies—units of identical size at this point, despite the different names—throughout New Hope.

"Hold one, Captains," he told his COs, and turned to the technician. "What have you got, son?"

The Yin might have three inches of height on him, but it had been some time since James could regard anyone under the rank of O-5 or E-5 as anything but a kid. His husband said he was getting old.

His husband was probably right.

"We've got a final vector on their approach," the tech told him quickly. "They haven't deviated from their course since they cleared beam range of the Navy picket."

"Where are they headed? To New Hope?"

"No. They're going to almost the exact opposite side of the planet, somewhere near the Corellian Plateau," the enlisted alien told him. "All eighteen of them are on the same vector, we'll be able to target them with surface-to-orbit missiles in just over two minutes, but..."

"That's a long way out of the way," James concluded. "Captain Sommers," he addressed the man whose company had been on Hope the longest, "what the hell is at the Corellian Plateau?"

"Nothing, sir," Naheed Sommers replied. "I don't think anyone has even set foot on that continent—we did overflights before the colonization and again last year for mapping, but the Plateau is a frozen mess of ice and rock.

"There's nothing there."

"Well, eighteen hundred heavily armed aliens apparently disagree with that assessment, Captain," James told him. "Which changes our plans dramatically."

"What do you want to do, General?" Indus asked.

"I want you, Battalion Commander, to stay here with my Charlie and Delta companies," he told her. "I'm going to take every suit of power armor we have, load them onto our assault shuttles, and go after the bastards.

"I don't know what they're after, but everything on this damned planet belongs to the Centauri Development Corp and the Duchy of

Terra, and I am not going to let them get away with blowing away half a Navy picket."

"We don't have shuttles for our force," Indus admitted.

James grinned.

"And that, Battalion Commander, is why I'm leaving two of my companies behind: because I have shuttles for them and I'm taking your people instead."

"You're taking, sir?"

"Oh, yes," the Ducal Guard's commander confirmed. "I'm taking command of the counter-strike myself."

THE DUCAL GUARD'S Asteroid-class assault shuttles were purchased from the Rekiki, another member race of the A!Tol Imperium that the humans had come to get along with well. Like the orbital satellite constellation that James was wishing Hope had, Terra hadn't got around to establishing military-level shuttle factories.

They had *some* home-built military shuttles, but they weren't enough to meet the voracious needs of both the Militia and James's Guard, so they'd purchased the Asteroid-class ships from the Duchy of Reki.

The Asteroids were smaller ships than their enemy had brought, only able to carry fifty humans or Yin in power armor each, but the Ducal Guard had primary responsibility for search and rescue in Alpha Centauri. They'd brought sixteen of the sublight ships— enough to carry the entire battalion.

Now those shuttles blazed through Hope's frigid atmosphere at several dozen times the speed of sound. They could go faster if they went higher, a suborbital skip would get them to the Corellian Plateau ahead of the incoming shuttles, but that would make them more vulnerable to their enemies.

Demonstrably, James didn't want to expose his people to whatever godawful weapons the attacker's shuttles carried.

"We are tracking the incoming shuttles," Indus told him over the tactical net his people were running. "Opening fire with the SOM launchers."

"Good luck," James replied, continuing to check over his gear. Unlike the bulky armor worn by the Guards and Marines around him, he wore a low-profile suit designed for Imperial Commandos. At three times the price of the standard armor and only somewhat less survivability, the only suits of Commando armor in the Duchy were used for the protection of high-profile VIPs.

The leader of the Ducal Guard qualified and it wasn't like he'd had time to be fitted for a regular suit of power armor before boarding the shuttle.

"We got one!" Indus reported. "Lead shuttle is coming apart over the oceans...what in blue suns?!"

"Battalion Commander?" James asked after the curse settled to silence.

"They disappeared, General," the Yin told him. "We nailed one of them with our first pair of missiles and *might* have got a second— and then the rest disappeared. Some kind of stealth field, I'm guessing, but that's—"

"Way out of what's supposed to be the Kanzi's league," James agreed. "We'll maintain course for their estimated landing site. Contact Governor Harper. She should be able to retask the survey satellites to give us overhead.

"Between that and our shuttles' scanners, we should be able to find the buggers once they touch down."

"Understood, General. Good luck."

———

THE SHUTTLES CAME in low and fast, skimming over the frozen plains of Hope's southern hemisphere. This section of the planet would have been called a desert if it weren't so cold, which left it classed as simply "useless".

Running down the middle of the plains of permafrost, nearly featureless at this height and speed, was a mountain range where two of Hope's continental plates collided. The rocks were icy and jagged, though some stubborn scrub that wouldn't have looked out of place in Terra's Arctic clung to their slopes to soften their starkness with Hope's dark green vegetation.

"Corellian Plateau is coming up," the pilot of James's shuttle noted. "You'll know it when you see it, trust me."

"You've flown this before?" the General asked.

"Ha! No," the pilot confirmed with a grin. "I don't think anyone has, but looking at the overhead from the survey sats...damn."

James looked at the screens showing the mountains in front of his shuttle and understood immediately both what had shut the pilot up and just what the man had meant.

The mountains gave way to a massive plateau, taller than many of the mountains and edged in pitch-black rock. The Corellian Plateau stretched for dozens of kilometers in every direction and was easily a kilometer high, towering above the icy plains around it.

"Slow us down and link into the survey satellites," James ordered as he gazed at the immense natural wonder in front of him. "Where the hell did these bastards land?"

"If they're even half-decently equipped, we could just swan around up here until someone fires an antiaircraft missile at us," the pilot suggested.

"Look to your scanners, Lieutenant," James replied. "I'd rather find them without being shot down."

"Scopes are clear so far." The Guard Captain shook his head. "How do that many shuttles just disappear?"

"Stealth fields," the General told him. "We know they exist, even if we have no idea how the damn things work. I wouldn't have thought they'd work well in atmosphere, though—"

"We've got something," Captain Sommers interrupted over the radio. "I've got what looks like a perimeter sweep on my sensors. They're trying to be sneaky—but they ain't Triple-S."

"Neither are we anymore," James said with a sigh. The Special Space Service attached to the United Earth Space Force had been the elite of a planet, every officer and enlisted already a proven veteran of their national military.

Since those national militaries no longer existed, his own Ducal Guard *couldn't* be as elite. Their training and prep made up much of the difference, but you couldn't make up for using a hundred different armies as a filter.

"Anything showing up around them?" he asked.

"Negative," Sommers told him. "I'm guessing they've still got stealth fields over their shuttles and whatever encampment they're setting up."

James considered it for a moment and then made a snap decision.

"Pass the coordinates on to all shuttles," he ordered. "We'll do one peeping-tom run over the area and air-drop the troops on any concentrations or encampments we find."

"Understood. And, sir..."

"Yes, Captain?"

"They're definitely Kanzi."

CHAPTER FOUR

JAMES WATCHED THROUGH THE VIDEO FEED FROM HIS LEAD shuttles as they flashed over the top of the plateau, looking for any sign of Terra's blue-furred enemies. Stealth fields, to his understanding, blocked every form of sensor but created a distortion that could be seen by the sentient eye.

"There!" his pilot snapped, the younger man's eyes picking out what the General had missed. He dropped a blue caret on James's screen, highlighting a section of movement that he'd missed.

Like Sommers had seen before, it was a perimeter-scouting patrol, half a dozen short and delicate humanoids clad in dark gray power armor. Two points weren't enough to necessarily draw a bead on the enemy landing site, but it was enough for him to start.

"Alpha-Two, you see them," James snapped. "You are go. Drop. Drop. Drop."

The computer running the display in his helmet was smart enough to recognize his focus and relay him updates as the Ducal Guard's Second Platoon, Alpha Company, Centauri Battalion engaged the drop system on their shuttle. One moment, they were locked into their shuttle, blazing across the plateau at six times the speed of sound.

The next, all fifty suits of power armor were blasted out the bottom of the spacecraft, the floor of the shuttle sliding aside barely in time for the soldiers to be fired downward.

The A!Tol Imperium's idea of a *safe* air-drop system didn't line up with any of its member species' idea of a *comfortable* system, but James couldn't argue with its effectiveness. Alpha-Two went from airborne above the enemy to on the ground *around* the enemy in under six seconds.

The ensuing firefight was over almost before it began, the Kanzi troopers down before they'd fired a shot.

"Flag the suit locations for analysis," James ordered. "We need to know if the tech these guys are carrying is as out of the expected parameters as the tech on the starships."

"Bravo-Two has another patrol," Captain Steffen reported. "They're dropping now."

"Alpha-One has dropped on the original patrol," Sommers added. "We have three target locations."

"Which means we have a central point," James agreed. "Imperial Marines, you're with me: right into the middle!"

"Oorah!"

Company Commander Donald Carver had, the Guard's commander reflected, been a *United States* Marine before signing on with the Imperium.

You could put a Marine in a new uniform and have them serve an alien empire, but you couldn't make them any less of a USMC Marine.

TEN SHUTTLES CONVERGED like moths to a flame, flying just above the surface of the plateau to thwart any waiting antiaircraft missiles. With only a vague idea where the Kanzi might have set down, James locked himself into the drop pods with the rest of his personal detachment, ex-SSS to a man, and left the call over when to drop them to the pilot.

Then the entire spacecraft *lurched* as if they'd run into a brick wall, feeling for a moment like they'd stopped in the air, and then the pilot was cursing on the channel.

"Holy shit. Drop! Drop! Drop!"

James didn't even have time to pull the sensor data to see what they'd found before the shuttle fired him into the air and the entire process of falling consumed his entire attention.

The same built-in inertial management systems that allowed the suit to take a tank round without flinching managed the acceleration, while an add-on belt of hyper-dense chemical rockets blazed to life to control his descent and deliver him to the ground intact.

The system might be entirely automated, but the sentient still had to decide where to land, and that was when he realized just what they'd stumbled into.

Sixteen heavy assault shuttles of an unfamiliar design had been arranged in a circle, spaced evenly apart—presumably close enough to keep their stealth fields linked together and shield the encampment —while power-armored Kanzi began to fill in the gaps with barricades and other, unarmored, aliens were setting up a series of prefab structures inside the impromptu fortification.

If James's people hadn't already been on their way and tracking the shuttles, he wasn't sure they'd have ever found the camp. Most early-stage Imperial colonies didn't have combat shuttles, and the Centauri Battalion had them only because they'd already been assigned to the unit when it had been flagged for deployment to the new colony.

That, it seemed, might have just saved the day. Five hundred power-armored soldiers, mostly Imperial Marines but with a hundred Terran Ducal Guards in the mix, dropped out of the sky on a half-built camp that wasn't truly expecting them.

The armored troops, however, were clearly *very* good at their jobs. Their weapons were free before James's people had even hit the ground, and the *hiss-crack* of plasma weapons filled the air.

He had a moment to be grateful that these Kanzi didn't appear to have any super-weapons for their ground troops, and then his helmet started flagging targets as he hit the ground. His plasma rifle swung free, tracking toward the first set of armored soldiers and opening fire.

In the back of his mind, he noted that there were fewer troops than he'd expected. The shuttles would have been enough to carry over fifteen hundred soldiers, but there were dozens—hundreds—of visible unarmored personnel, presumably civilians and only about four hundred soldiers.

Even including the unarmored Kanzi, however, there were only half the people he'd have expected. Potentially, the stealth fields took up much of the space, but it was also likely there was more gear on the spacecraft.

The Kanzi had been planning on sticking around. James had no intention of letting them.

"Watch your fire," he snapped at his people. "Shit happens, but let's *not* kill anyone unarmed or blow up those shuttles. I want to know what they brought here!"

He spotted what appeared to be some kind of tripod-mounted heavy weapon with half a dozen power-armored Kanzi struggling to get it set up. He had no idea what kind of system required external support when power armor was available, but he didn't want it opening fire on his men or the Marines.

He flagged it to his computer and set his rifle for maximum power, then opened fire. The computer helped track his fire to make sure he was shooting at the right time and place, and on maximum power, each round hit with the impact of ninety kilograms of TNT.

It also emptied the rifle's internal capacitor in four shots, but the strange weapon disappeared in a ball of fire and he dodged behind one of their prefabricated barricades to let his suit recharge the weapon.

One of the unarmored Kanzi was also behind the barricade and leveled a very human-looking pair of eyes on him. Kanzi and human body language were close enough that he could usually read them, but he had no idea what the alien in the strange burgundy uniform was thinking.

And then the Kanzi bit down in a strange gesture that James had been trained to recognize once, long before, and spat at the General's feet as his mouth began to foam up and his body stiffened. The apparent technician crumpled to the ground, some kind of poison pill killing him instantly.

A horrifying realization hit home and James slammed himself into the ground.

"Everyone, *down*! They're going to blow the shuttles!"

The Kanzi troops were outnumbered by his first wave, and he had another three hundred power-armored soldiers closing on the encampment as well. Their only chance had been to throw back his first assault, and his people had been down and among them before they'd reacted to the unexpected attack.

If one of the unarmed techs running around was willing to commit suicide to prevent capture, and the shuttles contained tech that the A!Tol Imperium didn't have, then...

Sixteen fusion cores overloaded simultaneously and the world tried to end in fire and thunder.

WHEN THE SHOCK FADED, James was still in the dark. After mentally making sure he wasn't dead, a system self-check showed that the Commando armor's sensors and screens were still working. There just wasn't any light reaching him.

His limbs didn't want to move either. He was buried. The armor happily responded to his query and confirmed that there was no oxygen and he was using the suit's supply. He had a day or so of air, give or take, but he also wasn't sure quite how buried he was.

"Company COs, report," he ordered. "What's our status?"

"My people are moving into the perimeter of the blast zone," Sommers replied instantly. "We're having interference with communications and safety beacons; your suit has better transmitters than most."

"For a reason," James confirmed. "I'm buried, looks like under one of their prefabs and probably a few tons of debris. Everyone else, sound off."

"I've lost contact with half my men," Carver told him. "Can't be certain how many are actual casualties versus interference or suit damage," the Imperial Marine continued, "but I'm coordinating everyone aboveground for search and rescue."

"I am with Carver," Company Commander Vildar added. The translator easily picked up the precise but exhausted tone of the Yin's speech. "More of my people have reported in, but many are buried. We are beginning to dig them and the Guard out."

"Alpha is with Bravo; we're securing the perimeter and sweeping in," Captain Marković reported. "I've lost contact with the entire platoon that was on site," she concluded grimly. "They were far too damned close to the shuttles."

"We didn't expect them to blow themselves up," James replied, cutting off any self-recrimination before it could start. "The Kanzi might run a theocracy, but they're not usually fanatics. This whole mess just stinks, and not just because I'm buried in three tons of dirt and half-melted ice."

Or because, in a worst-case scenario, he'd just lost the best part of three hundred sentients.

"We can prioritize you, sir," Sommers offered.

"Not a chance," James ordered. "My suit is undamaged and I have air and coms. I'm the last damn priority, not the first."

He managed to clench his fist, clearing a tiny pocket that he could move in. It was a start.

"Besides, I'm pretty sure I can dig myself out soon enough. Focus on the wounded and those in damaged suits," he continued. "Then, once we've dug everyone out, I want to go over this damn plateau with a fine-toothed comb.

"Whoever these people are, they sacrificed four Core Power–level destroyers to land this expedition and then blew it to hell the moment it was compromised. That's not normal Kanzi MO, people.

"They were looking for something and I want to know what."

CHAPTER FIVE

DIGGING EVERYONE OUT TOOK MOST OF ONE OF HOPE'S THIRTY-two-hour days. Despite his optimism, even James ended up having to be dug out by the search-and-rescue sweep from his Guard companies, but their actual losses were far lighter than he had any right to expect.

One Guard platoon had been entirely wiped out, too close to the shuttles when they blew. Another fifty humans and Yin, mostly Marines but with a dozen or so of James's men, had been killed either in the landing or the explosions. A hundred of both species and services had been wounded and evacuated back to the hospitals at New Hope City.

Eight badly wounded enough to be evacuated up to *Liberty*. There were few wounded from the space battle, but the Militia cruiser had the best medical facilities in the star system. Two of the badly wounded would need be cryogenically suspended until they could be returned to Terra or another major world with modern medicine.

That report made James shake his head. Injuries that severe would have been classed as dead on arrival by Terra's best medicine five years before. Technically, they *were* dead: their hearts had stopped beating but their suits had an emergency system to provide nutrients and warmth to the brain.

It wasn't clean or pretty, but at the point the heart was stopped or missing, having to rebuild a chunk of the soldier's skull was a minor concern.

James stood on the edge of the crater, studying the pattern the fusion overloads had created. It resembled nothing so much as a sixteen-petalled flower, an oddly poetic and pretty pattern for having been forged of fire and death.

"Have we managed to retrieve anything useful from the shuttles?" he asked Sommers.

"Nothing," the Captain admitted. "We're still picking through the debris of what they'd off-loaded, but the shuttles and their contents were completely vaporized." The blond Guard shook his head. "Yeah, a fusion-core overload is quite a boom, but that level of complete destruction... They were designed for it."

"To be destroyed without a trace?" James said.

"Exactly. Whoever launched this op wanted to be damn sure there'd be nothing left if it went sideways. They wrote off, what? Four destroyers, half a battalion of ground troops and the same in support techs and what might have even been civilians?" Sommers shook his head again.

"You're right, sir: they were looking for something. This wasn't an invasion attempt or they'd have come down on New Hope City and held the damn colony hostage with those fusion cores."

"Fanatics," James confirmed. He'd been a member of the United Kingdom's Special Air Service before he'd been Special Space Service. He knew how fanatics of any stripe worked.

"It was a do-or-die op," Sommers agreed. "A moon shot with a million ways it could go wrong. So..."

"So, everything they sent was expendable—including destroyers that could go head-to-head with our cruisers," the Ducal Guard

General concluded. "If the Kanzi have enough of those that they can throw them away, that's a problem."

"I'm not sure these guys are Theocracy, sir," the junior man said. "Dana's people were pulling together what gear and bodies we have, and there's a lot of things that don't line up. They're Kanzi, but..."

"But?"

"Go check in with Dana," Sommers suggested. "I've just been eavesdropping on her channel; she's the one with the bodies."

THERE WERE SURPRISINGLY few bodies left of the invaders. Even with the explosions, James would have expected there to be at least some of the power-armored soldiers left, but when he found Captain Dana Marković and Company Commander Vildar speaking softly next to the lines of the enemy dead, he counted fewer than fifty bodies.

"Ah, General," Marković greeted him. "Come to stare at the macabre and the curious like the rest of us?"

"I suppose?" he replied. "What have you found?"

"Well, firstly, we have no intact samples of their armor," she said immediately. "A suicide protocol overloaded the internal ammunition storage, vaporized the systems, most of the armor itself, and the occupant."

James winced. That was *not* a protocol he'd authorize installing on his people's gear. It could go far too wrong far too easily.

"How do we have *any* bodies, then?"

"Some of the unarmored landing parties were far enough out that they survived the explosions intact." She shrugged. "Not sure how many of them lived through the explosion, to be honest. At least one poisoned herself, but most of the rest we'd need to autopsy to identify the exact cause of death.

"We've also got a couple of suits of armor far enough out from the blast to survive intact, but close enough in to the blast to be completely crippled. We're not getting anything useful from their systems, but their occupants were intact-ish."

"Hence *the macabre and the curious*, I suppose. Anything I should know?" he asked.

"Fucked if I have a clue," Marković said in a tired voice. "But come take a look."

She led him to the row of bodies covered in white sheets, picking a specific body and pulling the sheet back.

"This was one of the soldiers," she noted, gesturing at the blue-furred corpse. "Suit failed in the blast; he died from heat and impact." She paused. "The scarring predates that."

James knelt down by the body and studied it, immediately seeing what she meant. Chunks of the Kanzi's fur had been burnt away as they died, but his face was mostly undamaged—but at some point, someone had burned patterns into the skin there. The Kanzi's fine facial fur had mostly grown in around the scars, but there were still lines of flesh visible through the oddly white lines of fur.

"Do these symbols mean anything?" he asked softly.

"Nothing the translators have loaded," Vildar replied. "I've relayed to the Navy contingent, but I understand us to have full files on the Kanzi languages. Those are definitely intentional symbols, but they're not in any language we know."

"I didn't think the Kanzi went in for ritual scarification," James noted. "Being 'the perfect form of God' and all."

"They don't," Marković told him. "I've been studying them—they *did* try and conquer our planet—and the main Theocracy cultures do *not* go in for bodily modification at all. This kind of scarring would be the equivalent of you or I intentionally chopping off an arm for style points."

"So, we're looking at a Kanzi from an unusual subculture," James noted. "They've got them, same as we do."

"That's what I thought when I first saw it, but..." The Captain shook her head and glanced over the corpses, comparing the bodies to a map on her helmet screen. She walked down the row and uncovered another body.

"This one was probably a civilian," she concluded. "No uniform, no weapon. Some kind of scanner gear...but she's the one who survived the blast and poisoned herself."

The Kanzi female had been about four and a half feet tall when alive but, other than that and the blue fur, probably would have been considered quite attractive as a human. The foam around her mouth from the poison hurt that image, though, as did the ritual scarification across her face, neck and breasts.

"Civilian but still scarred-up," James noted. "All of them?"

"All of them intact enough for us to be sure," Marković confirmed. "That's not some weird subculture, unless that culture manned this entire op. There's no question these guys are Kanzi, but..."

"Tech the Kanzi aren't supposed to have," the General said slowly. "Universal body modification the Theocracy regards as abhorrent. Suicidal fanaticism the Kanzi reserve for elite units. All of that, wrapped up in a symbiology we have no records of..."

"They're Kanzi, but I don't think they're Theocracy," his junior concluded as he trailed off. "Which is *weird* and makes no sense."

"Agreed." James rose from the bodies and looked around the Corellian Plateau again. With a sigh, he linked into the main communications network.

"Link me to Governor Harper," he ordered.

———

GOVERNOR KAGNEY HARPER was a cheerfully bubbly blond woman who reminded James of Duchess Bond herself, at least physically. *Bubbly* was not a word one tended to apply to the woman who'd once been nicknamed "Bloody Annie" for sheer stubborn pigheadedness.

"Greetings, General Wellesley. How may the Imperium's government in Centauri assist you?" she asked brightly. "I must extend my thanks and the thanks of the Imperium for your rapid and successful intervention in this incident, as well as for the intervention of *Liberty*."

"I don't speak for the Militia, Governor Harper," James reminded her. "I hope you've extended your thanks directly to Captain Rolfson."

"I have, but we all know you speak for Her Grace of Terra, General," Harper said. "The Board of Directors made it very clear to me that you hold Duchess Bond's full proxy with regards to the Centauri Development Corporation."

The governance structure of Hope was...odd. Harper reported to both the A!Tol Imperium, who ruled Hope in a strictly governmental sense, and to the Board of Directors of the CDC, who owned Hope in a strictly economic sense.

And the CDC, in turn, was sixty percent owned by the Duchy of Terra, with the remainder owned by various private interests across the Imperium who'd underwritten humanity's first colony.

Hope was not part of the Duchy of Terra, but Duchess Bond's authority over the Board of Directors stretched a *long* way.

"I need your survey teams," James told Harper. "Your planes, your ground teams, your satellites. Everything. If we need to take the Corellian Plateau apart stone by stone to find what the Kanzi were after, we will.

"My shuttles and Guards will be on site for a while, though we are sending the Marines back to New Hope City. For the moment, I'll remain here as well."

"Of course, General," Harper replied after a moment of hesitation. "Those teams and vehicles belong to the CDC, after all. They'll be glad to place them at your disposal."

She paused.

"Just what are you expecting to find?"

"I have no idea," he admitted. "But someone sacrificed four

destroyers and over a thousand people just to get a *chance* at finding it, so I'm going to bet it's worth our time."

Harper coughed delicately.

"Will you be leading the expedition yourself?" she asked. "My schedule says a courier will be arriving to pick you up tomorrow evening."

For a few long moments, James considered exerting his considerable independent authority to stay. Hope didn't even have a starcom *receiver*, let alone a starcom transmitter. That meant that the courier coming to pick him up was the fastest way to get the news about what happened back to Sol and the Duchy's full starcom—and hence to the rest of the Imperium.

"I'll talk to Rolfson," he concluded. "I want a high-level Ducal representative involved, Governor. Whatever this is, I suspect it's going to be of concern to the species, Governor, as well as the Imperium."

———

JAMES STUDIED *Liberty* with a careful eye as his shuttle approached the big cruiser. It was easy for someone who'd served aboard *Tornado* during Bond's year-long exile from Terra to see where the newer ship drew inspiration from the original experimental cruiser.

Liberty was leaner and more rakish than the old ship, better designed for her shields and armor and energy weapons, but she retained the same double-ended-spindle design and was painted the same gray color.

The Ducal Guard's commander wasn't fully up to date on the latest compressed-matter-armor designs, but the armor and the associated defensive suites were what fed and drove the Duchy of Terra's economy now. He understood enough to realize just how unusual the visible dimples on the armor, easily fifty meters across, that marked the impacts from the battle were. Compressed-matter plating didn't dent. Its supports broke. The plates could be detached from each other. The armor could be blasted off the ship...but it didn't *dent*.

But then, none of the tests they'd conducted had involved missiles dramatically faster and more dangerous than the A!Tol Imperium possessed.

"We're docking now, sir," his pilot informed him. "Captain Rolfson has prepared a side party."

James was a descendant of the original Duke of Wellington, who had fought Napoleon, with a dozen and more generations of stiff-upper-lipped British nobility behind him. He understood the need and importance of pomp and circumstance in the military.

Sometimes, however, he was in a hurry. But the rituals and traditions of the Duchy of Terra's still-fledgling militaries had to be nurtured and encouraged, to rebuild the spirit of Earth's defenders that had been shattered by the Annexation.

With a smile that concealed his impatience, James squared his shoulders to the task ahead.

AFTER THE FORMALITIES WERE OVER, the two old comrades took a seat in Rolfson's office, the Captain producing an excellent bottle of wine and pouring glasses for them both.

"How is *Liberty*?" James asked. "You took more of a beating than I thought."

"We're combat-capable, though we could use a reload," Rolfson replied. "The...dents are cosmetic, really. We've replaced the support matrix behind them, but I'm not sure anyone in the Imperium actually has the gear to pound out dents in *compressed matter*."

"Those missiles..." James shook his head. "I don't suppose they gave you any valuable insight, easily missed by an old ground-pounder, as to where these strange Kanzi came from?"

"Other than being quite certain the Theocracy doesn't have anything like them?" Rolfson sighed. "Nothing. What intel the Navy passes on to us suggests that point eight five cee seems to be about the absolute limit of what the interface drive can reach. All of the Core Powers use a point eight five missile, even if it's a secondary weapon for most of them now."

"I shudder to think what their primary weapons look like," the General said dryly.

"The only one of them we're sure of is that the Mesharom use a hyper-capable FTL missile that can enter and exit hyperspace significantly closer to gravity sources than any hyperdrive we have," Rolfson told him. "The Core Powers are easily two or three hundred years ahead of both the Imperium and the Kanzi. More, probably. It's hard to judge."

"And these Kanzi-manned ships were carrying Core-tier tech."

"Not quite," the Militia Captain disagreed. "Core-tier missiles, but...our scans suggest a more patchwork collection of tech. Compressed-matter armor and super-advanced interface engines, but their shields are only next-generation, not next-next-next generation, if that makes sense?"

"Sort of," James conceded.

"And we're frankly not sure *how* they were powering everything, because what scans we got of their power systems suggests that their fusion-core tech is actually *behind* the current Theocracy military. On the other hand, we have no idea why the last of them imploded, and I'm guessing those are related."

"Was there any useful debris?"

"No." Rolfson shook his head. "Space combat doesn't tend to leave much unless you're trying to take prisoners. Nobody was trying yesterday, especially not after Division Lord Harrison died."

"That's going to have consequences I can't predict," James admitted. "He and Tanaka were the only Lord-ranked human officers in the Imperial Navy. Death in the line of duty, defending an Imperial colony, *should* look good, but..."

"But Hope is a human colony, so who knows how Imperial politics will take it," Rolfson agreed. Humanity had been part of the

Imperium for four years, but they still wore their membership uncomfortably at best.

"Exactly. Commander McPhail's courier will be here to pick me up in about two hours," the General told the younger man. "I considered staying, but I think I need to get back to the Duchy and let Annette know everything that's happened. I suspect the aftermath of this is going to give us all a massive headache."

"Agreed." *Liberty*'s Captain sighed. "Make sure both the Duchess and Admiral Villeneuve know we had to use the plasma lance," he noted. "We've been keeping the fact that we've built any of them under wraps, but I needed to be certain we took them down."

James nodded. Technically, the Duchy hadn't incorporated any Laian technology into their new ships—but the members of the Laian Exiles who'd run one of the most notorious pirate ports in that region of space who'd immigrated to Sol had been involved in the design of the new ships.

They hadn't brought a single schematic or technology sample with them, but it turned out that some of the Laian engineers had forgotten more about starship technology than many A!Tol engineers would ever learn. Just having them on hand making suggestions and pointing out where the human research teams were going wrong had been a huge advantage for the *Thunderstorm* development teams.

"The Imperium knows we have the tech," James reminded him. "As I understand, we're negotiating licensing the *Thunderstorm* design to several other yards and the Navy has contracted with us to build one of the several *squadrons* they've ordered."

"It's not the Imperium we're worried about," the Captain replied. "It's the *Laians*. We're not sure how the old Laian Republic is going to react to their long-lost exiles upgrading the tech of an outer-galaxy power."

"Fair," James nodded. "The Duchess, the Admiral and I will deal with it, I suppose. I need you here, of course."

"Playing watchdog until the Navy can reinforce the picket?"

"Pretty much. I also, however, want you to personally take

control of the survey expedition looking for what the Kanzi were after," James ordered. "We need to know what they were willing to sacrifice so much for even a chance of finding."

"I'm hesitant to leave my ship, sir," Rolfson objected.

"This is a critical priority, Captain," James said flatly. The Ducal Guard and the Militia might not share a chain of command, but neither of them had any illusions about the Guard General's ability to give a Militia Captain orders. "We *must* know what they were after.

"It might be important enough that we simply don't admit to the Theocracy that we saw these people, Captain. I want a senior Ducal representative on the ground when we find it, and right now, that means you.

"Understood, Captain?"

Rolfson nodded.

"I understand, sir," he conceded. "It'll be a delicate balancing act, but we can make it work. What I do need, though, is ammunition resupply. We shot off almost our entire missile magazines taking down those destroyers."

"I'll see to it," James promised. "We'll probably end up sending a full battle group. If there is something on Hope worth all of this effort, then I'm quite certain both the Duchy and the Imperium want to see it defended—and the Militia's capital ships are closer than the nearest Imperial battle squadrons."

CHAPTER SIX

HAROLD WATCHED AS THE COURIER *HERMES FOUR* DISAPPEARED back through her hyper portal, heading towards Sol with the news of the strange events in Alpha Centauri, then turned his attention to the planet beneath him and the remains of its Imperial defenders.

Liberty outmassed the remaining four destroyers of the Imperial picket, but there were always niceties and traditions to observed, regardless of the actual balance of force.

Commander Teykay of *Plainsfang* was now the senior officer of the picket, the Rekiki officer resembling nothing so much as a massive, dark green crocodile centaur to human eyes. His body language was unreadable to Harold, but the translator handily picked up his concerned, overwhelmed tones.

"Per Imperial rules, Captain Rolfson, I remain in command here as the senior Imperial officer," Teykay told him. "I would appreciate your advice and suggestions, however, as I was fourth in this picket's sequence of command."

Plainsfang was a Terran-upgraded *Capital*-class destroyer and should have been able to eat her Kanzi equivalents for breakfast.

Instead, a mere three Kanzi destroyers had functionally destroyed the picket.

His "request" basically amounted to surrendering command to Rolfson and they both knew it, but it would also cover the big alien's posterior when the Imperial Navy started poking around just what the hell had happened there.

"I understand completely, Captain Teykay," Harold confirmed. The A!Tol words for the rank of "Captain" and the title of "Captain" as the commander of a ship were actually different, but the English problem remained. Fortunately, the translation program they were using was very, *very* good at context.

It wasn't a universal translator. The portable devices only contained thirty or forty languages, and even the program running on *Liberty*'s computers was limited to languages it knew and had problems with rarer cultural metaphor inside those languages, but it made the A!Tol's multi-species interstellar empire possible.

"I suggest I pull *Liberty* into the high guard position," he continued. That would put the heavy cruiser at roughly a light-second out from the planet in a long, slow orbit that would allow her to intercept any approach to the planet. "I think your ships would be better off directly positioned above New Hope City, to protect the colony in the case of another attack."

That kind of layered defense was more effective at defending against planetary bombardment than an invasion, but Harold had the grim suspicion that any second wave would focus on removing the "human problem" before continuing their search.

Sneaking past them hadn't worked, after all.

"I agree with your logic," Teykay said gratefully. "We will deploy as you recommend. We should remain in close contact, Captain. We don't know if there's a second herd to this stampede."

Harold smiled at the translation. Some metaphors didn't cross species. Some metaphors, while unfamiliar, were still quite clear.

"My orders are to deploy with most of my small craft to the

surface," he warned the Imperial officer. "The Duchy of Terra wants to keep a close eye on the survey of the Corellian Plateau."

"Of course," the Rekiki acknowledged. "Our paths align, Captain. I would happily contribute our own shuttlecraft and sensor drones to the search. Without more knowledge, we risk missing a strategic threat."

"I appreciate the assistance, Captain," Harold said. "The risk clearly already exists. We need to know what it is!"

PERMAFROST AND ROCK were generally safe for one landing, but reactionless, relativity-less, and mostly inertialess as the interface drive was, it still put out a *lot* of heat when bringing a multi-hundred-ton spacecraft in for a soft landing.

By the time Harold arrived, on the first wave of *Liberty's* five-thousand-ton heavy lift shuttles, the Development Corp's people had already addressed the problem. In two of Hope's thirty-two-hour days, they'd sprung into action at a site just outside the blast zone from the self-destructing Kanzi shuttles and assembled an entire work camp.

Central to it was a two-hundred-meter-diameter nano-concrete landing pad, created by loosing specially designed nanotech converters into the soil along with some feedstock. The dirt, stone, ice and chemical stock were rapidly transformed into a hardy black surface that could easily withstand the heat from any shuttlecraft ever built.

And since the nanites only had a power supply for ten minutes, there was no danger of turning anything you didn't want into concrete. Like many of the more mundane technologies the Imperium had brought to humanity, it was simple, elegant, and effective.

Off to the side of the landing pad were several massive tent hangars, each big enough to handle three of *Liberty*'s big military shuttles. A prefabricated control tower rose out of the hangars, festooned with sensors and scanning arrays as a small crew handled the chaos of shuttles, planes and survey drones sweeping over the plateau.

"We're down in thirty seconds," his pilot reported crisply. "And we then have two minutes to get off the pad and into one of the hangars; there's a bird inbound from New Hope City with a temporary medical clinic."

"Carry on," Harold ordered, leaning back in his chair. The Centauri Development Corporation were efficient; he had to give them that. They had had access to the best of Terra's people, though, plus the ability to hire expertise from twenty-eight species and over a hundred star systems.

Both the Duchy of Terra and the A!Tol Imperium had been determined to make sure the first human colony was a massive success, and they'd put their money, their people, and the resources behind making that a reality.

His shuttle landed with a gentle thud as the interface drive shut down and wheels extended, the spacecraft already moving toward the hangar.

Given the cycle of operations already in place at the Corellian Plateau, it appeared they needed to get off the landing pad before they could exit the shuttle.

A HARRIED-LOOKING LOGISTICS team took over offloading *Liberty*'s shuttle's cargo moments after they came to a stop, with an even more exhausted-looking manager waving Harold over to her.

"Linda McWilliams," the graying and stocky woman introduced herself briskly. "We're in barely-controlled-chaos mode here, Captain Rolfson, though from what I hear, that's not something you're unfamiliar with."

"Hardly," Harold agreed with a small smile. "This looks positively calm compared to most of my time aboard *Tornado*."

McWilliams shook her head at him.

"I've got a note that you and an escort need quarters?" she queried.

"Help setting them up, more likely," the Captain replied. "We brought down military prefabs that will handle about a hundred souls. They're military, so they have officers' quarters, and I'm laying claim on those right now," he continued with a larger smile, "but my understanding is that I'm only bringing down about forty of my people, including my Guard security detail. The other three prefab units are at your disposal."

"Oh, thank Goddess," she said. "We're *good* at rapid setup at CDC, it's been our job for eighteen months, but we didn't have an entire additional major regional survey on our schedule. Our people and our gear are already allocated, so we're robbing Peter, James, Philip and Thomas to pay Paul."

Harold winced. He was intimately familiar with that kind of arrangement from the aftermath of the desperate defense of Earth against the Kanzi.

"How can my people help?" he asked.

"Hands and gear, Captain, hands and gear—and you've just promised both," she said with a grin. "What *you* can do, however, is get over to the survey command center and, well, take command."

"This is a civilian op," Harold pointed out carefully. "I'm just the Militia and Duchy rep."

"Which means you aren't part and parcel of eighteen months of Centauri Dev Corp politics," McWilliams told him. "Not my place to judge who's right or who's in charge, but Ramona and Jonah are going to *kill* each other if someone doesn't take charge and tell them to work together."

That, too, Harold was familiar with.

"Who are they?" he asked. Walking into a minefield was a lot safer with a map.

"Jonah Trudeau is the head of CDC Survey. He's a geologist with thirty years of experience finding useful junk on asteroids," McWilliams replied. "I've worked with him for ten of those years; he's smart as a whip."

"But?"

"But. Ramona Wolastoq is humanity's first Goddess-blessed xenoarchaeologist, trained by the A!Tol themselves," the logistics manager said flatly. "And when she says there's a way we should be looking, I'm not going to disbelieve her!"

THE COMMAND CENTER was a prefabricated building like the rest of the encampment, though unlike most of the rest, it was two stories tall and had a hefty communications array attached to the top.

A pair of Ducal Guards stood watch outside the entrance, one of them holding a flimsy—a datapad built into a sheet of paper, old Terran tech—and subtly checking faces against it, while the other not-so-subtly leaned next to the door with a plasma carbine slung over his shoulder.

"Captain Rolfson," the man checking faces greeted him. "The Director is upstairs. He..." The soldier glanced around and shrugged. "He's in a meeting, but I doubt he'll mind being interrupted."

If even the security guards knew there was a problem, things had progressed downhill far faster than Harold's worst fears.

"Thank you, Corporal," he told the Guard non-com as he entered the building, his own trio of Guards trailing in his wake.

The ground floor of the center was a mixed array of cubicles and computer screens, some analysts going over data brought back by the early survey teams, while other analysts prodded at maps and radios, trying to coordinate efforts across the entire plateau.

They were also, to a man, woman, and alien, studiously hard at work. Very obviously at work. The kind of "obviously at work" that meant they were pretending not to notice something.

Harold walked through the studiously oblivious crowd to the stairs, then stopped and glanced back at his escort.

"Wait here, people," he ordered softly. "I'm not expecting assassins to jump out of nowhere."

This wasn't, after all, Earth. While the organized Resistance born from the UESF's emergency Weber Protocols had surrendered, there remained individuals horrified by Earth's annexation who would happily take potshots at the collaborators.

Anyone who made it to Centauri would have passed psych screening to make sure they were at least reconciled to the current state of affairs, if not necessarily happy about it.

Harold still wasn't sure he was happy about it, but his oaths and his loyalty to Annette Bond had dragged him from the UESF's uniform into the Duchy of Terra Militia's uniform.

And here. To an unusually empty upper floor with a closed conference door. A door that *probably* should have been guarded, except the guards had decided that securing the entire building instead was the better part of valor.

"I know my damn job, Wolastoq," a male voice snapped through the door as Harold approached. "I will not sit here and be lectured just because the Governor has an overinflated idea of your ego!"

"My *ego*, Director, is not the one refusing to listen to sensible advice," a melodious female voice replied. She was speaking significantly more softly than Director Trudeau, but she sounded no less aggravated. "Governor Harper asked me to join this expedition for a reason, but if you continue to waste my time, I'm not even sure why I'm on this warmth-forsaken planet!"

Harold sighed and pushed the door open, stepping in before Trudeau could respond to Wolastoq's words.

"Director, Miss Wolastoq, please...take a moment."

"Doctor," the woman replied harshly, eyeing him levelly. He returned her frank gaze, studying the calm-voiced woman. She was tall, with wide shoulders and broad, tanned features under thick black hair drawn back into a heavy braid.

Her eyes were flashing and her lips were pressed together enough to turn them white.

"It's Dr. Wolastoq," she repeated. "I did not earn a PhD on Earth and recognized academic credentials on A!To to be referred to as 'Miss', whoever you are!"

"Doctor," Harold conceded. "I am Captain Harold Rolfson, and I have been sent here as the representative of the Duchy of Terra." He turned his best "Captain's gaze" on the two CDC officials.

"Which means, in case you aren't up to speed, is that I speak for the majority shareholder of the company that employs you both, as well as being the man in the command of the *heavy cruiser in orbit*."

He let that sink in and then smiled at them.

"You now have about thirty seconds to convince me I shouldn't have the Board of Directors haul you both back to New Hope City and declare this entire expedition under military command," he said sweetly. "Go."

"We know our damned jobs, Captain," Trudeau repeated. He was a slim man of average height with night-black hair, and he hadn't moved from glaring at Wolastoq since Harold had arrived. "We've been surveying this planet grid by grid for eighteen months. We may be surveying here instead of around New Hope as planned, but we know the drill.

"High-level air searches, followed by ground surveys on areas of interest." He shrugged. "There's nothing *complicated* to this, Captain."

Harold nodded and looked over at Wolastoq. *She* was ignoring Trudeau and glaring at the Militia Captain, with a fire in her eyes that intrigued him.

"And, Doctor?" he asked simply.

"Trudeau knows his job," she allowed.

"*Thank* you!"

"But he's doing the wrong job," she said, holding up a hand to silence the director. "His people are geographic and resource survey-ors. Sure, by the time they're done, they'll know the location of every

source of minerals or hydrocarbon over a thousand tons in the area...
but I doubt the Kanzi risked war with the Imperium again for *raw
materials.*"

"We'd find anything else of interest, too," Trudeau objected.
"We're not going to miss anything."

"Yes, you will," Wolastoq snapped. "Your high-level air survey
will miss any sign under ten meters wide. Your scanner resolutions
aren't set up to detect small manufactured objects.

"We're not going to find a settlement or a facility or whatever
they were looking for on the surface," she continued. "All we're going
to find on the surface is minor debris, small amounts of discarded or
damaged manufactured objects. Hell, Director, your scanners
wouldn't even pick up concealed *power sources.*"

"There's not going to be—"

"There might," Harold cut Trudeau off. "We don't know what
the Kanzi were looking for, but they seemed to have a damn good
idea of what it was—and Doctor Wolastoq is quite correct. We're
looking for a facility or a settlement, not a mineral outcropping.

"They came here looking for something of enough value to know-
ingly lose thousands of people just for the chance. That's not raw
materials, as the lady says. That's tech. Tech they expected to be
intact and retrievable."

"That's nuts," Trudeau replied. "What kind of tech could they
want? Hell, as I heard it, the buggers had stealth fields."

"Weird ones," Harold said. His analysts were still puzzling out
the fields the Kanzi had used. "Too small for starships, and they
required atmosphere to function properly. If we hadn't followed
them down, we never would have found them. They'd have had
weeks to find what they were looking for.

"Dr. Wolastoq." He turned to the woman, whose glare had
become somewhat less hostile and somewhat more curious. "Can the
sensors Director Trudeau's people have be used for that kind of
search?"

"Yes, but not from altitude," she told him. "Fifty meters at most."

"We won't cover much area at all with the scanners at that height," he protested.

"But you won't *miss* anything, either," Wolastoq replied. "Better to take the time, Director, and do it *right*."

"I have to agree," Harold said. "People died because of whatever the Kanzi were looking for. We are going to find it, and if that means we need to take longer than you'd like, Director Trudeau, that means we take longer.

"Do you understand me?"

Unspoken was that if he *didn't*, Ramona Wolastoq was going to end up in command of this expedition.

"Yes, Captain."

CHAPTER SEVEN

In Annette Bond's opinion, her current status represented an utter betrayal by her husband, the people who'd put together the Charter for the new Duchy of Terra and her own body.

She'd thought the requirement for "an heir of the body" was a cute bit of poetry, until her newly elected Ducal Assembly started asking her when she planned on getting pregnant. Blonde and curvaceously attractive or no, Annette Bond was closer to fifty than forty and had built her career on being a hardass.

Unfortunately, the same sense of duty that had resulted in the United Earth Space Force's last Captain ending up as the Duchess of Terra had eventually led to her conceding the point—mostly because it would help with the politics around the A!Tol Imperium's newest member species and Duchy.

Ducal Consort Elon Casimir, however, had neglected to mention that his family tended towards twins and his own only-child status had been an anomaly until *after* they'd conceived.

The worst betrayal of all, however, in the mind of the woman who'd led a cruiser into exile, stopped an interstellar war, and dragged Earth's resistance kicking and screaming back into the fold, was that of her body.

At four months pregnant—with twins!—the doctors told her she was healthier than she had any right to be, and, beyond feeling slightly more tired than usual, she felt better than she had in years.

Plus, she *glowed*.

Her tailor was putting in a manful effort to help her suits conceal her pregnancy, and that state was the only reason she now employed a full-time tailor. She was making a very specific point to minimize the perks and benefits she claimed for her position.

Her stepdaughter, Morgan Casimir, was happily helping her dress. At a touch over eight years old, the blonde cherub wasn't *very* helpful yet, but she was at least better than Annette trying to dress herself.

"Are you ready?" a machine-generated but still-familiar voice asked, as a bullet-shaped body with a black beak navigated into her room on thick tentacles. The A!Tol Ki!Tana was an unusual specimen even among her own race, towering three meters tall when in motion and old enough not to remember how old she was.

She'd also survived the A!Tol version of menopause, which was almost universally fatal for assorted reasons, so she was basically immortal.

"As ready as I'm going to be until I'm no longer acting as a living incubator," Annette groused.

"Your young do not eat you alive," Ki!Tana pointed out. "Consider yourself lucky."

There was that. The A!Tol led the galaxy in artificial gestation technology for a reason.

That, of course, was why that "heir of the body" phrase was pissing her off.

"Are you coming with us?" she asked Ki!Tana.

"There is, unfortunately, a male A!Tol amongst the Imperial delegation," the Ki!Tol noted. Part of the price of her continued survival was avoiding the males of her species. A!Tol hormonal problems were...unimaginable to most species.

"I will need to avoid the meeting, but you and Elon and Orentel will be there," she continued. "I feel our world and family are well-represented."

"You had as much to do with *Manticore* as anyone," Annette said. "You deserve to be there."

"I had as much to do with this Duchy existing as anyone," Ki!Tana replied. "That doesn't mean I want to be visibly credited. That is not...how Ki!Tol work."

The survivors of the Birthing Madness were regarded as wise advisors by their race, but their history and legend had its similarities to old Norse kings and Odin. They were wise and they were helpful, but they were not often *safe*.

"Let's be on our way, Morgan," Annette told the child hovering at her elbow. "Villeneuve will never forgive us if we make the ship late."

"Unc' Jean will forgive me anything," the youngest Casimir said brightly. "He gonna be there?"

"Is he going to be there?" the Duchess of Terra corrected the child with a smile. "And yes, Admiral Villeneuve will be there.

"We are commissioning his new battleships, after all."

THE MASSIVE FORM of Annette's Councilor for the Treasury, Li Chin Zhao, waited outside the room for them. Zhao was a shaven-headed man dressed in a light pink suit that was carefully tailored to minimize as much of his obesity as possible.

He was also the former Chairman of the Republic of China and still the leader of the China Party. The Party was more of a social and philanthropic organization now, but it retained a degree of political power and influence—power and influence that Li Chin Zhao, as a member of Annette's Council, had made certain was thrown behind keeping the fledgling ducal government afloat.

Two of his ever-present white-suited young male bodyguards slash nurses hovered at his shoulders, trading professionally wary and amused glances with the Ducal Guards waiting for Annette.

"Captain Amandine sends his regards," the Councilor said warmly. "Your shuttle is landing on the roof of the Wuxing Tower as we speak, and I understand that the tram is waiting for us in the basement."

Annette lived on the top floor of a condominium building two blocks away from the Hong Kong skyscraper that had been acquired to house the Duchy's government. One of the reasons for choosing that particular penthouse had been the underground tram line that ran to Wuxing Tower.

"You are *not* my personal assistant," Annette pointed out with a chuckle.

"Yes, well." Zhao shrugged. "But since Jess and Maria are on maternity leave, poor Rianne is run off her feet. She's on her way up, but my staff have been helping her out so I knew the plan."

Maria Robin-Antionette was Annette's personal assistant and Jess Robin-Antionette was her press secretary. They'd met in Annette's service, married, and decided to have babies in one shot. *Both* of them were roughly eight months pregnant, which the Duchess of Terra regarded as the bravest thing she'd ever heard of a couple doing.

It also meant she'd lost two of her key staff members, and their replacement, Rianne Zhao Ha—a relative of both her Councilor for the Treasury and the Municipal Governor of Hong Kong—was still learning her job.

As Zhao finished speaking, in fact, Ha emerged from the elevator outside Annette's apartment, a tall dark-haired Asian woman who moved with surprising grace despite her clear rush.

"Your Grace!" she exclaimed at the sight of Annette. "Your shuttle—"

"The Councilor filled me in," Annette told Ha gently. "You're doing fine, Rianne. Please slow down and breathe."

"Yes, Your Grace. Thank you, Your Grace."

The Duchess of Terra looked around at the cavalcade she seemed to acquire wherever she went.

"All right, people. Let's not keep Admiral Villeneuve waiting. He's getting grumpier in his old age."

FOUR YEARS, give or take, was more than enough time for the Duchy of Terra to develop its own traditions, separate from both the A!Tol Imperium to which it owed its allegiance and the governments that had come before it.

One of those traditions, which Annette Bond would admit in her quieter moments was almost certainly her fault, was that the Duchess of Terra almost always traveled aboard the cruiser *Tornado*, now Militia hull number CA-001.

Three people had now commanded the ship after her, with Amandine taking over from Rolfson six months before when the *Thunderstorms* had commissioned, but *Tornado* remained unquestionably Annette's ship.

Of course, regardless of what Annette thought, the men and women who made up her Militia were never going to allow their Duchess to travel in Terra's oldest and least powerful heavy cruiser, even if *Tornado* remained more powerful than her Kanzi counterparts. Two *Duchess*-class super-battleships, each sixteen million tons of the best defensive and offensive systems the Imperium possessed, flanked the heavy cruiser as Annette's shuttle approach.

President Washington and *President de Gaulle* were the third and fourth super battleships to have entered the Duchy service...which also meant they were the oldest *still* in service, with *Queen of England* and the original *Emperor of China* having been destroyed driving back the Kanzi.

The upgraded *Majesty* class represented the current state of the art in Imperial military technology. The *Majesty*-class super-battleships they'd started as had been top-line warships—and then the Terrans had added compressed-matter armor and the Sword and Buckler systems.

Very few forces—outside, Annette supposed, the far more advanced Core Powers—could get past those ships without massively overwhelming firepower.

And that firepower would run into the defensive constellations around Earth, and the Duchy of Terra Militia's *other* five super-battleships, and the four *Thunderstorm* heavy cruisers, and...

And, well, the ships they were heading out to see today. Annette's shuttle tucked neatly into *Tornado*'s hangar bay, and she smiled as she saw the two men waiting for her. They were a study in contrasts, and each, in his own way, was utterly precious to her.

Short, dark-haired and noticeably chubby, Morgan Casimir's father Elon stood to one side of the deck with a wide grin on his face. The father of the twins currently making Annette glow was the mastermind behind today's events.

Next to him was the tall, white-haired and almost frail form of Admiral Jean Villeneuve. Once the commander of the United Earth Space Force, Villeneuve now led Annette's Militia and was her strong right hand, her shoulder to lean on, her trusted sword.

The years had been kind to him, but his job had not. With Imperial medical technology, the eighty-five-year-old Admiral should have another century in him, but Annette couldn't see it, looking at his worn face. She resolved herself to talk to him about Vice Admiral Pat Kurzman, the commander of the Solar Squadron, and succession planning.

When she exited the shuttle, however, Villeneuve beat her husband to her with the familiar spring in his step. He swept her into a brief but fierce embrace, and then stepped back to allow her and Elon to reach each other.

"How are you doing, Your Grace?" Elon asked her after she'd stolen a brief kiss from her much younger husband.

"Apparently, my body is a fan of pregnancy," she told him bitterly. "I am unimpressed and continue to regard this as your fault."

"*I* wasn't even part of the Charter Convention!" he replied with a laugh. "Blame Nash and Rutherford."

"Nash is on A!To," Annette replied. She'd sent Teddy Nash, once one of America's most famous actors, to the Imperial homeworld to sit in the House of Duchies as the speaker for Terra. The speakers in the House of Worlds and House of Species had been elected, but she had held on to the right to appoint the man who spoke for *her* on the capital planet.

"Rutherford, however..." She smiled grimly. Graham Rutherford was her Councilor for North American Affairs and had been a major organizer of the Charter Convention. "Would execution be too much for that 'heir of the body' clause? Should I just have him publicly flogged?"

"I believe you delegated your corporal-punishment authority to the First Ducal Court," Elon reminded her. "You'd have to convince them of his crimes, and you picked a stubborn collection of Judges."

"For a reason," she agreed with a sigh. She'd selected the nine Justices of the First Ducal Court from the former members of the various national supreme courts. Her criteria had been harsh, but she'd had quite a list of very qualified people. "For a reason," she repeated.

"Shall we get this show on the road? I believe we have an Imperial Echelon Lord to show off to!"

CHAPTER EIGHT

Annette and her collection of senior officials took over *Tornado*'s flag deck, currently unused as all of the cruisers in the system were simply attached to the Solar Squadron, commanded by *Tornado*'s former Captain.

"Greetings, Your Grace," Captain Cole Amandine told her over a video channel once she'd settled in. "We've been under way for a few minutes; we're just clearing the Terra drive-safety zone now and will be bringing the gravitational-hyperspatial interface momentum engine up to full power shortly."

She shook her head at him.

"Does *anyone* still use that entire mouthful, Captain?" she asked.

"The formal records, at least. You're looking fantastically well, if you don't mind the impertinence." Amandine was an unusually tall and skinny man—one of a still-small number of humans born and raised in the off-world asteroid colonies—though Imperial medicine had allowed him to give up the powered braces he'd once required to stand in regular gravity.

"It is somewhat impertinent," she noted, dropping into her frosty "the Captain's personal life is not your business" tones for a moment. Amandine recoiled for a moment, and then she smiled at him.

"But everyone seems to insist on it, so I won't be asking for your head *this* week, Captain," she continued. "To my displeasure, the twins and I are getting along stunningly well. This was *not* how I expected pregnancy to go for me!"

Amandine chuckled dutifully.

"We'll be in position over the Raging Waters of Friendship Yards in just over twenty minutes," he replied. "*A Dawning of Swords* and her escorts have already arrived with Echelon Lord Kas!Val. She sends her regards and looks forward to meeting you on Yard Station Bravo One."

The Duchy of Terra was a one-third partner in the Yards. Nova Industries, the company Elon Casimir still owned but no longer managed, owned another third. The last third was owned by a syndicate of Indiri shipbuilding houses, who had underwritten most of the cost of its construction.

And named it.

The journey to the Earth-Sol Lagrange Point Three didn't take particularly long at fifty-three percent of lightspeed, and Annette watched on the holodisplay they'd added to *Tornado*'s flag deck as they closed with the Raging Waters Yards.

There were two clear sections to the Yards.

Orbiting at the outside relative to the Sun were the main structures of the yards, dozens of refit slips arrayed around processing plants that busily consumed entire asteroids to produce the massive slabs of compressed-matter armor that were Terra's primary export.

Hundreds of small ships guided the slabs of compressed matter and the massive chunks of prebuilt support matrix through space, locking them onto the calmly helpless echelons of Imperial warships. Other ships cut into the older hulls, finding places to install prebuilt Sword anti-missile laser turrets or the docking nodes for Buckler anti-missile drones.

No non-Terran Ducal warship had been upgraded yet. After

three years, they'd still only upgraded half of the Imperial Navy's super-battleships, and the refit yards currently held forty battleships and twenty cruisers.

Closer to the Sun and set away from the refit facility were the actual construction yards. Built after the first, larger part of the yard, there were still only ten slips in place here. Six held *Thunderstorm*-class heavy cruisers, the second tranche of the warships to be built in Sol.

Those were only a third built, still over a year away from completion.

The remaining four construction slips were why Annette was there. Four immense double-ended-spindle hulls, each sixteen hundred meters long and seven hundred meters across at their widest point and massing just under eleven million tons.

They were more heavily set than *A Dawning of Swords*, the delicately elegant A!Tol battleship that hung beside them, and wrapped in the sheets of compressed armor *Dawning* hadn't been upgraded with yet.

Two of the *Manticore*-class battleships were still a year from completion. *Manticore* herself, however, and her sister *Griffon*, were now complete and about to launch on their space trials.

They would be the first battleships in the Duchy of Terra Militia and the first hyper-capable battleships humanity had ever built.

What everyone knew, of course, was the price of membership in the A!Tol Imperium and the reason Echelon Lord Kas!Val was present. *Manticore* and *Griffon* would serve the Duchy—but their two sisters would be presented to the Imperium.

Kas!Val was there to assess whether or not the Imperial Navy was actually going to want them.

YARD STATION BRAVO ONE SAT "ABOVE" the construction yards, serving as the central hub and docking facility for the roughly three hundred and fifty spacecraft and fifty thousand workers assigned to the construction facility.

Bravo Two and Bravo Three flanked the construction slips but were barely half of Bravo One's size combined. Bravo Four was almost hidden in the hubbub of the construction but, as one of Sol's two production plants for modern point seven five interface-drive missiles, was at least as important as Bravo One.

Annette and her entourage were escorted through to the main observation deck, a four-story edifice of heavily reinforced transparent ceramic—rated to survive a nuclear explosion—that looked out over the yards.

Directly in front of the observation deck lay *Manticore*, her running lights still dark and several tugs still standing by. All of the physical connections would have already been dismantled, and her trial crew was aboard, but the battleship would be silent until formally released to her trials by the ceremony to come.

Captain Patience Van der Merwe stood stiffly by the window, flanked by potted trees that shadowed the black South African officer into near-invisibility. Two bodyguards stood with her, helping her maintain a very clear personal space bubble that was not normal for a Militia Captain.

Standing at almost the exact opposite end of the observation deck were the immense, multi-tentacled forms of the A!Tol contingent. The largest of them wore the insignia of an Echelon Lord, a massive older female Annette knew to be Echelon Lord Kas!Val.

She wasn't sure who the junior officers, one female and one male to her now-practiced eye, were—but both of them were flashing the mixed purple, orange, and yellow of what a human would call mortification.

Kas!Val was mixing orange and yellow. She was angry—and either lying or feeling dirty.

A!Tol literally wore their emotions on their skin. It didn't leave much doubt as to what they were thinking, but it also meant that they couldn't always be diplomatic even if they were trying.

Two massive four-legged, two-armed bodyguards flanked the senior officers. They wore the insignia of Imperial Marines, but it was unusual, to Annette's knowledge, for an A!Tol officer to have an escort that wasn't either of their own race or one of the other Imperial Races, the oldest members of the Imperium.

The Anbrai were extraordinarily intimidating, being built like meter-and-a-half-wide barrels with legs, arms and heads, but they were not an Imperial Race. For an A!Tol Echelon Lord to have them for her escorts was a not-so-subtle insult from her Marine commander.

"Ah, Duchess Bond," a familiar clicking voice interjected into her thoughts, and she turned to find the iridescent carapace of Orentel, one of the Laians who'd settled on Earth and once Dockmaster for the Laian Exiles at Tortuga.

Now Orentel's mate Tidikat was a Commodore in the Duchy of Terra Militia, and Orentel herself was a civilian contractor with Nova Industries. Most definitely *not* a member of the military or an employee of the Duchy of Terra or the A!Tol Imperium.

The gloriously multicolored alien remained one of the few Laian females Annette had met—her monogamous relationship with Tidikat was moderately perverted by Laian standards, as the Duchess understood it—but she was also one of the smartest people she'd ever met.

Orentel had forgotten more about shipbuilding and weapons technology than most engineers would hope to ever learn—and she had a photographic memory.

"Orentel. It's good to see you," Annette told her, trading slight bows with the scarab-beetle-like alien. "Any concerns with the launch?"

"Nothing," the Laian said quickly. "Your tentacled friend managed to infuriate Captain Van der Merwe in under a hundredth-cycle, though." Orentel paused thoughtfully. "I did not think that was possible."

Annette winced. *That* was not good.

"If everything is ready, let Fernandez know we're here," she told Orentel. "I'll go meet with the Echelon Lord."

"What is it you humans say?" The Laian clicked her mandibles. "'Better you than me'?"

"ELON, Li, if you can go check in on Captain Van der Merwe," Annette asked softly. "Jean, I think you and I should go talk to the Echelon Lord."

"She won't find my rank particularly intimidating," the Admiral pointed out. "So far as she's concerned, I'm sure, she outranks any Militia officer."

"That's her problem," the Duchess of Terra replied. "I have some frustration at the universe to work out, and it appears Kas!Val may have volunteered to help me do so."

She saw Elon wince out of the corner of her eye, but he took Morgan by the hand and led the little girl away toward *Manticore*'s new Captain, Annette's treasurer trailing in his wake.

"Come on, Jean," Annette told her old mentor. "Let's go talk to our overlord's representative."

The old Admiral sighed and fell in at her shoulder as she crossed the dock to the Imperial Navy contingent. One of the Anbrai stepped in front of her and grunted.

"Echelon Lord is busy," the big alien told her, and Annette met the much taller creature's eyes and smiled.

"This is my star system, Initiate," she told the very junior officer calmly. "You and your mistress have two choices: she speaks with me now, or all of you get back on *A Dawning of Swords* and get the hell *out* of my star system while I officially complain to the Empress about your attitude and actions.

"Do you really want to make that decision for the Echelon Lord, Initiate?" she asked very, very quietly.

Anbrai were huge and so were their throats. She could *watch* the big alien swallow hard before he backed away.

"No, Your Grace."

"Good boy," she said, quite certain the not-quite-friendly intent would carry through the translator, then approached Kas!Val.

"Echelon Lord Kas!Val," Annette greeted the A!Tol. "Welcome to Sol. Are you looking forward to watching the space trials for *Manticore?*"

The flag officer's skin darkened dramatically.

"No," she said, the translator carrying the condescension in her voice quite clearly. "I'm not even certain why I was sent. The likelihood that your homebuilt trash will suffice to meet your obligations to the Imperial Navy is quite low, Duchess Bond. This is waste of several five-cycles of my time, time that the Navy could get much better value from."

"Echelon Lord, has *A Dawning of Swords* been updated to the newest specifications?" Annette asked.

"Not yet," the A!Tol replied.

"That upgrade will be done here," the Duchess told her. "Every ship in the Imperial Navy is planned to pass through these yards over the next ten long-cycles. *Every. Ship.*

"Do you really think that our own designs are so worthless when the Navy has tasked us with upgrading every warship in the Imperium?"

Kas!Val made a flicking gesture with one of her manipulator tentacles.

"I warned them that such a program would make you arrogant," she noted. "Tan!Shallegh's strange attachment to your species appears to be risking the strategic stability of the Imperium. You should tread carefully, Duchess Bond."

"I remind you, Echelon Lord, that this is *my* star system." Annette echoed what she'd told the young bodyguard. "I will not be threatened, Kas!Val. And if you will not work with my people, I will ask the Empress to send me someone who will."

That probably wouldn't *end* Kas!Val's career...but it would be a huge black mark when she came up for promotion to Squadron Lord. There were only twenty-eight species in the A!Tol Imperium—and only thirty Duchies. Annette Bond spoke for both one of the Duchies and one of the species.

And the Empress had personally stated the depth of the debt the Imperium owed Terra for short-stopping the early stages of what could easily have been another war with the Kanzi. She would not appreciate an officer who got on Annette's bad side.

It wasn't a lever she'd pull often, but Kas!Val wasn't doing herself any favors—and her orange-yellow skin acquired whirls of purple and black. Stress and fear. The A!Tol was realizing she might have picked a bit more of a fight than she was ready for.

"I did not intend to threaten," she said carefully. "I am, of course, fully willing to work with your people and to assess these *Manticores*. It is necessary to note that the likelihood that these ships will meet Navy standards is low."

"I believe you underestimate them, and I suggest you keep an open mind," Annette told her. "But first, I suggest you tell me exactly what you said to one of my best Captains that I'm going to need you to apologize for."

"I said noth—"

Annette held up a hand.

"I know Patience Van der Merwe," she said flatly. "So, unless you want me to be powering up the starcom specifically to complain about you, I suggest you explain what you did—and I *require* that you apologize to her for it!"

ONE GRACELESS APOLOGY, undercut by the tone of Kas!Val's skin but as good as Annette was going to get, later, the Duchess of Terra stepped onto a raised platform against the observation deck's window. Behind her, the two dark lumps of the *Manticore*-class battleships floated in space, waiting for the command to bring them online for their space trials.

"By now, all of you know how I feel about speeches," she told the gathered crowd. "Believe me, being pregnant has *not* improved my opinion of standing up, blathering on and on. But today...today is important.

"Captain Van der Merwe, Captain Darzi, get up here," Annette ordered.

The two Captains could not have been a sharper contrast to Annette's own American Midwest pale skin and blond braid. Van der Merwe was a tall black woman, broad-shouldered and powerfully built if not necessarily conventionally attractive. Captain Arash Darzi was ten centimeters shorter but only a few skin shades lighter, the Iranian officer wearing a white turban that matched the two Captains' stark white dress uniforms perfectly.

"These are your formal orders," she told them, handing each Captain an archaic piece of parchment. "But we all know what they are: Captain Patience Van der Merwe, you will take command of *Manticore* in my service. Captain Arash Darzi, you will take command of *Griffon.*

"Fail in this charge at your peril, et cetera, et cetera," Annette said grimly. "These two ships represent a turning point for the Duchy, our first homebuilt capital ships.

"They have every innovation built into them that we have sold the Imperium, and while they are smaller than the super-battleships that have anchored the Militia so far, they are and will always be special.

"So, we entrust them to two of our finest Captains and we have faith in you to do us proud! Thank you, Captains."

Annette was relatively sure that Van der Merwe, at least, suspected that Villeneuve and Annette had tried to give one of the ships to Harold Rolfson, but *Liberty*'s CO had refused on the basis that he'd only been in command of the *Thunderstorm* for six months.

There was more going on there, she suspected, but she'd only been a mediocre counselor even when she'd been a captain. As a Duchess, her job description required her to leave that to others.

"Mister Fernandez?"

Tais Fernandez, Nova Industries' Chief of Construction, was a short and tanned Hispanic man. He'd once led the secret research facility that had developed Annette's *Tornado*. Now he led Earth's largest construction project.

And if BugWorks still existed somewhere, well, that was a task for more junior, less visible men and women now. And it wasn't something Annette would talk about in this public of a setting.

"Everything is in order, Your Grace. Captains, the ships are yours," he told them. "If Miss Casimir would do the honors?"

A pair of big blue buttons marked a panel at the end of the dais, and Annette waved her stepdaughter forward. Memories of *Tornado*'s commissioning, five years earlier, flickered through her mind as the little girl stepped up and hit the right-hand button.

A pneumatic cannon fired a bottle of champagne into space, glinting in the lights of the yard as it flashed across the fifty or so meters between it and *Manticore*. A zoomed-in image of the bottle overlaid several chunks of the window as it smashed home, scattering broken glass and golden bubbles across the battleship's prow.

Then her running lights flickered to life, a spiraling pattern of light and power as *Manticore* officially came alive. She still had six months of space trials ahead of her, but the lights marked her formal activation.

The second button repeated the process for *Griffon*, another glittering bottle of champagne smashing across a dark gray compressed-matter hull.

"There's a lot of work left to do, Captains," Annette reminded them. "But we also have a small party set up in your honor, and I suggest we be about it."

CHAPTER NINE

HERMES FOUR HAD, ACCORDING TO HER ORIGINAL SCHEDULE, been supposed to get James back to Sol in time for the launching ceremonies for the new battleships. Commander McPhail's apologies aside, however, he was hardly surprised to be late.

No matter how competent the captain—and Commander Mary McPhail was as confidently skilled as a courier skipper as she had been a shuttle pilot, with thankfully less opportunity to add to James's gray hairs—the currents of hyperspace were not entirely predictable.

A navigator could have a mostly predictable route if they had a chart of the local currents and avoided them...but it would be a very slow route. Most navigators took those charts and rode the currents instead, cutting as much as half or two thirds off of their travel time.

The hyperspace currents around Sol and Alpha Centauri were well charted now, but that merely made travel safe and quick. It didn't make it any more predictable.

His understanding, of course, didn't keep James from standing at the back of *Hermes Four*'s bridge, watching McPhail's navigator prepare to open the hyper portal back into Sol. Generations of social conditioning and years of practice meant that he was almost as calm and steady as he appeared, but he dreaded the conversations he was about to have with his husband—who had known Harrison well before the man had left Earth—and his Duchess.

"We're on approach for the Raging Waters of Friendship Yards," the navigator reported. "We have confirmed location on the system perimeter hyper buoys. Emergence in thirty seconds and counting."

A starship could detect an interface drive at a hyperspace distance easily equivalent to several light-months, but anything else had a far shorter distance. The solution the Imperium used for navigation in its core systems was to emplace thirty or so devices whose sole purpose was to have an interface drive up for pure location maintenance: hyper buoys .

They marked the point where it was safe to open a hyper portal. A good navigator would be able to tell that regardless, but they were a useful aid, so the Duchy had acquired them.

"Portal opening."

The strange grayness of hyperspace "tore" open in front of *Hermes Four* as her exotic-matter arrays energized. The hole in space they opened glittered with natural light, the familiar yellow glow of James's home sun.

Even as the courier flashed through the portal, a quick but uncomfortable process, that familiar light allowed him to relax a bit. He relaxed more as he saw spread out before them the glittering lights of the massive yard complex that provided over eighty percent of the Duchy's Imperial credit revenue.

"We are on target," McPhail told him. "We should have you to the main station in under five minutes."

The redheaded Commander shook her head.

"Lot of metal out there, sir," she continued, studying her repeater displays. "*Tornado* on one side with a pair of super-battleships for escorts, four Imperial cruisers and a battlewagon on the other. All playing nice so far."

"I wouldn't expect anything else," he said. "Even our Militia ships are, technically, Imperial warships, after all."

"Don't remind me," McPhail replied dryly. "I accept the Duchess's choice; doesn't mean I like being a subject race."

James chuckled.

"I'm English, Commander," he replied. "Being a subject race is just the universe's normal irony for us."

HERMES FOUR EDGED toward the station and James found himself with an enviable view of the two battleships coming fully online. The last few shuttles made their way over to the starships, and they finally began to move.

Both the new ships and the courier were going at a snail's pace relative to the capabilities of their engines as they passed, their total speed barely passing a single percent of light. *Hermes* continued on her way toward the station and continued to slow down, though, and *Manticore* and *Griffon* began to speed up.

By the time the courier finally docked, the two battleships had peaked at half of lightspeed and were well on their way to the outer system. Five percent of light faster than their Imperial equivalents, faster than any capital ship in the region except the Imperium's "fast battleships" that were half their size.

James wasn't entirely aware of what trade-offs had been made to build a compressed-matter-armored battleship that could out-pace her contemporaries, only that trade-offs had been made.

They were still damned impressive ships.

"Docking in just over a minute, sir," McPhail told him. "*Hermes* isn't a big ship, but it will take you more than that to get down to the hatch—and Station Control just told me you've got two Admirals and a Duchess waiting for you at the dock."

James smiled thinly. He wouldn't allow himself more than that, but if there were *two* Admirals, then one was almost certainly his husband, Vice Admiral Pat Kurzman—and if Pat hadn't been among his greeting party, McPhail would have told him that.

"Thank you, Commander. This ranks among my most pleasant flights with you," he said calmly. "We didn't end up embedded in an enemy base or *anything*."

"As I recall, sir, burying you in the middle of the base was the order," she replied.

"The order was 'get us down'," James corrected primly. "*Inside the planet* was a little extreme."

She laughed.

"Your husband, my boss, and the woman who is *both* of our ultimate bosses, are waiting for you, General. Get off my bridge. Shoo!"

ANNETTE BOND WAITED CALMLY while her second-ranked Militia flag officer and highest-ranked Ducal Guards embraced and kissed. Centauri was a calm backwater still; she had no worries about what might have happened while Wellesley was there—and it was two days' travel away, so a few minutes were hardly a risk either way.

However, once Wellesley stepped away from Vice Admiral Kurzman, a broad-shouldered stocky man who was a sharp contrast to his tall and slim husband, his face was even grimmer than his usual aristocratic British stoicism.

"We have a problem," he told his greeting party flatly. "Division Lord Harrison is dead. Hope was attacked by an unknown force."

Annette was suddenly glad that the two men had taken time to greet each other appropriately, because she knew what the rest of the day was going to look like. The sinking feeling of solid ground dropping out beneath her feet was all too familiar.

"How bad?" she asked.

"The Navy picket was shattered, over fifty percent losses, including both cruisers. *Liberty* identified the intruders before they arrived, however, and engaged them successfully in the end.

"There was a ground landing using stealth fields that we managed to localize and defeat before they could disappear, but..." He shook his head. "They were looking for something and they brought Core Power–level tech to the party. Faster engines, more powerful shields, some kind of energy weapon we'd never seen before."

"No idea who?" Villeneuve asked. "Because I've some guesses."

"Landing party was Kanzi," Wellesley confirmed. "But...while the *designs* were Kanzi and the troops were Kanzi, the tech was centuries ahead of what they're supposed to have."

"Half the picket?" Annette echoed. And Harrison. One of only two human flag officers in the Imperium, and a measurable percentage of the human personnel in the Imperial Navy with him. "We need to inform the Navy if the Theocracy is moving again..."

"I don't know, Your Grace," her Guard commander replied. "They were Kanzi, but everything was wrong for them to be Theocracy."

"The Theocracy would not permit a major rogue faction," Villeneuve argued. "They fought a civil war over that three hundred years ago."

"Even if they somehow weren't Theocracy, the Imperium will need to summon the Theocracy for answers," Annette said grimly. "There's no point in a peace treaty or recognition of the Kovius zone or all of the crap involved in the Sol Treaty if we make excuses for them, gentlemen."

She sighed.

"And we have an Imperial Echelon Lord on hand," she continued. "You'll need to brief us more completely, James, and sadly, I think we need to include Kas!Val."

ANNETTE WONDERED if the Echelon Lord—roughly equivalent to a Rear Admiral in her Militia or the old UESF—was always grumpy and uncomfortable, or if it was just that Kas!Val really didn't like humans.

She wasn't taking bets either way, but the A!Tol flag officer wore her orange and yellow skin tones with a degree of self-confidence she doubted many humans could carry if they knew everyone around them knew they were grumpy.

"I've been reviewing the specifications and performance of your battleships," the A!Tol told Annette. "That is a process I can complete more quickly without interruption."

The unspoken comment of *and everyone would like me to be gone, including me* was so obvious, Annette half-expected the translator to pick it up.

"We have a problem, Echelon Lord," Annette told the A!Tol quietly. "A potential strategic threat to the Imperium. We have reports that will be forwarded to Navy command and Fleet Lord Tan!Shallegh, but I wanted to pull you into the initial briefing so you can pass on your own thoughts as well."

That Annette expected those thoughts to be slanted against Terra didn't invalidate that need. *Not* including Kas!Val would appear disloyal, especially in a Duchy so new—and especially in a Duchy whose proximity to the border with the Theocracy meant they were pouring a lot more resources into the Ducal military than was common.

There were other reasons for that, and to Annette's amusement, while she was certain the *Imperium* knew about the new BugWorks project, Kas!Val clearly did not.

"As you must," Kas!Val conceded. She pulled up one of the wide stools the many-tentacled A!Tol used in place of chairs, and settled in.

"General Wellesley." Annette turned to the Englishman. "I know you gave us the high level before and that there are full reports we have access to, but I suggest you run through the sequence of events as you are aware of them for all of our sakes."

"I can do that," Wellesley confirmed, stepping up to the front of the conference room while Annette sank, more gratefully than she'd let anyone see, into one of the powered, self-adjusting chairs that surrounded the long black table.

The General faced the group, which included both of Kas!Val's aides as well as Annette, Kurzman, Villeneuve, Elon and Zhao. Between the Ducal Guards assigned to most of the Terrans and Kas!Val's Marines, there were easily twenty armed sentients guarding the relatively small doors into the room.

"I was not present for the initial portion of the incident," he noted calmly. "I can only summarize what Captain Rolfson told me.

"He and *Liberty* were on a courtesy patrol of hyperspace around the Alpha Centauri system when they detected four unscheduled arrivals making a high-speed—point six cee—approach to the system.

"He attempted to approach to a range he could challenge them at, per the Duchy's agreements with the Centauri Development Corporation, and they opened fire with missiles that are well beyond our current technology."

"How far beyond are we talking?" Kas!Val asked, clearly having engaged a professional brain Annette hadn't been certain the alien had.

"They were point eight five cee missiles," Wellesley told her. "Now, I'm a ground soldier, so I'm sure that means more to you all, but my understanding is that that's about the theoretical maximum of an interface drive. You can't build faster missiles."

"That's the fastest you can build an interface drive missile, yes," Kurzman confirmed for his husband. He seemed about to say more, but a glance at Kas!Val shut him up.

"The Mesharom have supposedly built a hyperspace-capable weapon," the A!Tol Echelon Lord said reluctantly. "But short of that, you are correct."

"Carry on, General," Annette ordered.

"*Liberty* returned fire and began a running engagement with the unknowns that eventually crossed into the Centauri system," Wellesley noted. "There, the Navy picket under Division Lord

Harrison moved to intercept, attempting to trap what appeared to be four destroyers between *Liberty* and his own force."

"Destroyers? I thought the *Thunderstorm*s were an effective design," Kas!Val noted.

"*Liberty* destroyed one of the four ships shortly after leaving hyperspace, but they possessed both extremely powerful shields and compressed-matter armor," the General replied. "They lacked active missile defenses, however, and the remaining three vessels proved unable to penetrate the missile defense of Lord Harrison's fleet.

"Unfortunately, upon reaching beam range, they demonstrated a defensive system we cannot identify that completely negated Lord Harrison's proton-beam armament," Wellesley continued. "They then closed to the range of an unknown weapons system with which they destroyed both of the light cruisers and several of the destroyers from Division Lord Harrison's task force.

"While doing so, they launched a ground assault that I deployed the Ducal Guard and local Marine garrison to neutralize. They used another unknown technology to stealth themselves once they reached atmosphere, something similar to a Mesharom stealth field but much less effective.

"Fortunately, we were able to localize their landing and engage them. *Liberty* intercepted the surviving destroyers on the way out of the system and took them all out."

"How?" the A!Tol demanded. "If the battle lasted as long as it sounds, *Liberty* must have been out of missiles, and you've told me the proton beams were nonfunctional."

Wellesley sighed.

"Captain Rolfson engaged them with his cruiser's plasma lance," he noted flatly. "He specifically told me that information was critical to convey to both the Militia and the Navy."

Annette echoed her General's sigh.

"It is," she agreed. "We had hoped to get the *Thunderstorm*s into general Imperial service before anyone became aware of the plasma lances. There is a chance that the Laians may attribute our deploy-

ment of the system to stripping the Laian ships in our possession—
and the Republic has already made noises about wanting to reclaim
those ships and the Exiles."

"They left the Republic hundreds of years ago," Villeneuve
objected. "They have no claim on Orentel and her people now."

"Aggravating the Laian Republic is unwise," Kas!Val replied.
"The Navy should not have approved this deployment. *Would not*
have approved this. What kind of game are you playing, Duchess
Bond?"

"Echelon Lord, the *Thunderstorm* design was assembled in cooperation with the Imperial Navy, and between us and our Indiri and
Pibo licensees, the Navy has ordered eighty of them. If your superiors
had a concern about the plasma lance," Annette said, "they'd have
mentioned it when they were ordering *five squadrons* of them."

Kas!Val's skin tone was mutinous, but she shut up.

"Explain what we know of who these people were to the Echelon
Lord," Annette ordered Wellesley.

"While the technology is far too advanced for the Theocracy, the
ship design was quite distinctly Kanzi in origin, and the landing party
was made up of Kanzi. They all had ritual scarring that is anathema
to the Theocracy, and committed suicide rather than be captured—
even what appeared to be a civilian research detail."

"Civilians?" the A!Tol asked.

"I think they were looking for something. I don't know what,"
Wellesley admitted, "but the CDC is focusing their efforts on finding
out. If there is something to find, something worth risking that much
firepower and life for, we will find it.

"In the meantime, we need to protect Hope."

"I agree," Annette confirmed. "Admiral Villeneuve?"

"Your Grace?"

"Can we spare a super-battleship division?" she asked. She was
unsurprised by his wince—until *Manticore* and *Griffon* came online,
that was a third of his capital-ship strength. "Plus at least two cruisers
and a destroyer echelon?"

He nodded.

"That's almost half our hulls, but yes," Villeneuve confirmed. He glanced at the other Militia flag officer in the room. "You're the only one I can send with that kind of deployment, Kurzman," he noted. "Sorry, James."

"I get back and he runs away," the General agreed. "We're used to it, Jean."

"Echelon Lord?" Annette said to Kas!Val. "I will be sending a request for additional units to the local Navy base as well as A!To. Your comments and analysis would be most welcome as an attachment."

A flash of bright blue crossed the Echelon Lord's skin—a sign of acceptance, the equivalent of a human nodding.

"I will send my assessment, yes," she confirmed. The A!Tol considered for a moment, the orange and yellow of her skin fading in a dark green-blue that Annette recognized as determined curiosity.

"I will hold my own vessel and escorts here," she continued. "I have been authorized to take some time to assess the *Manticore*-class ships, and having an additional Navy unit two days away cannot hurt."

"It will not," Annette agreed, surprised and gratified by the suggestion. "Thank you, Echelon Lord."

"Duchess, I will not pretend to like your people, and I feel that we have accelerated your development more than is healthy for you or us," Kas!Val said bluntly. "But you remain members of the A!Tol Imperium and your defense is the Navy's obligation."

CHAPTER TEN

THE SUPER-BATTLESHIP *DUCHESS OF TERRA* LED THE WAY through the hyper portal into the Kimar system, her escorting cruisers swinging wide around her as they followed through. Forty-five seconds after the seventeen-point-five-million-ton warship reentered normal space, *Majesties of Yin* followed her out, accompanied by her own quartet of cruisers.

Division Lord Harriet Tanaka hummed softly to herself as the ten warships under her direct command executed the maneuver perfectly. The rest of the echelon continued to exit hyperspace in sequence behind her ships, but that was Echelon Lord Kora Siyid Luat's problem.

Every capital ship in the echelon had been provided by the Duchy of Terra. Seven of their crews were entirely human as well. Newly blooded tradition required that *Duchess of Terra*, who had been deployed to defend Sol with a scratch multiracial crew, be manned by multiple races.

The cruisers were all Imperial Navy–funded, not Ducal Levies, with a mixed bag of races providing the crews. Since Harriet herself was the most senior human officer in the Imperial Navy, it had been inevitable that the human Ducal levy be commanded by a nonhuman.

Luat had been well chosen, in the Japanese woman's considered opinion. He knew when to lead, when to listen, and when to get out of the way—and that was all a junior could ask for.

"Captain Sier reports we've been challenged by Kimar Control," Commander Piditel reported. The Rekiki, small for his race but still massive by most sentients' standards, had attached himself to Harriet's rising star somehow. Once the communications officer of her ship, he was now her flag staff communication officer.

"He knows the drill," Harriet replied. The single echelon, an eight-ship half-squadron of capital ships that made up the Duchy of Terra's military levy, was permanently assigned to the Kimar fleet base and kept intact.

That wouldn't last forever, Harriet knew. Each one of the Imperium's twenty-four Duchies was supposed to provide a full squadron of capital ships and escorts. There were enough new ones still building up to their full obligation, like Terra, that the Ducal Levies made up twenty squadrons of capital ships and thirty-six of escorts—forty percent of the Navy's capital ships and roughly a third of its escorts.

"He does," Piditel agreed. "Just keeping you updated."

Behind them, the eighth super-battleship and her escorts flashed out of hyperspace and the portals collapsed. Echelon Lord Luat had taken them on a two-week-long hyperspace exercise, pulling them entirely out of starcom communication to practice their logistics and short-range coordination.

It had been, in Harriet's opinion, an unqualified success. And not just because Second Division had taken home the overall top rank in the unofficial competition, either. The grouping had been close enough that she had no concerns going into battle with the rest of the echelon behind her.

"Division Lord," Piditel suddenly snapped formally, his long, crocodile-like snout turning back toward her with disturbing suddenness. "Fleet Lord Tan!Shallegh is requesting your presence aboard the flagship as soon as possible."

"Are the other flag officers requested?" Harriet asked.

"No, Division Lord. Just you."

HARRIET'S TOSUMI bodyguard fell in around her as the shuttle docked with *Glory of Hearts*, Tan!Shallegh's new flagship. *Glory of Hearts* was a rare vessel indeed: one of the Imperium's handful of *Glorious*-class super-battleships and also one of the roughly half of the Imperium's super-battleships to be upgraded to the new defensive specifications in the yards at Sol.

To Harriet's knowledge, only four of the *Glorious*es had been so upgraded, which made Tan!Shallegh's possession of *Glory of Hearts* as his flagship a clear sign of how his superiors regarded the A!Tol Fleet Lord.

Male A!Tols found it hard to rise in the ranks, and while the *Tan!* at the start of the Fleet Lords name marked his close relation to the Empress, he'd earned his superiors' faith several times over—and also earned *humanity's* trust.

And even Harriet, who looked at the alien as something of a mentor now, found it somewhat ironic that the A!Tol humanity trusted most was also the being who'd conquered them.

Armored A!Tol Marines greeted her as she exited her shuttle, their size—and profession—guaranteeing they were female. They fell in respectfully around her as one of Tan!Shallegh's aides approached her.

"I am Commander Ioan," the small, hairless humanoid told her. Gray-skinned and black eyed with no visible ears or nose, Ioan was unquestionably a Pibo. Like the Tosumi, they were one of the Imperial Races, the three species that had been culturally assimilated by the A!Tol before they'd mastered uplifting.

"The Fleet Lord will be available for you in a tenth-cycle," the

Commander continued. "If you can follow me, we've set aside a conference room for this, and our steward has a pot of green tea brewing."

Harriet smiled.

"It appears I am being spoiled, Commander. What's going on?"

Pibo didn't smile the same way humans did. Harriet had known enough of them now, however, to recognize the tilt of the eye-wrinkles that was an equivalent gesture.

"Division Lord, I would lose my job if I spoiled the Fleet Lord's surprises!" The eye-wrinkles straightened into a moment of seriousness.

"Not all of them are pleasant," Ioan noted after a moment. "I can tell you this much: the colony at Hope was attacked."

The gentle amusement at Tan!Shallegh having a tea available that was still grown only on Earth vanished in an instant.

"I see," Harriet replied. "Then let's make sure we're ready to meet with the Lord, shall we?"

FLEET LORD TAN!SHALLEGH was one of the smallest adult A!Tol Harriet Tanaka had ever met, clad in a black leather harness that carried his decorations and rank insignia while covering very little of the ever-changing skin of his species.

His size, she was led to understand, was mostly due to his gender. The physical differences between the two genders were quite pronounced in the A!Tol, though their culture was *slowly* beginning to accept that the *mental* differences were much less than they'd believed.

"Division Lord Tanaka," he greeted her, his skin flushing light blue with pleasure. The flush faded quickly into the whorls of green and purple swirling across his skin. The Imperial flag officer was stressed but determined.

"Fleet Lord Tan!Shallegh," she replied, with a slight bow of her head. She was seated with a steaming cup of her home country's tea in front of her, but Imperial etiquette did not call for her or Ioan to stand in the presence of the Fleet Lord.

"Firstly, my more pleasant surprises," Tan!Shallegh told her. A black box emerged from his harness and dropped onto the table. "Open it, Tanaka," he ordered.

She did.

Her own uniform was a derivation of the UESF's old one, itself an evolution of the old US Navy dress blues, but cut in the black and white of the Imperial Navy. She wore at her collar the insignia of an Imperial Navy Division Lord, a pair of crossed spears.

The box in front of her contained an identical insignia...carved from pearl. She knew the stone had almost certainly come from A!To, not Earth, but the process of its formation was functionally identical.

The cultural baggage around it was quite different though. To the A!To—and the Imperial Races—pearl was a sign of surviving pressure, of courage in the face of adversity. The sign of duty.

Which made crossed pearl spears the insignia of an Imperial Navy Echelon Lord, equivalent to a UESF Rear Admiral.

"Yours, *Echelon* Lord Tanaka," Tan!Shallegh told her. "For service well rendered, over time instead of in one great battle like your last promotion. You have served our Empress and our Imperium well."

"Thank you, Fleet Lord," she said slowly, replacing the pin at her collar with the new one. Imperial Navy uniforms didn't use braids or chevrons to mark rank, as there were too many variations in the cut and style—Tan!Shallegh's simple black harness was the A!Tol uniform, for example—which meant that changing the pin made all the difference to her rank.

"Ioan told me that Hope had been attacked?" she asked.

"Yes," the Fleet Lord confirmed. "Part of why your promotion is today without ceremony rather in a five-cycle once I had the chance to pull together all the appropriate glittering waters."

"My life is service," Harriet replied instantly. That was the choice she had made to save her son's life when it had turned out that the Imperials could cure his rare disease—and while that medicine would be available to everyone eventually, it would be available to the families of Navy volunteers *immediately*.

"Hope was attacked by an unknown force," her superior explained. "Apparently Kanzi. If we believe the High Priestess's and the Priest Speaker's protestations—and to my surprise, I am inclined to—apparently *non-Theocracy* Kanzi.

"Even the existence of Kanzi outside the Theocracy is of extreme strategic importance," he noted. "Given the level of technology shown in the attack—near Core Power levels!—the importance only grows.

"Bond's Militia concluded that the attack was looking for something. They're hunting for it, but they need backup if these strangers come back with another wave."

"I see, sir."

"You're keeping *Duchess of Terra* and her division mate," Tan!Shallegh told her. "Normal currents suggest you'll want to keep your flag aboard her."

"*Duchess* and her crew and I have been through a lot together," Harriet confirmed with a thoughtful hum. "I think I will."

"Good. I am also detaching a half-echelon out of Squadron Lord Uan's Thirtieth Battle Squadron," he continued. "Fast battleships; they may not be big, but I suspect maneuverability may be more important.

"I'm also splitting the Kimar Station's currents to provide you with two squadrons of cruisers to reinforce the escorts from your ships and the two divisions of fast battleships I'm giving you.

"That will give you forty-four cruisers and six capital ships, Echelon Lord, a force that requires a commander of your rank," he noted. "You'll have a few cycles to work them up here as a unit, but you need to be in Alpha Centauri in, shall we say, twelve cycles."

It was a seven-and-a-half-cycle—slightly more than a week—flight from Kimar to Alpha Centauri with the latest charts. Plus or minus a half-cycle either way, with the currents.

Five cycles wasn't much time to work up fifty starships, but twelve days was as long as they could justify leaving Alpha Centauri uncovered.

Harriet nodded grimly.

"I understand, sir," she told Tan!Shallegh. "Do you have the contact information for my subordinate flag officers and Captains? We will need to get started immediately."

CHAPTER ELEVEN

HAROLD HAD TO ADMIT THAT CDC'S PEOPLE WERE IMPRESSIVE. In barely a week, they'd gone from bare rock to a bustling settlement resembling a small town, with prefabricated structures laid out in neat avenues.

The tents were gone now, replaced with more solid shelters with better heaters. The Corellian Plateau was bitterly cold, even for Hope, a world that received less heat than Earth did on average.

A nanocrete runway had joined the landing pad and more hangars had sprung up around the two structures. Harold's heavy-lift shuttles had helped out in a dozen ways, but the most noticeable was the installation of the massive set of fuel tanks that had been at New Hope City. None of CDC's shuttlecraft were rated to carry that much weight, but his shuttles had shifted them easily.

Now the runway was a buzzing hive of activity as manned aircraft and automated drones arrived and left at every hour of the day. Director Trudeau's people weren't used to the level of detail that an archaeological survey required, but they were no strangers to massive amounts of work or ungodly hours.

Dr. Wolastoq's personal team of xenoarchaeologists were operating out of a prefabricated structure that had probably been intended to be a school. While Wolastoq had been asked to assist in the Hope colonization effort, no one had expected there to actually be anything for her to find. Her team was entirely human, which meant that they were all students except for her. Any other experts that could be brought in would be alien, and CDC hadn't thought they would be needed.

As Harold stepped into the lab, however, he had to duck as a chunk of permafrost smashed into the wall next to him and shattered into a hundred pieces.

Ramona Wolastoq stood next to a series of machines that Harold didn't recognize, clearly glaring at the results of whatever scan she'd run on the piece of frozen dirt she'd just destroyed. Four of her students were gathered around the equipment as well, apparently unbothered by their leader nearly taking out a starship Captain.

"We're done for now," Wolastoq snapped. "Go get some rest; we'll have a new round of samples in a few hours."

"Yes, Doctor," the students chorused before trooping out. They'd all slipped out the door before Wolastoq even realized that Harold was there.

"What do you want, Captain?" she snapped. "I'm busy."

"Yelling at your students and breaking samples, yes, I noticed," Harold agreed, surprised at how much he enjoyed the flash of not-quite-anger that ran through her eyes in response. "I wanted to check in, Doctor, and see how you were doing."

"I don't need a nursemaid, Captain. I know how this works."

"Agreed," Harold said calmly, smiling as Wolastoq's eyes widened in surprise before she controlled herself again. "And I don't, so I was hoping you could give me an update."

"Fine," she snapped. "Come with me."

The Amerindian xenoarchaeologist led him past the equipment to an array of storage drawers, each neatly labeled.

"We have space to store twelve hundred soil or artifact samples," she told him. "We're full on soil samples; I'm starting to discard the oldest as new samples come in." She glanced at the mess by the door.

"Usually, admittedly, with more care than that." She sighed.

"No luck, I take it?"

"Well, I can tell you a lot about this plateau, but not much of use."

"Give me the rundown, Doctor?" Harold asked.

"Ice cores tell me that this rock is more habitable right now than it has been in the last million or so years," Wolastoq replied. "This is a permafrost zone now, but it has life. That's a development of the last fifty thousand years or so.

"Plateau or not, this place was under two meters of ice a hundred thousand years ago, and that's been its constant state for most of its history," she continued. "If anyone settled here, they had a far higher tolerance for cold than we do."

"Some of the races we've encountered do," he argued.

"But every race we've encountered requires liquid water," she snapped back. "Same for Imperial records. Average annual tempera-ture in this place is somewhere around minus fifteen Celsius right now, and it's *warm* compared to the historical average."

"So, any settlement would be technological, but anything that wasn't wouldn't have attracted the attention it did," Harold replied. "Any signs?"

"That's what all of this is," Wolastoq said flatly, gesturing at the rows of sample drawers. "Every one of these is a chunk of soil where *something* triggered as abnormal. We're finding a lot of little oddities, but nothing that will let us trace a source."

She shook her head.

"I can tell you, Captain, that there *is* something here." She gestured for him to follow her and led him to a map on the wall with a mass of glowing green, yellow, and orange dots.

"I don't know what," she admitted. "There's no pattern to any of this. Green dots flagged as abnormal but nothing unusual when we scanned them here. Yellow dots are samples where we confirmed artificial radiation of various ages.

"Orange dots are just weird." Wolastoq shook her head. "They all share a specific makeup, but it's like fragments of something ended up in them—but those fragments are like nothing I've ever seen or heard of."

She slid a hand into the haptic control field over the map and blanked the green dots.

"There's no pattern to what's left," she told him. "No center point I can identify yet—we thought we had one, but..." Wolastoq gestured to the soil sample she'd thrown at the wall. "That sample was from what I thought was the center point, and it shows no signs of any abnormality at all."

Harold studied the map. There was something there, something that the back of his mind insisted was a pattern, but he couldn't see it. He shook his head.

"I'm guessing you have the solution?" he asked brightly.

Wolastoq chuckled bitterly.

"The key is time, Captain. In two senses: first, that it's going to *take* time to analyze enough of the samples to break down enough of the pattern to find whatever we're missing; and second, that whatever we're looking is *from* a specific time, and there's enough movement in the permafrost here that things move quite quickly on a geological time scale."

She shrugged.

"So, we estimate the movement and backtrack in time," she concluded. "That gives us an idea, but...so far, I'm not getting anything useful."

Harold continued looking at the map.

"Can you run that backtrack for me?" he asked. "Something in here is ringing a bell, but I'm not sure what."

"Sure, certainly *I'm* feeling blind right now," Wolastoq told him.

The dots moved, following clear currents of the underlying soil and ice—currents that flowed on timescales of centuries, not minutes.

The yellow dots...there was no pattern there. Something had flooded seemingly random chunks of the plateau with hard rads.

"Wait, stop," he told her as the *orange* dots, the strange debris, formed a pattern he did know. "I think I know your problem," he continued as he studied the frozen source of samples. "I know *that* pattern, and it won't have a single point source."

"What do you mean?" the xenoarchaeologist demanded grouchily, her glare returning.

He pulled out his communicator unit, an updated version of the scroll-like device the UESF had used, and rolled it open. He didn't have access to Hope's network from there, but the communicator was still linked in to *Liberty,* and the heavy cruiser had the files he was looking for.

"Here." He passed her the unit. "That's the debris pattern for when the wreckage of *Geneva* went down over the Australian Outback."

He tried not to wince at the orbital photos. Like the video he kept on his desk in his office aboard *Liberty*, it was a reminder of loss. His lover had died farther out, the wreckage of *Queen of England* retrieved from deep space and scrapped to help build *Manticore* and *Griffon*, but *Geneva* had gone down in the same battle.

The pattern was clear and, while it didn't quite match the one on the Corellian Plateau, the similarity was there.

"*Geneva* was already dead when she came down," he half-whispered. "She was coming apart as she burnt up; very little hit the ground intact in the end. But irradiated soil and hull fragments were found all along a fifteen-kilometer track before that final impact."

"That...makes sense," Wolastoq told him, her voice and eyes gentler than they had been before. "A ship, damaged but not destroyed—so, less particulate but more radiation than *Geneva*. The track might help us find the crash site, but..."

She shook her head.

"What?" he asked.

"It's the timeline, Captain," she admitted. "The crash pattern lines up with the radiation dating, and that's part of why I was thinking the rad date was from something else.

"That pattern is fifty-six thousand years old, and *no one* we know of, not even the Mesharom, had space travel that long ago."

Harold whistled softly. Everything he'd heard put the rough "start of galactic civilization" with the first Mesharom hyperspace flights, forty-something thousand years earlier. If the Mesharom weren't inherently a slow-paced, slow-breeding, somewhat lazy race, they'd have ruled the entire galaxy.

A starship from before the start of known civilization was something very, very new.

Before he could say more, however, the com unit in Wolastoq's hands started flashing and she quickly passed it back to him.

"Rolfson here," he answered it.

"Sir, this is Lyon," his tactical officer greeted him. "We have a major hyper portal in the outer system. I recommend you get back aboard immediately."

Harold nodded instantly.

"I need to get to the shuttles," he told Lyon swiftly. "I'll be aboard in five minutes; get the ship ready to deploy."

He turned back to Wolastoq.

"Have fun, Doctor," he told her with a grin. "I need to go earn my paycheck."

Her responding smile was the first one he'd actually seen out of the woman.

VICE ADMIRAL PAT KURZMAN stood calmly on the flag deck of the super-battleship *Emperor of China*, second of its name after the first had died at the Second Battle of Sol. *Emperor* brought up the rear of his little formation, with *President Washington* leading the way through the massive hyper portal the first capital ship had opened.

Between the two immense warships was their collection of escorts and escortees. Four *Thunderstorm*-class heavy cruisers and eight *Capital*-class destroyers plus half a dozen freighters and colliers. Half of the Duchy of Terra Militia's cruisers and a third of their destroyers and super-battleships had been sent on this mission.

With the regular patrol deployments, like the one *Liberty* was on, that left *Tornado* and the three Laian attack cruisers under Commodore Tidikat as the only cruisers in Sol. Villeneuve had kept the lion's share of the Duchy's capital ships in Sol, but most of the Militia's lighter units were now scattered through the Kovius Zone, that forty-light-year sphere around Terra that was part of the Imperium—but belonged to humanity.

The Kovius Treaty guaranteed those systems to humanity, and the Imperium honored that by granting the Duchy ownership rights of those worlds. The Duchy only *ruled* Sol itself, but it would maintain an economic interest in every world in the Kovius Zone—and at least the first wave of colonists would be human.

For now, Hope was the only established human colony, and Pat was there—a small but still unfortunate number of light-years away from his husband--to make sure it was safe. No matter what.

Technically, that was the Imperial Navy's responsibility, but the nearest Fleet Base was almost two weeks' travel away. Sol was right next door and no one was going to argue the Militia had no interest in defending Hope.

"*President Washington* has handed over portal maintenance," his chief of staff, Commander Heng Chan, informed him. The tall and painfully gaunt Chinese man was part of the massive number of Chinese Party members who'd been trained in secret to counter the UESF if it became a problem—crews and personnel who'd eventually been used to man the Militia's capital ships against the Kanzi.

Many had died in Sol's defense, and many more had gone home once it was over, but there'd been enough of them, combined with the original large Chinese contingent in the UESF, that the Chinese were the single largest ethnic group in the Duchy Militia.

"Captain Fang reports that *Emperor*'s emitters are holding the portal without problems; we will be passing through in sixty seconds," Chan continued. "There are no problems with portal stability or any of the ships."

"Thank you, Heng," Pat replied. It had taken a few more days to get the task group in motion than he'd liked, but the Duchy of Terra Militia wasn't actually set up for rapid deployment. It was a primarily defensive force, after all.

"The colliers?" he asked.

"Transiting now," Chan confirmed. The true center of the Militia formation was the six colliers, loaded with missiles, spare parts, food and fuel. Hydrogen for the fusion cores could be acquired from any gas giant or ice asteroid, but the antimatter that fuelled the primary cores was harder to come by.

"We are thirty seconds from emergence, doing a final safety scan," Lieutenant Commander Tran reported. The bleached-pale Vietnamese officer studied his screens. "Wait, what is *that*?"

"What have you got?" Pat demanded.

"Fifteen seconds to emergence," Chan reported. "We can't break off now unless it's critical."

"No, just another portal opening. I've got—"

Emperor of China flashed through the portal into the Alpha Centauri system, normal space settling in as the portal collapsed automatically behind them.

"I've got nothing," Tran repeated after a moment. "*Somebody* opened a hyper portal as we were entering, trying to use ours as a shield from the colony's sensors, I think.

"They didn't get the timing quite right, but I didn't get anything on the ship, either. Too far away."

"Pull sensor data from the task group and inform Captain Rolfson and Commander Teykay that we'll need all of their sensor data as well," Pat ordered. "If someone was lurking in Centauri, I want to know who."

If he was being watched, he needed to know who was watching.

There were friends in the area, after all...but there were also enemies and people who could easily become either.

And the last people who'd been in Centauri with stealth fields had killed an Imperial flag officer.

IT TOOK NEARLY ten minutes after Harold arrived on his bridge to confirm that the battle division that had just arrived in Centauri was friendly. The Militia ships had emerged at "only" three light minutes, but that still meant a six-minute two-way communication lag.

"Vice Admiral Kurzman, welcome to Alpha Centauri," he greeted his superior officer. "I gladly yield command authority of the Alpha Centauri System to you. Things have been quiet since the attack, but I'm glad to see backup—and just as glad to see your munitions colliers and couriers!"

Plus, the two super-battleships had starcom receivers, which meant Sol, at least, could communicate with Centauri instantly now. Hope's starcom receiver was on order, supposed to arrive in a few months. A full starcom installation was a massive two-year construction project; Sol's was relatively new and it would easily be five to ten years before the minor colony at Hope could justify it.

He sent the message and glanced around his bridge.

"Any oddities on the sensors?" he asked.

"Nothing," Saab told him. "It's been dead as a doornail around here, like nothing ever happened." The XO shivered delicately. "It's creepy. Would almost have preferred a second wave."

"If there's a second wave, I'm glad they held off," Harold replied. "I'd rather run them into super-battleships than try and fight them with no missiles."

"Aye," his XO agreed. "The lance was more effective than hoped, but I wouldn't want to fight a battle with it as our *only* weapon."

Harold settled into his command chair, studying his repeaters as he refreshed himself with the status of his command. They still had no missiles but were over eighty percent on their antimatter and hydrogen stocks.

With the warships headed his way at forty-five percent of light-speed, the transmission delay was dropping rapidly, and it appeared that Kurzman had replied immediately.

"Captain Rolfson, it's good to see you," Harold's old Captain told him. "I assume command of the Alpha Centauri System.

"I'm glad to hear things have been quiet, but I'm now concerned that may have been a false impression," the Admiral continued. "We picked up someone entering hyperspace as we were exiting, trying to use our portal as a shield for theirs.

"We didn't get much information on them, but Captain Fang's staff have narrowed down the real-space locus of the portal. His people will be sending over the data momentarily, and I'll want you and the Imperial ships to review everything you have on that chunk of space.

"If nothing else," Kurzman noted grimly, "we know we can find a stealth field if we take enough time."

That was not good. The strange Kanzi had used stealth fields, but their version had required atmosphere to function. It had been useful for a landing assault but hadn't enabled them to hide in space.

The only people with proper stealth fields were the Core Powers.

"Do we have the data?" he asked Lyon.

"It's coming in now."

"Relay it to Teykay," he ordered. "And then have CIC take it apart with a fine-toothed comb. If someone was hiding in this system..." He shook his head.

"With that close of a locus, we'll be able to tell if there was a ship with a stealth field present," Lyon promised. "We'll find them, sir."

CHAPTER TWELVE

HAROLD REPORTED ABOARD *EMPEROR OF CHINA* SHORTLY AFTER the super-battleship made orbit, leaving *Liberty* once more in the charge of his XO. Commander Teykay landed shortly after him, and he waited for the Rekiki officer before heading to the conference room.

"It seems everything was less quiet than we thought," the big centaur-like lizard rumbled to Harold. "Too many mysteries in this system; you humans seem to attract trouble."

"I wish we'd stop," Harold told Teykay. "Three years of quiet was not enough—and that's if you even count the long-cycle after the battle as quiet!"

Teykay chuckled. For six months—an Imperial long-cycle—after the Kanzi had attacked Sol, the massed battle squadrons of the Imperium and the Theocracy had glared each other from border fortifications all along the line. In the end, there'd been peace, but it had been an uneasy few months.

Especially for the Terrans, who had had no ability to influence the outcome of events but whose vulnerability had been clearly demonstrated.

"Commander, Captain, come in, come in," Kurzman ordered as they reached the conference room. Captain Hu Fang stood at one end of the long dark-gray table while the Admiral occupied the other. The junior captains of the task group were scattered along it, though chairs had been left next to the Admiral for Harold and Teykay.

Well, a bench in Teykay's case. The Rekiki couldn't sit comfortably on human chairs.

"All right, everyone," Kurzman continued after Harold and the Rekiki were seated. "As of a few hours ago, I relieved Captain Rolfson as Station Commander, Alpha Centauri, for the Duchy of Terra Militia. We are, of course, subject to Imperial Navy authority as represented by Commander Teykay, but one hopes the Commander will listen to my advice."

Teykay stamped his foot with an accompanying hiss, a brisk laugh for his people.

"I have a handful of destroyers. This ship alone outmasses my entire so-called 'command', Squadron Lord. Until more serious Imperial forces arrive, I am more than willing to concede functional authority here to you."

"I appreciate that, Commander," Kurzman replied. "My understanding is that a significant Imperial reinforcement is going to be heading our way, but nothing had been confirmed when we left Sol."

"We can't let the death of an Imperial flag officer go unpunished," Teykay told him. "There must be consequences."

"And as soon as the Imperium is certain *who* was behind this, there will be," the Admiral confirmed. "The last I heard was that the Empress had summoned the Theocracy representative on A!To and demanded an explanation—and that the Priest Speaker claimed to have no idea what she was talking about."

"It wouldn't be the first time the Priest Speaker lied to the Empress," Harold pointed out. "He claimed to know nothing about the attack on Sol, and we *know* that was a sanctioned, if technically rogue, operation."

"Agreed. We have evidence to suggest these Kanzi weren't

Theocracy, but that ball is now out of our court," Kurzman replied. When Teykay looked at him questioningly, the flag officer chuckled. "We have no control of that situation, Commander. It's now a political question, for the Empress and the Houses, not us.

"*Our* responsibility is simple: no matter what happens, Alpha Centauri holds. We were hopeful that no one outside the Imperium knew what had happened here, but we now know we were at least partially wrong."

Kurzman tapped a command and a hologram of the Alpha Centauri system, centered on Hope instead of any of the stars, appeared above the table.

"Someone opened a hyper portal *here* just after we opened ours here," he told the assembled officers, highlighting two marks on the hologram as he spoke. "Their timing was all but perfect: no one in Hope orbit saw anything, and no one in the task group saw anything except *Emperor* herself—and all we confirmed was that a hyper portal was created."

"We're going over our scan data now," Harold told everyone. "We expect at this point to find a stealth-fielded ship in place. If we do, we'll try to trace back its movements until we find its entry into the system."

He shook his head.

"Likely they entered Centauri with their interface drive down or hiding behind someone else's hyper portal. It's certainly something our stealth scouts have done in the past, so we know it's possible even without a stealth field."

"We don't believe the observer was the same as the people who attacked us," Kurzman noted. "Which means we have at least one more player in this game and they are likely a Core Power.

"That's not a long list, and the list of those with interests out here is even shorter," he continued. "I'd *love* to think that we just saw the tail end of a Mesharom scout ship, but we know damn well the worms have us wired up six ways to Sunday.

"Which means we probably just saw a *Laian* scout ship, which is going to be a giant pain in the ass.

"But I remind you all, our orders and our responsibility, both to our Duchess and the Imperium, are clear: no matter what happens. No matter who comes calling. We hold Centauri."

ONCE THE MAIN meeting was over, Harold joined the Admiral in his day cabin, where Kurzman poured them both a glass of scotch over ice and passed one to the Captain.

"To absent friends," he toasted.

"To absent friends," Harold agreed softly, swallowing the whisky and letting it burn down his throat. They'd both made the wild ride as privateers aboard *Tornado* with Annette Bond, and there weren't many left in uniform who had. A good half of the old cruiser's crew had gone aboard *Emperor of China* and *Queen of England* with Andrew Lougheed and Elizabeth Sade, and none of those brave spacers had come home from the battle with the Kanzi.

"You were here, I wasn't," Kurzman said after a long moment. "How bad was it?"

Harold shook his head.

"Four destroyers, Admiral," he reminded his superior. "Maybe... half a million tons apiece. *Liberty* alone outmassed them and should have outgunned them.

"But each of them had shields as powerful as *Liberty*'s, backed up with compressed-matter armor and missiles ten percent of lightspeed faster than ours, plus whatever godawful thing they killed Harrison with."

The Admiral sighed.

"I knew Xander well," he admitted. "Back when I was a Nova Industries navigator and he was a Navy Captain, I dated his brother. We all stayed friends after, too. He was a good man."

"Everyone says that about the dead," Harold replied. "But that was my impression. Not many with the *framatanda* to sign on with the Imperials as a flag officer."

"Man had big brass balls," Kurzman translated from Harold's Swedish with a chuckle. "But...ton for ton, how would you stack our ships up against theirs?"

"Their missiles have twice the force and are damned hard to shoot down," the Captain replied. "Their destroyers have the shields of our cruisers and they appear to be able to ignore our short-range beam weapons other than the lances. They're faster than we are, but they lack active missile defense."

Rolfson swallowed more of the scotch and looked up at the Admiral.

"In a straight fight, those four ships could have taken *Liberty*," he admitted. "Neither of us was quite sure of the other's capabilities; that's the only reason we took them down. I'd say, ton for ton, one of their ships is worth two to three of ours."

"Damn," Kurzman murmured. "That's worse than I was hoping."

"Stack them up against the Laians or the Mesharom, eh, they're still coming up short," Harold said. "But we're not a Core Power and we all know it. Hell, I don't even know what the hell they shot Harrison with."

The Admiral nodded, and slid an open scroll-communicator over his desk. "Sign that, Captain."

"What the hell?" Harold asked, staring at the text on the page. It was a secrecy agreement, similar to half a dozen he'd signed to join the Militia. "What is this?"

"This is you agreeing to accept clearance to our deepest, darkest secret, Captain," Kurzman told him. "Sign it, and I can give you a few answers. Don't, and you're whistling in the dark when these bastards come back."

Harold glared at his boss for a long moment, and then dashed off a signature with his finger.

"What did I just get myself into?" he demanded.

"You're now cleared for BugWorks Two," Kurzman told him. "It's a short damned list, so far as people who aren't working at the facility go.

"Long and short of it, the Duchess decided to take advantage of our access to Laian engineers and Imperial technology and intelligence," the Admiral explained. "BugWorks Two is a black Duchy of Terra Militia project where we are attempting to study the technology of the Core Powers and reverse-engineer useful gear to help keep ourselves valuable to the Imperium."

"*Shit.* Seriously?"

"Seriously. The facility is hiding in low Jupiter orbit and has, to date, produced exactly zero useful technologies," Kurzman admitted. "What it *has* given us, however, is a solid idea of just what tech is out there.

"So, while I don't know *who* hit us, I can at least identify some of what they hit us with."

"Like?" Harold asked. The Admiral had his full attention.

"The Mesharom have developed a defense they call an antiproton curtain," Kurzman told him. "They're doing their best to keep it under wraps, because proton beams are still a staple of the Core Powers' arsenals and the curtain no-sells them *completely*. For a while, anyway."

"Weaknesses?"

"Being overwhelmed," the Admiral replied simply. "If Harrison had sustained proton fire on the bastards, he'd have taken down the curtains in three or four salvos. The same kind of maneuvers that extend shield life will work for the curtains, though, and they're *only* effective on proton beams."

"Who else has them?" Harold asked.

"That's the problem, Captain," Kurzman said grimly. "So far as we know, *only* the Mesharom have antiproton curtains. The Kanzi certainly don't—and perhaps worse, even the BugWorks Two teams, which include some of the best minds we've been able to quietly poach from four species, have *no idea* what they killed Xander with.

"Some of their gear was basically modern. Some was old Core

Power tech...but some was Core Power cutting-edge, and some was gear *nobody* has."

"I don't like the sound of that," the Captain agreed.

"No. That's why we showed up with a fleet and the Imperials are sending one as well," Kurzman told him. "I'm not going to argue with your assessment of our relative firepower, which means we need three times their tonnage if we're going to stop the bastards."

He smiled grimly.

"I'm hoping they stage up more slowly than we did. If they only send, say, cruisers for the next wave...they're going to have an ugly surprise coming."

THE MEETINGS HAD BEEN INFORMATIVE, though Harold would admit the productivity of them was probably questionable. If nothing else, lining up every Captain of the suddenly swollen Alpha Centauri Station and making sure they knew each other had some value, as had his briefing on what BugWorks Two knew about the strange Kanzi's weapons.

Most of it was "show and tell", however, and he did have real work to do. It was also exhausting, and he leaned back in his chair in his shuttle and was about to let himself drift off to sleep when his communicator buzzed at him.

He suppressed an entirely-un-Captain-like desire to ignore it and opened up the device.

"Rolfson."

"Harold, it's Ramona," Dr. Wolastoq greeted him. He couldn't remember ever telling the xenoarchaeologist to use his first name—and she'd definitely never told him to use hers!

She was smiling as well, a broad, friendly grin unlike anything he'd ever seen on her face. Combined with the eager glint in her eye, it transformed her face from somewhat plain into surprisingly attractive.

"Doctor, you looked pleased with yourself," he replied carefully.

"I am pleased with myself," she agreed. "And pleased with *you*, Captain. Your bit of insight was exactly the key we needed. We found it."

"'It' being...?"

"What is either a fifty-thousand-odd-year-old meteor impact or the crash site of an FTL starship," Wolastoq replied. "The source of our radiation and debris, and—I'll bet a nice dinner in New Hope City—what the Kanzi were looking for."

"I'll take that bet," Harold agreed, then paused. That came perilously close to asking the archaeologist out on a date, since he was quite certain she was correct.

She chuckled, far more relaxed than he'd ever seen her.

"I don't want to open this up without you here, Harold," she told him, her voice soft. "We found it because of you, and after everything that happened...I want you there."

Her voice firmed up a moment later.

"And we need a starship specialist, a Navy officer," she continued. "I know something about excavating and studying starship wrecks, but you know ships better. We can use your help."

Sleep, it seemed was going to be a long time coming—but it was going to be *so* worth it.

"I'll have my pilot redirect," Harold told her. "We should be on the ground in under ten minutes."

CHAPTER THIRTEEN

ADMIRAL JEAN VILLENEUVE WAS TIRED. HE WASN'T OLD, NOT BY the standards of Pre-Annexation Earth, let alone the A!Tol Imperium, but he'd given the UESF sixty years of his life only to watch everything they had built fail before the A!Tol.

He'd given Bond and the Duchy another four years since, and some days, he swore those weighed on him more.

All of that, however, was forgotten as he stood on the flag deck of the battleship *Manticore* and surveyed the results of his work. Orentel and her mate stood slightly behind him, the two man-high beetle-like aliens sharing in this moment of delight as the two brand-new battleships pirouetted through a series of maneuvers with Commodore Tidikat's attack cruisers.

"Our cruisers are still faster," that worthy noted, adjusting the straps of his uniforms across his broad, carapaced chest. "Not just the attack cruisers, all of our ships."

If Jean understood correctly, the three Laian ships that had joined his little fleet had been laid down while Earth was still experimenting with getting into orbit. Despite that, they were, without a doubt, the most advanced ships in the Militia.

They'd also been thoroughly boobytrapped to make sure that the Terrans didn't tear them apart for that technology. There was an *etiquette* to how the Arm Powers were allowed to try and acquire Core technology, even centuries-obsolete Core technology.

"We don't need them to outrun cruisers," Jean said. "Just Kanzi battleships."

"They can do that," Orentel agreed, her eyes glittering as *Manticore* and *Griffon* executed a position exchange at half the speed of light. In combat, the switchover would have moved incoming fire from one warship's shields to the other, potentially saving a pressured vessel from destruction.

"And catch many people's cruisers, at that. What they can't do is go pincer to pincer with super-battleships."

"They don't need to," Jean replied. "So long as they can fight battleships on an even keel."

The ex-Dockmaster's mandibles chittered in laughter.

"Oh, there is no 'even keel', as you humans say, between the *Manticore*s and your blue-furred friends' ships," she told him. "One on one, *Manticore* would crush any Kanzi warship or last-generation Imperial ship with ease.

"Super-battleships would be out of their range, though working together..." her mandibles chittered again, a slower, more thoughtful sound. "The two of them could handle any Arm Power's super-battleship. Against a Core ship, though..."

"If we have to fight Core ships, we're dead," Jean said grimly. "And we all know it." He shook his head. "We've done fantastic work with the *Thunderstorm*s and the *Manticore*s. Your people's assistance was invaluable."

"You gave us a home and solid ground beneath our claws, Admiral," Commodore Tidikat said. "We are grateful. We did not bring technology with us, only our minds. I am pleased that my mate's mind has been so valuable."

Orentel's mandibles chittered in laughter again.

"I have many ideas," she told the two males. "Even limited to the technology of the Imperium, I think there is much we can achieve that will surprise those who would threaten our new home.

"Give me time, Admiral, and I will make your Militia the envy of the galaxy!"

Jean chuckled.

"That's more attention than I expect we want, Orentel," he admitted. "We're the back end of nowhere by everyone's standards—and both we and the Imperium want to keep it looking that way!"

The two Laians were intimately involved with BugWorks Two, which was part of why the Duchy was so determined to avoid the Imperium taking official notice—and why the Imperium was very careful *not* to take official notice.

Jean, after all, had no illusions about the likelihood they'd concealed the project from their overlords. They weren't hiding BugWorks from the *Imperium*.

"Beneath notice is good," Tidikat agreed, watching the five ships dance around each other on the screen. "Beneath notice is a safe place to raise our broods."

And that thought, Jean reflected, was why he wasn't going to be hanging up his stars anytime soon. The Duchy of Terra was not yet safe for the generation being born—and he owed it to the people he'd once failed to provide that safety.

No matter how much it took from him to do it.

A SHUTTLE CARRIED the gaunt Admiral back to his flagship, *Empereur de France*. The super-battleship, along with *President De Gaulle*, hovered protectively over the testing area. They were close enough to Earth to arrive inside fifteen minutes if there was a problem, and far enough away that no one was going to be peeking at the Duchy of Terra Militia's space trials.

His pilot was taking the flight at a leisurely pace. *Empereur* was only a few hundred thousand kilometers away, which meant the full half-cee capacity of the shuttle's interface drive was not only unnecessary but dangerous.

It still wasn't a long flight, but it bought Jean Villeneuve a few quiet moments where he couldn't justify working, a rare luxury in his current work.

Or his previous work, which was part of why his wife had divorced him so many years before. She'd understood—she'd *always* understood—but it had eventually become more than she could handle.

Jean didn't begrudge her that. He'd made his choice long before—and then made it again when Annette Bond had formed the Duchy of Terra and asked him to command her new Militia.

His reverie was broken by a pinging alert on his communicator.

"Villeneuve," he answered briskly.

"Admiral, this is Chief Shang," the senior non-com of his flag deck staff immediately greeted him. "One of the hyper buoy just translated into normal space with an emergency alert: we have multiple unscheduled hyperspatial anomalies headed toward Sol. ETA: twenty minutes."

Merde.

"Understood, Chief," Jean said, his outer voice perfectly calm. Six decades of practice made that easy. "Inform Captain Ruan that I will be aboard *Empereur de France* in just over two minutes."

"Yes, sir."

Jean dropped the channel and eyed his communicator darkly for several long seconds. The anomaly scanners on the hyper-beacons were small, relatively low-resolution things. Their purpose was to provide a warning, not any details.

Of course, the beacons didn't have better scanners because anomaly scanners *couldn't* provide details.

That lack, however, left the decision of what to do up to an old man's discretion and an old man's hunches.

He tapped the communicator, linking it into the shuttles' transmitters and inputting a code that would have every Militia ship receive and retransmit his message.

"All Duchy of Terra Militia ships, this is Admiral Jean Villeneuve," he said, his voice still level and calm despite the shiver running up his spine. "We have unknown incoming starships and I am declaring Case Zulu. All ships are to go to general quarters and return to Earth orbit.

"This is not a drill."

BY THE TIME the hyper portal actually opened, Jean had managed to consolidate his fleet. Four super-battleships and two half-tested battleships hung exactly halfway between the shipyards and Earth, positioned to defend whichever came under threat.

The three attack cruisers of the Laian Exiles slotted into escort positions, along with a squadron of sixteen *Capital*-class destroyers. There were another dozen or so destroyers scattered throughout the system, and *Tornado* still orbited Earth, accompanied by Echelon Lord Kas!Val's task group, but Jean needed most of them exactly where they were.

The hyper portal itself was a warning sign. The seventeen-and-a-half-million-ton mass of his super-battleships made up an organic shape two kilometers long and a kilometer wide, with flowing curves and protruding, tentacle-like nacelles and weapons mounts. They were A!Tol designs, so more elegant than Jean would prefer, but still functional and deadly.

To enter or exit hyperspace, those kilometer-wide ships generated a roughly circular hyper portal about ten kilometers across. There were larger ships in the Imperium, massive bulk transports and mobile yards, and they generated equivalently larger hyper portals.

The portal opening two light-minutes away from Earth was *two hundred kilometers across.*

"All ships, move to point Zulu-Alpha-Two," he ordered, the

portal, despite its size, matching neatly to one of his defensive plans. His fleet would cut the newcomers, whoever they were, off well before they reached Earth.

"What the hell is *that?!*"

Commander Hochberg was not normally given to swearing, but Jean saw exactly what his staff tactical officer had seen, and had to swallow a few choice curse words himself.

Twenty-one vessels had emerged from the portal. Twenty were cruisers of some type, long domed shapes that looked familiar but paled into insignificance next to their mothership.

The central vessel of the formation was at least twelve kilometers long and a quarter of that wide. A long beetle-like shape; his scanners showed that it positively *bristled* with weapons, fueled by dozens of antimatter cores.

"Estimate sixty million tons mass, but she's moving at point five cee towards Earth," Hochberg continued crisply after a moment. "Armament unknown, shields unknown...wait, I have deployment of parasite anti-missile platforms. At least thirty."

"Admiral, I have Commodore Tidikat on the channel for you!" Chief Shang told him—and suddenly, Jean knew exactly why the cruisers had looked familiar.

"Commodore," he greeted the Laian correctly. "Am I looking at what I think I'm looking at?"

"Twenty modern Laian Republic attack cruisers and a war-dreadnought," the Exile said flatly. "We could probably take the cruisers, our capital ships outmass them two to one, but..."

"That war-dreadnought could wipe out a third of the *Imperial* fleet, let alone our Militia," Jean replied. "They're your people, at least theoretically, Tidikat. What are they going to want?"

The tall beetle like alien was even more inscrutable than usual, his jeweled eyes half-closed.

"There's only one thing the Republic would send a capital ship this far out for, Admiral.

"Us."

ZULU-ALPHA-TWO PUT the Militia force directly between the oncoming dreadnought and Earth, Jean put his fleet steadily, if not calmly, in the path of the storm and waited to see what the Republic commander would do.

"We're well within our missile range," Hochberg reported. "Flight time eighty seconds and dropping."

"Their missiles are faster," Jean reminded the Commander. "We've been in their range for a while. Fleet will hold position. Formation Delta-Charlie-Six."

DC6 put the destroyers out in front of the super-battleships and deployed their anti-missile platforms. The Terran systems were inferior to the handful of old Laian systems humanity still had, and Jean could only imagine how obsolete they were compared to the drones available to *today's* Laian fleets.

"Any communication from the Laians?" he asked Shang.

"Nothing. Radio silence so far. We've hit them with standard challenges, but they're ignoring us."

In about two minutes, the war-dreadnought was going to fly *through* Jean's fleet, and that he could not allow.

"Put me on, Chief," he told the NCO, then leaned into the camera.

"Unidentified Laian Republic vessels," he challenged them, "I am Admiral Jean Villeneuve of the Duchy of Terra Militia. You have violated A!Tol Imperial space and the Sol Kovius Zone. If you approach within ten light-seconds of my vessels, you will have committed an unquestionable act of war against the Imperium and I will have no choice but to open fire.

"Identify yourselves or withdraw."

The message was sent, winging its way across the void.

"All ships are to clear for action," Jean ordered. "If they approach within ten light-seconds, target the dreadnought with everything we've got."

His flag deck was deathly silent, but he could see the order go out on the screens. Across the fleet, the last few preparations that hadn't been made swung into action as his ships prepared for a battle they could not win.

If they fought the war-dreadnought, they would die.

But they would die under the eyes of an Imperial flag officer with access to a starcom. The consequences of that would ripple across the galaxy. The tentative balance of respect and fear that kept the Arm Powers in check could easily break. Even as simple an act as the Laians having their embassies in several Arm Power empires revoked would have economic repercussions that would damage or even cripple the Republic.

And the violation of the Kovius Treaty would put the Republic in the crosshairs of the first among equals of the galactic powers. The Mesharom would *not* let that go unpunished, and *no one* was quite sure how powerful the galaxy's elder race actually was.

"Forty light-seconds and closing," Hochberg reported. "Sixty seconds to the line."

"All ships report cleared for action. All launchers are loaded, all proton capacitors charged. The vessels with plasma lances report full plasma chambers."

Manticore and *Griffon*, like the *Thunderstorm*s before them, carried the crude-but-effective ripoff plasma lance Orentel had helped the humans design. It was a somewhat less-efficient weapon than the one carried by Tidikat's three attack cruisers, but with a battleship's power cores behind it, even the war-dreadnought would know it had been touched.

"Forty seconds to the line. No response."

Jean waited in stony silence. There was nothing he could do now. He'd picked a battle formation that would give his people the best chance of weathering the hail of terrifyingly fast missiles the dreadnought could unleash, but even if they made it to range of their beams and lances, the Laians had better energy weapons too.

"Twenty seconds to the line. All vessels standing by."

A part of the Admiral wondered if any of his people would blink. All of his Captains were well-enough briefed to know the odds. Most of his ships were fast enough to run, to break and leave the rest of the Militia to face the hammer on their own.

"*A Dawning of Swords* is moving!"

"What?" Jean demanded.

The A!Tol battleship and her four cruisers escorts were indeed moving. Heading out toward the Militia with a very clear intent to join the battle line. There was a small chance that the Laian Republic could brush over blowing away the Duchy of Terra Militia.

But an Imperial Navy capital ship with an Echelon Lord aboard? No. If they fired on *A Dawning of Swords*, there would be war.

"Ten seconds to the line!"

"Stand by," Jean ordered. Watching. Waiting. Just what would the Laians do?

"Dreadnought is breaking off!" Hochberg snapped. "Reversing course at point five cee, cruisers are following suit."

Terra's Admiral breathed a long sigh of relief.

"If they talk to Kas!Val, I want to know," he announced aloud. "Otherwise, we wait until they try and talk to us.

"Keep the fleet at general quarters. I doubt this is over."

THE LAIAN SHIPS WITHDREW, settling in at exactly one light-minute away from Earth with Jean's ships and the Imperial contingent fifty light-seconds from them. Ten from Earth.

At fifty light-seconds, the Imperial and Militia ships' missiles were in range, so Jean was grimly certain that the Laians were well inside whatever their missile range was—and he'd only know they'd opened fire seven or so seconds before the missiles hit.

So, his ships waited. Their Buckler antimissile platforms orbited in front of them while they watched the Core Power ships and waited to see what the Laians would do.

For over an hour, the three fleets orbited like that, the Laians continuing to ignore any attempt by Earth, Jean or Kas!Val to open communications.

It was an hour Jean spent in the command chair on his flag deck, refusing to so much as move. He couldn't show his nervousness to the crew around him. Couldn't vent to anyone. All he could do was wait —and be grateful that Bond had been an officer before she'd become a Duchess and knew better than to jog his elbow at a time like this.

"Sir, incoming transmission from the war-dreadnought!" Shang finally announced, the words landing like pins in the silence. "Standard interstellar protocol." The Chief Petty Officer shook his head. "The same one we've been hailing them on for the last hour and a half."

"Put it on, Chief."

The image of a massive insect, bearing a strong resemblance to a Terran scarab beetle, appeared on his screen. Unlike any of the Exiles Jean had known, this Laian's carapace was a dark red with gray and silver streaks, colors he had not seen on the Duchy's new citizens.

"I am Kandak, the Two Hundred Eighty-eighth Pincer of the Republic," the alien told them. The translator program carried no inflection or tone, and a quick glance noted that they were receiving the *Laians'* translation rather than sending Kandak's own speech and letting the Terrans translate it.

It was partly an insult and partly an attempt to avoid the Terrans reading Kandak's emotions, Jean figured. The rank was important too, and his computer happily explained it quickly. A Pincer in the Republic's service could be anything from a junior Admiral to a senior Captain, but there were exactly four hundred of them, and their ranking was by seniority.

As the two hundred and eighty-eighth of the four hundred, Kandak was too junior to command a division or squadron of capital ships, but a battle group based around a single war-dreadnought was about right.

The Laian was also junior enough to have been sent a long way from home on a what the officer had to regard as a low-priority, low-value assignment.

"I command *Harvester of Glory* and her escorts," the Laian officer continued. "I have been sent by the Council of Priors to respond to reports that your race has stolen Laian technology. I am charged to bring home the rebels from *Builder of Sorrows* and the ships they stole.

"You will turn them and their ships over to me immediately or I will take them by force."

The channel cut.

"Well that's that," Jean said aloud. "At least they're asking *politely*, right?"

He shook his head as the half-forced chuckle ran through his bridge.

"Shang, forward that to the Duchess and Kas!Val," he told the coms non-com. "Then get me a channel back to him. Let's see if we can at least get everyone down from waving missiles around long enough to talk."

A warning icon flashed up, letting him know he was recording again.

"Pincer Kandak," he greeted the Laian officer. "I am Admiral Jean Villeneuve, commanding officer of the Duchy of Terra Militia.

"I can assure you that we have not stolen Laian technology. I would be delighted to assist you in arranging inspections of our old Laian warships to show you how they have been modified to prevent us doing anything of the sort!

"As for the rest of your mission"—he gave an expressive shrug—"I am not authorized to discuss any potential deal around the three cruisers of Laian construction in our service. You will have to have that discussion with my Duchess, Annette Bond.

"What I can assure you, however, is that no member of the Laian community in the Duchy of Terra participated in the Anshokar Rebellions. Not least, Pincer Kandak, because the Anshokar Rebellions were three hundred and ninety-six years ago and your species has a maximum life expectancy with even your healthcare of three hundred.

"Neither the laws of the A!Tol Imperium nor, as I understand, the accepted laws of interstellar jurisprudence permit the punishment of someone for the crimes of their ancestors two to five generations in the past, Pincer."

Jean smiled. It was a false thing, more hostile than reassuring, but it was all he could force for the alien threatening his people.

"We will not surrender our citizens under threat of force for crimes they did not commit," he said flatly. "We are prepared to negotiate acceptable proof that we have not stolen Laian technology, but that line is fixed."

The message was sent and he leaned back. Fifty seconds' light delay each way was enough to make communications a slow, agonizing process. It also, however, meant that he wasn't at a range where the Laian dreadnought could simply wipe out his entire fleet with a single surprise salvo.

"What happens now, sir?" Hochberg asked quietly.

Jean looked over at his staff officer, who was suddenly looking very, very young.

"I don't know," he confessed, equally quietly. "But we appear to have short-stopped the actual attack, which means this is now a political problem.

"Which unfortunately means it's now Duchess Bond's problem."

CHAPTER FOURTEEN

THE ONE PART OF THE PREGNANCY EXPERIENCE THAT WAS living down to Annette's original expectations was morning sickness. Except that it wasn't always in the morning, and this bout had picked a *hell* of a time to strike.

Fortunately, Elon was actually around, and the source of her current discomfort was smart enough to know when to shut up and set up a portable holoprojector in the bathroom that would keep her updated on the developing affairs.

Once her stomach had *finally* settled, she took a seat back in her office and studied the situation.

"Rianne?" She summoned her secretary, who appeared with admirable speed. "How many of the Councilors are in Hong Kong right now?"

"About half, Your Grace."

Annette's Council was her brain trust, the collection of extremely smart people she used to help run the planet. Unfortunately, that meant she usually had them out around the world doing just that.

"Ping everyone who can get to Wuxing Tower in ten minutes or less," she told Rianne Zhao Ha. "They're to assemble in the Council chamber as quickly as possible. Elon will be there in ten minutes; I'll join them shortly afterwards."

Her secretary blinked in surprise.

"What will you be doing, ma'am?"

"I'm going directly to Wuxing Tower. Once you've got the Councilors in motion, I need you to contact Sol starcom. I need a channel to A!To by the time I make it to the Tower, Rianne.

"This is Imperial politics, which means today I speak for someone else—and I'm not going to do that without A!Shall knowing just what the hell is going on!"

Zhao Ha swallowed.

"The Empress, my lady?"

"I will not commit the Imperium to war without A!Shall at least knowing enough of what's going on when she has to go in front of the Houses and tell them what happened!"

A!SHALL was the Empress of some two-hundred-plus worlds and the unquestioned mistress of twenty-eight species. She was a constitutional monarch, her powers bound by a series of documents written across two thousand long-cycles—roughly a millennium, as humans tracked time.

She was advised by a tricameral legislature: the House of Races, the House of Worlds and the House of Duchies, who wielded what humanity would call the powers of purse and legislation. Justice and the military, however, ended with her.

A!Shall was also the smallest adult female A!Tol Annette had ever seen, barely matching the Duchess of Terra in height. Annette wasn't a tall woman, and she was *very* used to being overshadowed by the A!Tol she met.

From what she understood, A!Shall was still quite young to be Empress—and Empress was not a strictly hereditary position.

"Annette," A!Shall greeted her after the functionaries had finally connected them. Even for A!To's Imperial bureaucracy, live starcom communications were uncommon—they required something like three quarters of the capacity of the massive interstellar communication relays—and those from dukes and duchesses rarer still.

They'd managed to pin down the Empress of the A!Tol with surprising speed.

"The shadows of the currents tell me this is not a call for warmth," the Empress continued. "What has happened?"

"A Laian war-dreadnought and her escorts have entered Sol," Annette said crisply. "They have demanded that we surrender the Laians who accepted Imperial citizenship and the cruisers they brought with them."

The Empress had more emotional control than Annette had ever seen in another A!Tol. Her dull-gray skin barely flushed in response to that—but the Duchess picked out the orange of anger and the black of fear in the quickly suppressed flush.

"The Fleet Lords warned of this," she finally said. "They feared that your giving them a home would cause problems."

"I know."

"Do you expect me then, Duchess Bond, to turn the tides of history?" A!Shall asked calmly. "Do you expect me to allow the fears of my strong right hands to force me to step aside? To break the oaths I swore to you?"

"I fear for my people," Annette admitted. There was almost no one else in the galaxy she would admit that to. "And my children."

A!Shall flashed bright blue: an understanding nod. The Empress of the A!Tol would never have children. To stave off the birthing madness that killed all females of her kind, the Empress's eggs were extracted and destroyed. It would be a child of one of her sisters who would assume the throne when A!Shall passed on.

"I will not defy the waves of a thousand thousand long-cycles," the Empress proclaimed. "I will not break the oaths and sacred tablets that make your Duchy mine. I will speak to the Lords of my Fleets and Armies.

"I do not know, Annette Bond, what force we may send to your aid. But know this: the Imperium is one. Unified. An attack on any of us is an attack on all of us.

"And while your Laians may still call themselves Exiles, they are *not*. They are *my* citizens, and the tentacle of my Imperium stands above them.

"Negotiate if you can, Duchess Bond. Send all that you have seen to my warriors. But know you speak not just for one world but for two hundred—and that I have faith in your honor."

Annette felt her spine straighten as A!Shall spoke. Across cultures, across species, the Empress still managed to hit every button to give her strength. It wasn't hard, sometimes, to see why A!Shall was Empress despite her age.

"I will do what I can," she promised. "But thank you."

"I swore an oath to you as you swore an oath to me," the Empress replied. "We will both keep our oaths. That is how the Imperium is built, after all!"

ANNETTE'S COUNCIL was waiting for her and she walked into the room calmly. After four years together, she knew which way many of them would jump, but their skills, their advice, were worth their weight in gold.

"Your Grace, how are you feeling?" Dr. An Sirkit asked. The Thai princess—now a purely ceremonial title—was also Annette's Councilor for Health Affairs, charged with implementing Imperial medical technology across the world.

"There is a dreadnought orbiting within weapons range of our world and demanding that we surrender citizens who joined us of their own free will," Annette replied. "That is the focus of my energies, Doctor!"

"You are also pregnant," Sirkit said. "Even with our medical technology, twins at your age requires...caution."

"I am perfectly cautious," Annette snapped. "I also have a job to do, Doctor. Let's focus, shall we?"

The half-dozen others in the room had known better than to say *anything*. Elon and Zhao sat at her left and right hands as Annette took her chair. Karl Lebrand, still one of America's richest men despite it all being in blind trusts now, sat past Elon, facing Janice Philips, the dark-skinned woman who'd taken on the unenviable task of making sure that areas of the world neglected before the Annexation still benefited from the Imperium.

Pierre Larue, Councilor for European Affairs, sat at the end of the table with Hope Mandela, the Councilor for African Affairs. The two, a widower and a divorcee, had found a surprising middle-aged romance in their work together, and unless Annette missed her guess, they were holding hands under the table.

"Ladies, gentlemen, you have all reviewed the exchange between Pincer of the Republic Kandak and Admiral Villeneuve," she told them. "We know what the Laian Republic wants from us. While this shouldn't need to be said, I'm going to lay it out *very* clearly:

"Under no circumstances will we surrender our citizens, regardless of their species or origin. We have the *full* support of the Empress on this matter and should expect to see heavy firepower being relocated in our direction in short order."

"Doesn't that risk escalating the situation?" Lebrand asked.

"There isn't much escalation from sailing a capital ship into a foreign nation and basically demanding our complete surrender," Zhao snapped. "Any student of Chinese history can tell you that."

That sent a chill running through the room.

"The Empress and I both agree how loyalty flows, people," Annette said calmly into the silence. "The Laians came to us because we promised them a home, a safe harbor. We will *not* surrender our citizens. If that requires our Militia and the Imperial Navy to throw super-battleship squadrons at a Laian war-dreadnought, *that is what will happen.*"

"So, what do we do?" Mandela asked. "Until the Imperium can

reinforce us, we negotiate from a position of weakness with someone who wants something from us." The black South African woman glanced around the room. "As both Councilor Zhao and Councilor Sirkit can remind anyone who has forgotten, that hasn't generally ended well in our own history."

"Admiral Villeneuve has laid out our initial negotiating position," Annette told them. "We are prepared to prove that our plasma-lance program did not use any stolen Laian technology. That is all we are going to give them."

"Can we even prove that?" Philips asked. "I thought the Laians were involved in the development."

"They were," Elon confirmed, "but not in any major role. Orentel has been involved in other programs of ours, but the lance development project was as aboveboard as we could make it, because we knew this might be a problem.

"The base technology behind it was within the Imperium's grasp; the A!Tol just hadn't combined things in the right way. Knowing it was possible was half the battle; Orentel just told us when we were barking up the completely wrong tree.

"So, yes, Councilor Philips, we *can* prove that our plasma lance was entirely home-developed after seeing the Exiles' weapon in action."

"That might not be enough," Annette warned, "but that is where we're going to start. I'm not certain what concessions we can offer, but we will see. Once this 'Pincer of the Republic' is actually speaking to us, I will invite them to meet with myself and Admiral Villeneuve aboard one of the orbital stations.

"I would prefer a peaceful solution to this," she said grimly. "I am all too aware of the potential costs of the alternative."

CHAPTER FIFTEEN

"I'm not seeing anything," Harold admitted, looking out the window as the survey craft shot over the Corellian Plateau toward Wolastoq's destination.

"It's a fifty-thousand-year-old crash site," the xenoarchaeologist pointed out. "What are you expecting to see? Debris? A crash furrow?"

"Something?" he replied, filing away the woman's new grin and cheerfulness in the "not quite sure what's going on" category in his mind. "You told me you'd found it, so..."

"Look at the scanners, Captain," she told him. "We're seeing a higher density of irradiated soil. They were closer to the ground here."

A glance over her shoulder confirmed what she was saying. The radiation levels were still low, but they were high enough now that the survey craft, a glorified helicopter with added gravity controls for efficiency, could detect them from the air instead of needing the lab to go over them.

"This radiation is weird," he noted, looking at the spectrographic data. "It's not what I'd have expected to see from a crash site. Less decayed in many ways than I'd expect from fifty thousand years."

"I know," Wolastoq agreed. "The dating is solid, though. Weird, huh?"

"You sound far too excited," he said.

She laughed.

"We're about to poke at a spaceship that pre-dates known galactic civilization," she told him. "You *bet* I'm excited. Come on, we're coming in at what I think the final resting site."

There were dozens of nondescript lumps across the Corellian Plateau's surface. Rocks left behind by glaciers. Permafrost that had expanded under soil and refrozen at the higher level. There was nothing to make this particular lump of dirt and stone look unusual except for the calculations and maps that said the crash path ended there.

"Circle the mound," Wolastoq ordered the pilot. "Drop the sensor pylons in the *exact* locations I gave you. Even the tiniest of errors will extend the calibration time."

The mound was two hundred meters across, and the survey craft cut a three-hundred-meter-wide circle around it, dropping ten pylons for the xenoarchaeologist's scanner array.

"All right, put us down; I'm running the calibration cycles."

She was focused on the screen in front of her, a larger version of the scroll-handle flimsies the Militia used as communicators, as she ran through a series of tests and links. The survey chopper settled in to a gentle landing and she hummed softly to herself.

"And...there."

Something clicked through on the screen, and the page of read-outs and data resolved into a roughly three-dimensional map of the mound that Harold could follow. He couldn't read the iconography—but then, he imagined Wolastoq would be lost trying to read a warship tactical plot—but he could see the rough outline of the ground.

And he could see that there was *something* there.

"Calibrating pulses. All right." The xenoarchaeologist was talking more to herself than to him, but he waited patiently. Watching her work was fascinating in its own right.

"Lot of rock, lot of ice. The material we've been finding—it's weird, doesn't always show as artificial to our tests. Not metal, not as we would think of it, anyway. That's why the hull didn't show up on higher-level scans."

"The hull?" Harold asked.

"Calibrating for our samples of the debris and... There!" She highlighted it on the screen and he almost swallowed his tongue in shock.

The map of the hill was still there but it wasn't important anymore. Inside it, buried at a forty-degree angle facing downward, was a ship. It didn't look like any starship he'd ever seen, resembling nothing so much as an old flying-wing bomber.

Twelve meters thick. Fifty-six meters wide at the base of the triangle. Twenty-six long. It wasn't a big ship, similar in size to the handful of hyper-capable scouts Earth had built before Annexation.

"That's not possible," Wolastoq suddenly said sharply.

"I'm not arguing with you, Doctor, but it's there."

"No, Harold," she said distractedly. "Not the ship—I can *see* the ship. There's power."

He was distracted for a moment by her use of his first name, then when what she'd said hit home.

"It has power," he repeated. "It crashed fifty thousand years ago. What do you mean, *it has power?*"

"I don't know," she admitted. "But now I've calibrated for the hull, I'm reading some really odd signatures: heat, electricity, even what might be gravity manipulation.

"It's still alive, Harold."

He met her gaze for a few seconds, then looked out the window at the mound next to them.

"Please tell me we also brought earth-moving equipment."

"AYE, we can clear a hole any size you want through the dirt and rock with the surveyor's sonics," the pilot told them cheerfully.

Even with Wolastoq's horrified expression, Harold would have guessed that was the wrong response to getting into a fifty-thousand-year-old crashed spacecraft.

"Your sonics, Mr. Douglas, might well clear a hole *through the spaceship*," she snapped acidly. "They're designed for mining and mineral excavation, not archaeological work. Do you have anything more controlled?"

Isaac Douglas, an older black man with a half-chewed, unlit cigar in his mouth and salt-and-pepper hair, grinned back at her around the cigar.

"O' course," he confirmed cheerfully. "But after all the hell you've put the survey team through, did you think I *wasn't* gonna poke you?"

For a moment, Harold was worried the xenoarchaeologist was going to explode, and he made a distinct effort to smother his own almost-chuckle so Wolastoq didn't hear it.

Then she swallowed, exhaled, and that brilliant grin he was starting to find distracting returned.

"Okay, Douglas, I deserved that," she admitted. "What *do* we have?"

"The surveyor's sonics have a lot of settings," he told her. "I wasn't pulling your leg on 'any size'—I'd suggest we use them to clear down to about a meter of depth over the hull in our target zone.

"Then we have nano-cleaners and handheld sonics that should suffice to get us in without damaging the hull."

He shrugged.

"I don't know much about archaeology," he concluded, "but that's the process we use to try and access caves we think will have fragile crystals. If we can get into salt caves without breaking anything, I think a starship's hull should be able to handle it."

"We use much the same tools," Wolastoq agreed. "And using the surveyor's sonics to get close will save us time." She closed her eyes in thought, then opened them again to look at Harold.

"Harold, you know starships better than I do," she admitted. "We don't know the hull material well, but if it's a ship, it should have certain qualities, yes?"

"There's a lot of variation," he said slowly, "but yes. Plus, it survived a crash from orbit, so that gives me a minimum idea."

Liberty, for example, would survive such a crash due to her compressed-matter armor. The old scout ships, though, the closest he'd seen to this strange vessel's size, wouldn't have. Their titanium hulls would have crumpled under the impact of a crash.

"Could we get closer with the heavier sonics?"

Harold nodded in thought, considering. If the ship was armored like a modern warship, the CM would laugh at the sonics. On the other hand, they still had no idea what the hull material was—it could easily be far more vulnerable to sonic vibration than to direct impact.

"We should," he said cautiously, "but there are still risks. Probably...thirty centimeters? Maybe forty to be safe."

"We can do that," Douglas confirmed. "Just say the word, Doc."

Wolastoq looked at the image on her screen of the unknown, impossible starship.

"Do it."

AS HAROLD and Wolastoq exited the surveyor craft, the escorting Guard assault shuttle swung around to drop off several of his escorts. Four power-armored Guards was *probably* overkill, especially with the heavily armed interface drive shuttle hovering five hundred meters above.

"Here, those suits give you extra muscle; help me move this gear!" Wolastoq told the Guards. "Thank you."

The words were only half an afterthought, but they were enough to get two of the four soldiers moving, grabbing the heavy support pack for the handheld sonics and the canisters of nanotech goo that would do the final work.

"All right, everyone," Douglas announced over the surveyor's speakers. "I'm rotating fifteen meters to the left, and I'm going to clear a thirty-meter section down to forty centimeters with the surveyor's sonics."

He paused.

"You guys in armor would probably be fine, but I suggest everyone else stay at least this far away. Oh, and put in your earplugs. This will hurt otherwise."

Harold was already wearing universal translator earplugs, part of the Militia's standard-issue gear. Those would, along with their main purpose, protect his hearing from just about anything.

Wolastoq took a pair of white plastic plugs out of her suit jacket and popped them into her ears before flashing the floating surveyor a thumbs-up.

The aircraft swung around, extending a series of projectors as Douglas stabilized it in position above the mound covering the spaceship. A deep thrumming sound echoed around the plateau, even through the earplugs, as the sonic disruptors went to work.

At first, there was no visible change. Then the soil began to shake as the vibrations broke up the permafrost and other bonds tying it together. Then chunks of soil began to slough off the slope, followed by dust as rocks in the path of the focus beam of sound simply disintegrated.

In thirty seconds, a hole five meters by five meters by five meters opened in the side of the hill, its former contents shaken loose and spilled down onto the ground beneath their original home. Then the surveyor swung farther away from them and repeated the process.

Six times, Douglas fired up the sonic disruptors. Six times, massive amounts of soil, ice and stone were turned to dust and collapsed outward.

All that was visible inside the massive hole he'd cleared,

however, were more soil, ice and rock. The surveyor could clear all the way down to the buried hull, but they had no idea what fifty thousand years buried under permafrost would have done to the hull material.

It was time to dig.

IT HAD TAKEN LESS than ten minutes for Douglas to clear a massive section of the hillside away. It took Harold, Wolastoq and their helpful Ducal Guards over an hour to get a roughly two-meter-by-two-meter area cleared down low enough to unleash the nano-cleaner.

The semi-intelligent agent swarmed over the dirt, picking up anything it registered as dirt or rock or ice—the target "contaminants" programmed into it this time—and moving it away. When they started, there were a few small glimpses of a strange gray material under the soil, but most of what they were seeing was still rock and ice and dirt.

They watched all of that move, seemingly of its own accord, and add itself to the pile of debris created by the surveyor's sonic disruptors and their own work. As it moved, it revealed a smooth, unbroken surface underneath.

The hull was a waxy gray material with a slight sheen. There was none of the pitting or scoring Harold had expected from a crashed ship. It was perfectly smooth, with no sign of any kind of entrance, and he looked at it with a sigh.

"I suppose it was too much to ask to uncover an airlock straight away," he admitted, then glanced over at Wolastoq. "I don't suppose your sensor pylons can give us some kind of interior map?"

"I'm barely able to register that the hull exists," she said. "I'm getting nothing clear from inside the ship—from these scans, the inside might as well just be dirt, but I *think* that is just this material screwing with me."

She reached out and tapped the hull, her eyes glowing with wonder. "That's much softer than I would expect," she murmured.

Harold joined her in touching the hull, running his fingers along the impossibly smooth surface.

"No metal or ceramic I've ever seen," he agreed. "But...tough. Obviously *very* tough."

"We have debris from it across the plateau," Wolastoq objected. "Can't be that tough."

"There's not much that's harder on *anything* than unplanned reentry," he said. "And if there was any damage, it repaired itself." He hesitated, considering. "Oh, what the hell. Corporal!" he shouted back to the Guards. "Bring me that handheld!"

"What are you doing?" the archaeologist demanded.

"Science," he replied with a big red-bearded grin. "I'm testing a hypothesis."

The handheld sonic disruptor, linked to its power source by a long cable, landed perfectly in his outstretched hand, and he saluted the Ducal Guard with it.

Before anyone could stop him, he turned it to full power and activated it on the hull.

The waxy material rippled slightly but otherwise was undamaged. He held the focused beam of sound on the hull for several seconds, then released it.

"That hull isn't going to be bothered by the sonic disrupters," he told Wolastoq calmly as she glared at him. "I suspect it might even laugh at *Liberty*'s missiles. I suggest we bring up the other surveyor craft and sweep the entire ship clean."

He shook his head, stepping back to study the mound.

"I want to see just what this planet was hiding."

THERE WERE seven of the surveyors available in total, a sign to

Harold that CDC really had taken this project seriously, as there were only ten on the entire planet.

He and Wolastoq retreated from the mound as the aircraft moved in. A dozen or so meters and ear protection were enough for one set of sonic disruptors, but seven of them needed a far larger safety radius.

"Double-checking the safety perimeter," Douglas said over the radio. "Is everyone clear?"

"Check," Harold confirmed. "I have confirmed with the Guard: they've swept the area on the ground and surveyed it from the air."

"All right. This is gonna be *fun*. Initiating synchronized disruptor sweep."

Even from a quarter-kilometer away, the vibration rattled Harold's teeth this time. Seven sonic disruptors opened up with carefully targeted full power, sweeping around the buried ship with constantly varying waves of focused sound.

A sonic disruptor was an utterly ineffective weapon, but when it came to reducing mountains and hills to dust and loose dirt, there was no better tool. Entire chunks of the mound disintegrated, exposing the strange ship section by section.

The flying-wing comparison was apt. It was a slightly off-centered triangle, with the south side longer than the north in its current position. There was no visible cockpit or bridge, the entire ship being the same smooth, waxy gray material.

Some of the dirt underneath the ship disintegrated, and Harold inhaled sharply as the ship slowly settled. The advantage, however, of turning the mound that had covered it into loose dirt and soil was that the ship now had a soft bed to settle into as it slowly leveled out, sliding down to rest on the Corellian Plateau.

"You can move into the safety zone," Douglas announced. "We're done here. One...whatever the hell that is, cleared of dirt and ready for investigation."

"Thank you, Mr. Douglas," Harold told him. "I don't suppose you can see an access point from up there?"

"Captain, all I see from up here is gray wax. I'm half-expecting the thing to be full of old cheese at this point."

Harold chuckled. "It has power," he reminded the pilot. "There's *something* in there."

"We've cleaned her off. Getting in...getting in is up to you."

CHAPTER SIXTEEN

THE STRANGE WAXY HULL MATERIAL RESISTED HAROLD'S fingers. It *felt* soft and waxy, but there was no real give to it as he pushed.

"How safe is that, exactly?" Wolastoq asked from a couple of meters behind him.

"Potentially not in the slightest," he agreed cheerfully. "But I'm running out of ideas and getting pissed off."

With the rock and soil removed, they'd moved the sensor pylons closer to the now-level starship, pulsing the hull with every sensor they could think of to try and learn something about the ship.

Anything.

"It's cold," he told her. "Feels soft, but I can't put my fingers inside it or anything like that. Laughed off our sonics, and I hesitate to try real weapons on it."

"That does strike me as a bad idea," the archaeologist said dryly. "I would prefer to get into it with it still *intact*, after all."

"I suspect, my dear Dr. Wolastoq, that we could line up *Emperor of China*'s main proton beam batteries and not make much of an impression," Harold said. "It's deflecting every sensor we send at it.

I'm impressed by the battery of tools you have available, but all they are telling us is that there is a ship here."

"And that there is a source of heat and odd gravity waves inside," Wolastoq reminded him. "There has to be *some* way into the ship, doesn't there?"

"I can think of a few reasons there might not be," he admitted, studying the massive gray shape. "If the builders had some form of short-range teleporter, they wouldn't need an airlock. Or the self-repair mechanism that fixed the damage from the landing accidentally closed over the entrances. Or if we aren't looking at a ship at all."

The last thought was disturbing and he laid his hand back on the waxy hull, listening for something he hadn't checked for before: a pulse.

"What do you mean?"

"If this was *alive*—or was alive, once—then it wouldn't have crew or an entrance," the red-bearded Captain said. "There are spaceborne life forms out there, after all."

Most of them were very large, very delicate creatures that lived on sunlight and ice and had roughly the intelligence of a placid herd beast.

A stoned placid herd beast.

He'd never heard of any space creatures that could move particularly quickly or survive a crash into a planet, but after the last five years, Captain Harold Rolfson was not going to assume humanity knew everything about the universe.

Wolastoq stepped up next to him, carefully pulling her braid back and laying her hand on the waxy hull as well. She was doing the same thing he was, feeling for some sign of life.

"I don't think it's alive," she admitted. "I feel like we'd be able to tell—we'd feel *something*."

Harold nodded, looking over the ship thoughtfully. They'd been making the assumption that they'd be able to *see* the airlock, but this hull material had clearly repaired itself. What if it was self-motile in other ways?

It would require power, but their scans suggested there *was* power.

"If it's a ship," he said slowly, "I don't know anything about the builders, but at this point..."

"Harold?"

"I speak fluent starship," he told Wolastoq with a grin. "And if I was building this thing, I'd put at least one of the airlocks *here*."

It wasn't exactly where they were standing, but it was pretty close. Right beneath what they thought was the "front" point of the triangle. He walked over to the spot, studying it, and then tried to slide his hands into the wax again.

This time, the wax responded. He felt the hull warm under his hands, the strange material coming to life and *moving* against his skin. One moment, he was touching another expanse of gray wax—and the next, a ten-foot-tall by four-foot-wide opening had appeared in the hull.

All he could see inside it was a featureless, gray cocoon-like space. Probably the airlock.

"Well, that looks welcoming, doesn't it?" Harold said cheerfully. "That said, I suggest we go get oxygen masks and lights.

"We have no idea what the inside of this thing is going to look like."

THERE WAS enough space in the cocoon for one Guard in power armor or two unarmored people, and Wolastoq wasn't letting anyone else go inside the ship before her.

"We may need to find additional controls to open it from the inside," she noted after overruling the trooper protecting them. "It may not open again without being fed more power. No offense, Corporal, but I don't want a soldier with no archaeological training being the only person inside the ship!"

"What about you, sir?" the Guard turned to Harold, who gave the trooper a grin.

"I, Corporal, am going armed to make sure the good doctor is safe," he told them, patting the heavy plasma pistol slung on his hip. "And since I'm the only starship officer down here—and I'm the one who worked out how to get in."

Most of his argument was half-directed at Wolastoq, who he was expecting to argue. Either she had been planning on bringing him with her already or he successfully convinced her, as she simply nodded and gestured for him to enter the opening in the side of the ship with her.

Both of them put breathing masks over their faces, hanging the compressed-air supply—two days' worth, to be safe—on their backs. They also had wrist-mounted flashlights, and Harold still had his Militia earbuds, which normally gave him communication to *Liberty* in orbit.

He was quite certain his earbuds could reach outside the ship.

Wolastoq was carrying a bag of tools, and with the confined quarters of the airlock, the bag was the only thing stopping them from being fully pressed against each other.

Which was a far more distracting position than Harold had expected. In the three years since Elizabeth Sade had died, no other woman had even caught his eye, and the xenoarchaeologist crammed into the side of the ancient spaceship with him couldn't have been more different from the gracefully ethereal woman he'd loved.

"So, Captain, entertaining as being squeezed into a coffin with you is," Wolastoq said after a moment, "how are we getting *into* the ship?"

Thankfully, it was already shaded enough that he was relatively sure she didn't see him flush. Starship captains weren't supposed to blush like guilty schoolboys, after all!

"If it works the same as the outside, I should just be able to... Here."

He tried to slide his hand into the wax on the middle of the inner wall, hoping it would respond. For a moment, nothing happened.

Then the whole opening seemed to warm up and he half-felt, half-saw the outer "door" close. That was when Wolastoq's coffin comment really began to take on a life of its own. There was no space, no air. No light.

You could, thankfully, not be a starship captain or a xenoarchaeologist if you were a claustrophobe. It still wasn't a comfortable experience, and if a readout on his contact lenses hadn't been telling him the atmosphere was changing, he might have panicked for reasons that had nothing to do with claustrophobia.

"Pressure is dropping," he noted aloud. "Oxygen percentage rising. Temperature rising. This is...impossible. The airlock is fully functional."

Then the interior wall *flowed* open...and the carefully balanced atmosphere and temperature that the airlock had created collapsed back into the general atmosphere of the ship—which closely resembled that of the outside Corellian Plateau. A bit warmer from insulation, but the same pressure and oxygen levels.

"The rest of the ship, it seems, is not so intact," Wolastoq replied. It took her several moments longer to extricate herself from the airlock—and Harold—than it probably should have, which his lizard brain enjoyed *far* too much for his sense of comfort.

He eventually managed to focus on the here and now and look around with his light.

"That makes me feel a lot better," he admitted. The room the light showed was the same gray wax material as the outer hull, the walls just as clean and undamaged as the outer hull. The *contents* of the room, however, were not.

At some point, it had contained a relatively normal-looking set of lockers and humanoid spacesuits, if scaled for bipeds eight feet tall with four arms. Those lockers had been smashed free and scattered across the room during the crash. They'd never been cleaned up, and several shattered suits filled the antechamber.

"So, the ship isn't *entirely* impossible," Harold continued. "Self-healing, semi-motile hull. Presumably needs power, but we *knew* there was power."

He shook his head.

"The hull alone, Doctor," he told the woman with him. "If we could duplicate the hull alone, that would advance our materials science by decades, if not centuries.

"What the hell else is in here?"

"I don't know," she told him. "But I do think that if we're going to wandering around an abandoned starship in the dark together, you should call me Ramona."

He laughed. She'd never asked his permission to use *his* first name, but he'd never dared to use hers.

"Very well, Ramona," he conceded. "Where do you think we should start?"

She pulled a multi-sensor scanner pack out of her bag and started setting it up.

"First, I want to get some readings and see what we can get from in here," she told him. "Then, well, you're the one who 'speaks fluent starship'. I suggest we go looking for what you think is important."

THE PULSES from Wolastoq's handheld unit were both more and less helpful than Harold had hoped. Part of him had expected that the scanner would be completely useless, blocked by the interior walls as thoroughly as the hull had blocked the more powerful sensors outside.

On a modern ship, however, the scanner would have given them a complete interior map.

The end result on this strange ancient vessel was somewhere in between. The sensors appeared to be able to pulse through about one interior wall of the strange waxy material the ship was built from and down corridors and hallways. They had a map of their immediate surroundings but not much more.

"Where are the gravity signatures?" he asked. "I'm guessing that whatever is still giving off power is in Engineering and related to that."

Wolastoq fiddled with the device and then pointed. "I can't get an exact range, but that way."

"Well, then, shall we see if the airlock door still works so we can get out later, and then go take a look?"

He stuck his hand in the wall, much the same as he had to get in, and was quietly relieved when it flowed away to reveal the cocoon-like airlock.

"This ship is creepy," he noted. "But to still be functioning, however minimally, after fifty thousand years..."

"It's unlike anything I've encountered in A!Tol records," Wolastoq said. "It's incredible."

"Are you recording?" he asked.

"Everything," she confirmed. "Everything I see, everything light goes on, and everything the scanner picks up. You?"

"Same," he said. He checked an icon in his contacts and winced. "I don't have a live link outside, though," he warned her. "The hull is blocking my transceiver."

"I'm not surprised," she said calmly.

"I am. That transmitter can reach *Liberty* from outside."

"And we couldn't get a single detailed scanner reading through this hull," Wolastoq replied. "We know we can leave, so let's go check out what we find. Don't touch anything."

"I'm a soldier, Ramona, not *stupid*," he replied. "If the gravitic source is that way, then..." He studied the hallways. "...this way."

―――――

DESPITE THE STRANGE material the ship was built from, the hallways followed a pattern that made sense to Harold. What made no sense, at least initially, was the complete lack of doors—until they hit the end of a corridor where he was *certain* there should be an access to continue.

"Run your scanner again," he suggested to Wolastoq. "See if there's anything different about this section of wall ahead of us."

The xenoarchaeologist studied the device's screens and shook her head.

"Same material, same color, same...everything."

"We know that," he told her. "Look for...thickness, temperature. Is there something to mark that this is a door?"

"There's...all right," Wolastoq replied. "Right, speaking starship, huh?"

"When was the last time you did archaeological work on something that was still half-functional?" Harold asked.

"Never," she agreed with a chuckle. "Okay, take a look at the screen. I've highlighted an orange section that's about one point five degrees Celsius warmer than the hull around it and seven millimeters thinner."

The orange highlighted section on the screen looked vaguely like a doorway—if a doorway was nine feet tall and an even oval. Harold sighed.

"Well, I guess there's the method that worked on the airlock."

He pushed his hand into the center of the "door" area. It resisted for several moments, and then flowed away from him to open up the entire highlighted area.

"That was much slower than the airlock," he said. "That's...probably not a good sign."

"Might be the design?" Wolastoq asked.

"More likely, we're using up whatever power reserves this thing has left," Harold admitted grimly. "Or the reserves are localized and prioritized. God knows *I'd* be more concerned with making sure the airlock worked than—"

He shut up as his light swung through the now-open door and

settled onto the body. If you could even call it that after fifty thousand years had had their way with it.

"Ah," Wolastoq said softly as she saw why he'd stopped speaking. "My turn. Can you stand there and hold the light steady, Harold?"

"Sure," he agreed. He'd seen more bodies than he liked to think about, and he supposed he should have known there would be dead aliens in the ship, but he hadn't been expecting to open a door and find one.

The figure was tall, roughly eight feet in height, but narrow-bodied with a doubled set of shoulders and four arms.

More than that was hard to see. It wore a black uniform that covered it from the base of its neck all the way to the tips of its feet and fingers. The black material had a similar waxy look to the hull, like it had almost grown on the spacer as it covered its gangly height and six-fingered, two-thumbed hands.

"Mummified," Wolastoq said calmly as she knelt next to the corpse. "The ship couldn't stop itself from ending up with the same atmosphere as outside, but there wasn't much alive out there to sneak in in the first place.

"Cold, dry air did the rest." She shook her head. "After fifty thousand years, there still isn't much left. If I try to take a sample, he'll disintegrate. Not that I need a sample to know how he died."

The xenoarchaeologist pointed at the dead alien's head, which was hanging at an angle that was survivable for *some* species but not most.

"He broke his neck in the impact. Nobody survived to bury him."

"Creepy," Harold replied. "Any idea *what* he was?"

"A sentient spacer aboard a starship that predates the oldest known civilization," she replied dryly. "As for species? No. Doesn't match anything I've ever heard of."

"Or I. And the Imperium briefed us on every race they knew of."

Which was a lot. The A!Tol had twenty-seven subject races. The Kanzi had nineteen enslaved species. There were nine Core Powers with members from sixteen species. There were another nine major powers in the Milky Way's spiral arms, with another fifty-two major species between them.

Harold couldn't remember everything about every one of the hundred-plus alien species he'd learned about, but he couldn't remember any eight-foot-tall humanoids with four arms.

"We have gear that should be able to take a sample in the camp," the archaeologist told him. "For now, I've taken readings and pictures. I suggest we leave him and find Engineering. If this place still has power, that's where it is, right?"

"Exactly," Harold confirmed. "And if they've got a power plant that's still running after fifty thousand years, I *want* it."

THEY PASSED two more corpses along the way to what Harold estimated to be the engineering section. Neither was more than dust in the black uniform now, the warmer air as they approached the core having done what the cold near the hull hadn't.

"No signage. No symbols," Wolastoq observed. "I don't know much about starships, Harold, but every one I've been on had signs and directions."

"They all do," he confirmed. "The nature varies from species to species, but visual cues are almost a universal constant. And yet none..."

"You sound like you have a thought," she said.

"Only two possibilities I see right now," Harold replied. "Though I'm sure people will come up with hundreds more. First, that everything *was* labeled, but either in something that didn't survive fifty millennia or at visual wavelengths you and I can't see."

"The former seems more likely," Wolastoq told him. "Though if it's the latter, we'll pick it up when we go through the footage."

"The second," he said slowly as he knelt by the third corpse, "is that they had some kind of computer implant in their heads so they didn't *need* signage, which, given how much this gentleman has decomposed..."

He poked the debris pile that *had* been a sentient creature very carefully with the tip of his flashlight and was unsurprised when the dust settled again—and revealed a much-corroded collection of small wires and a blackened waxy material similar to the hull and uniform.

"Neural implant," Harold concluded. "None of the Core Powers use them; too many potential problems with people hacking your brains. None of the Arm Powers have the tech for them, so far as I know.

"Who the hell would trust circuits in their brain?" he asked rhetorically.

"Someone who thought all of the bugs were worked out of the tech," Wolastoq replied. "I know I'd risk quite a bit for a reliable way to expand my memory and reduce the number of references I need to look up."

Harold shivered.

"I can see the advantages on a warship, but I've always been told even the Core Powers find the tech is too dangerous." He sighed and rose, checking his bearings. "One more of those weird doors and I think we're in the core."

If the crew had used neural implants to navigate around, the doors had probably opened and closed automatically for them. The "stick your hand in the middle and it will flow open eventually" method was probably an emergency failsafe.

The last door slid open into a significantly larger open space than he'd expected on the relatively small ship. It probably stretched from the top of the vessel to the bottom, an open void ten meters on a side.

Struts of metal—not the waxy material of the rest of the ship—held a spherical containment chamber in the center of the room. Harold thought he recognized the struts and he stepped over to rap one.

Wincing, he gestured Wolastoq over to him.

"Can you scan this, Ramona?" he asked. "I'm not sure I believe it."

She ran her device over it, flipping from one sensor to another, then met his gaze.

"Compressed matter," she confirmed. "I don't know what the numbers it's giving me mean, though."

He leaned over her screen, feeling her breath on his neck as he did so, and sighed.

"That means the it's roughly seventy-five percent more compressed than the CM that armors our warships," he explained. "Last intelligent estimate I saw put even *Mesharom* armor at only forty percent denser."

"Everything about this ship is more advanced than it should be," Wolastoq agreed. She hadn't moved away, the two of them still well inside each other's personal space as they looked at the containment chamber.

"What is that?" she asked.

"What does your toy say?"

"It's the source of the gravity waves and the heat. The waves are too weak for us to feel yet, but they're stronger as you get closer to it."

Harold nodded. That made sense, and he shivered as he looked around the engineering core, realizing what was missing.

"No hyperdrive."

"What?" Wolastoq asked.

"This ship doesn't have a hyperdrive. That, that and that." He pointed at three cylindrical objects against the back of the engineering space. "Those are fusion cores. Smaller than I'm used to, but I wouldn't bet against their power output.

"*That*, I have no idea what it is." He pointed to a set of long-dead mechanisms that occupied the port and starboard walls, converging to a single point about the spherical containment chamber.

"And the orb? The thing they have *compressed matter* holding in place?" Wolastoq asked.

Harold studied it for a long moment, then shook his head.

"We're talking something that's only at the remote edge of theory for the A!Tol," he said quietly. "Something even the Core Powers regard as a technological pipe dream. *That*, Ramona, is a singularity power core. Over fifty thousand years old, it's decayed to the point where it can barely run the doors, but when it was built, it could probably have sustained an entire planet.

"We can't recreate the singularity that fed it, but even learning how it was contained could revolutionize power generation across the galaxy."

He shivered again.

"We need to get outside and commandeer one of Admiral Kurzman's couriers," he told her. "We need to do that *now*.

"The Duchess needs to know what we've found. Hell, the *Empress* needs to know what we've found."

Because as soon as anyone else found out, the single division of super-battleships Terra had sent to protect their colony wasn't going to stand a chance.

CHAPTER SEVENTEEN

THE SOL SYSTEM'S EXPLOSIVELY EXPANDING SPACE INDUSTRY had called for large numbers of interface-drive ships. They didn't need to be hyper-capable; they just needed to be able to move around the system at a quarter of the speed of light.

Humanity was the twenty-seventh species the A!Tol had incorporated into their Imperium, however, and far from the first to only barely have scratched the surface of what the interface drive could do. The very first installation the Imperium had arranged to be built on Earth's surface had been a factory to build cheap, durable, low-velocity interface drives.

The rich being the rich, several of those drives had ended up attached to luxuriously appointed civilian ships, and through means Annette chose not to question too hard, Zhao had managed to commandeer one of those space yachts for her meeting with the Two Hundred and Eighty-eighth Pincer of the Republic.

Despite his many duties, Wellesley had somehow managed to reclaim command of her personal bodyguard, leading the eight power-armored Guards—all human today, despite there being several species, including Laians, represented in the Ducal Guard—out around her as they exited her shuttle and formed up to wait for Pincer Kandak's craft.

The yacht *Jessica*, named for the owner's daughter, as Annette understood, hung exactly halfway between the Laian war-dreadnought and the assembled fleet of Terran and Imperial capital ships. She was outside of energy weapon range of either force...and well inside the missile range of both.

If someone wanted to kill the Duchess of Terra and the Laian flag officer in one fell swoop, all it would take was a single missile. *Jessica* had no defenses. That was why the Duchy had suggested her as a meeting place.

Well, that and the fact that her crew quarters could be sealed off from her guest quarters and landing bay, and the landing bay was large enough to accommodate two shuttles. The crew would never see the meeting taking place aboard her, and both Annette and Kandak were arriving by their own spacecraft.

The Laian shuttle was a small disk thirty meters in diameter, a design from a species that had used the interface drive for so long that aerodynamics only barely factored into their shuttle designs.

It hovered in the empty space in the hangar for several moments, then folded out four large legs and settled down onto them. A ramp slid down from the middle of the ship, and four armored Laian soldiers, their power armor suits an inky black that seemed to suck up the light, strode down it.

They ignored Annette's waiting party, sweeping out to scan the entire hangar bay before returning to the ramp.

Four more soldiers and three officers, unarmored and wearing simple harnesses over their dark carapaces, followed them down the ramp. Annette recognize Kandak in the center, the dark red Laian bigger than his escorts—which meant older, though he was hardly the largest Laian she'd met. The High Captain of Tortuga, the leader of the Exiles her Laian citizen had abandoned, had been much bigger than Kandak.

"Pincer Kandak," she greeted him. "Welcome aboard *Jessica*. I have had a space arranged for our discussions and set up some Laian-compatible food."

She could have just provided Universal Protein, the hyper-processed, tofu-like food that was biocompatible with every species known. But since she *had* a Laian enclave, she had access to food that Laians could eat.

Politeness cost less than missiles and starships, after all.

"My guards will sweep the ship," he said flatly. "Once they have confirmed you have no surprises or traps, we may speak."

He gestured a pincer, and half of the armored Laians charged back into the ship.

"I do not know what purpose you seek to gain by this meeting," he continued. "My orders are clear."

"Unless your orders are to start a war, Pincer of the Republic, I hope you have some flexibility," Annette replied. "I am prepared to alleviate the Republic's legitimate concerns, but this is the sovereign space of the A!Tol Imperium.

"We will not be bullied."

KANDAK PROVED UNSURPRISINGLY silent after that until his guards returned, presumably notifying him by radio that all was clear as they said nothing Annette heard.

"Very well, Duchess," he finally spoke again. "Since you seem to believe your words can change something, I will allow you to speak. You had a space set aside?"

"Yes, Pincer," she told him. "If you and your officers will follow me."

His mandibles clicked in a gesture she recognized as equivalent to a human grunt. If she had to deal with a representative of one of the Core Powers, at least it was one from a species whose body language she had some familiarity with.

Jessica's one meeting room was right off of the hangar bay, and the owner had laid in seats for a variety of species, including Laians. Three chairs designed for the upright, carapaced aliens were set up along one side of the black marble conference table, and three of Annette's favored powered auto-adjusting chairs occupied the other side. Zhao and Villeneuve took the seats on either side, leaving the center one to Annette. She waited on Kandak.

The Pincer took a seat, his body language radiating surprised pleasure that Annette was *quite* sure he didn't think she was picking up. Once he had positioned himself, Annette sat herself down, watching the alien and waiting.

A robot delivered a tray of Laian-compatible snacks and drinks to the three seated officers. Kandak managed to control his emotions enough not to have an audible mandible-chitter of delight.

Neither of his subordinates was so self-controlled. The Laians on Earth didn't have access to much of their homeworld's native flora, but they'd managed to find Earth-native plants that could provide the same chemicals and nutrition, and several had set themselves to the task of making the best food they could from Earth's supplies for their people.

From what Annette had been told—and the two junior Laians' reaction—they succeeded, at least so far as smell and appearance went.

"We are not swayed by food and small luxuries, Duchess," Kandak told her, though he didn't *refuse* the food either, snatching up one of what would be canapes for a human and eating it neatly.

"I do not expect you to be," she told him. "But a certain respect is owed the representatives of one of the Core Powers."

"The only respect I want is for you to hand over our rebels and their stolen ships, as well as any technology you have extracted from them," he told her. "Once that is done, Duchess, I will be on my way back home."

"We have never extracted technology from the ships here," Annette replied. "And the ships are centuries obsolete by your standards, aren't they?"

"There are rules, Duchess Bond, about technology transfer from Core to Arm," Kandak said. "They are ironclad and forbid what you have done with our ships."

"We have done nothing with those ships," she replied. "They are manned by Laians, and at no point have we attempted to dismantle or even examine them. They were trapped by your kindred so we could do no such thing."

Kandak laid a small silver disk on the table and tapped something on a long black panel on his left arm. A hologram sprang up from the disk, showing the final exchange between *Liberty* and the strange ships that had attacked Alpha Centauri.

Including Captain Rolfson's deployment of his ship's plasma lance.

"*That*, Duchess, is one of our plasma lances," he said calmly. "A technology the A!Tol Imperium does not possess but that you, apparently, do. One I must assume you were given by these rebels."

"That is *a* plasma lance," she confirmed. "A Terran-developed, Terran-built, and Terran-deployed plasma lance. Its development was partially funded by the A!Tol Imperium, and ships of that design"—she gestured at the hologram—"are shortly to enter Imperial service.

"Which makes it, Pincer, a technology that the A!Tol Imperium *does* possess."

"A technology you stole."

"No," Annette denied. "It was developed based on watching a Laian plasma lance in use, yes. But we have a saying on Earth: once you know it is possible, everything that follows is just engineering.

"While based on the concept we saw demonstrated, our plasma lance was developed by ourselves—something that, while it is frankly disrespectful to demand, we can prove if we must."

Kandak was silent for several moments, sneaking a second snack. Annette suspected that laying on a snack board that the Laians would *enjoy* was the smartest idea she'd had for this negotiation.

"I will need to see proof of that," he finally said. "But all that would change, Duchess, is that I would not need to demand that surrender of your new cruisers.

"I still will require you to surrender the stolen vessels and the rebels who stole them. If you do not do so, I am required to take them by force."

"By force," Annette echoed softly. "You fly into a star system of a sovereign nation and inform me that I *must* surrender sentients who have voluntarily become citizens and the ships they arrived on, or you will take them by force?"

She gestured to Villeneuve.

"I believe Admiral Villeneuve has stated his position on the surrender of the Laians who have immigrated here, and it seems I must reiterate.

"And to be clear, I *have* spoken with Empress A!Shall," she assured the Laians. "She was quite specific in her instructions to me, which leaves me with little more choice in my answers than you would have me believe you have."

Annette leaned forward against the table, grateful that the powered chair was smart enough to pull her slightly back as she did so, to avoid the indelicacy of bouncing her pregnant stomach off the gorgeous black table.

"There are no Laian rebels here," she said calmly. "There are, I will concede, the descendants of Laians who fought in the civil war between the Ascendancy and the Republic—though I must note that the Exiles are descendants of the Ascendancy, which was the ruling government of your race before the war. That does raise interesting questions of *who* were the rebels, does it not?"

"The attaintment travels by hive and lineage," Kandak told her. "They remain enemies of the Republic. The ships remain ours, with technology more advanced than the A!Tol have developed. You have no choice, Duchess. You *will* surrender them to us."

"Neither Terran nor Imperial law recognizes any such transfer of guilt," Annette replied. "If you could prove specific war crimes by a specific individual, we would be prepared to consider extradition, but the Laians in the Duchy of Terra are now citizens of the A!Tol Imperium. Simply being descendants of the losers of your civil war is not enough for me to blithely hand them over."

"Then I will regretfully be forced to take them," the Pincer of the Republic said levelly.

"Past my Militia," Annette said. "Past the Imperial Navy. Past my Ducal Guard and the Imperial Marines on the surface, because both of those forces will defend the Laian enclave as fiercely as any other city on my world.

"Are you truly prepared to start a war over this, Pincer of the Republic Kandak?"

"My orders do not leave me flexibility, Duchess. Surrender the criminals, or I will be forced to take them."

"I know perfectly well, Pincer, that the Republic has solved the starcom mobility problem and that your *Harvester of Glory* has the ability to 'phone home'," Annette told him. "Neither I nor my Empress are prepared to be dictated to by the Laian Republic, Pincer."

She and her companions rose as if they'd been reading her mind.

"There may well be compromises we are prepared to consider," she allowed, "but so long as you claim that we must either abjectly surrender or you will attack my world, then all I can say is: bring it on.

"And either you will fail, or when the fragile bonds that keep galactic civilization together collapse and the Republic burns as the Ascendancy did, you will *know* it was your choice that started it all."

CHAPTER EIGHTEEN

Super-battleships had one distinctive advantage over their smaller siblings: none of the fast battleships and only a small number of battleships carried starcom receivers. Super-battleships were large enough, however, that all of the A!Tol Imperium's super-battleships had the receivers.

They couldn't transmit at all and the bandwidth was atrocious while in hyperspace, but it meant that Echelon Lord Harriet Tanaka could still receive updates as her new task group made its way toward Alpha Centauri.

Not that the updates were anything she *wanted* to hear, just what she *needed* to.

Laians.

Not the ex-pirates turned immigrant settlers of the Exiles and Earth's enclave, but the communist-on-crack fanatics of the Core Power Laian Republic. The Republic wasn't the strongest or most advanced Core Power, but they were far from the weakest.

And even the weakest Core Power was *completely* out of the A!Tol Imperium's weight class.

Fifty starships followed the currents of hyperspace from Kimar to

Alpha Centauri, the cruisers and fast battleships forming a rough defensive sphere around the two super-battleships at the heart of the formation.

It wasn't the most powerful force Harriet Tanaka had ever seen —*that* honor still went to the ten-squadron battle fleet the Imperium had mustered after the Kanzi attack on Terra, a fleet that had never had to go into action.

It was, however, a more powerful force than she'd ever commanded, with almost fifty thousand sentients of twenty-one different species under her command. It had been a force level selected to make certain that any logical follow-up wave to the four destroyers they'd seen would be utterly outclassed.

She had just under a hundred million tons of warships, equal tonnage to the Laian task group at Sol, but the technological advantage was more like four or five to one...in the opposite direction.

A!Tol intelligence on Laian war-dreadnoughts was limited, but Harriet went through what they had. She didn't even have enough information to identify the warship's age, let alone its class. What data she had suggested somewhere between two and four hundred missile launchers, each firing missiles rated at point eight five cee, plus multiple versions of whatever the Laians had replaced the plasma lance with.

The Republic was quite cagey about that. Their internal politics required a large amount of publicity around the military, but they'd managed, despite it all, to keep the exact specifications of their warships secret.

"Captain Sier, to my office, please," she ordered over the intercom.

If she was going to have this kind of headache, she might as well share it and see if her Yin flag captain had any thoughts on the next step.

WHEN THE TALL, blue-feathered Captain arrived at Harriet's office, she had two sets of holograms hovering in the air, humming as she regarded them thoughtfully. One had four smaller ships, the other a single, absolutely immense vessel.

"Echelon Lord," Sier greeted her. "How may I assist?" He looked at the two floating holograms. "What am I seeing here?" he asked.

"These"—Harriet gestured at the four smaller ships—"are the vessels that attacked Alpha Centauri. Destroyer-sized, near–Core Power tech levels. Fast, dangerous, complete unknowns."

"The ships that we are on our way to make certain don't show up again," Sier agreed, eyeing the other, far more immense vessel. "And this...this is a Laian war-dreadnought."

"Yes," she confirmed. "Specifically, *Harvester of Glory* under Two Hundred and Eighty-eighth Pincer of the Republic Kandak. With twenty attack cruisers for escorts, though they didn't seem worth including in the screen.

"Currently, *Harvester* is in a trailing orbit of Terra, demanding that the Duchy surrender the Laian Exiles and their ships, seeing as how they are apparently still regarded as rebels against the Republic."

"Shadowed clouds," Sier cursed. "And we, of course, are the closest task group to either system. What are our orders?"

"We have no new orders," Harriet said grimly. "Our objective remains to secure the Alpha Centauri system, but I cannot see leaving a *war-dreadnought* moving around our territory as a secondary priority."

She hummed softly again, studying the two ships.

"We don't know enough about Laian capital ships for me to be happy trying to engage or intimidate her," she said quietly. "I wish we could communicate with Admiral Kurzman—on the one hand, we need somebody in Alpha Centauri, but on the other, I'd feel somewhat more comfortable trying to convince the Pincer to back down with eight super-battleships instead of six."

"I'm not sure even twelve A!Tol capital ships would intimidate a Laian dreadnought," Sier admitted, studying the hologram of the massive vessel. "She was designed to fight Wendira, after all, and the Grand Swarm is...well, a lot scarier than we are."

The Wendira and the Laians were both insect-like sentients with exoskeletal carapaces...and that was where the resemblance ended. The Laians' culture discouraged nuclear families in favor of lineage marriages that raised children in common, but that was a *cultural* thing, not a biological thing.

Only one of the four Wendira castes/subspecies was actually capable of having children. The other three subspecies—Warrior, Worker and Drone—were all hatched from eggs laid by Wendira Royal females.

Harriet wasn't quite sure if the clash between the Laians and the Wendira was biological, cultural or political, but they were the two Core Powers most regularly in direct conflict with each other. The Laian war-dreadnought's most likely enemy was a Wendira star hive —what Harriet's race would call a supercarrier.

Harriet wasn't sure how the Wendira had designed a one-sentient spacecraft that moved at point eight cee without killing the occupant with hyperspace radiation—and A!Tol intelligence suggested that to a large degree, they simply hadn't. Wendira Drone-castes weren't exactly expendable, but they were functionally infinite in number, after all.

"Which leaves us with one specific problem," Harriet concluded. "We can either continue on our current mission, which would position us where we could support Terra if the Laians *do* pick a fight... assuming Villeneuve could spin the fight out for a few days, at least. Or we can go to Terra and hope to help talk this Kandak down but leave Alpha Centauri vulnerable."

"If I may make a small suggestion, Echelon Lord?" Sier asked slowly.

"There's no other reason I asked you to meet me," she said. "Please, Captain."

"You're thinking like a Division Lord, not a task group comman-der," he pointed out. "You have *fifty warships*."

Harriet paused, her hum cutting off as she considered.

"Sixteen of our *Stalwart*-class cruisers would be more than enough to deal with, say, four cruisers on the same level as those destroyers, wouldn't they?" she murmured. "And the cruisers are going to be irrelevant to any attempt to intimidate Kandak into standing down."

"I would suspect so, Echelon Lord."

As Harriet opened her mouth to thank her flag captain and begin to give orders, her intercom pinged again. She tapped it.

"Tanaka."

"Echelon Lord," Commander Piditel greeted her over the channel. "We have just received an encoded message over the starcom. It appears to be from Fleet Lord Tan!Shallegh—and is marked as for your attention only."

"Forward it to my office," Harriet ordered swiftly, then turned to her captain. "Thank you, Sier. Once I've heard what Tan!Shallegh has to say, I will pass orders to the task group."

———

AFTER SIER HAD RETURNED to his duties, Harriet slowly locked down the security measures on her office. Attached to her flag deck, it wasn't necessarily the most physically secure or safest location on the ship, but once she'd activated the full confidentiality suite, it didn't matter if someone had bugged her office somehow.

No message was getting out through the Faraday cage her office had temporarily become.

The full suite rendered her unable to communicate with the rest of her flagship, which meant it could only be used for the most restricted of communiques—and was almost never used outside of hyperspace.

The codes attached to Tan!Shallegh's message required it, though, and she sealed herself in before activating the video.

A hologram of the A!Tol Fleet Lord appeared above her desk. He looked tired, his skin mostly gray despite shocking streaks of black and green.

"Echelon Lord Tanaka," the recording began. "This message is classified Lowest Void. While I expect you to use this information to make your plans, it is *not* to be distributed to any of your staff or Captains."

That had Harriet's attention. She was aware of the "Lowest Void"–level classification—somewhere well past Top Secret, as the UESF had classified things—but nothing in her current files had that level of secrecy.

"Nothing at Lowest Void is kept in digital records," Tan!Shallegh told her. "This message will purge itself one cycle after being received. These are not affairs we can officially acknowledge the existence of, but be aware that we will be advising Duchess Bond of the same information.

"We have certain allies among the Core Powers, individuals and factions that act to keep the old races from abusing their power as much as possible. We have deep, dark channels they can communicate with us through, but those channels are slow.

"They risked much to pass on Ki!Tana's warning at Sol six long-cycles ago fast enough. Such risks were not taken this time, but that has left us a problem."

The gray on his skin was exhaustion. It wasn't a shade Harriet had seen on A!Tol often.

"We have now, somewhat too late, been warned about *Harvester of Glory*," Tan!Shallegh noted. "But that was one part of a longer message, and the rest is...disturbing."

The Fleet Lord gestured his manipulator tentacles, and an image appeared on the hologram.

"We know why the Laians are here," he told her. "We are not entirely surprised by their presence.

"Nobody knows who the strange Kanzi who attacked Alpha Centauri are. We're watching for them, but they're an unknown factor—which means they cannot be our priority compared to what we *know* is coming."

The image was a vessel, something entirely outside of Harriet's personal experience. A broad-based cone formed of increasingly smaller stepped circles. Without scale, it was hard to guess the size... but then she recognized just what she was looking at.

"Our contacts have also confirmed that there is a Wendira star hive in the region," Tan!Shallegh said. "They are...hunting something. It's not *Harvester*; our contacts don't believe that Hive Commandant Ashtahkah is aware of *Harvester*'s presence.

"The Wendira think there is something in the Terran Kovius Zone worth deploying a hundred-million-ton carrier to search for. *Harvester of Glory* is bad enough, but *Wing's Nightmare* is easily equivalent to Pincer Kandak's entire battle group.

"And either of them could take multiple squadrons of our best."

Harriet stared at the star hive. It was *ugly* to human eyes, but she could pick out the launch decks, the missile launchers, the beam weapons. A star hive could deploy starfighters to swarm any lesser ship. Conquer a planet with the Warriors and Drones aboard. It was the ultimate multipurpose vessel, and powerful enough to be able to do each of its tasks well.

"My fear, Echelon Lord, is that the Hive Commandant is hunting the same thing the Kanzi were," Tan!Shallegh concluded grimly. "Whatever it is, it has attracted the attention of a Core Power and an unknown player to your species region.

"I have requested reinforcements, but..." He fluttered his tentacles, an A!Tol shrug. "I would not engage either vessel without a minimum of four squadrons of super-battleships. I have been promised those ships and more, but it will take time to gather them.

"I need you to buy me time, Echelon Lord. You and the Duchy of Terra Militia must keep the Wendira and the Laians from starting a depths-sunk war before we can get there."

There was a long pause in the message, but the recording didn't end.

"Our contacts didn't tell us everything," he finally admitted. "They don't pass on the sources of their information or any validating sources, though we have found them reliable. What we are quite certain of, however, is that our contacts specifically do not provide us with information on Mesharom movements in our region of space.

"We have reason to believe that there is a Mesharom Frontier Fleet deployment near Sol as well. I would like to say they are potential allies, but the Mesharom have their own plans and objectives."

Harriet sighed. Of course it couldn't be *simple*.

"There are a lot of players on the move around Sol right now and we don't know why," Tan!Shallegh told her. "We will gather reinforcements and move as quickly as possible, but I *must* gather sufficient force to make the gesture meaningful.

"All I can offer is information and warm waters. Good luck, Echelon Lord."

THREE CORE POWERS. Plus an unknown group with basically Core Power–level tech.

Harriet wasn't sure just what the hell anyone was looking for, but it couldn't be worth this level of attention!

Whatever *she* thought, however, those four players had wandered into the area around her homeworld, and dealing with them was going to fall on her as one of the senior Imperial officers in the region.

She had to decide what to do, and much as she hated the idea, splitting her forces was looking like the only option. With a sigh, she wiped the message from Tan!Shallegh and took down her office's security suite

"Piditel," she pinged her coms officer. "I want an all-Captains, all-Lords video conference in twenty minutes."

"Yes, Echelon Lord."

The plan she and Sier had worked up while they were only looking at the Laians was going to have to do. Without more information on the Mesharom, the strangers or the Wendira, all she could spare was a cruiser squadron.

The only change she was going to make was sending the lion's share of her courier ships to Alpha Centauri. If someone else showed up there, she wanted to know as soon as possible, not have to wait for a warship to be broken free and sent over.

They needed to spin out the clock for Fleet Lord Tan!Shallegh to gather his fleet—but at the same time, she doubted time was the A!Tol Imperium's friend.

CHAPTER NINETEEN

VICE ADMIRAL PATRICK KURZMAN MASSAGED THE BRIDGE OF his nose, studying the imagery that Rolfson had sent back up from the planet.

"All right, people," he finally said, glancing around the small gathering in his flag briefing room aboard *Emperor of China*. Rolfson was there, as were the flagship's Captain Fang and Pat's aide, Heng Chan. Commodore (retired) Kulap Metharom, a tiny Thai woman who'd been instrumental in developing the original Terran interface drive and had emigrated to Hope, had agreed to join them by video from the surface.

Commander Teykay of *Plainsfang* joined them to speak for the Imperium, the Rekiki clearly surprised that *Emperor* had chairs for his race. Clearly, despite being assigned to humanity's first colony, he hadn't looked into the history of just how Terra had *become* a Duchy.

There weren't many Rekiki left in the Ducal Guard, but the lizard-like centaurs who'd followed Tellaki into Bond's service—and sadly survived him—were all heroes so far as Earth was concerned.

"I've kept up with our active technological development, but I'll freely admit I'm lost as to the high end of Imperial research and science," he noted. "Would someone care to fill me in on just *what* we're looking at?"

"A number of things," Rolfson replied. "Dr. Wolastoq continues to go through the ship, *carefully*, but we have no idea what else we're likely to find.

"What we have found so far is that the hull is semi-motile and semi-organic, sustained and manipulated by artificial microorganisms and similarly sized robotic controllers. We haven't done too many tests so far, but we know it's self-repairing and extremely tough."

The big red-haired Swedish Captain shrugged.

"I wouldn't want to replace compressed-matter armor with it, but I'd *love* to have my support matrices made of the stuff. It's not a world-changing discovery, but reverse-engineering it would still be huge.

"The big discovery, though, is the power core." Rolfson tapped a command, focusing the image Kurzman and everyone else were watching on the suspended sphere.

"Further scans suggest the core contains a decaying singularity with a mass approximately eleven percent of Earth's—nine percent of Hope's. The gravitational effects are almost entirely contained, and the decay of the singularity is used to produce power for the ship.

"It is basically in standby and decaying at a natural rate, hence it still being functional after fifty thousand years."

"That's insane," Pat objected. "*Fifty thousand years* and it still has *power?*"

"Best guess that, when crashed, the core had mass roughly equivalent to Earth's and was somewhere between one fifth and one fourth of full capacity," Metharom told them crisply. "Not sure what power needed for. Small ship, but core..." The research engineer shook her head. "Core would power *Emperor* on own. No need for secondaries."

"Those two discoveries we think we can reverse-engineer," Rolfson noted. "Not necessarily fully, but enough to get significant value out of.

"The last one, we have no idea what the hell it is, how it worked, or how we'd get value out of it, but..." The image moved to showed the strange V-shaped mechanism from the ancient ship's engineering section.

"We *believe* this was their FTL drive," the Militia Captain concluded. "She was not a hypership, but she was definitely an interstellar craft, I'd guess a scout ship or courier of some kind, as we have yet to find any weaponry aboard her, and she was too small for significant cargo.

"The only known method of faster-than-light travel in our galaxy is via hyperspace," Rolfson said. "This represents something we did not think existed and have almost no chance of understanding—and also something that every power in the galaxy will literally kill to possess."

"And it's sitting on our first colony," Pat said with a sigh. Humanity had been lucky so far, but this was starting to look like bad karma.

"I've already forwarded your report to Sol," he told the junior officer. "*Hermes Nine* should be entering hyperspace in the next five minutes. The Duchess will know what we've found and so will the Imperium.

"For now, however, what the *hell* do we do, people?"

"We cannot allow this discovery to fall into the hands of the Kanzi," Teykay told them grimly. "Or the Laians. Or...anyone else. Can the ship be moved?"

"No," Rolfson said instantly. "We don't know nearly enough about her to do so. Her self-repair appears limited to the hull itself; most of her interior systems are still trashed from the impact.

"Wolastoq continues to survey the vessel, and with your permission, Admiral, I'd like to take a team back down to the surface to assist."

"Agreed," Pat told him. The Admiral paused thoughtfully, then sighed.

"*Emperor* has a significant arsenal of 'just in case' equipment," he reminded the others. "Including six surface-to-space heavy missile launchers. We will deploy those, as well as our heavy ground vehicles and Guards, to the surface.

"I hope to stop any further incursions in space, but I think we have no choice but to make certain that this discovery is protected at every level by every means we have available!"

———

HAROLD'S SHUTTLE touched down at the landing pad at the Corellian base camp amidst a swarm of activity. CDC was breaking the camp down as rapidly as it had gone up. Much of the equipment and personnel were returning to New Hope City.

The rest was moving twenty-three kilometers away, into a new camp around the crashed alien ship. A new nanocrete pad was already taking shape, but it wasn't complete enough yet to take the military shuttle he'd returned on.

The new pad was supposed to be bigger, too. Designed to handle several of the Militia's big heavy-lift shuttles at once so they could bring in the defensive launchers and heavy weapons for the Ducal Guard.

For about twenty-four more hours, however, everyone was landing here, at the original base camp. A company of Hope's Ducal Guard guarded each site, and a dozen or so more came down with Harold and the specialist engineers he'd brought with him.

Kurzman's words left Rolfson with an itch between his shoulder-blades, though. There'd been no further sign of trouble, but he wore a heavy plasma pistol on his uniform belt anyway. They could not risk anything happening to that ship, not now.

He was surprised, however, to find Ramona Wolastoq waiting for him when he left his shuttle. The xenoarchaeologist was standing aside from the crowd, studying the specialists with an appraising eye, but cracked a slight smile when she saw him.

"Bringing me anyone useful?" she asked bluntly when he approached her.

"Three chief engineers, a hyperdrive specialist, two cyber-technicians I wouldn't trust within ten feet of my entering a password, and half a dozen other senior techs and scientists," he confirmed cheerfully. "The best people in the Admiral's task force for this mystery. Even Kulap Metharom is flying down from New Hope City."

"That's good," Wolastoq replied, giving him a quick and thoroughly unexpected hug. "I can handle the 'what happened here' side of this, the archaeological side, but I'm not qualified to poke at strange alien tech."

He returned the surprise embrace and grinned at her.

"And we don't have a clue how to deal with things that are fifty thousand years old. We need everybody's skills today, so we'll make it work."

"And security?" she asked softly.

"Once the new pad is in place, we're landing surface-to-space missiles and pulling together about two battalions from the Guard contingents aboard the Militia ships," Harold told her. "We've got power armor, some heavy weapons... We're going to make damned sure nothing happens, Ramona."

"Good. This whole thing just makes me...feel like a target."

"I know what you mean."

"CAPTAIN SOMMERS, we're inbound from the main base camp," Harold overheard the surveyor's pilot saying into his radio. "Please confirm IFF ID; I'd rather not be shot down today."

The pilot waited a few moments.

"Captain Sommers? Hope Charlie Company, anybody there?"

"What's going on?" Harold asked, stepping into the cockpit.

"I can't raise the camp at the ship," the pilot replied. "I'm not even getting a system response."

"May I?" Harold gestured to the equipment. He poked at it for a moment, not seeing anything the pilot hadn't, then shrugged and activated his earbuds.

"*Liberty*, can you ping Captain Sommers from orbit?" he requested. "We're not getting a response on the ground, they may be having system issues."

"Roger," Popovitch replied lazily. There were a few seconds of silence, then the laziness was gone as the communications officer spoke again. "I have no response, sir," he said formally. "Nothing—not the company communications setup, not individual suits of power armor, nothing."

"That doesn't make sense," Harold replied, "unless..."

"Even if they'd been blown to hell, this ping would get me locator beacons from the armor, sir," Popovitch told him. "It's clean, because I can pick it up, but they're being jammed."

Harold's blood turned to ice.

"General message to the task force, Popovitch: drop all Guard contingents on the dig site. Drop them *now*, assault mode.

"The camp is under attack."

"Yes, sir."

Harold barely heard his coms officer's acknowledgment; he was turning back to the pilot of the surveyor plane he was in.

"This thing isn't armed," he snapped. "Turn us back; get us out of here."

If it was just him and his Guard escorts, he'd go in. But his shuttle was full of critical specialists...and he was *not* going to risk Ramona Wolastoq.

Douglas obeyed instantly—but not instantly enough. As the aircraft slowed to begin its tight turn, the white flash of plasma fire passed through where they *would* have been.

"Shit!"

The surveyor jinked upward, evading a second burst of deadly-hot plasma.

"I can't evade long enough to get us home," he told Harold. "I gotta put us down!"

The man didn't wait for permission or approval, turning off the engines and the antigravity generators in one swift gesture. The survey helicopter did not have nearly enough wing area to support its weight without power and promptly plummeted out of the sky—just underneath a *third* set of plasma bolts.

Harold's stomach tried to escape out his throat as the aircraft fell. They'd only been half a kilometer in the air—there wasn't *that* much space to fall!

The pilot had it in hand. Ten meters above the permafrost, he slammed the surveyor back to full power. Antigravity slowed their fall while the engines converted most of the downward momentum into forward velocity.

It wasn't enough to keep them in the air—but it *was* enough to allow the pilot to coast them to a surprisingly soft landing.

"These things are designed for rough terrain," the man told Harold. "But they aren't designed to be shot at—and I doubt whoever shot at us thinks they actually shot us down."

"No," *Liberty*'s Captain agreed, checking his plasma pistol. "I very much doubt that."

"MOVE OUT, MOVE OUT!"

The Ducal Guards in the back of the surveyor were already in motion by the time Harold made it back out of the cockpit, but they'd only been able to fit four of them in with the specialists they'd thought were more important.

"What's going on?" Wolastoq asked.

"Someone is jamming the camp at the ship and just tried to shoot us down with a plasma cannon," he told her grimly. "I don't know who, but I've got one solid guess."

"Who?"

"The Kanzi," he concluded. "They must have snuck at least one force away as a follow-up team, and they've been waiting for us to dig up the ship so they could try and steal it."

"There's an entire *fleet* in orbit," she said. "What are they planning on doing with it?!"

"I don't know," he admitted. "Fifty-fifty between they think they know enough to fly it and they have a second wave coming in."

"It doesn't have enough power to fly," Wolastoq objected.

"I know that and you know that," Harold agreed. "But these guys haven't been inside it and checked the singularity core."

"So, what do we do?"

"We take cover, because the buggers with the plasma cannon are going to come check on us," he said grimly. "Otherwise? We keep our heads down. Reinforcements are on their way."

HAROLD LEFT it to the Guards to corral the half-dozen engineers and specialists he'd brought with him while he took charge of Wolastoq. He didn't have power armor, but the xenoarchaeologist was being significantly more sensible than the Militia officers.

"Are we abandoning the plane?" she asked, her tone almost conversational.

"For now," he said. "They know where it went down; they're going to be heading right here."

He checked his earbud and shook his head.

"On the other hand, we are definitely inside whatever jamming field they're running. Nobody else is going to be quite sure where we went down. Come on."

Harold drew the heavy plasma pistol he was carrying and checked the charge. The weapon could, theoretically, take down someone in power armor. If fired at maximum power and relatively short range—but the power pack could only handle three maximum-power shots.

He dialed it to max power anyway. He knew how good a shot he was—with three shots, he was pretty sure of getting one hit, and one dead Kanzi trooper was better than half a dozen lightly scorched ones.

The Corporal leading the guard detachment waved him into a nearby ravine, one of the cracks in the permafrost that ran through the Plateau, nearly invisible from the air.

"We've lost coms," the Guard said without preamble. "Even short-range is gone—but we *do* have our scanners and we have incoming."

"How many?"

"Six, maybe seven," the trooper told him. "Five suits of armor and we've got definite movement and thermal separate from the armor." He pointed an armored finger at the plasma pistol in Harold's hand. "Can you use that?"

"I won't hit with every shot, but I'll hit with some," the Captain promised.

"Good. Take this and get back in the ravine with the rest of the squishies," the Corporal ordered, passing him two spare power packs from his suit storage panels. "We'll hold them, but if any get past us, you'll be all they've got."

Technically, the NCO had no business giving Harold orders—but the Swede wasn't stupid.

"Come on, Ramona," he told the archaeologist. "Let's go dig in."

He smacked the Guard on the armored shoulder.

"Backup is coming from on high; I called it in before we went dark," he promised. "These guys are fucked."

"I know," the Corporal agreed, waiting a few seconds in silence as the civilian moved farther back down the ravine. "The question is if we'll still be here when they get here. Go watch them, Captain. We'll buy you every second we can."

THE WINGS WERE the first clue that the attackers weren't Kanzi. Even as plasma fire started to echo down from the mouth of the ravine as power-armored soldiers inevitably found each other, four winged creatures, entirely alien to Harold's experience, flew *over* the ravine.

They were strange golden insectoids, appearing to only be about four feet tall but with six limbs, the middle ones being the rapidly buzzing wings keeping them gliding through the air.

His attention, however, was riveted on their dark gray uniforms and the deadly-looking plasma carbines the flying aliens had in their hands. Whoever these new strangers were, they weren't friendly.

They were also unarmored, so Harold spent a precious fraction of a second dialing down the power on his pistol before opening fire. Thankfully, they didn't see him until he started shooting—and the accuracy of his first shots surprised even him.

Three glowing bolts of plasma hammered into the closest flying alien, sending it collapsing from the sky in deathly silence. Its companions, however, returned fire immediately. Harold had better cover, but they landed almost immediately, throwing his second salvo off.

Plasma blew chunks off of his cover, but he ignored it as best as he could as he aimed carefully and shot down a second insectoid attacker.

Then the pistol was suddenly slipping from nerveless fingers as a larger chunk of debris hammered into his shoulder. His uniform had some anti-ballistic properties, but not enough to stop a six-inch-long dagger of stone from punching through fabric, skin, and bone alike.

It hit with enough force to fling him to the ground, gasping in pain as his arm simply refused to respond to his orders to grab the pistol again. He twisted, trying to reach the gun with his left hand, only for pain to force him to crumple back into the ground as Wolastoq reached him.

"Son of a *bitch*," the Amerindian woman swore. "Who are these people?"

Even if Harold had been able to speak past the pain, he didn't have an answer for her. Before either of them could say more, a mechanical voice echoed over the ravine.

"You surrender now. We claim battle right."

He could hear them approaching, feet scuffing on the permafrost, but he could barely move. Wolastoq clearly heard them as well and snarled.

"*Not* happening," she whispered to him, grabbing up the pistol and checking its settings.

"You surrender," the translated voice repeated.

Ramona Wolastoq shook her head and suddenly kissed Harold fiercely.

"You, Captain Rolfson, are not permitted to die. I'll be right back."

She strode away, the plasma pistol in her hand, and stepped around the ravine corner. The sharp *hiss-crack* of plasma weapons firing echoed in the tiny crack in the frozen soil. Two shots. Half a dozen. Ten. Fifteen?

Then silence and only pain kept Harold from shouting after Ramona before she came back around the corner. There was a burn across her cheek from a near-miss, and another across the shoulder of her suit jacket, but she was alive.

He had never seen anyone more beautiful.

CHAPTER TWENTY

"Someone get me *some* kind of update," Pat Kurzman snapped. "What the hell is going on down there?"

"It looks like we lost communication with the dig site just over thirty minutes ago, but there were no scheduled coms, so we didn't notice," Heng Chan reported grimly. "We got an emergency pulse from Captain Rolfson calling for a full-court drop on the dig site six minutes ago, which our Guard commanders executed immediately.

"Our first wave of assault shuttles will be touching down within ninety seconds," the chief of staff continued. "Orbital surveillance shows no movement at the site. At all."

"That is not good," Pat said grimly. "What about Rolfson?"

"His aircraft went down and we detected heavy plasma fire in the area," Chan said. "We have to assume he's been shot down."

"Do we have a source on the plasma fire? We have to be able to see *something*."

"Nothing so far. Orbital surveillance is drawing a blank; it's...weird."

"It's someone jamming our sensors," Pat replied. "Our sensors, our coms...it's like a stealth field in turbo-charge mode, covering an entire attack."

"That's..." Chan swallowed. "That's possible, I suppose."

"Unfortunately. Any sensor feeds from the shuttles?"

"Nothing different from what we're seeing."

That wasn't good.

"Do we have a solid lock on Captain Rolfson?"

"No," Chan admitted. "We know where he transmitted from, but he went silent a few seconds later, just as we registered plasma fire. No origin, just the bolts themselves."

"I am *very* sick of being behind the tech curve," Pat said conversationally. "All right. Get me Captain Fang. I have an idea."

Fang appeared on the screen almost instantly, the shaven-headed and heavily muscled Chinese man looking almost as aggravated as Pat felt.

"Sir?" he asked flatly.

"I'm guessing you're not magically seeing anything I'm not," Pat said.

"No. What do you need?"

"We're looking at a modified stealth field," the Admiral told his flag captain. "What I *need*, Captain, is eyes. And you're going to give them to me."

"How? *Emperor*'s sensors can't see through whatever they're doing!"

"But *Emperor* has a full suite of class IV autonomous multi-environment sensor drones," Pat reminded Fang. "You're going to crash one into the ground next to the dig site, and then you're going to use as many damned drones as it takes as relays to get the sensor data up to the Guard and to us.

"And yes, Captain, I'm aware of what a AMESD costs. Do it."

Fang didn't look like he'd even been considering objecting.

"You'll have whatever eyes we can give you before the Guard touches down."

"Make sure *they* have them too."

THEY LOST contact with the assault shuttles first. One moment, every channel was live. The next, they could still *see* the shuttle formation—but there were no communications getting through.

Ten seconds after that, they lost sight of the shuttles. Whatever godawful nightmare tech was shielding the attack on the surface was *terrifying* to Pat.

It was not, however, magic. Between them, the ships of his task force carried over three hundred AMESDs, and, following Pat's orders, they deployed every single one of them.

They didn't crash one drone into the planet. They crashed *six*, each of them relaying up to rapidly flying drones immediately above them.

Thirty-two meters. That was how far the radios on the drones, designed to communicate across entire star systems, could transmit inside the field. With each layer of relay occupying three drones, it took over a *hundred* drones to get the transmissions clear of the stealth field—but they did it.

"Who the hell *are* these people?" Pat demanded as he finally resolved the dig site—and the ongoing battle that was raging through it.

Most of Captain Sommers's company was gone. Some remained, taking cover in the handful of prefabs around the site and using the nanocrete landing pad as a shield against the winged soldiers trying to move in on them.

Both sides were carrying plasma weapons, and the entire force trying to take the camp, at least, was in power armor. The only thing in Sommers's favor was that the numbers were more even than Pat had feared: the Guard captain had a full company of two hundred troops, and it looked like the aliens had "only" landed about twice that.

Somehow. Through *everything* Pat had in orbit.

"With what we've got, can you localize the source of the jamming?" Pat asked.

"Yes, sir," Fang confirmed. "Looks like multiple sources, I don't think we've got them all locked in, but we have at least three."

"Kill them from on high, Captain. You are authorized."

The standard ship-board weapons of any galactic power could *shred* a planet. Deploying them against surface targets was done very, very carefully—and only on the authority of the highest-ranked officer in the system.

Fang had clearly been expecting the order, however, as less than ten seconds passed from Pat's words to *Emperor of China* shifting course to allow her broadside to bear on the planet.

Three proton beams fired. They'd lose much of their energy passing through the atmosphere, with attendant negative effects, but it was still better than sending cee-fractional hammers into a planet they wanted to keep.

"And one more," Fang noted calmly. A fourth proton beam fired, incinerating the emitter that the destruction of the first three allowed them to localize.

"We have coms," Chan announced.

"This is Sommers," a voice echoed over the radio. "Zulu. Zulu. Zulu. We are being fucking overwhelmed. *Someone fucking answer me!*"

"Captain, this is Vice Admiral Kurzman," Pat told the man crisply, checking the timing and smiling grimly. "If you would like your answer, I suggest you look up."

The first wave of Guard shuttles crashed down onto the dig site seconds later. Plasma bolts and autocannon shells walked their way around the perimeter of the dig site, followed by power-armored troopers.

One moment, the Guard were about to be overwhelmed, their communications blocked and the enemy all around them.

The next, they had communications back and the odds were flipped. Surrounded and facing air support, the strange aliens were suddenly the ones without a chance. Half of their force was wiped out in the first strafing runs and gunfights.

The rest of the battle was short and ugly, but at least, unlike the strange Kanzi who'd attacked before, *these* aliens proved willing to surrender.

"Find their ship," Pat ordered. "Do whatever it takes—I'm assuming we're looking at a stealth-fielded transport."

Fang coughed.

"Already did, sir," the Captain admitted. "It was the last stealth field source. It's, ah, scattered across about a kilometer of permafrost."

"Damn," Pat said, then shook his head. "So be it, Captain. It had to be done."

"Sir, I have Commander Teykay on a channel for you," Chan reported.

"Put him through."

The Rekiki's now-familiar face appeared on the screen. Pat Kurzman had worked with Rekiki for five years now and he could easily read the fear...no, the *terror* on the Commander's crocodile-like face.

"Admiral Kurzman, I know who these aliens are," he said urgently. "They shouldn't be here—they shouldn't be here at all.

"Those are Wendira Warrior caste, sir."

CHAPTER TWENTY-ONE

ANNETTE HAD LONG ACCEPTED THAT, AS THE DIRECT VASSAL OF the A!Tol Empress, the ruler of Earth, and the direct owner, in several senses, of about fifteen star systems, she didn't ever truly get "time off".

Birth was probably going to force her to change that, at least temporarily, but she was still some months away from that, and the twins were being surprisingly cooperative.

For now, she had a private meeting room built into her penthouse with the best security the Imperium's technology could offer. She, Elon, Villeneuve and Ki!Tana were gathered there, staring at the image that Tan!Shallegh had sent them.

The ten-foot-tall winged creature in the hologram was surprisingly beautiful to human eyes. Her carapace glittered with silver and gold and her wings, massive even relative to her size, were a glittering translucent white.

"Hive Commandant Ashtahkah," Annette said simply, gesturing at the image. "A Royal-caste Wendira. Past her egg-laying years now but mother to approximately seventeen *thousand* Wendira of the four castes."

"The higher ranks of their military are split between Royal-castes who are too old to breed and Warrior-castes who have earned their rank in blood," Ki!Tana told the others in the room. "I have had only limited encounters with Wendira, but none have been positive.

"Why they are here? I do not know."

"And the Mesharom?" Annette asked. When Ki!Tana had wandered back into her life, shortly before the Second Battle of Sol, she'd done so in a borrowed Mesharom scout ship.

Whirls of yellow-green flickered across the Ki!Tol's skin before setting into green and purple.

"You know there are secrets I cannot betray," she said finally. "What I will promise you is this: the Mesharom are not your enemy. They may not help us against the Laians or the Wendira, not if they lack the force, but they will not strike against Terra themselves."

"That's not exactly reassuring," Elon argued. "Not with *three* Core Power battle groups wandering around the area. I'm starting to feel very small and very neglected, and I much preferred that feeling to go along with being very ignored!"

"You knew when you took in the Exiles that there might be consequences," Ki!Tana said. "There is a reason no one did it before you. They knew the Republic would come."

"The Mesharom and the Wendira are here for different reasons, though," Villeneuve replied. "And we don't know why."

"I'm guessing the same damned reason why those strange Kanzi showed up on Hope," Annette said. "There's something there they all want. The Laians just happened to be here at the same time, which means if we manage to satisfy them, somehow, they may go away. Given the number of players that seem to be intruding onto our little corner of space, that is worth quite a bit to us now."

"But...how much?" Elon said softly. "We won't betray the Laians. What *can* we give the Republic?"

"The ships," she told her consort. "I'll hate to lose them, but if we give Pincer Kandak the attack cruisers, he gets to go back to the

Republic with solid proof of *something*. And we get to remove one player from the damned board."

"Will he accept?" Ki!Tana asked. "He seemed quite determined before."

"It's been thirty-six hours that *Harvester* has just sat there looking intimidating," Annette reminded her staff. "I doubt he's willing to offer a compromise himself, but he is also hesitating to start a war.

"I think it's time he and I spoke again."

"You're taking a risk every time you meet with him," Elon told her. "We cannot necessarily trust the Pincer not to do something stupid."

"We have no choice," Annette said. "Right now, Kandak holds the military balance of power in this system. We can't stop him and he knows it. At the same time, if he tries to take the Exiles by force, we will fight him—and he doesn't appear willing to accept the consequences of that!"

"Yet," Jean Villeneuve said quietly. "But sooner or later, if we don't find a compromise, someone back in the Republic may give the order—and he *will* obey."

"Then like I said," Annette concluded, "it's high time he and I spoke."

JESSICA FOUND herself once more pressed into service as a neutral meeting point, the Laian flag officer and the Terran Duchess meeting in her hangar bay again.

There were fewer escorts this time. Annette hadn't brought any members of her Council, and Kandak, perhaps sensing the tone of the event from the fact that the brief communications arranging it had all come directly from Annette herself, had come without aides.

Their escorts were only two troopers each, though one of Annette's was Wellesley and she suspected that Pincer Kandak's guard probably included someone of similar seniority. She'd also have been surprised if there weren't backup still aboard the Pincer's shuttle—certainly, there were another half-dozen Guards in power armor aboard hers—but the appearance of a modicum of trust was important.

The Laian was silent until they entered the meeting room once more, leaving even the handful of guards behind. He chittered in undisguised pleasure at the sight of the tray of snacks, however, followed by a sharp silence that in a human would have been an embarrassed flush.

"I take it," Pincer Kandak noted slowly, as he picked up a snack, "that you are quite familiar with my people?"

"I dealt extensively with the Exiles at *Builder of Sorrows*," Annette confirmed, using the Laian name for the semi-mobile pirate station rather than its human nickname, Tortuga, or its A!Tol name, A!Ko!La!Ma!—which meant, roughly, "hive of bandit bugs".

"I also have spent time with our Laian citizens here on Terra," she continued. She didn't stress the word *citizens*, but she could tell that Kandak caught the emphasis regardless. "One of them sits on my Council and another is one of the senior officers in my Militia."

Kandak's mandibles clicked in a Laian nod and he took a seat, considering her with black, multifaceted eyes.

"Some truths must be spoken," he finally said. "The Voices of the Republic had their orders from the Grand Parliament as to what was to be done about the Exiles."

As Annette understood it, the Voices of the Republic were the twenty senior officers of the Laian navy. The Grand Parliament was their elected leadership and a quite politic choice of words on the translator software's part.

A more literal translation, she knew, was the *Big Hive*.

She waited for Kandak to continue. There was presumably a point to his history lecture, and she'd let him get to it on his own time.

"Your...defiance required the Voices to ask the Parliament for direction," Kandak admitted. "And your choice of cause, Duchess Bond, has touched certain factions' chosen paths."

That took a moment to process. The translator was *smart*, but it wasn't perfect. If she'd interpreted what he said correctly, though, the way she'd phrased the challenge had linked into a portion of the Grand Parliament's pet causes.

"The Grand Parliament is divided, which has left the decision to fall back to where it began: *Harvester of Glory* and myself."

"And what is your decision, Two Hundred and Eighty-eighth Pincer of the Republic?" she asked carefully.

"I have not made one," he said crisply. "In the absence of clarification, however, it seems to me that I must follow my original orders. So, I must once again, Duchess Bond, summon you to surrender the Exiles and their ships to me."

"I can't do that," Annette said steadily. "The laws of the Imperium do not recognize any authority on your part over them or any crime they are guilty of. I cannot—I *will* not—surrender the citizens of our sovereign Imperium under threat of force."

"Then we find ourselves still at an impasse, Duchess Bond, and I do not think I need to remind you of the balance of military power present here."

"You do not," she agreed. "But I do not think I need to remind *you* of the potential consequences if you were to take our citizens by force."

"I do not think they will be as severe as you hope," Kandak warned her. "You are a very small player in a very small game. There are not many who will protest for you, Duchess Bond."

"Perhaps not. But I do not think the consequences for the Republic would ignorable either," Annette told him. Despite herself, she cupped her stomach protectively under the table. The next few minutes could easily decide what kind of world her children grew up in.

"I have a compromise to offer," she continued. "We are prepared to acknowledge the *legitimate* concerns of the Laian Republic, with regards to the warships of the Laian Ascendancy and a potential uncontrolled technological transfer.

"My staff have assembled what we believe to be sufficient documentation of the development process of our plasma lance to prove that we did not take any technology from the cruisers in our possession. The Exiles locked the vessel down in such a way that we could not have," Annette explained.

From the soft chitter of his mandibles, Kandak didn't quite believe that assessment, but he remained silent, hearing her out.

"While under no circumstances are we prepared to surrender our citizens for the crimes of their forefathers, we *are* prepared to turn the three former Ascendancy Navy warships in our possession over to the Republic," Annette said finally, in a rush.

At least one of those ships had been built by *Builder of Sorrows* long after the civil war, but it was clear that the Laian Republic, at least, regarded anything in the possession of *Builder*'s Crew as Ascendancy Navy.

Kandak was silent for several seconds, considering.

"I appreciate your willingness to make concessions, Duchess Bond," he finally told her. "I understand the difficulty in a sovereign facing this kind of demand.

"But I am afraid that your compromise may be insufficient. The Grand Parliament has always been very clear that the attainment of the rebels' treason passes down their lineage. After this much time, there may be mercy, but they must be returned to the Republic to face its judgment."

"Then the Republic must be prepared to break all laws of interstellar decency and sovereignty," Annette replied. "I will yield the ships if I must. I will submit to an intrusive assessment of our research programs if I must.

"But I will not surrender citizens who immigrated to my world in good faith. I have offered as much as the Imperium is prepared to give, Pincer of the Republic.

"The choice is now yours."

CHAPTER TWENTY-TWO

MOST PEOPLE WOULD NOT HAVE BEEN ABLE TO TELL THAT THE Duchess of Terra was furious merely from how she walked when she left the conference room. Many might have picked it up from the fact that she and Pincer Kandak had entered together and she had left without him.

James Wellesley, however, had served Annette Bond as her body-guard and ground force commander since before Earth had fallen to the A!Tol. He *knew* her. And when his visibly pregnant boss *stormed* from the meeting room, he knew things had not gone according to plan.

He and the other armored Guard trooper fell in behind her in silence. Now was not the time to be asking questions.

Halfway back to the shuttle, his suit communicator pinged.

"James, this is Villeneuve," the man in charge of Sol's defenses said in his ear. "Do you have Bond with you?"

"Yes. I'm guessing the negotiations didn't go smoothly, because she'd about ready to chew cars and spit nails at the next person who talks to her."

"*Magnifique*," Villeneuve said. "She has her earbud turned off.

You need to get her back onto the shuttle ASAP and into space, General."

"What's going on?" James asked.

"*Hermes Nine* just emerged from hyper portal squawking a priority-one Imperial security code. They're refusing to transmit details, since we have a foreign warship in the system, and are heading straight for the starcom."

James took a second to process that, letting habit and training keep him moving after Bond.

"I'll advise her as soon as we're aboard the shuttle," he concluded. "And then we'll get ourselves over to the starcom platform. I suggest you have as many Councilors as you can find on short notice meet us there—plus Echelon Lord Kas!Val.

"I suspect Commander Sadik will appreciate only having to give that kind of briefing once."

"Agreed," Villeneuve confirmed after a moment. "Casimir and Ki!Tana are already on their way. The living-room cabinet will be there; I'm not sure who else I can get into orbit in time."

"I don't suppose there's any chance of hiding all of this from the Laians?" James asked.

"I'm still only eighty percent sure how *many* stealthed scout ships they have around the system, let alone where the three we know of are," the Militia's commander admitted bitterly. "I'm relatively sure they already decrypted the message from Commander Sadik, and I'm not even entirely confident they won't have broken *Hermes Nine*'s firewalls and airgap security before she reaches the starcom.

"It's entirely possible that Kandak will know about whatever's going on in Alpha Centauri before we do, so I suggest you get Annette moving. We're on a time limit—and I don't know how long it is!"

AS SOON AS they arrived on the shuttle, James sent a text order and course to the pilot. Then he removed his helmet and dropped down opposite Bond.

"I take it he didn't like our compromise," he said genteelly.

"He feels he has his duty," the Duchess replied. "That's a word I'm very familiar with and sometimes wish wasn't quite so barbed and explosive." She shook her head. "We need to get Villeneuve on the line. I don't think Kandak is going to move immediately, but he's functionally ruled out any chance of a peaceful resolution—and it sounds like his superiors have dumped the whole mess on him."

"We're heading to meet Villeneuve now," James told her. "We have a problem. *Hermes Nine* has arrived from Centauri and has requested a hard link to the starcom and an in-person briefing. I don't know what they found in Centauri, but I suspect it's about to blow up in our faces."

"With three fucking Core Powers circling like vultures," Bond said in disgust. James carefully did not notice her protectively cupping her stomach. "They're not leaving us a lot of choices, are they?"

"What are you going to do, Your Grace?" James asked softly. "We can't fight Kandak, or the Wendira—or the Mesharom, for that matter. Peaceful annexation isn't an option this time either," he concluded.

"No, it's not." Bond shook her head at him. "Let's see what Commander Sadik has for us—and operate on the assumption that Kandak's people have hacked it out of his systems by the time we hear it."

"Shouldn't Sadik's confidential data be on cold, unlinked storage?" James asked. He'd been wondering that since his conversation with Villeneuve.

"Yes," Bond confirmed. "And we have reason to believe that *isn't enough* against some of the data-extraction tools the Core Powers have available. The Imperium has some guesses as to how it works, but the basic conclusion from Intelligence is to assume that a Core Power ship has complete access to your databases."

James swallowed.

"What about BugWorks?" he asked softly.

"They have to know the database *exists* to access it," she reminded him. "And BugWorks Two isn't mentioned in a single database on Earth. We made *damned* sure of it."

"Is there anything from Two we can use?" James suggested. "If we're down to the wire against Core Powers..."

"Nothing yet," Bond admitted. "We're at least two years from prototype hardware, let alone any usable ships.

"No, my friend, we will fight this battle with the weapons we have to hand—but believe me, we will fight it."

She smiled grimly at him.

"I will not leave a broken Duchy to my children."

ONE OF THE reasons the starcom transceivers took so long to build was the sheer size of the station required. A starcom platform took the form of a central sphere with four equilateral triangular "wings" that acted, roughly, as antennae.

The sphere was forty kilometers across, most of it taken up by power-generation equipment. A super-battleship ran on six antimatter power cores backed up by sixteen hyper-compressed fusion cores. A starcom required *sixty* antimatter cores and over two hundred fusion cores, enough power to run half of Earth's cities and industries.

The "wings", each containing nearly incalculable amounts of gold and platinum wiring, plus multiple exotic-matter arrays, were sixty kilometers high, two thick and fifty deep.

Combined, a starcom platform was sixty kilometers tall and over a hundred and twenty kilometers across, requiring a crew of some twenty-two thousand sentients and enough robots, drones, and semi-sentient AI programs that Annette wasn't sure anyone had a total count.

Hermes Nine was linked up to the docking spire, a deceptively frail-looking tower on the "top" of the sphere. Frail as the tower appeared, it was thicker than the courier was long, with lots of space for the shuttle to tuck in and dock as well.

Manticore and *Griffon* hovered above the docking spire, their own immense bulk dwarfed into near-insignificance by the starcom. Villeneuve was apparently there already, and the Duchy's two most modern warships would defend their Admiral and Duchess until the end.

"Docking complete," the pilot reported, and Wellesley offered her his hand.

"Shall we, Your Grace?" the English General asked.

"Lead on, General."

Her smile tightened as the rest of her Guard detachment fell in around them. Unlike Wellesley, the other seven Guards still wore their power armor. Even there, the most defended facility in Sol, her Ducal Guard were concerned for her safety.

After the last few years, she couldn't blame them.

———————

COMMANDER SADIK WAS a short and squat Turkish man, his eyes and hair dark as he stood at the front of the briefing room, visibly sweating as the senior members of his government and military organization took their seats.

"You wanted a personal briefing, Commander," Villeneuve told him, and Annette could hear the reassuring gentleness in the old Admiral's voice. "Now you have us all. Why don't you begin?"

"Yes, sir," Sadik said loudly, then swallowed and wiped his face with a linen handkerchief.

"Vice Admiral Kurzman locked everything we were carrying down under a Council-only seal, though he said he believed you'd want to pass this on to the Imperium as quickly as possible."

"I understand," Annette confirmed. Whatever they'd found, it was enough that Kurzman was leaving the call over whether or not to inform their overlords to her. It was unlikely she wouldn't, but Kurzman had always chafed under being a subject race.

"Dr. Wolastoq found what the Kanzi force was looking for," the courier captain said simply. "They traced a series of radioactive particles and debris to what appeared to be a crash site for a starship.

"An *old* starship. The details are in the files, but the estimate I saw was that the ship was fifty-five thousand and seven hundred years old," Sadik said levelly. "Dr. Wolastoq and Captain Rolfson managed to successfully enter the vessel, which still has some limited power."

"Wait, you're telling me a *fifty-thousand-year-old ship* has *power?*" Villeneuve demanded.

"The details are in the files," Sadik repeated, "but my briefing is, well..."

He tapped a command on his communicator, and the screen behind him lit up with an image of a strange chamber, clearly inside a ship but unlike anything Annette had ever seen before. A single metallic orb was suspended by gray-black struts in the middle of the space, and the walls were a gray, waxy material.

"This appears to be some form of power core based around a gravitational singularity," Sadik told them after wiping the sweat from his face again. "The struts are compressed matter, but the hull is a semi-motile organic material controlled by interlaced nanotech. The hull is self-repairing, though most of the ship's equipment is nonfunctional—but the core is still producing a small trickle of power."

There was a hard snap and Annette glanced over at Ki!Tana. The A!Tol's skin was black as night, a shade of pure fear and terror that she'd *never* seen on the old alien before.

"Ki!Tana?" she asked softly.

"Not here," the alien answered instantly. "Finish your briefing, Commander. I apologize for the interruption."

"There isn't much more for now," Sadik admitted. "The details are in the files," he repeated for the third time, "but that's the core of it. We have found an unknown alien vessel that dates to before known galactic civilization and contains technology we do not understand.

"Admiral Kurzman stated his intent to hold his force at Centauri to protect the ship and recommended the immediate deployment of whatever forces we could find to reinforce him. I'm not sure if he was aware of the Laian presence when he gave that recommendation," the Commander told them, "but he felt that this discovery was..."

"Of the highest strategic importance," Annette finished for him. "And it is. Thank you, Commander Sadik. Please make sure the files are available to us all, and have a copy prepared for transmission via starcom.

"We need to inform Imperial Navy HQ as soon as possible."

The Duchess of Terra smiled grimly.

"The situation has grown more complicated. Again."

CHAPTER TWENTY-THREE

The conference room was silent for several long seconds after Sadik left the leaders of the Duchy of Terra alone. Annette turned a questioning gaze on Ki!Tana, but the A!Tol didn't elaborate on her earlier comments.

Her skin remained the inky black of fear, though, which was far from reassuring.

"So, what do we do?" she said into the silence, looking to her husband and Villeneuve. "Obviously, we pass all of this information on to the Imperium, but where do we go from there?"

"Fleet Lord Tan!Shallegh has promised significant reinforcements," the old French Admiral reminded her. "The same multi-squadron force that he was gathering to shield the Imperium from Pincer Kandak and Hive Commandant Ashtahkah can be used to shield this ship from potential claimants as well."

"It's a matter of timing," Annette explained. "And politics. We don't want a war, but if someone else takes possession of Alpha Centauri ahead of Tan!Shallegh's arrival, a war is the only way he'll dislodge them."

"We know this wasn't what Kandak was looking for," Elon said.

"But it seems likely that it's what the Kanzi raiders and the Wendira were after. Do we know how they knew about it?"

"Hell, the Theocracy are claiming they had nothing to do with it," Zhao replied. "They might even be telling the truth, which begs the question of who *is* looking for this and what they'll do to seize it."

"Everyone."

Annette turned back to Ki!Tana as the alien spoke harshly.

"*Everyone* is looking for Those Who Came Before, even if they don't know it," she told them. "The Wendira and the strangers, unquestionably. How either knew there was a ship of Those Who Came Before in Centauri, I do not know, but it is the only thing they can be seeking."

The A!Tol's tentacles fluttered in uncertainty.

"This specific ship is not why the Mesharom are here...but the hunt for artifacts of Those Who Came Before is why the Mesharom Frontier Fleet exists," she concluded. "Everything else the Frontier Fleet has done over the thousands of long-cycles it has existed has been in service of that search."

"You know more than you have told me," Annette accused Ki!Tana, but there was no heat in the words. She *knew* Ki!Tana had secrets she hadn't shared. From what Annette understood of the process of becoming a Ki!Tol, Ki!Tana had secrets even *she* didn't know she did.

"Always," Ki!Tana confirmed. "These secrets are not mine to share, and there are oaths I have sworn, stories that would break the history of our sector. I must...speak to others before I say more."

Others almost certainly meant Ki!Tana's contacts with the Mesharom Frontier Fleet. Ki!Tana was technically under an indentured-servitude contract to Annette, but the Duchess knew the Ki!Tol had other loyalties, other allies.

"Do what you must," Annette told her, giving her alien friend the permission she knew Ki!Tana didn't need.

She turned to the rest.

"For now, we must consider how much we can afford to spare," she told them quietly. "With *Harvester of Glory* in the system, I don't think we can afford to send any of our ships to Alpha Centauri—but Echelon Lord Tanaka is due to arrive within the next forty-eight hours.

"I intend to contact her via starcom and divert her to Alpha Centauri. Whatever is going to happen here is going to happen regardless of whether Tanaka's half-dozen capital ships are present, but they may make all the difference at Hope."

"We have an entire world to protect," Villeneuve said quietly, but it wasn't truly an objection.

"I know. But...Kandak can smash us anytime he chooses. Tanaka's task force wouldn't change that; it would only add to how many ships died trying to stop him."

Annette looked around the room, meeting each of her Councilors'—her *friends'*—gazes in turn.

"We must begin to face the reality that we will not be able to stop Kandak and may not be able to negotiate a compromise," she told them. "I see no choice but to activate Operation Denmark."

"Denmark requires...sacrifices," Zhao said bluntly. "Do the Laians know what we need to ask of them?"

"Orentel and Tidikat are aware of the plans for Denmark," Annette confirmed. "They... *Fuck.*"

The Duchess of Earth swallowed angry tears, placing her hands on her pregnant belly and facing her Treasurer.

"They understand what must be done," she grated out.

Operation Denmark called for hiding much of the Laian population on Earth—but the Republic *knew* there were Laians on the surface.

To save as many as possible, the only plan they had left called for roughly one tenth of the Laian Enclave to allow themselves to be captured or killed, along with the crews of Tidikat's ships.

THE MEETING HAD BARELY BROKEN up and half of them were still in the room when Villeneuve's communicator suddenly blared an emergency alert. Annette froze, staring at the device in her Admiral's hand like it was a pair of snakes as he yanked it open.

"Villeneuve here," he snapped.

"*Harvester* is moving," a vaguely familiar voice said quickly. "And her escorts—on a direct course for the fleet."

"*Merde*. Understood. I will be back aboard *Empereur de France* immediately."

Annette shared a helpless look with Villeneuve. They'd delayed too long. They needed *time* to execute Denmark, to hide most of the Laians on Earth. The price had been too high and they'd failed.

"Get to your ship, Admiral," she ordered. "I'll get aboard *Defense One*."

"You need to return to the planet, Your Grace," Villeneuve told her. "We cannot lose you. Not now."

"I will not stand by and watch men and women die on my orders without sharing their fate."

"Yes. You will," Wellesley said, stepping up beside her. "Because the succession isn't unquestioned. Because the Duchy needs you. Because if you die, your children die with you."

"You bastard," Annette hissed, her hands half-instinctively covering her stomach.

"I am a son of the Duke of Wellington," her General replied. "I am an *asshole*, but I am quite certain I am not a bastard.

"I am also right."

"He is," Villeneuve agreed. "You have to return to the surface. My people need to know you're safe."

"My place—"

"—is on Earth, showing people that things are going to be okay," the Admiral told her. "It is not with the fleet. This is no longer a political affair."

She shook her head, glaring at them both.

"You're right," she conceded. "I will remain aboard the starcom, where it's *safe*. But if I am to step out of the way once it is 'no longer a political affair,' then as God is my witness, I am going to *make* this a political affair."

"I suspect Pincer Kandak is done listening," Villeneuve replied.

"*Harvester* was already in range of the Militia," Annette said, the realization sinking home as she spoke. This was still political. There might still be a chance to save her people. "If he was truly done listening, he'd already have started shooting. I don't know what Laians call it, but I think our friend is playing chicken.

"And I will *not* blink first."

IF THERE'D BEEN any question left in Annette's mind as to what the Pincer of the Republic was doing, it passed as soon as she entered the command center aboard the starcom platform. *Harvester of Glory* was moving toward Earth at only twenty percent of lightspeed.

That was a *crawl*. It was a speed that was intended to give her people time to panic, time to do something stupid—time to make up Kandak's mind for him.

It had still cut the range down to barely fifteen light-seconds by the time Annette was in the command center and able to bring up a communications system. Her secretary was still catching up to her and the command center's crew was sparse and unprepared, but she'd commanded a warship once.

She was able to place a glorified phone call.

"Pincer of the Republic Kandak," she said calmly into the camera. "Your course is a clear sign of hostile intent. Please clarify your actions or we will be forced to engage you in defense of the Imperium's sovereignty."

In the time it took her message to reach the Laian ship, *Harvester* had cut several seconds off the transmission lag. It still took over thirty seconds for Kandak's response to arrive, the war-dreadnought now barely one and a half million kilometers from the Militia formation.

"Duchess Bond," the Pincer greeted her. His mandibles chittered in amusement and he waited for a long moment, clearly enjoying leaving her in suspense.

Then *Harvester* came to a sudden and complete halt, exactly one light-second away from her fleet.

"We have decided to accept your compromise," he told her. "Your crews have fourteen minutes to evacuate the Ascendancy cruisers. At that point, my marines will board them and take control of the vessels to return them to Laian space.

"Resistance will be met with overwhelming force. Your Militia will not be harmed if they stand down immediately."

Fourteen minutes was a Laian "clawspan", less random than it sounded to human ears.

Annette immediately hit a second series of commands, linking her into Villeneuve's shuttle.

"Jean, they took the compromise," she told him immediately. "We need to evacuate Tidikat's ships *now* and keep the rest of the Militia out of the way."

"What if it's a trap?"

"Then we're no more fucked than we would be trying to fight him at missile range," Annette pointed out. "Let him have the ships; we can build more ships more easily than we can fight the Republic right now."

"I'll pass on the orders," he told her. "There's got to be a catch, though. He was too determined until now."

"I know," she agreed. "They hacked *Hermes Nine*. He knows everything we know about the ship. He's resolving the situation here so he can go straight to Alpha Centauri."

CHAPTER TWENTY-FOUR

THE STARCOM MESSAGES HAD BEEN FAST AND FURIOUS OVER THE ten days since they'd left Kimar, and Harriet Tanaka was feeling the frustration of being able to receive messages but not send them.

At least Tan!Shallegh was a smart enough alien not to give her *orders* via starcom, just situation updates. The Imperial Navy was well aware that the inability of their officers to communicate *back* to their superiors meant that the information loop was entirely one-way. It wasn't—it couldn't be—a command-and-control loop.

"Echelon Lord," Piditel said brightly, the Rekiki turning from his station to look over at Harriet's seat next to the central hologram on the flag deck. "New starcom transmission for you."

"I'm going to suggest that Tan!Shallegh just schedule a daily update," she replied. "This mess is getting out of hand."

"This one is from Terra, Echelon Lord," Piditel told her. "Duchess Bond sent it, under a priority key."

Harriet exhaled and nodded. She trusted Bond's judgment on what was important enough to ping a capital ship in motion.

"Relay to my office," she ordered. "Let me know if anyone else decides there's something I need to know!"

Piditel hissed and stamped his feet, the lizard-centaur's version of chuckling as she stepped into the small room off from her flag deck. The door slid shut behind her and Harriet dropped into her chair, tapping a command that caused the built-in robot to bring her a tea.

Sipping the fragrant beverage, she opened Bond's message.

"Echelon Lord Tanaka," the Duchess greeted her formally. "I hope that your task group has had no issues and is on schedule. My last update from Kimar would put you roughly thirty hours out from Sol.

"I presume Tan!Shallegh has updated you on what we found in Alpha Centauri, but I've attached the files under a your-eyes-only seal for your perusal. The ship is from a race the Imperium knows nothing about, using technology we are completely unfamiliar with.

"She is the prize of the century, and even the Core Powers want her," Bond concluded bluntly. "Unfortunately, our data security is clearly insufficient in the face of modern Laian electronic warfare.

"Pincer of the Republic Kandak has seized the three Laian Exile warships in my Militia in lieu of attempting to arrest every Laian in Sol—and is leaving. I am...extremely confident that the Pincer and his battle group are heading to Alpha Centauri.

"I'm not certain what he plans on *doing* there. We have a super-battleship division guarding the planet, but they're no more able to stop *Harvester of Glory* than the Militia here in Sol was."

Bond shook her head, the woman's eyes shadowed.

"I haven't quite decided what my response is going to be—but the threat to Terra that you adjusted your deployment to counteract has relocated to Alpha Centauri. I suggest you do the same, though I have no intention of giving you orders."

Harriet shook her head. Unless she misjudged her old comrade-in-arms, if she went to Centauri, she was going to be seeing Bond soon enough.

"There are two hundred thousand people at Hope," the Duchess said softly. "We owe them our sword arms. That was our oath—and the Empress's.

"I cannot order you to Alpha Centauri," Bond concluded. "But I beg of you, Harriet: redirect immediately. The Duchy's Militia can't beat Kandak to Hope—but with the charts you have of the region, you can."

The message ended and Harriet sighed, rubbing her face with her hands as she considered. She'd redirected her task force, except for a single squadron of sixteen cruisers, to Sol from Alpha Centauri. Now...it seemed the Laians were going to be leading her on a chase.

"Commander Piditel," she raised her coms officer. "Orders to the task force: the Laians are moving on Alpha Centauri. We are redirecting again."

CHAPTER TWENTY-FIVE

"I DON'T SUPPOSE OUR WINGED FRIENDS ARE BEING particularly helpful as to where they came from or what the hell they wanted?" Kurzman demanded.

"No," Harold admitted. "We're getting the Wendira equivalent of name, rank and serial number. They're all Warriors, not Drones, which means we got hit by one of their higher-tier units, according to Imperial Intelligence."

"We've got what, fifty of them?" the Admiral asked.

"Fifty-six, about half wounded," Captain Naheed Sommers confirmed. The conference was being held via radio, but Harold and Sommers were in the prefabricated camp rapidly growing around the alien ship.

"They're being model prisoners," the Guard officer continued. "They follow orders; they've let us know what their needs are." He shook his head. "I'm pretty sure if we'd captured half of an old Triple-S troop, we wouldn't have got half the cooperation they're giving us."

"I suspect they think we won't be holding them for long," Harold said. "Which either means someone is going to show up asking us to turn them over, or—"

"Or someone is going to show up and try and take the damn system away from us," Kurzman agreed with a sigh. "Someone *other* than the Laians."

That piece of news had just reached him and made Harold's bandaged shoulder twinge. He was still restricted to light duty and had been forced to temporarily turn command of his ship over to Saab.

His "light duty" currently consisted of overseeing the engineers picking through the ancient hull and the surface-to-space missile batteries they'd assembled around the site. New Hope had surface-to-orbit missiles, designed to shoot down landing shuttles.

The dig site now had true SSMs, all up interface drive missiles rated to take down starships up to thirty light seconds away from the planet. Not that the six launchers they'd set up had enough ammunition to fight anything heavier than a destroyer, but they still gave Harold some peace of mind.

"What are we going to do about them?" he asked the Admiral.

"Tanaka is supposed to be redirecting our way; her ETA's about the same as Kandak's," Kurzman added. "I don't know what Bond and Villeneuve's plan is yet, but I can guess."

"Steer to the sound of the guns, from what I know of our Duchess," Wolastoq said. Harold wasn't entirely sure how the xenoarchaeologist had ended up in the meeting, other than the fact that she'd barely left his side since the brief battle.

He was sure she couldn't be around as much as it felt like—she *was* still running the dig, including taking over directing his technical staff—but her presence was starting to acquire a comforting familiarity.

"Quite possible," the Admiral agreed. "This system is even more of a backwater than Sol right now, but I have the horrible feeling we're about to see the biggest confrontation between Arm and Core Powers in several hundred years. If both the Wendira and the Laians are now looking for this ship..."

"We're going to find ourselves in the middle of a battle we can't fight," Harold replied.

"That's why I'm hoping for as many reinforcements as possible," Kurzman admitted. "For now, however, that ship is the key. What have we learned?"

"That it's weird," Wolastoq told them. "I'm sure no one is surprised to discover she'll never fly again. But what's strange is we can't work out how she *ever* flew. She doesn't have an interface drive. She doesn't have a hyperdrive. She doesn't have reaction thrusters.

"Even stranger, she doesn't even have a complete electrical network, according to your Militia engineers. She's got a partial network of gold and copper wiring, much as we'd use, and then three sets of what *look* like electrical systems but are made out of materials that don't conduct enough to be useful."

"That makes no sense," Harold said.

"We run, what, a primary and a secondary power network, right?" Wolastoq asked.

"Yeah, but the cabling is basically identical for both," Harold replied. "You're saying they had four power distribution systems but three of them don't work anymore? We're talking material decay or what?"

"I checked that after the engineers told me their thoughts," the xenoarchaeologist said. "They're stable materials, nothing that would degrade or change over time. It's like...they somehow *could* transfer power through them.

"And that's not the only thing that doesn't make sense." Wolastoq shook her head. "From what your engineers are saying, as we understand physics, this ship didn't work. Not doesn't work anymore, it *definitely* doesn't work anymore—it never should have worked."

Kurzman massaged the bridge of his nose.

"So, whoever Those Who Came Before were, their tech is completely out of our experience," he concluded.

"Not just out of our experience," Wolastoq objected. "Impossible.

Half of the systems in that ship shouldn't work at all." She shivered. "And one of the ones that doesn't? Their brain implants."

"What do you mean?" Harold asked.

"Every body we've found had an in-head implant to interface with the ship, but they were made up of materials we wouldn't have expected to work as electronics," she said. "It's like...something made the implants stop working all of a sudden—and given how pervasive the implants are..."

"That may have been what killed the crew?" Kurzman said softly.

"So far as I can tell, those implants should never have worked," Wolastoq repeated, "but clearly, they *did*. But if they stopped working...any of these guys who wasn't already dead died damned quickly."

HAROLD HADN'T FELT QUITE SO MUCH of a sense of impending doom since they'd learned about the Kanzi fleet heading for Sol ahead of the Second Battle of Sol. The Wendira had apparently been searching the area for this ship, and if their quiet effort had failed, then the next one was going to be loud.

The Laians were on their way. Once again, the Imperium was charging to the rescue—though at least Tanaka was going to be there before the rocket went up, hopefully.

He'd spent the Second Battle of Sol aboard *Tornado* as her executive officer. He was looking to spend the Second Battle of Alpha Centauri as an invalid on the surface, his right arm still useless and locked in a cast as the regenerative matrix went to work on the large hole he'd torn through it.

He was doing his best to be useful, collating the data assembled by the engineers on the ancient ship into something remotely coherent. The ship itself seemed to be a barrier to that, so many of its systems destroyed and so much of what was left not making any sense at all.

A sharp knock on his door shattered his concentration, and he dismissed the file with a wave of his hand.

"Come in," he barked.

Ramona Wolastoq stepped through the door of the officer's quarters in the prefabricated Guard barracks he'd brought down with him on the first day. She wore a dusty lab coat, which she quickly removed and hung up before sitting down on his bed, facing him while she looked at him appraisingly.

"How are you holding up?" she finally asked.

"Feeling injured and useless," he replied. "The Militia I serve is about to go into only its second real major battle, utterly outclassed, and I'm stuck down here."

"You realize that left to its own devices, your body would take weeks to recover from that injury—and you'd potentially be crippled for life?" Wolastoq asked conversationally. "I've done archaeology on Earth, too. I've seen skeletons of people who died from less-extreme injury."

"I know," he admitted. "It's just..."

"You want to do more," she said. "So do I, and I'm completely unqualified to help!"

He chuckled.

"Any great inspirations on the starship?" he asked.

"It's weird," she echoed her earlier words, patting the bed beside her in a clear invitation.

He shook his head, suddenly awkward. They hadn't really discussed their kiss during the battle, and he didn't really regret it, but...

"I'm sorry," Ramona said quickly. "I...thought..."

"It's not you," he told her. "I...I lost someone very dear to me at the Second Battle of Sol, and I'm not really over that yet. You're the first woman to actually interest me since, but...it doesn't feel right."

"That was three years ago," she said. It wasn't an argument, really, just a statement. Perhaps a question.

"Seems like yesterday, sometimes."

"I know that one," Ramona agreed. "Been five years since my divorce; still feels as much of a shock some days as it was when he walked into my office and told me it was happening. He 'felt like he was a second husband to my work.'"

She shook her head.

"I probably screwed up half a dozen ways," she admitted, "but I didn't expect that. Let a lot of things go in that divorce I might have fought for, had I seen it coming—had I wanted it."

"Aren't we a pair?" Harold said with a chuckle. "Sade and I had almost nothing in common except that we'd been stuck in exile with Bond together. That was enough for then. Might not have been enough for forever, but the Kanzi didn't give us time to find out."

"And you feel guilty because you lived."

"Survivor's guilt?" He snorted. "Yeah, there's a chunk of that. And regret. And grief."

"At least you don't know it ended because of you," Ramona said. "That one... That wound hurts, even now."

"Bullshit, 'It ended because of you,'" Harold told her. "There's a lot of steps short of 'I want a divorce,' you know. Man was an idiot."

She chuckled.

"Glad to hear someone say it, I suppose. Doesn't silence the gremlin."

"No." He carefully rose and joined her on the bed, and she rested her head on his uninjured shoulder. "Between the Annexation, *Tornado*'s exile, and the Second Battle of Sol...we don't have a lot of captains or flag officers who haven't lost friends and family in the service of Terra and Imperium.

"The gremlins—the nightmares—they're par for the course. Villeneuve hired some *damn* good counselors, but there's only so much they can do."

"Sooner or later, you have to move on on your own," Ramona said quietly, and Harold realized that, without thinking about it, he'd moved around to face her. She was still leaning on him, they were barely inches apart.

"My shoulder is still locked in a cast," he reminded her.

She smiled.

"I'll be gentle, I promise."

CHAPTER TWENTY-SIX

"AND BREATHE FOR ME."

Annette obeyed with a vague attempt at grace. Regardless of how busy or complex matters had become, she understood the reality of being an almost fifty-year-old pregnant woman, and the attendant necessity of extremely regular checkups.

She didn't necessarily *like* it, but she understood it. *Empereur de France*'s chief surgeon was trying not to appear too intimidated by having the Duchess of Terra in her med bay for a prenatal checkup, too, and succeeding quite well.

Given that Commander Bauer was a petite and gorgeous blonde woman, Annette suspected she had a lot of practice in appearing more intimidating and less intimidated than she was. Certainly, Annette wasn't much taller than Bauer and had spent much of her military career cultivating a reputation as a harsh battleax to help maintain her authority.

"All right, you can put your shirt back down," Bauer told her, wiping the ultrasound gel off Annette's stomach and then putting away the tools. "You're doing extraordinarily well. Neither of them is showing any problems or difficulties—and neither are you."

"I suspect you'll understand me, Doctor, when I say that discovering that pregnancy comes easily to me is *not* in line with my self-image," Annette said dryly. "Anything I should be paying attention to?"

"No morning sickness anymore?"

"It's mostly passed. No strange cravings or anything, either."

"You might be surprised by those as you hit the third trimester, but the description of it coming easily to you is about right," Bauer agreed. "Given your age, you still want to be careful, though. I'm guessing, though, that telling you to try and avoid stress is a waste of my time?"

The Duchess of Terra chuckled. She didn't need to say anything. Around them, *Empereur de France*'s corridors hummed with activity as the Duchy of Terra Militia prepared to move. If Annette had had her way, they'd already be halfway to Alpha Centauri.

None of her Militia ships carried the supplies for extended flights, though. The supplies were on hand, easily available for when the cruisers went out on their patrols, but none of the capital ships or escorts kept more than a week's consumables on board.

Now every ship in the Militia was being stocked. Shuttles swarmed the four super-battleships and two battleships, loading magazines, filling antimatter and hydrogen bunkers, and delivering crates of food and supplies.

"The entire Militia will be in motion in fourteen hours," Annette finally said aloud. "The situation remains political enough that I'm half-tempted to go with them.

"Reduced stress is *not* an option just yet." She sighed. "I know once the babies are born, I need to take some time, and I *will*, but this crisis needs to be resolved."

"You're the Duchess of Terra," Bauer said. "There is always going to be a crisis; you are going to need to *make* time."

"There are crises and *crises*, Doctor," Annette replied. "And this is definitely the latter. I'll do what I can."

As she was sliding off the table, there was a knock on the door.

"We're fine," Bauer announced. "What is it?"

Rianne Zhao Ha opened the door and stuck her head around the corner, Annette's secretary looking as energized by all the activity as anything else.

"Can we borrow your room, Doctor?" Ha asked. "The Duchess needs to have a meeting that nobody knows about."

"The room is secured but not *that* secured," Bauer said. "You can use it, but..."

Rianne stepped through the door with an Imperial privacy generator.

"We thought of that," she said cheerily.

"Well, then, Your Grace, I think I shall simply disappear and note this appointment took longer than expected," *Empereur de France*'s senior doctor said brightly. "Good luck."

ANNETTE HADN'T BEEN EXPECTING the sudden intrusion, but she was somehow unsurprised to see Ki!Tana edge her way into the private treatment room. The three-meter-tall alien filled much of the space, and the room would have been *very* claustrophobic if the Ki!Tol hadn't long since become a comfortable presence.

"You realize that we spend enough time together that any meeting between us would go unremarked," she told the alien.

"Perhaps," Ki!Tana agreed levelly, "but I must speak today not merely of things that I am sworn to keep secret but of secrets that I am no longer supposed to know."

The alien's skin was dark green—determined despite fear. Just what did Ki!Tana have to *say*?

"You're making me nervous," Annette admitted. "What is so terrifying, Ki!Tana?"

"You know how an A!Tol becomes Ki!Tol," the old alien told her.

"We are mad for a very long time. It takes tens of long-cycles for us to adapt to our body's final attack on our sentience to force us to breed or die."

A!Tol did not have wombs or anything of the sort. Live birth involved the young eating their mother alive. For some strange reason, the A!Tol had some of the best artificial gestation technology in the known universe.

Technology that damned "heir of the body" clause had prevented Annette from using.

But their biology had had one last nasty trick for them once they'd established the ability to separate reproduction from death: a female A!Tol was a large, powerful sentient with a regenerative ability unmatched without technology, but all of that was designed to enable her to survive gestation.

And her hormones *demanded* that she breed. And those hormones didn't recognize it even if all of the eggs had been removed and the A!Tol in question couldn't breed—that such a removal extended the life expectancy of an A!Tol was part of why it was traditional that the Empress had them removed and destroyed.

Between medication and technology, the A!Tol had bought themselves time, but eventually, all A!Tol females succumbed to "the birthing madness." At which point they usually suicided or died of starvation.

A small—a *tiny*—minority managed to force themselves through it to the other side, a new level of sanity where they could endure for centuries. These were the A!Tol's wise elders and trickster demons—the Ki!Tol.

"We remember *nothing* of our lives before we are Ki!Tol," Ki!Tana reminded her. "Or...or so we let everyone believe."

Annette sat up straighter, studying her oldest alien friend. That was news. That was...a deception that could cause serious trouble in Imperial culture.

"We don't remember much," the alien told with a raised manipulator tentacle. "Just flashes. But if you have enough flashes, and they're of events that are in the historical record, you can put the pieces together."

"You're losing me," Annette admitted.

"I told you once that I had seen a starkiller fired," Ki!Tana reminded her. "Did you ever wonder how? Who would have been there when the A!Tol fired the first of them they ever built, the only one they ever used?"

"I honestly assumed there were a lot of people there," Annette said. "Things were strange enough then that I barely remembered anything you'd said."

During *Tornado*'s exile, Annette had come into possession of a new generation of starkiller: a missile-sized weapon instead of a starship-sized one. They hadn't been supposed to exist and had been in the hands of a conspiracy plotting to start a new war with the Kanzi.

She'd earned her Duchy by destroying them.

"No," Ki!Tana said softly. "There were only a few. *I* wouldn't permit the guilt to be shared."

"You," Annette echoed, looking her advisor in her ink-black eyes and understanding what she was saying. "*You* ordered it fired."

"Piecing together the pieces of flashbacks and bits of memory I have, I was Empress A!Ana," Ki!Tana said quietly. "And I know things that were meant to die with A!Ana."

"Like?"

"We did not develop the starkiller ourselves," the A!Tol said flatly. "Our program to develop one was no more successful than the Kanzi's. We were *given* the answers to develop it, in exchange for a very specific favor."

And suddenly Annette began to understand why this was coming up now.

"We were involved in a three-way war with two factions of Kanzi at the time," Ki!Tana told her. Her voice was distracted, half-recalling memories and half-recalling history. "One faction wanted to enslave all non-Kanzi bipeds, those they call mockeries of their God.

"The other wanted to exterminate them. *They* found a ship of

Those Who Came Before. They were reverse-engineering it, and something about those ships, that technology, *terrifies* the Mesharom."

"What did they do?" Annette asked, her voice very quiet.

"They gave the Kanzi one chance to give it up. And then they gave us the starkillers on the condition that we use it to destroy the entire star system the ship was in."

Annette was silent, waiting for Ki!Tana to finish.

"That turned the tide of the war. The slavers won the civil war; we beat them both back and secured the borders of the Imperium. All it cost was six billion sentient lives."

"My god. And now..."

"And now you have found something similar to what those Kanzi found," Ki!Tana told her. "You must speak to the Mesharom. I do not know what they want, what will happen, but you *must* speak to them."

"Is that possible?" Annette asked. "I am prepared to negotiate, but..."

"I can arrange a meeting," the old alien told her, admitting what Annette had always known—that Ki!Tana was still in contact with the big worms. "There is a Frontier Fleet detachment in the area. It is...sufficient to engage *Harvester* or the Wendira. If you can convince them to help."

"Set it up," Annette ordered. "Let's see what the galaxy's elders want."

She wasn't necessarily willing to give up the ship—but if the alternative was to see an entire star system destroyed, there were *many* things she'd consider that she wouldn't normally!

"You will need to meet them in person," Ki!Tana warned. "And... while I know few of your Council will approve, I think that whatever happens, *you* need to be at Hope.

"Too much rides on what will happen there for you to leave it to another."

"I HAVE to go with the fleet."

From the sudden silence in the room, Annette could just have easily dropped a time bomb in the middle of the room that everyone was staring at.

It wasn't a very full room. Elon and Zhao would end up running Terra while she was away, and Villeneuve would be personally commanding the Militia fleet going to Centauri—they were sending *everything* heavier than a destroyer, after all.

"No," Elon said immediately. "You can't—you're needed here!"

"The situation remains both fluid and political," Annette told her consort levelly. "I carry more of the Empress's authority and trust than anyone else available—and I'm *including* the two Echelon Lords we have to hand!

"There is no one better placed to speak for the Imperium in what is going to become a bitterly dangerous set of negotiations. Without an active starcom link to A!To, *someone* has to speak for our nation.

"That someone has to be me."

"No, it *doesn't*," her husband objected. "Any of the 'living-room cabinet' can speak as well as you can. Hell, Jean is just as trusted, just as respected as you are. He can speak for the Empress as well as you can."

"I'm the only human who has met A!Shall," Annette said. "I am the only available Duchess. There is no one else who can speak as well."

"But there are others who can speak almost as well who aren't *pregnant*!"

"I remain the Duchess of Terra, Elon," she snapped. "You knew that when you married me. There are duties I cannot pass on—and there are lines even my *Consort* should not cross."

Elon recoiled as if she'd slapped him—which, for all that she hadn't touched him, she might as well have. Once one of the richest and most powerful men on Earth, he'd traded much of his power—though not his wealth, which had been moved into several massive blind trusts—for the role of husband to the Duchess. He would have had an important role in the Duchy's governance either way, but his current position *looked*, at least, dependent on who he'd married.

"Jean, Li, help me out here," Elon said to the other two men.

"You are her husband, Elon," Villeneuve replied with a smile. "You are welcome to argue with her if you wish to be stupid—but I am her *Admiral*, and I have learned when to shut up and obey."

Li Chin Zhao shrugged expressively.

"She is the Duchess, Elon," the immensely fat man said, leaning back in his chair. "And she is correct. For different reasons than you, I would rather see her and her children-to-be safe behind every barrier and army we could muster—but *she is the Duchess.*

"And she is correct," he repeated with a sigh. "No, Annette Bond must speak for both Terra and Imperium as this whole mess evolves—and it will evolve at Hope."

Zhao turned back to Annette and shook his head at her. For all that he was actually younger than his Duchess, his gaze was paternal—Zhao had no children, no interest in romance or family at all. He had dedicated his life first to China and then to the Duchy of Terra.

Any legacy Li Chin Zhao would leave would be forged by service—and would be nurtured by Annette's children.

"I have to go," she said softly, turning her gaze from Zhao to her husband. "And you and Li have to stay. Someone has to run Terra while I'm gone."

Elon exhaled and bowed his head.

"Promise me you'll stay on the super-battleships?" he asked. "I understand, but please...stay safe."

"You know me," she said lightly, but his gaze swallowed her false cheer.

"Yes," Elon confirmed. "That's why I say it. You will do what you must—that's why I love you—but come back to me."

"I'll stay on *Tornado*. *Behind* the super-battleships," Annette promised, taking his hands. "I need to be there; I need to talk to people. I don't need to be on the front lines getting my eye cut out again!"

CHAPTER TWENTY-SEVEN

"HYPER PORTAL!"

The shouted report echoed across Pat Kurzman's bridge, and he shook his head somewhat repressively at the young officer who'd given it.

"The timing is wrong for it to be the Laians," he concluded gently. "They only left Sol fourteen hours ago, and hyperspace is hyperspace. No one's worked out any way to travel faster in it that I know of!"

In truth, given the quality of Imperial charts for the area around Sol now, Imperial or Militia forces should be significantly faster to move than the Core Powers. Hyperspace currents weren't always of a predictable strength or course, but there were highest-probability zones.

"Nonetheless," Pat continued, glancing over at Commander Chan. "Heng? Please bring the task force to battle stations. Let's see who our new visitors are."

The timing was, in fact, wrong for every single group he was expecting. Not, of course, that Imperial intelligence was sure where the Mesharom or Wendira forces in the region were. The timing, would, actually line up with...

"Captain Fang is reporting Imperial IFFs," Chan noted. "Sixteen ships, *Stalwart*-class heavy cruisers. IFFs mark them as one of the squadrons attached to Echelon Lord Tanaka."

"Ah," Pat noted. "So, she decided not to leave us swinging when she was diverted to Sol. Nice to know we were remembered."

"We have a Division Lord Torandus reporting in, they are taking command of the Imperial forces in the system—they're an Ivida neuter."

The Ivida were one of the Imperial Races, a dark red-skinned hairless biped with double-jointed limbs.

"Any coms for us?"

"Not yet," Chan replied. "Wait." He focused on his screen. "I have a transmission from Torandus directed to you, sir."

"Classification?"

"Encrypted in standard codes. Clear for flag staff, sir."

"Put it on my screen, then," Pat ordered.

Despite their mostly-humanlike appearance, Ivida lacked anything humanity would call a nose or ears. Their head was a smooth, dark red broken only by bright white teeth and eyes.

"Vice Admiral Kurzman, I am Division Lord Torandus, commanding the Hundred and Fifth Cruiser Squadron," the Ivida greeted him. "My squadron was split off from Echelon Lord Tanaka's task force to assist you in the defense of this system against further attacks.

"I have taken command of all Imperial forces in this system, but I have no intentions of ordering around the sentient with the super-battleship division. If you can make yourself available, I would like to come aboard your flagship once we have arrived in orbit and speak with your intelligence team for an update on the situation.

"We have been out of communication for eight cycles, and I worry what we may have missed."

Pat sighed. Enough had changed in the last week that Torandus's commander was already on her way to back them up—Pat's own superiors would be leaving Sol within a day.

"Sensible sentient," he said aloud. "Chan—start having our people put together a briefing package on the events of the last eight cycles. Can we *feed* an Ivida?"

"UP and spices, but yes," Commander Chan replied confidently. "Our chefs will consider it a challenge."

"All right. We'll invite him and his senior captains for dinner, brief them on the *clusterfuck* that has been this last week."

Pat smiled grimly.

"Misery loves company, after all."

"THE BRIEFING FILES your staff sent over were illuminating, Admiral," Torandus told Pat as the two flag officers and their staffs settled down to the meal *Washington*'s crew had put together.

"This strange ship you have found is fascinating to me," they continued. "The Imperium has no knowledge of races before the Mesharom. Not even legend or myth—though one is forced to wonder about the Kanzi idea of god when such a race who predates us all was bipedal like so many of us."

"Form follows function," Pat replied. "Evolution on a thousand worlds seems to have settled on only so many designs for the body of a tool-using sentient."

"And yet," Torandus said. "So many variations, but so few patterns. Half of all known sentients are bipedal, Admiral. That seems unlikely to be pure happenstance."

"It frees up the upper limbs for delicate tasks like toolmaking," the human officer replied. "Certainly, we know humanity was around more than fifty thousand years ago, even if we were still working out fire at the time."

The Ivida made a deep rumbling noise it took Pat a moment to identify as laughter.

"For all of our protestations of high culture, none of the Imperial Races were far ahead of you," they said. "A hundred thousand long-cycles ago, my ancestors were just working out that if you followed the thunder-mountain-beast herds as they migrated, it was easier to keep track of your main source of food. Domesticating them wouldn't occur to us for another thirty thousand long-cycles."

It was telling, in many ways, that the Ivida used the A!Tol long-cycle to measure time, something humanity still did only in official Imperial documents. It wasn't even particularly suited to their home planet...but whatever measurement they'd use for time before the A!Tol came was lost to myth and history now.

Give it another few thousand long-cycles, and the A!Tol *might* start getting over their collective guilt about the set of accidental cultural genocides that had created the Imperial Races. Maybe.

"I'm more concerned about today," Pat replied. "There seem to be a lot of players in this game, and I don't know any of them well. Doesn't even feel like we even know the Kanzi well anymore."

"Indeed. What is the estimated time on the Laian battle group?"

"Twenty-six to thirty-eight hours, depending on which currents they know about and how well hyperspace cooperates," Pat told him. "Tanaka is...thirty to thirty-five hours out. The Militia is forty-four to forty-six."

"A race, then, between my Echelon Lord and this Pincer of the Republic."

"And that's assuming no spoilers from the Kanzi, the Wendira or the Mesharom."

"Indeed." A shadow passed over the Ivida's white eyes. "I have met Wendira Royals," they said. "They are very aware of the castes of their race...and class any non-Wendira beneath even the lowest Drone."

"That doesn't sound promising for negotiation."

"The Wendira do not negotiate unless they are certain they cannot simply take," Torandus replied. "The Mesharom will make an offer first. The Laians...will ask. Once."

"And if we aren't prepared to surrender the ship to any of them?" Pat asked.

"That, Vice Admiral, is why Lord Tanaka is bringing a task force. If we will not surrender to the Core Powers' whims, then no matter how the tide turns, we will have to fight *someone*."

CHAPTER TWENTY-EIGHT

WITH THE RESUPPLY COMPLETE, THE SOLAR SQUADRON OF THE Duchy of Terra Militia finally moved out. Even more than usual, it was a horrendously unbalanced force. Four super-battleships led the way with *Empereur de France* in the lead.

Echelon Lord Kas!Val's *A Dawning of Swords* followed them, her four escort cruisers tucked in close around her as the Imperium joined its vassal in preparing for war.

Behind *A Dawning of Swords* came the two *Manticore*-class battleships, flanking the only Terran cruiser in the force: *Tornado*.

Last of all, a single echelon, eight ships, of *Capital*-class destroyers trailed the rest of the fleet.

Once the Solar Squadron left the system, only eight destroyers and the orbital platforms would remain to defend Sol. It was a calculated risk—one the weight of the defensive orbital platforms made reasonable.

But still a risk.

Annette, in the end, was actually traveling on *Tornado* again. The old XC cruiser was unique in the galaxy now, with her combination of Pre-Annexation Terran technology, Laian Exile technology, and the blend of Imperial and Terran tech that had become the hallmark of the Militia.

There had been two incomplete hulls like her that had survived everything. Both had been claimed by the Imperial government in the end, though the payment had been more than sufficient to salve wounded Terran pride.

"Is everything in order?" she asked Villeneuve from *Tornado*'s flag deck. Her chief Admiral was back aboard *Empereur*, leading the fleet from the front.

"So far as I can tell," he said. "I am...*mal à l'aise* with both you accompanying the fleet and leaving Earth so lightly defended."

"No one is coming to attack Earth—this week," she replied. "But if we can't short-stop this disaster before the shooting starts, we could find the Imperium at war with at least one Core Power."

"I don't need to be told how that scenario ends," the man who had led Earth's failed defense against the A!Tol said sadly. "My memories of that kind of technological mismatch are vivid."

"We do what we must, my old friend," Annette told him. "We take the risks and the sacrifices we have to. The galaxy moves on."

"Whether it moves on with us included is an entirely different question," Villeneuve told her. "Captain Amandine has orders to do whatever you command, you know. No one is going to question if *Tornado* is late to the party."

Annette hadn't told the old French Admiral anything, but he winked at her.

"If I turn into a stereotypical pregnant woman and have to return to Earth for fries and anchovies?" she asked sweetly.

He laughed.

"*Ma chère* Duchess, the day you turn into a stereotype of any sort is the day I retire!"

She chuckled.

"I hope, Jean, that your return to retirement will be sooner than that," she said gently. "I feel guilty for dragging you back into the harness, you know."

"I wouldn't be anywhere else in the universe," Villeneuve said. "My world needs me. *You* need me."

"I do," she admitted. "You're my strong right arm, as Zhao is my left and Elon is my support. I'd have made this work without you three, I'm arrogant enough to think that, but you made it so much easier."

"You're talking like we're going to die, Annette," her Admiral replied. "I don't plan on it anytime soon. This is a show of force, nothing more. If everything goes right, we won't have to fight a battle."

She chuckled bitterly.

"When has it *ever* gone that smoothly for us, Jean?"

He sighed.

"There is always a first time, *n'est-ce pas?*"

ANNETTE FOUND herself counting the minutes after they passed through the portal into hyperspace, the strange gray dimension swallowing her entire fleet like it had never existed. Only *Manticore* and *Griffon* were still within the one-light-second range where they could actually be seen.

The rest were visible only on the anomaly scanner, blips in the void that contained tens of thousands of her friends and people. They looked to her for leadership, never realizing that it was *she* who owed *them* everything.

An hour passed and it was time. Ki!Tana and Wellesley fell in with her as she made her way from the flag deck to the bridge. There were two Guards waiting for her there, flanking the door—a normal security measure, but these had been briefed in advance.

They saluted and overrode door security, allowing her onto the bridge without announcement.

No one on the bridge even blinked. There was no one aboard *Tornado* who would question anything Annette Bond chose to do. If she wanted to half-sneak onto the bridge of her old ship, no one here was going to stop her.

She crossed to the Captain's command chair and stepped up beside Captain Amandine.

"Cole."

"Your Grace," the ethereally tall, space-born Captain replied. "What do you need of me?"

"We need to shut down the interface drive," she told him. "Drift for a bit, let the rest of the fleet get out of range of the anomaly scanners."

"Ah."

Amandine didn't even question or hesitate.

"Mister Lawrence," he barked. "All stop. Bring the drive down."

"Yes, sir!"

"I presume Captain Van der Merwe and Captain Darzi know something is up?" the Captain murmured.

"No details. I'm not even going to give you details—sorry, Cole—but they know we're going to drop out of formation. No one will ask questions."

Amandine chuckled.

"Your Grace, it's *you*. No one would ask questions."

Without the interface drive, *Tornado* went from moving along at point four five cee, keeping pace with the super-battleships, to a relative halt. The distance between her and the Militia formation expanded quickly, inasmuch as such things could be judged in hyperspace.

"Mister Lawrence." Annette waved the navigator over. "I need you to surrender your station to Ki!Tana. Where we're going is classified at the highest levels."

"Of course, Your Grace," the Lieutenant Commander agreed instantly. "I'll send my staff off-duty and stand by myself for any assistance needed."

"Good man," she said. "Ki!Tana?"

"We need more distance," the A!Tol replied as she slid in behind

Lawrence's station. The powered chairs aboard *Tornado* had been updated to adjust for multiple species back when Annette had run the ship with a crew of exiled Terran officers and recruited alien pirates.

The seat adjusted to hold Ki!Tana's immense bulk with ease.

"How much time do you need to set up your course?" Annette asked.

"None," Ki!Tana said. "It's all preset. As soon as we're clear of the sensors of the rest of the fleet..."

"Always hard to judge that," Amandine noted. "We'll lose them in about thirty seconds, but they may still have us on their scopes for a bit after that."

"We'll give them ten minutes to be clear," Annette declared. "Then we'll move. This meeting is necessary, but time is of the essence."

"And you're not going to tell us where we're going?" the Captain asked.

"I don't even know myself," she said. "I know who we're meeting, though, and that's enough."

TEN MINUTES SEEMED to take an eternity to pass, but Ki!Tana finally took over control of the ship, bringing up the interface drive and taking off at a course almost perpendicular to their original one.

Without needing to stick with the rest of the fleet, she quickly brought them past half of lightspeed, then dropped them into a hyperspace current that the Imperium was aware of but found useless, as it didn't go anywhere.

They followed that current for three and a half hours, the entire bridge watching as the Ki!Tol made careful adjustments, guiding them to a point in space Annette wasn't even sure Ki!Tana knew with certainty.

"Here."

The single word echoed in the soft quiet of the bridge, with the undercurrent of clicks that was Ki!Tana's actual voice. As she spoke, she changed the direction of the ship, pulling them out of the hyperspace current and out into the featureless void.

"There's nothing here," Amandine reported. "No gravity sources. No planets. No sun...nothing."

"Do you understand, then, why getting here wasn't as easy as it looked?" Ki!Tana asked. "Opening hyper portal."

Annette was used to the hyperspace portal spilling the light and warmth of a star system into the gray void when it was opened. Here, in the depths between the stars, it simply opened up the gray void to reveal black void.

Slipping through the portal, however, it quickly became clear that the "void" was filled with stars. There were stars too dim to be seen in any star system, but they were clear when you were this far out into the middle of nowhere.

"There's still nothing here," Amandine said.

"Wait," Ki!Tana replied.

They waited.

The stars shimmered.

Three massive egg-like white shapes, each easily five times *Tornado*'s size, appeared out of nowhere as they dropped their stealth fields.

"What are *those*?" someone asked.

"Mesharom Frontier Fleet battlecruisers," Ki!Tana told them. "And today, we are their guests. Please be polite."

THERE WAS no communication from the enigmatic white ships, but Ki!Tana knew the protocols. She and Annette took a single shuttle, with just one crew member to pilot it, and flew over to the center ship.

"There's no airlock or hangar," the pilot told them as they approached. "Just...hull."

"I know," Ki!Tana told him. Her manipulator tentacles fluttered across the controls. "Take the course I just plugged in and transmit the code on the frequency I gave you."

"That's...a collision course."

"Trust me," the A!Tol said brightly. "I've had to do this myself, and it is unnerving. But follow the protocol and we'll be fine."

The young man at the controls swallowed hard but obeyed. The shuttle continued to approach the battlecruiser.

"They're what... six million tons? Twelve hundred meters?" Annette asked her alien friend.

"Twelve million tons," Ki!Tana corrected. "About fourteen hundred meters long, six hundred at the widest. They have significantly less living space than an Imperial ship and heavier armor, so Mesharom ships are much denser."

They were slowing as they approached. Now the shuttle was moving at a crawl for an interface-drive ship, barely a dozen meters per second, as they approached the coordinates and pulsed the code that Ki!Tana had provided.

For a moment, nothing happened and Annette was terrified they were going to crash into the side of the alien ship—then the hull seemed to *ripple*. The white exterior flowed away, exposing a surprisingly normal-looking compressed-matter hull with a hangar airlock door.

"Okay, that's just *weird*."

"Outer hull is an ablative layer of microbots," Ki!Tana said quietly. "Similar in concept to the hull of the ship you found on Hope, though less advanced."

That was a terrifying thought, one that Annette found herself fixating on as the shuttle drifted closer to the Mesharom warship.

The Mesharom were the unquestioned galactic elders, the most advanced race known. Their own cultural and psychological peculiarities kept them from advancing as fast as most other races, so they were slowly losing ground—but they'd had a twenty-thousand-year head start over even the other Core Powers.

But the crashed fifty-millennia-old ship on Hope was *more* advanced than the Mesharom ships were.

———

ANNETTE ROSE to exit the shuttle and was surprised when Ki!Tana remained seated in her couch.

"Aren't you coming along?" she asked. "I don't know the protocols from here."

"There are few protocols from here," the Ki!Tol told her. "But they'll only talk to one person at a time. By Mesharom standards, the Interpreter on each ship is insanely extroverted, which means they *will* speak to aliens."

"But only one at a time."

"That's...strange."

"Mesharom don't like each other, let alone anyone else," Ki!Tana reminded her. "The only reason they manage to get six genders to work together for reproduction is because they only need two of them in one place at a time.

"I don't know who you will be meeting, only that it will be the ship's Interpreter. Be straightforward, be honest...be *you*. You'll be fine."

"And if I screw it up?"

Ki!Tana's tentacles fluttered in uncertainty.

"I don't know," she admitted. "I think the worst case is you'll have to agree to give them the ship. So long as you're willing to do that, I think our people are safe."

Annette shook her head.

"I hate dealing with the Core Powers."

"So does everyone. Good luck."

———

ANNETTE STEPPED out of the shuttle and into the hangar bay. This clearly wasn't the main small-craft hangar for the ship—it was far too small, barely large enough for the Terran craft to safely land. The walls were the same stark white as the outer hull, though, so it was possible they were made of the same active microbots as the outer hull and the rest of the hangar was simply closed off.

Two metallic figures wormed their way over to her. They were clearly robots—if for no other reason than they were far smaller than she understood the Mesharom to be. Serpentine constructions built of flexible plates and a smoothly flowing black fluid she guessed to be similar to the hull.

"We are your escorts," the left robot announced in perfect English. "Interpreter-Captain Adamase is waiting in the meeting space. Please follow us. Divergence from the designated path is not permitted."

The two mechanical serpents weren't visibly armed, but Annette presumed there were weapons of some kind concealed inside their shells. Breaking protocol would be uncomfortable at best—and quite possibly fatal.

"Lead on," she told the escorts.

The one that had spoken turned and moved away from her. The other waited, clearly intending to fall in behind, and Annette followed the first one.

Fortunately, she wasn't bothered by snakes, or the escorts would have been terrifying. As it was, they were disturbing, slithering across the unmarked floor as they led her away from her shuttle.

A gap in the stark white wall opened, leading her into a thankfully ordinary-looking ship's corridor. The escorts continued to guide her through the ship as she noted signs and symbols that, despite being in a different language, were otherwise familiar.

Her translator earbud could tell her what the signs meant if she asked, but for now, the robots knew where she was going and she simply followed. When negotiating with dragons, one did not ask questions about the art collection in the foyer.

As she moved through the ship, the sheer scale of it all began to sink in on Annette. Initially, it had all seemed normal, but...the scale was off. This was not a ship built for bipeds two meters tall at most.

This was a ship built for creatures that could squash down to a meter tall if they wanted, but were much, *much* larger. The doors were easily three and a half meters tall and perfectly square. The robot serpents escorting her came up to her waist in motion, but could easily rear up to dwarf her—and they were tiny compared to their masters.

"Here." The lead serpent stopped at a door, which promptly slid open in front of them. "The Interpreter-Captain is here."

With a likely-unnecessary nod to the robot, Annette walked through the door into the meeting room. Based on the rest of the ship, she'd expected something stark and white, but the room was quite different from what she'd seen so far.

It was lit in a soft blue, calming but easy to see detail in. The walls were gentle hues, carefully guiding the eye around. She could feel her breathing ease and her blood pressure drop.

The room had been *designed* to ease a human's stress levels, to make her as comfortable as possible. She suspected it was easily changed, lights and colors and sounds adjusting in a matter of moments to prepare for whichever species the Interpreter was meeting with.

A moment later, she understood why, as the Interpreter moved. She'd missed them in the relaxing vibe of the room, but the Mesharom reared up to be clearly visible and Annette had to suppress an instinctive urge to run—or to vomit.

Interpreter-Captain Adamase looked like nothing so much as a four-meter-long, dark-green furry millipede. Dozens of long feelers, equally capable of tool manipulation or locomotion, fluttered around on their underside as they rose to face her. Massive crystalline eyes, reflecting the soft lights of the room, turned their attention on Annette as Adamase studied her.

"I have not met a human before," they finally said. "Yet...a life beats within. *Two* lives. You bear?"

That took a moment to process.

"I am pregnant, yes," Annette confirmed.

"Are you first or final bearer?" Adamase asked, then shuddered. A nerve-wracking gesture, possible a head-shake equivalent? "Right. Your species is dual-gendered, two gametes, one bears. You are...female?"

"Yes."

"I am final-bearer," Adamase told her. "I have delivered two litters into this world for my parenting circle. Is it as incredible an experience for your kind?"

Annette laughed.

"I do not know, Interpreter-Captain," she admitted. "I haven't done this before, and my understanding is that the process is much different for Mesharom."

Those crystalline eyes blinked rapidly, the reflection of the light in them almost blinding. Laughter, Annette thought.

"This is true. Is the meeting room comfortable, Duchess Bond? We can make changes if you wish."

"It is more than sufficient," Annette replied. "If there is a seat somewhere, at least."

A feeler separated from the rest of Adamase's limbs and pointed to a seat that Annette had missed. She took the chair carefully, mindful of her stomach, then turned her gaze back on the Mesharom.

Adamase was silent, watching her.

"Ki!Tana told me I needed to meet with you," the Duchess of Terra finally said. "We found a ship of a species she called 'Those Who Came Before', and we wish to avoid conflict with the Core Powers—but you, the Laians, and the Wendira are all here now."

"The Laians came for their own reasons," the Mesharom replied evenly. "So did we. The Wendira, however, were hunting the ship. Which is *fascinating*, but now we all know it is there, and you are correct, Duchess Bond, in that it could far too easily trigger conflict."

"The ship offers immense opportunity to my people," Annette argued. "Both Terra and the Imperium would benefit greatly from researching it."

Adamase was silent again. The crystalline eyes stayed focused on Annette for a long time, then slowly closed and reopened.

"You are not prepared to fight us for it," they said. It wasn't a question, and Annette wondered just how obvious her thoughts and emotions were to this creature. "But you want to know *why* you must surrender it to us."

"If it is the price for you to protect us from the Laians and Wendira, I will pay it," Annette said bluntly. "But yes, I do not understand why."

"Because you do not know what we know of Those Who Came Before," the Mesharom final-bearer told her. "I think...yes. We must tell you what we told your friend, that which she has forgotten and *you*, Duchess Bond, must share with your Empress...and *only* your Empress.

"Do you understand?"

Annette was taken aback.

"What is this secret you would have me keep?" she asked.

"The nature of the universe and how what was shapes what is," Adamase told her. "I do not need to explain. You simply need surrender the ship to us. But you are owed the explanation, if you will die with it."

"Tell me," Annette instructed.

THE INTERPRETER-CAPTAIN WAS silent for a minute or so, presumably marshaling their thoughts into a form of explanation that they figured Annette could understand.

"You must realize," Adamase finally began, "that our civilization has never advanced quickly or in giant leaps. Steady development as a culture and a technological race has always been our way.

"However, we never suffered the mass cultural and technological setbacks so common to other races from wars or the collapse of empires. We...did not fight wars on grand scales. Do not think we were pacifistic," they warned, "we simply cannot organize armies as other races do.

"Our wars were fought by small groups of champions. We have always been more individualistic than many races, our distaste for others' company outside of breeding cycles a long-term impediment to us in many ways."

Annette knew that the Mesharom she was speaking to was arguably insane by their species' standard, willing to associate not merely with other Mesharom for extended periods—a requirement to be starship crew—but also with aliens.

The ship she was on required as many hands as a Terran ship, but most of those hands were robots. Mesharom did *not* like each other's company. Or anyone else's, for that matter.

She'd never really thought through what that meant for a civilization. Everything from war to science were group efforts for most races...but not for the Mesharom.

"What that slow progress has given us, however, is a written history longer than any other known race," Adamase noted. "We have detailed records stretching back sixty thousand orbital cycles."

Annette managed not to audibly whistle. That was somewhere between ninety and a hundred thousand years. The Mesharom had started keeping records—and storing them carefully, if they still had them!—before Cro-Magnon man had *existed*.

"It took us twenty thousand orbits to get from writing to the steam engine," the alien said, "And another five thousand to get to rockets and in-system exploration.

"And then Those Who Came Before arrived. They came from the stars in great ships and they taught us technology that even then seemed like magic."

Adamase was silent for several seconds, their crystal eyes reflecting the lights of the room as they stared blankly into space.

"For four thousand cycles, we were what your Imperium calls vassals," they admitted. "We were not wise enough to realize what they kept from us. We and others were their...pets. Their science experiments.

"Those Who Came Before ruled. The rest obeyed, providing resources and labor for their grand projects—and their projects, Duchess Bond, were grand beyond any current dreaming of power."

"If there was an empire that spanned half the galaxy, what happened to them?" Annette asked.

"They were arrogant. Beyond any current dreaming of arrogance," Adamase said. "Their technology was vastly different from what you see now. We cannot duplicate it. What the records tell us of their ship engines still reads as magic—there was no hyperspace, no travel time.

"Once they knew where they wanted to be...then they were there. A spatial repositioning system, not a hyperspace portal."

"That isn't supposed to be possible," Annette replied. She wasn't a scientist, but she'd commanded experimental starships and kept up with what her people said could and couldn't be done.

"It isn't," the Mesharom agreed. "The laws of physics would not allow it. *Now.*"

She stared at the alien in horror as just what Adamase had said sunk in.

"According to our histories, Those Who Came Before wanted their repositioning system to have a greater range," the Interpreter-Captain told her. "They built a grand device, a machine around the galactic core, and attempted to deploy a system that would vastly increase their jump radius, seeking to visit other galaxies."

"And?"

"And they changed the laws of physics," Adamase concluded. "They broke reality, Duchess Bond. Fundamental constants of electricity, gravity, sub-quantum forces...all changed. Not enough that life stopped working; they were arrogant but not...careless.

"But enough that most technology stopped working."

That would explain the collapse of the Empire, but not what had happened to its member races...except...

"We found bodies with neural implants," she said quietly.

"Implants that were based on a circuitry that could no longer conduct electricity," the alien told her. "Implants that had become essential for life for every member of Those Who Came Before and the vast majority of their subject races.

"We were always stubborn. A smaller portion of our race was implanted than many others—and we were more prepared to survive on our own when most of our technology stopped working.

"Many died," Adamase said calmly. "Even with all that we knew, it took us five thousand more orbits to reach the stars once more. A thousand more to develop the hyperdrive.

"And then we went looking for our old masters and fellow servants. We found our own worlds, some more advanced than others, some less. We reunified.

"Our masters were gone. Their other servants were gone. We were alone in the Core, but rapid expansion was not our way."

The alien shivered in what might have been a shrug.

"And then other races came. We helped some, ignored others. We had competition, but more than anything, we feared what Those Who Came Before had done."

"How does any of their technology even still work, then?" Annette asked.

"Anything that still functions was designed for far higher electrical conductivity than it currently has," Adamase told her. "If it still works, it is no longer as efficient. The ship you have found appears to be one of the most intact samples of their technology we know of, but that is a danger, Duchess Bond."

"Why? If none of it works..."

"Attempts to duplicate their star drive are how the starkiller was invented," the alien said flatly. "We cannot predict what their technology will do now. It is better locked away, safely, where it can harm no one."

"Surely, some of it is still of value," Annette argued. "The singularity core and the active hull my people describe—they're still functional. If we work together, we can all benefit."

"Whose system are you prepared to risk for this study, Duchess?" Adamase asked her. "We did not challenge the Syana when they sought to study the ship they found. *They destroyed their homeworld.*"

Annette winced from the words, spoken with a fierceness that crossed even through the translator.

"We fear the technology of Those Who Came Before," the Mesharom continued. "The Frontier Fleet exists to contain it, store it. We cannot even risk destroying it—failure of the containment of the singularity core has a significant chance of destroying Hope. We have the capacity to safely move it.

"No one else will," they warned her. "That ship *must* be taken into safe storage, Duchess Bond. We cannot risk what happened before happening again."

The Mesharom had watched their entire galactic society self-destruct. No wonder they were terrified of the technology left over—Annette was actually impressed that they weren't trying to stop technological development in general!

"You understand that I cannot simply hand you the ship for nothing," she finally said. "I understand, even if I don't fully agree with, your reasons. But you have told me I cannot share those reasons, which means I must have *something* to show my people and my Empress for the exchange."

"A Laian war-dreadnought. A Wendira star hive," Adamase observed. "We will protect you from these."

"You'll have to convince them to stand down anyway," Annette replied. "Or they won't let you take the ship."

"The Laians can be convinced. The Wendira can be intimidated," the Mesharom Captain said simply. "This is not a negotiation, Duchess Bond."

She laughed.

"Of course it's a negotiation, Interpreter-Captain," she told Adamase. "We've established that you're taking the ship, but there remains the question of price."

They'd given Ki!Tana—well, A!Ana, but that name was a dangerous one to have in her mind—the starkiller technology to make sure the Kanzi didn't have access to technology from Those Who Came Before.

The Mesharom didn't know she knew about that, but there was no way she was giving them the ship for free.

"There are rules around the transfer of technology to non–Core Powers," they noted.

"The Mesharom wrote them," Annette agreed, pleased to see that Adamase recognized at least the *currency* they'd be paying in. "Would it be the first time the Frontier Fleet has broken them?"

"No."

Annette waited in silence. She had only the vaguest idea of what she could ask for in exchange, and that struck her as the best time to let the other side make an offer.

Negotiations weren't her strong point, but she hadn't spent three years watching Zhao and Elon dissect people across the negotiating table without learning something.

Adamase also waited and Annette smiled at the alien. The Mesharom were intimidating and more than a little repulsive, but the bit of history Adamase had shared with her put their entire foreign policy into perspective.

The Mesharom only had one goal: to make sure galactic civilization didn't destroy itself again. That was a cause Annette was willing to help them with.

"I am authorized to provide certain assistance in exchange for artifacts of Those Who Came Before," the Interpreter-Captain finally told her. "Retrieving the ship would require us to drive off the Laians and the Wendira. I am prepared to commit that we will make certain that the Imperium is protected from their actions now and from retaliation for this in future.

"I can also..." A pause. Thoughtful.

The Mesharom, it seemed, never rushed to anything.

"I can also provide your BugWorks Two facility with certain schematics and specifications," they concluded. Annette tried not to cringe. The Mesharom *really* shouldn't know that facility existed, but she'd suspected the Frontier Fleet had Terra completely wired up.

"They will not be sufficient to allow you to build anything immediately," Adamase warned, "but they should provide the groundwork for you to construct folded-hyperspace communications and...other systems."

Annette blinked. "Folded hyperspace?"

The crystalline eyes glittered with inner light of laughter.

"The problem the Arm Powers always have is that you keep trying to miniaturize starcoms, and then wonder how we fit one into a ship that moves," Adamase murmured. "And the truth is that we use a completely different type of communicator. Your scientists will see.

"If, of course, that is a sufficient price for you?"

The capacity to have ship-to-ship communication—hell, even just to have ship-to-planet communication—was huge. It was the biggest gap in the command-and-control loop of the Imperium, and having those communicators would all but guarantee victory in the next war against the Kanzi.

And given the attack at Hope, Annette couldn't help but feel there was going to be a next war against the Kanzi.

"That will suffice," she agreed levelly.

"Good. Return to your ship," Adamase instructed. "We will meet you in Alpha Centauri."

CHAPTER TWENTY-NINE

THE FIRST ARRIVAL WAS ONE OF PAT'S "SPOILERS". Unfortunately, whoever it was also chose to remain a mystery.

The sensor platforms scattered through the system and augmented by the Militia and Navy's recon drones picked up the hyperspace portal, despite the attempt to hide it behind the farthest-out planet, one of the ones with an odd double loop around both of Centauri's stars.

Unfortunately for whoever was being sneaky, Alpha Centauri AB2 had been the location of an old secret supply cache, one of the ones that had enabled *Tornado*'s exile years before. There wasn't *much* there, but there had been no point in wasting the carefully concealed and dug-in underground facility.

AB2 hosted the central processing center for the outer-system surveillance network. It had a six-person crew, all of whom had pissed off *somebody* to get the job—and to protect said crew, the planet itself had been seeded with passive sensors to cover every approach.

It had been enough to pick up what had been intended to be a covert hyper portal. What those sensors *hadn't* enabled, however, was to see what had come through.

"Stealth fields," Commander Chan observed as he studied the same screen as his Admiral. "I'm starting to very much hate stealth fields."

"I'd be a much larger fan of them if *we* had them," Pat replied. "Get CIC on the reprocessing. If we can track a course for the bastard, we can send a destroyer to go say boo.

"If nothing else, I want to know *whose* stealth ship it is."

It was six hours too early to be the Laians. Unfortunately, right now, that wasn't reducing the options by nearly enough.

"THIS IS *BUENOS AIRES* ACTUAL, we are in zone delta-six and sweeping for the target."

Pat couldn't help but wonder when destroyer skippers had started sounding so young. Like the rest of his ship commanders, Commander Ognian Andreev had been a UESF officer before the Annexation.

Like a rising proportion of them, he'd been a *junior* officer, the assistant tactical officer aboard the single battleship Bulgaria had funded. He was only thirty-four years old and made Pat Kurzman, who was barely a decade his senior, feel ancient.

"*Buenos Aires* Actual, be advised, all other delta zones are reporting clear," Chan told the Bulgarian starship captain over the radio. Lightspeed delay was a problem in these kinds of operations.

Pat had ten destroyers out sweeping for the stealth ship that had snuck into Alpha Centauri, and it was taking between five and ten minutes, depending on the ship, for communications to pass around.

With the rest of the delta zones clear, CIC was calling delta-six an eighty-percent probable for the stealth ship. *Buenos Aires* could easily be about to step into a world of hurt—and the battle group was sixteen minutes away at best speed.

The other destroyers were closer and they'd get an emergency ping faster, but...if one half-million-ton destroyer was in trouble, Pat suspected a second half-million-ton destroyer wasn't going to make that much of a difference.

But he couldn't risk uncovering Hope, either. The super-battle-ships and cruisers were going to stay right where they were.

The *Capital*-class destroyer's sensor data continued to ripple in for post-processing by *Emperor of China*'s far more powerful computers. The hope was that *Emperor* could identify the stealth ship and warn *Buenos Aires* of its presence before the unknown vessel dropped their field and opened fire.

"This process is taking too damned long," Chan complained. "Someone could have brought an entire fleet through that damned portal, and we could have missed them."

"No," Pat said calmly. "CIC already confirmed it was only one ship. They localized a vector and speed. They could have *changed* either of those, but I don't think they realized they were detected."

That particular illusion would have been shattered when ten Imperial Navy and Terran Militia destroyers swept out, looking for the alien ship.

"What the hell is that?" The transmission from *Buenos Aires* was entirely off-protocol, a panicked shout as Commander Andreev spotted something that absolutely should *not* have been there.

The ship they were pursuing hadn't dropped its stealth field or fired a single weapon. It had, at some point, dropped parasite craft that now brought their drives online.

Eight ships, roughly the size of a Terran assault shuttle, went from cold in space to point seven cee in just over three and a half seconds. They started at ten light-seconds from *Buenos Aires* and cut that to one in barely twenty seconds.

Pat's orders had been clear: Commander Andreev was not to open fire unless there was a clear danger to his ship. He wasn't going to argue that eight starfighters charging at your ship didn't qualify.

Andreev's crew reacted quickly. Missiles were in space within five seconds; proton beams lashed out at the starfighters when they hit a million kilometers.

Buenos Aires killed two fighters before they reached the single-light-second mark—and then the fighters unleashed their own weapons. Rapid-fire pulses of plasma, coherent bursts of super-heated matter the A!Tol Imperium could never duplicate, hammered home across the destroyer's shields.

The shield collapsed in moments. The *Capital*-class destroyer's compressed-matter armor held under the pounding for several seconds longer—long enough for her proton beams to shred another two fighters.

Then the sensor feed cut off as *Buenos Aires* came apart. The blast of her fusion cores overloading was bright enough for *Emperor of China* to pick it out of the background radiation from eight light-minutes away.

Pat swallowed a curse word. Then several more as he stood, staring silently at the screen.

"Have CIC..." He coughed to clear his throat. Something was stuck there. "Have CIC run an analysis," he ordered. "We should have enough sensor data to confirm if those were Wendira."

"Yes, sir," Chan replied. "It has to be, doesn't it? I'm not aware of anyone else who uses starfighters."

"Given the events of the last few weeks, I am *not* relying on that assumption," Pat Kurzman said softly.

IT TOOK fifteen minutes to confirm what they'd all but known from the beginning. CIC had to borrow updated warbook files from Division Lord Torandus to be absolutely certain, but with those, Commander Chan and his people had it dialed in.

"Wendira *Flying Sword of Fire*–class starfighters," he concluded. "Either they were lacking in munitions or they badly underestimated

Buenos Aires—they should carry a pair of point eight five cee missiles, but they closed to use their plasma guns instead."

"The *Capital*-class destroyers are heavily upgraded from the old Imperial standard for the targeting software and slew capacity of their proton beams," Pat pointed out. "I doubt they expected to run into heavy beam weapons designed to act as backup missile defense systems.

"With the Sword and Buckler turrets, it was being questioned whether we wanted to keep that functionality on the new designs. I think that argument just got buried forever."

"Agreed."

"Did we catch where the fighters disappeared?" the Admiral asked, studying the tactical display and noting that the icons for the remaining four fighters had vanished.

"We have the location, yes," Chan confirmed, dropping an icon onto the display. "They dropped back under somebody's stealth field, but unless their commander is an idiot, they're long gone and we have no way to track them."

"Damn. Thoughts, Commander?" Pat asked.

"That they could retrieve the fighters means we're not looking at a scout ship with a few starfighters strapped to the hull," his chief of staff noted. "Probably a specially designed stealth carrier, quite possibly a specialist covert-ops ship."

"Like the one that landed the ground force," Pat concluded grimly.

"Exactly," Chan said. "Probably the exact same type of ship, in fact, only that one did a better job of sneaking in."

"So, at this point, the Wendira know exactly what we have in place," the Admiral said slowly. "They're going to be *wrong* in less than twenty hours, but..."

"They may well arrive before then," Chan agreed. "Along with the Laians and Gods alone know who else."

"And we have no idea how much weight of metal they're bringing to the party." Pat shook his head. "We have prisoners, right? Get me Rolfson."

DUCAL GUARDS and Imperial Marines alike fell in behind Captain Harold Rolfson as he stalked through the camp set up around the crashed starship. Ramona Wolastoq was busily poking through the corners of the ship, testing to see if there were any other systems intact that might be useful.

He wasn't sure she'd find anything, but he was glad it kept her occupied. His own inability to return to his ship was grating on him, and only Ramona's presence was keeping him sane. His "light duty" for convalescence had become direct military command of the encampment now.

And included in that encampment was the set of cargo containers that had been retrofitted with additional security and turned into a prison camp for the frustratingly uncommunicative Wendira prisoners.

They'd had difficulty even establishing which was the senior bug. There were no Royal or Drone-caste in their collection of prisoners, only Warriors. They'd given up the equivalent of name-rank-serial-number, but even Imperial records on Wendira ground-force ranks and organization were limited.

"This one," the Yin Imperial Marine leading the way told him, tapping on one of the cargo containers. "I had my Marines pull out the one you want to talk to."

"Who have we got?" Harold asked.

"Third of Eyes Tarish," the Speaker replied. "Roughly... Company Commander or one of your Majors. They weren't in command of the operation, but they're the senior survivor."

"All right. Let's see what this Tarish has to say," Harold said grimly.

THIRD OF EYES Tarish was unlike any creature that Earth had ever seen. A Warrior of the Indira, Tarish stood just over one hundred and sixty centimeters tall, every bit of them a dull layer of black or dark gray carapace that would blend into almost any terrain on almost any planet.

Their wings were folded in against their back, but Tarish had extended their secondary eyestalks, the second pair of eyes watching as Harold entered the interrogation chamber—even while the larger primary eyes stayed staring directly ahead. Sharp mandibles flanked a small mouth and breathing orifice, creating a face that was both quite insect-like—and utterly alien.

"You are Third of Eyes Tarish?" Harold asked calmly. His translator turned his words into the clicking, buzzing noise of the Wendira's primary language.

Tarish didn't respond and Harold stepped closer, into the line of sight of all four of the alien's eyes.

"You've already given us your name and rank," he said reasonably. "You may as well confirm for me. You are Third of Eyes Tarish, the senior survivor of this strike force?"

The Wendira was silent for several seconds, then blinked all four eyes, one at a time, in a slow, disturbing sequence.

"I am."

"Why did you attack us?"

Tarish stared at him wordlessly.

Harold pulled up a chair and sat down, bringing himself down to the level of Tarish's primary eyes.

"I am Captain Harold Rolfson," he introduced himself. "I command one of the starships in orbit as well as this camp. I was injured when your force attacked us. I think you at least owe me an explanation of just what I got shot over."

The same long sequence of blinking.

"The ship of the Gods of Light. You are unworthy and it shall be taken from you."

"Ah."

That was about what Harold had figured.

"I don't suppose you considered *asking* us?"

The secondary eyestalks retracted sharply, right down to the carapace, and Harold wished the Imperium had better information on Wendira body language.

"No one would surrender or sell a ship of the Gods. You are unworthy. We have been seeking and we shall claim."

"All right. So. Your force was attached to Hive Commandant Ashtahkah and *Wing's Nightmare*?"

The eyestalks remained retracted but the visible portion shivered some more. Harold was reasonably certain he was hitting a nerve, but Tarish was silent this time.

"I'm guessing Ashtahkah is coming," Harold said. "There's at least one ship already in this system: your people killed more of my friends. There's going to be a reckoning for that."

"Release me," Tarish suddenly snapped. "Release my men and surrender the ship. You cannot stand against the Swarm."

"One star hive?" Harold replied. "You underestimate us if you think we can't stop Ashtahkah. The price may be high, but we will pay it before we surrender."

"You are unworthy," the Wendira repeated. "You are not ready. You are *weak* and you will burn before the Swarm of War."

"Will we?" the Captain asked softly. That suggested...*something*. He didn't like the implications.

"We will see," Harold continued. "Thank you, Third of Eyes Tarish. You will be exchanged back to the Grand Swarm once this is over, I think."

He smiled, somewhat viciously. "I doubt you'll be alone."

CHAPTER THIRTY

"HYPER PORTAL."

The announcement was calmer this time, which was strange to Pat. The timing was right and the location was right for it to the Laian war-dreadnought. They were still an hour short of the earliest window for Tanaka's arrival and fifteen hours from the Terran fleet's.

The last update was that Fleet Lord Tan!Shallegh's squadrons were on the move as well. Ten capital-ship squadrons of the Imperial Navy—a hundred and sixty battleships and super-battleships, and the best part of a *thousand* escorts—were converging from eight different fleet anchorages.

The plan had been to have them converge at Kimar, but with the progression of the situation, they'd apparently been ordered to converge at a rendezvous point barely a light-month out of Alpha Centauri.

That order, though, said everything to Patrick Kurzman. If the Imperial Navy expected Tanaka's task force and the Duchy of Terra Militia to *hold* Alpha Centauri, they'd have been ordered to converge on the system.

Tan!Shallegh wasn't bringing a fleet to relieve Alpha Centauri. He was fully expecting to have to *retake* Alpha Centauri.

"Well, the timing is right for the beetles," Pat said aloud. "I don't suppose we can count on our Wendira ghost to fuck them up, can we?"

"So far as we can tell, they're still out there, but I doubt they had much more than the eight starfighters they threw at *Buenos Aires*," Commander Chan concluded. "I doubt they're feeling brave enough to throw four starfighters against... Well, CIC has their analysis."

The main tactical hologram zoomed in on the incoming force, and Pat nodded his understanding as the images and numbers of the Laian task force emerged.

Harvester of Glory held the center point, just as she had at Sol. There were only sixteen modern assault cruisers flanking her now, though, and the three ancient ones they'd commandeered from the Militia were completely missing.

"It's definitely *Harvester of Glory*?" Pat asked.

"Yes, sir. All metrics confirm." Chan shrugged. "The other ships were all with her at Sol too, so far as we can tell."

"It appears Pincer of the Republic Kandak sent some of his ships home with our old Laian cruisers," the stocky Vice Admiral concluded. "Get me Torandus on the line."

The Ivida's motionless face appeared on his screen almost instantly.

"Vice Admiral," Torandus greeted him. "In the face of the enemy, I see no reason to insist on protocol. I recognize your command authority in the Alpha Centauri System. What are your orders?"

Pat had been planning on giving suggestions, so the Division Lord's decision to make the chain of command absolutely clear was a relief!

"Your *Stalwarts* are fully upgraded with the new defenses, correct?" he asked.

"That is why my squadron was sent instead of one of the others," Torandus confirmed. "All of my ships have passed through your

Raging Waters of Friendship Yards and received the full Sword and Buckler package."

"I need you to rendezvous with our *Thunderstorm*s and take up screening positions around *Emperor of China* and *President Washington*," Pat ordered. "We're going to be facing missiles significantly faster and longer-ranged than our own, so we'll want the maximum depth of defense possible."

"Understood. I will coordinate with your escort commanders; we will do all within our power to protect the capital ships." Torandus paused. "Will we attempt to communicate?"

"I'll try," Pat said. "But given that the Two Hundred and Eighty-eighth Pincer of the Republic isn't even supposed to *be* here..."

"It is always worth the attempt. Secondary forms of communication are always available."

"Secondary forms?" the Terran Vice Admiral asked.

"Missiles," Torandus clarified. "When talking fails, violence remains a form of communication, does it not?"

PAT TOOK a moment to compose himself. The Laian battle group was still ten light-minutes away, putting them at least ten minutes from weapons range. That gave him time to breathe, to make sure he didn't appear panicked when he talked to a sentient whose flagship outmassed the entire defensive force.

"Put me on," he finally ordered Chan. A small light on his chair controls told him he was live, and he smiled thinly at the camera.

"Two Hundred and Eighty-eighth Pincer of the Republic Kandak," he greeted the alien. "I am Vice Admiral Patrick Wellesley Kurzman, commanding officer of the Duchy of Terra Militia First Task Force.

"Your presence in this system is an unexpected surprise. Our understanding is that you were returning to the Republic with the vessels you commandeered.

"While your presence here is not necessarily *unwelcome*, I must ask you to clarify your intentions before you approach Hope any closer. There is at least one unknown, apparently hostile force present in the system that has already attacked our ships, and we are currently on high alert.

"If you approach within one light-minute, I will have no choice but to regard it as a hostile act and engage your vessels. I don't believe either of us desires that, so please clarify your intentions to avoid potential complications."

Ten minutes to reach the Laian ship. Except, of course, that the war-dreadnought was trundling toward Hope at half the speed of light itself. Even though the interface drive didn't play remotely fair with Einstein in terms of time dilation—the ship was, from that perspective, immobile—communication timelines got...complicated.

"Mark the one-light-minute perimeter," Pat ordered Chan. "Pass the orders to the task force: if the Laians cross that line, we hit *Harvester* with everything we've got."

"Will that be enough?" the chief of staff asked.

"Two super-battleships. Twenty-one heavy cruisers. A dozen destroyers." Earth's second-most-senior naval officer shook his head. "I'd like to think so, Commander. I really would."

"But?"

"*Harvester of Glory* alone outmasses our capital ships two to one," Pat said. "Hell, that war-dreadnought outmasses *our entire fleet*. And his tech is, at best guess, four hundred years more advanced than ours.

"That's *ignoring* the fact that we have a damned Wendira covert carrier wandering around the system, a star hive somewhere in the region, a Mesharom Frontier Fleet detachment around, and *someone* with super-advanced, apparently Kanzi warships."

"I won't feel particularly certain of our odds until Tan!Shallegh arrives," he admitted. "And even then...with four Core Power–level players in the game, I'm not sure even ten squadrons will be enough to feel safe."

Chan shivered.

"With the Militia and Tan!Shallegh's fleet, that's over a thousand warships," the chief of staff said.

"Do you know how many of those war-dreadnoughts the Republic has?" Pat asked. "Because Imperial Intelligence *doesn't*—but their best estimate is five hundred."

He shook his head.

"Keep that quiet, Chan," he ordered, glancing around his flag deck to make sure only his chief of staff had heard his depressing musings.

"We will do our duty. The truth is, the Imperium isn't important enough for the Republic to go to war with us. That's a sad shield to hide behind, but it's no less real for that."

"INCOMING TRANSMISSION," Chan reported. "Directed to you, sir, from the Pincer."

"Well, at least he's talking this time," Pat said. "Put him on. What's the time delay?"

"Still about five minutes. They're still closing, sir."

"Understood."

The image of the scarab beetle–like Laian commander appeared on the screen. His claws were shivering, a trembling disquiet that Pat had only seen in Laians once or twice before. It had never been good news.

"Vice Admiral. There has been much talking between your race and mine," Kandak snapped. "I am a warrior. I will not claim honor or law when such is irrelevant.

"You too are a warrior, a guardian of your homes and worlds. So, I will be blunt."

That was probably not a good sign.

"There was flexibility when I came to your Duchy. Your Duchess spoke of honor and equality, and these are words of meaning to the Republic.

"But there are other words of meaning: survival. Power. The harsh necessities of history."

Kandak's claws calmed and he leveled his large black gaze on the camera.

"You have a Forerunner scout ship on the planet you have colonized," he said flatly. "My orders from the Grand Parliament are clear, specific, and direct."

Which meant that the politicians hadn't even gone through Kandak's superiors. He'd received a direct order from the Republic's leaders. What the *hell* had Wolastoq found down there?

"You will surrender the Forerunner ship to me. If you do not, I will destroy your fleet, seize the ship, and bombard your colony to make certain there are none to carry word of what happened here.

"I do not desire to hold your civilians hostage, but if I must destroy you, the galaxy can never know what happened.

"You know how this will end if you fight me, Vice Admiral. Yield."

The message ended and Pat exhaled, looking around his bridge.

"Well, at least that makes it straightforward, doesn't it?" he said with forced cheer. "I don't see a reason to send the Pincer a response. Orders to the task force, people.

"Prepare to engage the enemy."

———

THE TERRAN/IMPERIAL task force began to move. The Militia's *Capital*-class destroyers, accompanied by the four Imperial ships under Teykay, swept out first. They put half a light-second between them and the heavy cruisers, with their Buckler platforms moving out another fifty thousand kilometers.

Then the sixteen Imperial *Stalwart*-class heavy cruisers and five

Terran *Thunderstorm*-class heavy cruisers followed, their own Buckler platforms fifty thousand kilometers ahead of them.

Pat Kurzman and his two super-battleships came last, a full light-second behind the destroyers. A third shell of Bucklers hovered fifty thousand kilometers in front of *Emperor of China* and *President Washington*, creating a three-hundred-and-fifty-thousand-kilometer-deep, six-layered missile defense network to protect the two super-battleships.

Pat wasn't one for speeches, but the moment seemed to call for one, and he activated his camera again.

"All hands, all hands, this is Admiral Kurzman," he said calmly. "The Laians have informed us that if we do not surrender the alien ship we discovered on the planet beneath us, they will destroy this fleet, take the ship, and bombard the colony to remove any witnesses.

"Neither the Duchy of Terra nor the A!Tol Imperium is prepared to negotiate in the face of threats of terror. We will not be bullied. We will not be threatened. If the Laians want this damned ship, then they can come and take her.

"I trust that every sentient of this fleet will do their duty. That is all."

The message went out. Hopefully, it was enough. Pat didn't expect to *win* this fight—the entire formation was set up to mitigate the Laians' overwhelming advantage in missiles—but he had no choice but to fight it.

"Captains," he continued, linking in all of the ship and formation commanders. "We don't know what the Laians have for beam weapons, only that they completely replaced the plasma lance in their service with it. I want us to keep the action at at least ten light-seconds and focus on self-defense.

"We're going to hammer *Harvester* as hard as we can, but our job isn't to win this fight. Our job is to drag this mess out until Echelon Lord Tanaka gets here. Our first and primary objective is to keep the Laians away from Hope—but our second task, almost as important, is simply to stay alive."

"Estimated range of the Laians' missiles in sixty seconds, sir," Chan reported quietly.

"We must test their resolve," Kurzman told his people. "And we must still be here when our reinforcements arrive.

"Let's make this happen."

KANDAK'S RESOLVE, as it turned out, was pretty solid. Thankfully, A!Tol Imperial Intelligence's estimate of the range of Laian missiles had actually been too high. They'd estimated that the Laian weapons had a ninety-second flight time at eighty-five percent of lightspeed.

The reality appeared to be seventy-five seconds. It was still a range of well over a light-minute, and ten light-seconds more than Imperial missiles, which had five seconds' less flight time and a tenth of lightspeed less velocity.

And...

"My god, they're thick enough to fucking *walk on*," Chan exclaimed.

Pat wanted to tell off his chief of staff, but he was certain the thought was being shared by everyone else aboard *Emperor of China*.

The Laian battle group had launched over two thousand missiles. The massed launchers of all thirty-five of Pat's ships could only put out a thousand.

This was going to suck.

"Open the range," Pat ordered. "Hold us at fifty light-seconds for as long as you can."

"He's got a point oh five lightspeed edge on us," Captain Fang reported from the bridge. "Plus...we can only keep the range open for so long without leaving him a clear path to Hope."

"Do what you can."

The tsunami of metal flashed toward them and hit the outer perimeter of the missile defenses. Buckler drones spun in space, rapid-cycling lasers lashing out at the cee-fractional weapons desperately.

The salvo crossed the defense perimeter in under three seconds—but the Duchy of Terra Militia had spent three years writing the Imperium's missile defense doctrine, and the A!Tol Imperial Navy had proven able students.

Hundreds of missiles hit the perimeter—and hundreds died. Failing interface-drive bubbles popped like sparks of starlight, a cascade of flickering diamonds on Pat's tactical displays that reached for his two super-battleships.

Shields flickered as missiles hammered home and held.

"Return fire."

A second Laian salvo was already in space, but now the Terran and Imperial ships' launchers thundered. They turned away from the incoming battlegroup, their curve a course that would keep the range open while holding position between the inbound Core Power fleet and Hope.

"Range is dropping," Chan reported. "Twelve million kilometers. Time delay is causing both of us major targeting issues. If they close the range, sir..."

"Then our defenses won't hold. So, we keep the range open and pound him."

"Plasma fire on the scopes," a report echoed. "Their drones are out and sweeping. Zero penetration. I repeat, zero hits."

"Damn," Pat said, studying the screen. Humanity's Buckler drones were based on old Laian rainshower defender antimissile drones, and he guessed it wasn't a surprise that the Laians had advanced their defenses along with everything else.

"Hard to localize them, but I think we're looking at at least half again as many drones as we have," Chan concluded after a moment. "And they could easily be...three, four times as effective. We're not going to get any missiles through, sir."

Warnings flickered on Pat's display. Both of his super-battleships were taking missile hits. They were stopping over ninety percent of the Laian missiles, but that was still splitting a hundred missiles between the two ships.

They were super-battleships. They could *take* those hits.

But not forever.

"We may need to bring them to beam range, sir," Chan suggested. "Our proton beams and the *Thunderstorms*' lances—"

"Are almost certainly shorter-ranged and weaker than whatever the *hell* that war-dreadnought is carrying for beam weapons," Pat replied. "Switch target priorities. Hit the drones—open a gap and start picking off cruisers."

"That won't let us hurt *Harvester*," his chief of staff objected.

"No. But if we take out even one of his ships, I think we'll make Kandak blink."

PAT KNEW that if the Laians broke their single-minded focus on his super-battleships, he'd start losing escorts. For now, however, the war-dreadnought and her cruisers were only targeting his capital ships—a targeting decision that was saving lives for now and would doom his force the instant even one of the two went down.

His own refocus meant they gave up completely on hitting *Harvester* herself. Their missiles swarmed in on the much smaller targets of the plasma-cannon drones. The defensive drones were harder targets than the capital ships, but they were also closer and *much* less heavily shielded.

"Six hits," Chan reported. "That's what its taking us to take each drone out. And we're only getting a quarter of our missiles even to the drones."

Pat nodded silently. The massed firepower of his entire fleet had taken out barely ten percent of the Laians' drones. That exchange rate...wasn't going to work.

"*President Washington* reports they have a localized shield failure. Multiple hits—armor is holding, Captain Robertson is rotating the ship to protect the damaged shields."

Four salvos. It had taken the Laians four salvos to start collapsing the shields of his most powerful ships. *Emperor of China*'s shields were still intact, but that wouldn't last. He wasn't bringing down enough drones.

"We've got new drones deploying," one of his officers reported. "Their screen will be back up to strength by the time our next salvo arrives."

"This isn't working," Chan said.

"No." Pat shook his head, searching for an answer in the tactical display. "Step down the velocity of the next salvo," he ordered. "I want two salvos stacked to arrive target at the same time at lower velocities, targeting the drones.

"We'll lose a higher percentage, yes, but we'll get more hits over-all. Focus them *here*." He highlighted the lower left portion of the Laian drone screen. "Then I want a full-speed salvo arriving two seconds *after* those missiles, heading straight for *these* two cruisers."

"We could be throwing away three salvos for nothing," Chan warned.

"We're throwing away *every* salvo right now," Pat snapped. "It's a Hail Mary, but it might be all we've got. Do it!"

President Washington lurched as another series of Laian missiles struck home, overwhelming the battleship's shields. The super-battle-ship seemed to tremble—but kept firing, her shields snapping back up in time to intercept the next salvo.

"Robertson reports they're still here, but their shields are fluctu-ating on them. He's not sure they can take another series of hits."

"Fang is moving *Emperor* to shield her," Chan reported. "Thirty seconds to your Hail Mary."

The super-battleship rang like a bell. Safety straps kept Pat in his chair as the starship jumped.

"Report!"

"Twelve hits to *Emperor*'s hull. Armor is compromised in several sections; we have casualties."

His flagship's survival was Captain Fang's concern. Pat turned his attention back to the tactical display, just as his doubled salvo went in. None of the missiles were moving at anything approaching full speed, and the plasma drones took a brutal harvest.

But enough made it through to completely gut a quarter of the Laians' defenses—and a thousand missiles followed their slower sisters at full speed into the gap.

At over ten million kilometers, Pat couldn't tell how many missiles actually made it through. They had no idea how many missiles crashed home on the two attack cruisers he'd marked for their attention. At least dozens. Possibly hundreds.

When the radiation cloud of the missile impacts cleared, however, both ships were still there, still moving in formation alongside *Harvester of Glory*.

One slowed as he watched, however, dropping out of formation as its crew slowed, reducing the demands on damaged engines as they struggled to keep her together.

The second stayed at full speed, cruising alongside the rest of the formation, apparently undamaged, for five seconds. Six. Seven.

And then it came apart in the bright flash of an overwhelmed interface drive, the strange interface between real-space gravity and hyperspace that propelled the ship suddenly unleashing all of its energy *into* the ship that had ridden its thunder.

"We got one," Chan breathed.

"And they're breaking off," Pat said. "Watch."

A moment later, what he'd seen became clear to the rest of his staff. *Harvester of Glory* was swinging around to cover the damaged cruiser with her own hull, and the entire Laian battle group was withdrawing at the point four cee that was all the battered ship could reach.

"Let them go," Pat ordered. "Time is *our* friend, not theirs."

CHAPTER THIRTY-ONE

HAROLD WATCHED THE BATTLE UNFOLDING WITH ILL GRACE from the surface. There was very little the type of person who commanded a warship liked less than sitting on their hands doing nothing, but even he had to acknowledge his injury.

If nothing else, he knew that the pain blockers and regeneration meds he was on slowed his mind, dulled his thoughts. He could still get to the same place, but it was taking him longer—and that delay could be deadly in combat.

His brain finally catching up to his paranoia, however, resulted in his walking calmly into the military command post at the dig site with Ramona Wolastoq following behind him.

"Captain Sommers, what's our status?" he asked.

"We have heavy armor on patrol, one company suited up and ready for action," the Guard officer replied crisply. "Antiaircraft systems are online. We're keeping our eyes open, but the space forces should be able to warn us before anyone reaches us."

"How?" Harold asked.

Sommers looked at him strangely.

"Sir? They're in orbit, we're not..."

"And did we spot the Wendira coming, Captain?" Harold asked gently. "Did we see those Kanzi after they entered orbit?

"Hell, Captain, we *know* there's a Wendira covert carrier out there, and I'd be shocked if she doesn't have stealthed landers."

Sommers looked vaguely ill.

"We...didn't think of that, sir."

"My area of expertise, not yours, Captain," Harold replied. "Ramona." He turned to the woman behind him, feeling a warmth thrill through him at the sight of her, despite the situation.

"How quickly can we get the civilians out of the site?"

"A full evacuation?"

"The Militia and the Navy can't stop people sneaking stealth-fielded ships down," he told them. "But they can't steal the ship without going through the Guard and the Marines. This place is going to be a battlefield, and we don't need civilians in the middle of that."

She nodded.

"Of course. We kept it in mind after the first attack," Ramona admitted. "We can have most of the people off site in twenty minutes. I'd rather have an hour; that'll let us get most of the useful samples away, too."

"Start now," Harold told her. "Make sure we get at least one sample of the hull away with us, too. If all of this goes to hell, what you take with you right now might be all we get out of this damned mess."

"All right," she confirmed. "I'll get started."

"Good luck."

She gave him a meaningful nod and exited the command center, leaving Harold alone with the other military officers—and Sommers giving him an odd look.

"The good doctor has definitely mellowed," the Guard said calmly.

"She got to poke around the guts of the most important artifact in *Imperial*, let alone human, history," Harold pointed out genially. "If

I'd been handed that kind of dream opportunity in my own field, I'd be happy too."

"Our field doesn't lend itself so well to that kind of opportunity," the ground-pounder admitted. "I'm passing orders for the entire battalion to suit up. Anything else you'd suggest?"

"Start scanning for atmospheric turbulence," Harold recommended. "Most of the satellites we have upstairs are glorified weather satellites—which means they can tell us if there's an air pressure wave that's out of place."

"Because, say, an invisible ship is coming down at several thousand kilometers an hour," the Guard said. "We'll get on it."

"I also need to see the list of what we brought down," Harold continued. "I saw something unusual on the list, something I wasn't sure why we brought down...but that we might just need after all."

HAROLD BARELY HAD time to confirm that the giant pile of military hardware they'd brought down from the super-battleships had contained what he thought it did before Ramona returned and gestured for him to step outside with her.

"Civilian evac is moving," she said. "Is there anything you need from us?"

He shook his head.

"I want you to babysit that hull sample yourself," he told her. He looked around, making sure that no one was close enough to hear him. "I don't know how this is going to end, Ramona. But I don't think it's going to end with us in possession of the ship. Take two samples of the hull, two copies of all of the data."

"You want me to bury one."

"Exactly. Bury it deep. I'm worried we might have to give somebody everything we've learned before this is over, and I want to be sure we've got as much as we can salvage."

"I'll make sure of it," she promised. She paused, looking him directly in the eye. "Are you ordering this evacuation to keep *me* safe?"

Harold laughed and waved a hand in the air.

"Fifty-fifty," he admitted. "I'm ordering the evacuation to get everyone out of the line of fire. I'm tasking *you* with making sure we keep a secret copy of everything because otherwise, I'm half-certain you'd try and stay."

"I'm tempted," she said.

"I know. But you're no soldier," Harold told her. "Hell, *I'm* not a soldier. I plan on leaving the actual fighting to the Guard and the Marines."

"Then why are *you* staying?" Ramona asked.

"Because someone has to take responsibility for what happens here," he said. "And, like it or not, the Admiral put me in charge. So, whatever happens down here, it's under my orders. Which means I stay."

"Captain goes down with the ship?"

"Something like that. I'd rather be *on* my ship, but I know the meds mean I'd be a liability."

"And you're not down here?" she asked.

"Down here, I'm leaving the split-second decisions to others," Harold told her. "Mine are bigger decisions with more execution time. Like getting you to take those samples back to New Hope."

She shook her head, glanced around to be sure no one could see them, and then stepped in to kiss him fiercely.

"You are *not* allowed to get yourself killed, Captain Harold Rolfson," she told him. "That's an order."

He smiled and nodded cheerfully, watching her as she walked toward the shuttles that would take her to safety.

Then he went back into the command center to give more orders.

———

BATTALION COMMANDER INDUS had joined the crew in the

command center while he'd been speaking to Ramona, and Harold gave the curvaceous blue-feathered alien a crisp salute. He was in charge of the *camp*, but there was no question that Indus—who now had two battalions under her command, with Marines borrowed from the *Stalwarts,* and hence outnumbered the Ducal Guard—was in command of the ground troops.

Once he'd finished giving his instructions to Sommers, Harold joined her next to the tactical hologram portraying the area around them.

"Do we have any hits yet?" he asked the tech running the analysis.

"Only normal weather patterns," the Pibo technician replied. "Is a stealth-field ship likely to be that obvious?"

"It's designed for space, Initiate," Harold said. "The Kanzi had a version that only seemed to work in atmosphere, but if the Wendira are coming...I'm betting that their version doesn't handle atmosphere well."

"They're a Core Power," Indus objected. "Their tech is—"

"Still limited by physics," the Terran officer interrupted her. "And if we assume our enemies have godlike technology, Battalion Commander, then we may as well surrender now.

"And I refuse to consider that."

The Yin snapped her beak in sharp laughter.

"Agreed," she said. "Keep scanning, Initiate," she ordered the Pibo. "If nothing else, we are preparing for their attack."

"No one was expecting to fight an open-field battle on the Corellian Plateau," Harold said.

"No, but our power armor and tanks can handle the conditions," Indus told him. "We are in trouble if they land on top of us. Can you prevent that?"

Harold glanced over at the small section of naval technicians running the control panel for the surface-to-space missiles they'd brought down.

"How close a target lock do you need with your birds, Chief?" he asked the middle-aged Chinese woman in charge.

Chief Petty Officer Kun Hu shrugged. "In space, direct hit," she told him. "In atmosphere? Near-miss is good. Within half a klick or so."

Harold turned back to Indus.

"If nothing else, we can make them blink," he promised.

"*Red tides*," the Pibo tech suddenly cursed. "It worked." They paused. "That's bigger than I was expecting."

"Show me."

The tactical display zoomed in, marking out the disturbance pattern of an invisible warship descending toward the Corellian Plateau. There was no way to be sure how large the actual ship was, but the zone of air it was heating up and shoving aside was almost two kilometers wide.

"Chief Hu!" Harold barked. "Two missiles, right up the middle of the anomaly, if you please!"

"Roger."

The command center rumbled as the launchers, spaced in a ring five kilometers away from the dig site, activated. The initial stage of an SSM remained a chemical rocket, blasting the weapon clear of the surface so it could activate its interface drive semi-safely.

Cee-fractional speeds weren't possible in an atmosphere—but thousands of kilometers a second were. The two missiles went from zero to several hundred kilometers an hour as the rockets lifted them up—and then to just over one percent of lightspeed.

The ship never had a chance to dodge. They saw the missiles coming with only fractions of a second to spare. Somehow, they still managed to eject landing craft before the hammer of god ripped the stealth carrier to pieces.

"ID those ships," Indus snapped. "Get me a number and tell me who they belong to." She hissed, her beak opening to expose a dark blue tongue. "Please tell me they're someone we're *expecting* and not somebody new."

"I've got ten transports, probably platoon level," the Pibo tech replied instantly. "They are...Wendira. Definitely Wendira."

Harold sighed.

"Well, it could be worse. Battalion Commander, I believe the rest of this is yours."

CHAPTER THIRTY-TWO

"WENDIRA." PAT SHOOK HIS HEAD. "WELL, I CAN AT LEAST hope that they only had one damned stealth ship in the system, right?"

"You can hope," Chan agreed, but his tone wasn't hopeful.

"Rolfson," the Admiral pinged his subordinate on the surface. "Do you have this under control?"

"Civilians are evacuating; Guard and Marines are moving out," the Captain replied. "They came down hard and fast, before we could hit them with more missiles. Best guess is the ground force is thirty minutes away—and the civilians will be out by then."

"Can you hold?"

"Indus thinks she can overwhelm them," Rolfson said. "I'm not going to argue with the specialist. The ground gear we saw before wasn't that much better than ours. I think we can hold. They won't get the ship, sir."

"I'm relying on you, Captain," Pat admitted. "If the Wendira take the damned ship, this whole fight up here is for nothing."

"Hell, maybe we should tell Kandak they're here and ask for help," the Captain replied. "It's not like we can piss him off *worse*."

"I'm not taking that bet," Pat said. "Watch your back, Rolfson. We'll keep the skies clear."

"Wilco, Admiral. Good luck."

Pat turned his attention back to the system projection. The Laians had withdrawn well out of range and were hovering protectively around the damaged cruiser. He was quite certain Kandak hadn't expected to lose anybody in this attack, and the destruction of the cruiser had been a rude awakening.

Somehow, his entire task force had made it through intact. There were damage and casualties, and they'd lost a good third of their deployed Bucklers, but every ship was still with him—and with the Laians licking their own wounds, the colliers had moved forward to resupply the warships.

Missiles and defensive drones drifted across space in carefully guided swarms. *President Washington* had been rearmed first and now stood watch as *Emperor of China* uncovered her vulnerable magazines to reload the munitions expended.

The Vice Admiral was far too aware of just how many missiles could be fired off in a deep-space engagement. One of the problems they'd had during *Tornado*'s exile was the discovery that the cruiser's magazines simply weren't large enough for any kind of extended engagement by galactic standards.

The *Thunderstorm*s had incorporated that lesson along with many others, and the *Majesty*-class super-battleships had been designed by the Imperium. Nonetheless, he wasn't going to pass up the opportunity to reload.

It was going to be a long few days.

"Any sign of Tanaka?" he asked quietly. They were *finally* into the window where he might luck into seeing reinforcements.

"Nothing so far," Chan replied. "We don't know exactly where she was when she turned for Centauri." The chief of staff shook his head. "We don't even know for certain that she *did*, except that she'd already be at Sol if she didn't."

"And the Duchess is a minimum of fourteen more hours." Pat

shook his head. He didn't *want* Duchess Bond in the middle of this mess—but he wasn't going to turn down four more super-battleships and three battleships, either.

"Let me know the moment the Laians even twitch," he told Chan. "I'm going to grab a coffee. I need a moment off this damn flag deck."

"WE ARE NOT ALONE OUT HERE."

Lesser Speaker Piotr Han was a half-Chinese, half-Russian officer and one of the first humans to have entered the Imperial Navy as a raw recruit. Barely a year out of training, he'd earned his first promotion—to the equivalent of a junior grade Lieutenant—just before the task force had left Kimar.

Right now, he was holding down the sensor relay panel on Tanaka's flag deck while his supervisor grabbed some much-needed nutrition. They were still twenty minutes from Alpha Centauri, and Harriet Tanaka was quite certain they were going to be busy upon arrival.

"That's not very informative, Piotr," she told the junior officer gently. "Anything further you can tell me?"

"Sorry, ma'am," Han replied crisply, "but not really. I thought the first contact was a ghost, but it's repeated ten or eleven times now. I'd say we're looking at at least one, possibly more ships in hyperspace, closing on Alpha Centauri."

"What kind of range?"

"I can't be sure," he confessed. "The computer is only assigning a fifty-percent probability that there's an actual contact out there, but given the briefing on what we're expecting..."

"Anyone know what a stealth-fielded ship looks like in hyperspace?" Harriet asked conversationally.

"They're not supposed to work in hyperspace," Piditel told her.

"At least, not against anomaly scanners. The anomaly should still register."

"Well, I agree with Lesser Speaker Han's assessment," Harriet replied, pulling the young officer's data onto her repeater screens. "Too much repetition, especially when we're expecting contact."

She hummed to herself as she ran the data through a filter.

"Two contacts," she agreed. "Each might be more than one ship, but...the radius translates to several light-weeks in real space."

There was no way they could identify a ship from the hyperspace anomaly, either. The flickering ghost wouldn't even let them assess speed. It could be the Mesharom. It could be the Wendira or the Laians. Or it could be the mystery Kanzi or someone completely different.

Her money, however, was on the Mesharom. No one else was supposed to have more than one ship out there.

"The Terran Militia is almost twelve twentieth-cycles behind us, people," she reminded her flag deck staff. "Tan!Shallegh is at least three full cycles, easily as many as five. We can't jump at ghosts, not when we *know* the Laians have almost certainly beaten us here."

If they had beaten the Laians, they'd have been close enough that she'd have expected to see *Harvester of Glory* on her anomaly scanners. Whoever these ghosts were, they had to be her second priority.

"Our time is up, in any case," she continued. "Signal to the task force: all ships to battle stations. We will assess the situation once we arrive, but we must assume that we are entering a combat environment and will need to relieve Hope's defenders."

And if she was very, very lucky, she might not have to avenge men and women she'd once called comrades and the sentients she'd sent to fight by their sides.

ANOTHER HYPER PORTAL flared on Pat's screens, and this one he hadn't been expecting.

"I don't suppose their whole fleet is running away?" he asked, looking at the portal in the middle of the Laian battle group.

No one bothered to answer him. It took a few seconds for the sensors to resolve the sequence of events, but it was quickly clear that *Harvester of Glory*, at least, wasn't leaving. The portal wasn't big enough.

The cruiser they'd damaged disappeared into the portal, accompanied by one of her sisters. Only thirteen cruisers remained to escort *Harvester*—but all of them settled into a calm course back toward Hope.

Whatever hesitation the loss of a ship had instilled in Kandak, the Laian had clearly decided that he could absorb any further losses and take Hope.

That wasn't an assessment Pat Kurzman could disagree with.

"Course?" he asked aloud, but he could see the pattern already.

"They're heading directly for Hope, ignoring us," Chan said. "We can either fight them or watch them drop into orbit and take the ship. And if we fight them—"

"They'll pull us into range of whatever they're using for beams," Pat agreed. "Well, it would have been nice to have shocked the Pincer of the Republic into retreat, but we didn't expect it.

"The Task Force will go to battle stations and maneuver to intercept the enemy," he ordered. "We will vector for a zero-range intercept—they've got something in store for us, but our beams and lances will have their part to this conversation."

If any of his ships had actually stood down from battle stations, he'd be surprised. With the Laian battle group in system, they'd all known this moment was going to come again.

"Any report from Rolfson?" he asked.

"No new updates," Chan answered. "The evacuation is complete; Indus is estimating contact in ten minutes. She has them outnumbered almost two to one, she seems confident."

"And all of that goes to shit if the Laians drop another regiment on their heads," Pat said grimly. "So, let's see what we can do, shall we?"

"Last I checked, the Laians and the Wendira hate each other's guts," his chief of staff replied. "It seems like there should be *something* we can do with that."

"I'm unenthused with the 'find a bigger fish' method of diplomacy these days," Pat told him. "The Republic are egotistical *bastards*, but I know Laians. I don't know Wendira, and the Laians have at least *tried* talking."

"The Wendira just started shooting," Chan admitted. "So what do we do?"

"We fight. And if you have a deity you like, I suggest you start praying for Tanaka to show up!"

"Sir! Vector change on *Harvester*!"

Pat turned to look at the display. It was true. The Laian warship was suddenly breaking off, at a ninety-degree angle to his original course. He'd swing well clear of both Hope and the First Task Force now.

"What am I missing?" he murmured.

"Hyper portal!" Chan snapped. "Big one—I've got at least half a dozen capital ships, plus escorts." The chief of staff turned a massive grin on Pat. "I hadn't started praying yet, so I'm giving credit for this one to you, sir.

"The lead ship is definitely *Duchess of Terra*. Tanaka made it in time."

HARRIET STUDIED THE SCREEN GRIMLY. There were a lot fewer Laian cruisers out there than she'd expected—and a lot more Terran and Imperial ships than she'd dared to hope. Either there hadn't been a battle yet, or it had gone a lot more her people's way than she'd been expecting.

"Laians are breaking off," Han reported. "Vector is away from us, maintaining distance from Hope and the Militia task force."

"Let's demonstrate what we think of Pincer Kandak's activities," Harriet replied. "Orders to all ships: pursue the war-dreadnought. Form on *Duchess of Terra* in standard combat formation."

Her cruisers and fast battleships fell in around the two super-battleships. Other than the fast battleships, each barely a quarter of *Duchess*'s size, her force wasn't that much heavier than Kurzman's.

Unlike Kurzman's force, however, hers wasn't primarily Militia. If the Two Hundred and Eighty-eighth Pincer of the Republic decided to fight an Imperial task force, *that* meant war.

"Piditel, record for transmission," she ordered.

"Laian war-dreadnought *Harvester of Glory*, Pincer Kandak commanding," she greeted the hostile ship. "Your presence in this system is unexpected and unwelcome." She glanced at the sensor data filling in her displays and managed to conceal a grimace.

"My sensor data is showing an exchange of fire between you and Imperial forces. I have no choice but to regard you as a hostile force.

"You have one twentieth-cycle to withdraw from this system. Failure to withdraw or further hostilities towards Imperial forces will be an unquestionable act of war and will leave me no choice but to destroy or intern your forces."

Internment wasn't going to happen. Not with eight Imperial capital ships against a Laian war-dreadnought, even with a dozen destroyers and almost fifty cruisers in support.

"We're getting an update tight-beamed from *Emperor of China*," Piditel reported. "It's...not good."

Harriet pulled the data onto her repeaters with a gesture. Her coms officer was understating it. *President Washington* was damaged but combat-operational, but the Militia had already had one ugly exchange with the Laians.

An extremely uneven exchange that they'd forced to a draw only because Kandak hadn't expected to lose any ships. That wasn't promising.

And the surface situation...

"Battalion Commander Indus may be confident she can defeat that ground force, but she is assuming we don't have *more* stealthed transports in system," Harriet said aloud. "The fast battleships are to deploy their Marine contingents for a combat drop on the Corellian Plateau. *Duchess of Terra* and *Guardian* will both deploy their second battalion as well."

The fast battleships only carried a half-battalion of Marines. Her two super-battleships each carried a short regiment of two battalions. Four battalions, with assault shuttles and power armor, would double the odds against the Wendira.

"Yes, Echelon Lord."

"The assault shuttles will deploy directly from here," she continued after a moment's humming thought. "The task force will continue its pursuit of *Harvester of Glory*. Piditel—see if we can coordinate with Admiral Kurzman.

"I'll feel a lot happier standing off against Kandak with eight capital ships than with six."

CHAPTER THIRTY-THREE

JEAN VILLENEUVE STOOD IN THE CENTER OF HIS FLAG DECK, doing everything in his power to radiate *calm, wise elder*. He had a lot of practice with that by now and was quite confident in his ability to appear completely calm and in control, regardless of his surroundings.

"The currents are against us, sir," Captain Ruan, *Empereur de France*'s commander warned with a dissatisfied grunt. "The transit is taking longer than we hoped. We're going to be late."

"We allow a window for travel times, Captain Ruan," Jean reminded him. "While I would certainly prefer to arrive early, we know hyperspace is not controllable."

"Sir, I mean that unless something changes, we are going to arrive *after* our expected window," Jun-Ho Ruan said. The Chinese-Korean officer, once a member of the Chinese Party's secret spaceborne military, was a squat man who looked more Mongolian than either of his official ethnicities.

"I see. How late?"

"At least two hours," Ruan told him. "We are still at least sixteen hours out."

"A lot can happen in sixteen hours," Jean said. "But we must accept that we cannot change it. Thank you, Captain Ruan. Keep me updated."

The private channel from the bridge closed, and Jean continued to survey the holograms aboard *Empereur de France*'s flag deck. The data on the fleet was unreliable at best, relayed ship-to-ship via the one-light-second bubble each could transmit in. The anomaly scanners let them stay in formation, but it took time for the absence of a ship to be noted.

He'd picked out that *Tornado* was missing some time before, though even *he* hadn't been briefed on Bond's plans.

"Sir." A staff officer approached from behind.

"Commander Soun," he greeted her, recognizing his intelligence officer, Commander Channary Soun, by her voice. Her normal role was an interface with A!Tol Imperial Intelligence, though in combat, she was an electronic warfare specialist.

Neither of those roles gave her much to do while the fleet was in motion.

"I've been reviewing our ship-to-ship relay communications," she said quietly, standing close enough to him that no one else could hear their conversation. "*Tornado* is missing. There's a program loaded in *Empereur*'s computer that is faking her status updates."

"Ah," Jean acknowledged. "I wondered why no one had mentioned the absence."

"Someone covered their tracks." The intelligence officer paused. "While I hesitate to make accusations, sir, the code appears to be Consort Casimir's."

Jean chuckled.

"Why am I not surprised Elon got dragged into this?" he observed. At some point, the Ducal Consort had caught up with Imperial programming as well as technology. There was a *reason* Elon Casimir sat at the Duchess's right hand, and it certainly wasn't because he was pretty.

"What's going on, sir? Shouldn't I have been briefed on any kind of covert mission?"

"Commander Soun, *I* wasn't briefed," Jean told her. "I have my guesses, but all I know for certain is that Duchess Bond detached from us on a secret diplomatic mission."

He shook his head, minimally but enough that Soun would see it.

"I will not share my guesses," he warned her, "only my hope that we will see her again at Alpha Centauri—and that, as usual, Her Grace may save us all."

"Yes, sir," Soun replied stiffly. She paused for a moment, then continued.

"I've reviewed what little data there was in the briefing Imperial Intelligence provided on the Wendira, sir."

"And?"

"Something doesn't quite add up," she admitted. "We, ah, may have had some off-the-record conversations with Pincer Kandak's intelligence staff."

"Spies," Jean said with a sigh. "Regardless of the species, you're all the same."

"We bought a listing of Wendira officers from them," Soun told him. "Cheap, too. They're perfectly willing to screw over the Wendira."

"And?" the Admiral asked.

"Hive Commandant Ashtahkah does command a star hive, yes, but...she's a Royal, not a Warrior. She's only been an officer for two years; her rank is due to her blood, not her talents."

"So, she might be less of a threat than the weight of metal suggests," Jean concluded with a sigh.

"Yes, but..." Soun sighed, still standing out of his line of sight. "They wouldn't send an inexperienced Royal on this kind of detached duty, sir. The Royals command most of the star hives, but they're aware of the limitations of the freshly commissioned ones."

"Meaning?"

"They'd send a Warrior Hive Commandant on this kind of op,

sir. Ashtahkah commands *Wing's Nightmare,* but there is *no way* she's in command of the deployment."

Jean sighed.

"There's a second star hive, isn't there?"

ANNETTE TOOK the flag officer's seat on *Tornado*'s flag deck, watching the tactical holograms as her old ship fell into formation with the three Mesharom battle cruisers.

"We're receiving course information from the Mesharom," Amandine reported. "I take it we're going with them?"

"I'm not going to argue with the battlecruisers that outmass, out-tech, and outgun us ten times over if they're sending us an invitation, Captain," she told him. "If they want us to go with them, we go with them."

"Yes, Your Grace. Just wanted to confirm," the Captain replied. "Falling into formation now."

He chuckled a moment later.

"Damn, look at their positions, Your Grace. Makes me feel all important!"

One battlecruiser had fallen in directly ahead of *Tornado,* and the other two were flanking her. It was a clear escort formation. The Mesharom apparently wanted to be sure that Annette made it through this intact—and while *Tornado*'s mix of tech meant she still punched above her weight class by Imperial standards, she was an obsolete toy compared to the ships around her.

"They're opening a hyper portal," Amandine reported. "Um. Duchess? They're asking us to shut down our interface drive."

"Why?" Annette asked, looking over at Ki!Tana. The A!Tol fluttered her tentacles in an alien shrug.

"They aren't being that communicative," the Captain said. "There's no talking. Just...instructions and data. I get the feeling they don't like us."

"They don't like *anyone*, Captain," Ki!Tana reminded Amandine. "It's not personal; it's just what the Mesharom are like. If they want us to shut the drive down, I suggest we do so. They have no reason to harm us and every reason to help us."

After all, if Annette didn't get to Alpha Centauri, no one there would know about the deal they'd agreed to.

"You're probably right," Amandine said. "Your Grace?"

"Do it," Annette ordered.

For a moment, *Tornado* halted in space. With proper shutdown, the interface drive's momentum and energy were lost back to hyperspace and the cruiser returned to her original velocity from Earth orbit.

That wasn't nothing, especially given how far away they were from Earth, but it wasn't the point five cee she'd been maintaining before.

The stop was only momentary, however, before *Tornado* leapt forward again.

"Captain?"

"They appear to have extended and merged their interface-drive fields to include us," Amandine reported. "We are now moving at point six cee and the Mesharom are taking us through the hyper portal."

The usual momentary sense of discomfort washed over Annette, and they were in hyperspace, continuing to be pulled along by their new...allies? Friends? Customers?

Annette wasn't quite sure what to think of the Mesharom, but they appeared to mostly be on her side so long as she was prepared to pay their price.

Perhaps that made them mercenaries.

"That current wasn't there before," Amandine said quietly, and she turned her attention back to the hologram.

He was right. The upgraded anomaly scanners *Tornado* carried were capable of picking out hyperspace currents—that was how they were mapped in the first place. She could see the one they'd arrived on, at the limits of the scanners' range.

And there was another one, right in front of them. A new one, exactly on the course they needed to follow...

As she watched, it extended forward and their escorts tucked into it.

"They can create hyperspace currents?" she asked Ki!Tana.

"I...I did not know that," the Ki!Tol admitted. "But it explains a lot. That is a level of control over hyperspace I did not believe was possible."

"They're pulling out all of the tricks today," Annette said, half-amazed and half-shocked.

The Mesharom were afraid. *Terrified*, it seemed, of the potential consequences of the ship of Those Who Came Before falling into the wrong hands.

"Given the current, what's our ETA?" she asked Amandine.

"The fact they can make it at all is incredible, but it's not that strong a current," *Tornado*'s Captain admitted. "I call it eight hours. Maybe seven."

Annette nodded and leaned back in her seat. The race, it seemed, continued.

CHAPTER THIRTY-FOUR

THE TANKS WENT FIRST.

The A!Tol Imperium's H25-AC-K main battle tank was an impressive piece of machinery, far more expensive than the Terran Ducal Guard had been able to justify acquiring. It was a multirole combat vehicle, capable of hovering anything from one centimeter to one kilometer above the battlefield and carrying enough intelligence and firepower to act as both air and ground support.

It was also, despite the best efforts of its Imperial designers, approximately as stealthy as a giant bonfire. Indus sent all twelve of them forward ahead of the rest of her force, testing to see just what her enemies could throw at them.

The tanks could take a lot more damage than her power-armored soldiers, but they were also bigger targets.

Harold watched them advance from the command center, hoping they would be enough.

That meant he got to watch them die.

The force that had landed wasn't a small, covert team using jamming and stealth fields to cover their approach and take their enemies at close range. This was an *assault force*, with the full technology and will of a Core Power behind it.

The sky ahead of the advancing Imperial Marines lit up with a thousand golden glowing sparks, rising from launchers the Wendira had brought with them as they deployed. With access to the full array of satellites overhead, Harold could tell that those sparks were drones. About thirty centimeters across. Maybe a kilogram.

They jumped over the horizon, scanned for their enemies, and struck. They carried no weapons, just interface drives.

They couldn't manage the velocity of the missiles Harold had shot down their transport with, but a thousand or so kilometers a second was more than enough. Each of the drones hit with the force of over a hundred tons of explosive.

The shields and armor of the A!Tol armored vehicles had laughed at Earth's best when they'd landed on Earth. They stood off the first drone. The second. In some cases, even the third or fourth.

A dozen drones swarmed each tank—and the rest went after the front line of the Marines.

"Antimissile defenses!" Indus snapped.

Harold was already moving. The Marines didn't have much to hand that could stop high-velocity weapons—they generally relied on shooting down the source, but the Wendira attack drones were coming from launchers well out of sight.

The mobile surface-to-space launchers Harold had brought down with him, however, each carried a stripped-down version of a Sword turret. It was a last-ditch system, almost as dangerous to the launchers as what it was shooting at, but they could protect the launchers or a nearby city when anything else would fail.

And now those turrets sprang to life. Systems intended to target missiles moving at eighty-five percent of the speed of light had no problem with drones that had to stop in the air to orient themselves.

But there were *so many* drones.

"I'm covering you as best we can, Battalion Commander," Harold told Indus. "And you've got reinforcements dropping from on high. I don't know what else to tell you!"

"Keep covering us," the Yin snapped. "And relay every scrap of visual data you can to those assault shuttles—*someone* needs to kill those drone launchers for me!"

———

THE MARINES DID the only thing they could do while under fire— they charged. With power armor augmenting their limbs, it didn't matter which species a given soldier was. They all moved at about the same speed—and with Harold's turrets providing them cover, they made it through the hail of hyper-velocity-missile drones.

The first line of troops they hit were physically smaller than the soldiers that had assaulted the camp before. Maybe a hundred and thirty centimeters tall in power armor, these were Wendira drones. Despite their lack of bulk, their armor was easily a match for the Imperium's.

Plasma fire lit up Harold's scanners, and the HVM drones were still hammering the rear of Indus's formation—and some were now trying to target the surface-to-space missile launchers as well. The defense turrets were working so far, but they weren't intended for this heavy of a use.

He wasn't surprised when the first turret threw up an overheat error.

"Indus, watch the sky," Harold barked. "I'm down one turret and—"

The ground rumbled as the drones struck home and one of his launchers came apart under the pounding.

"Make that two turrets," he continued grimly. "They're all over-heating; you're going to lose your cover far too damned quickly."

He didn't need acknowledgement from the Yin. She had more important things on her mind, so he focused on pulling through the data he had, localizing the launchers.

There!

They were monstrously ugly things, basically just big tubes mounted on ten robotic legs and followed around by ammunition hoppers. Shields and stealth screening covered them, protecting them from counter-fire and surveillance—but each clump of drones localized another launcher.

"Incoming assault shuttles; I'm sending you target coordinates," he transmitted to the inbound Imperial Marines. "Hit them as soon as you can with everything you've got!"

"This is Battalion Commander Diti!," a calm-sounding translated voice replied. The underlying clicks and tones told him the speaker was A!Tol. "We have received your coordinates. We are still at least three thousandth-cycles from landing, but we can launch bombardment from here.

"Confirm distance of local forces," the Battalion Commander requested.

Harold ran the numbers. Four minutes from landing, but...

"Closest elements are still six kilometers from the target zone."

"Understood. Please pass on orders for Battalion Commander Indus to hold position. Sky fire incoming."

Harold nodded and switched channels.

"Indus, hold position at your current distance," he said briskly. "Fire from on high inbound!"

Marine assault shuttles didn't carry any weapon capable of threatening a starship. Their limited arsenal of interface-drive missiles was designed to two do things: shoot down other shuttles and bombard landing sites.

They were designed to do those two things *very* well.

Harold's crudely rigged sensor setup promptly failed to count how many weapons had been launched. At fifteen percent of lightspeed, each missile hit with the force of a twenty-five-megaton bomb.

The bombardment only lasted ten seconds, but when it was done, the drone launchers were gone.

So were the enemy transports and at least half of their troops—

and Diti!'s shuttles swept in barely two minutes later with several thousand more Marines.

"Admiral Kurzman," Harold pinged *Emperor of China*. "Ground site is secure. For now."

"The Laians appear to be trying to lure us out of position to try and get their own troops down," the Vice Admiral warned. "I wouldn't count on those being the last troops you have to face, Captain."

"Understood, sir."

CHAPTER THIRTY-FIVE

HARVESTER OF GLORY WASN'T RUNNING.

Harriet Tanaka was quite certain of that. The Laian war-dread-nought still outmassed every other capital ship in the system combined, and while her thirteen remaining escorts weren't much bigger than the Imperial and Terran heavy cruisers, they were definitely more dangerous.

But Pincer Kandak was trying to keep his options open. By maneuvering away from *Duchess of Terra* and her escorts, he was keeping outside of missile range and potentially luring Vice Admiral Kurzman away from the planet.

He also wasn't responding to her attempts at communication and he wasn't heading out-system.

"Sooner or later, he's going to come for us," Captain Sier noted. Harriet's flag captain had been with her since her first ship and had stood at her side when *Duchess of Terra* had been given an impromptu commissioning into the Imperial Navy and sent to Earth's defense against the Kanzi.

"If his orders are as definitive as it sounds like from his conversation with Kurzman, he has to," Harriet agreed. "He's just weighing how much it's going to cost."

She sighed.

"Also, quite likely, he's waiting for the Parliament to decide whether or not they really want to commit an act of war against an Arm Power. If he follows through on his threat to bombard the colony, the lack of witnesses would work just as well despite our larger naval detachment."

"Assuming he stopped our couriers from getting away," Sier pointed out. Kurzman's couriers were too close to the planet. There'd been no way they'd have escaped past Kandak's fleet.

There was equally no way that Kandak could stop Harriet's courier ships from making it to Sol and the starcom there, unless...

"If our ghosts in hyperspace were his, he might be able to rely on that," she said.

"We *know* what the Laians can do," Piditel objected. "Stealth fields, sure. We're pretty sure the random stealth ship that Kurzman saw when he arrived was Laian, despite the Wendira ships running around the system. But hyperspatial-anomaly cloaking?"

The big Rekiki shook his long snout.

"That's beyond them."

"We thought it was beyond *everyone*," Harriet said. "I'd buy it of the Mesharom; we don't have their abilities nailed down quite as well as most of the Core Powers."

"Agreed, but the Laians are the *closest* Core Power to us," Piditel replied. "We've spent quite a bit of time making sure we know them better than anyone else."

"And is the Grand Parliament really likely to want a war?"

"It's a war they'd win," Sier said. "It would be an unimaginable mess that would likely see the largest deployment of starkillers ever, but they'd win."

"I don't know the Laians well," Harriet admitted, "but from the couple I met on Earth, they don't seem the sort to make a desert and call it peace."

The Yin and Rekiki both stared at her in confusion.

"The Grand Parliament, for all their flaws, seem to have at least some degree of commitment to protecting their people," she clarified. "I have to wonder if they're actually willing to embrace a war that would see billions of *Laians* dead in exchange for whatever the hell is down on Hope."

"They accepted the chance of it," Sier said slowly, "but now they face the *certainty*. They may blink."

"We can hope."

"The problem is that the Wendira and the Mesharom won't."

EMPEROR OF CHINA curved in space, the small fleet of warships they'd assembled to defend Hope moving with her as they maneuvered to stay between *Harvester of Glory* and the planet beneath them.

Pat Kurzman watched the hologram display silently. There wasn't much for the Admiral to do at this point. Once the Laians made their move or someone else arrived, that would change, but for the moment, his task force simply had to stay between *Harvester* and Hope.

"Have we found any signs of more stealth ships?" he asked Chan. "The post-processing should be complete now, correct?"

The A!Tol Imperium had learned ways to find stealth ships. Unfortunately, those ways required as much as an hour of processing of the data after the sensors picked it up. It wasn't enough to find or engage a stealth-fielded ship, but it was enough for them to at least confirm if one was present or not.

"We're assuming we can find Wendira or Laian stealth ships," his chief of staff reported. "But...given that we *did* manage to find signs where that Wendira carrier arrived, that seems reasonable."

"And?"

Chan shook his head.

"There's at least one ship out there," he admitted. "We can't say more; they're moving around a lot and the data is an hour out of date. Maybe two."

"Any idea of size?" Pat asked. "I don't think the Laians stealth-screen war-dreadnoughts, but the Wendira might hide their star hives."

"Nothing that big. They might be able to wrap a stealth screen around a ship that big, but the scan processing would find it pretty clearly. I'm guessing there may be another damned Wendira covert carrier and probably a scout ship or six of *somebody's*."

"Those stealth carriers are giving me a headache," Pat complained. "They've got the firepower to walk right over us. What the hell are they playing at?"

"Being cute," Chan said. "Probably wanted to steal the ship before anyone knew it was there."

"At least two groups knew it was there before we did," Pat said. "The Wendira and the Kanzi. Everyone else started showing up after we dug the ship out. I suspect the Wendira are going to be answering some pointed questions from the rest of the Core Powers once this is over."

"I just hope we're around to hear about the consequences." Chan paused. "But since *Harvester of Glory* just gave up on playing matador, I'm not taking bets on that."

Pat turned his attention back to the hologram. His chief of staff was correct. The Laian battle group was now bearing directly for Hope.

"Get me Tanaka," he said quietly. "Pincer Kandak has volunteered us to be the anvil. It appears my old friend gets to play the hammer."

"WE'RE COMING in behind him as fast as we can," Harriet told Kurzman. "We'll range on him forty seconds after you do."

"He's giving us the best opportunity we're going to get," the Militia Admiral replied. "He's got to know that, which means he thinks he can take us."

"I think the odds are more even than that," she said. "We'll crush him between us, finish this mess before it gets any worse. *Kichi* to you, Admiral. We'll meet you in the middle."

Harriet linked in her capital ship commanders and escort squadron leaders with a swipe of her hand.

"All right," she told the collection of sentients facing her. Only two of her capital ship commanders were human, and none of the escort formation leaders were. Between the twenty-eight cruisers and six capital ships of her task force, seventeen of the Imperium's races were represented, and seven of those species were on this channel.

"Pincer of the Republic Kandak is done playing and he's heading straight for Hope. We're going to intercept him and demonstrate just *why* he shouldn't have decided to fuck with the Imperial Navy.

"If any of your ships are not fully ready for action, *fix that*," she told them. "We range on the Laians in eleven minutes."

Harriet smiled coldly.

"Battle formation K-17," she concluded. "Let's stick to the plan and beat the big bastard to death."

K-17 assembled her entire force into a three-dimensional wall of battle, allowing every one of her cruisers and battleships to maneuver independently to avoid fire but also stacking their missile defenses and offensive firepower.

Two of her fast battleships and a third of her cruisers didn't have the new armor, anti-missile turrets, or drones. Three years wasn't nearly enough time for the Imperium to have upgraded every ship in a fleet almost three thousand vessels strong.

Twenty-eight cruisers, four fast battleships and two super-battle-ships still made for a *lot* of launchers. And proton beams, too, though if they got close enough to use those, they were going to be in trouble.

Minutes ticked by as the three forces moved toward each other, massive chunks of the system passing beneath both *Harvester* and

Harriet's force while Kurzman's fleet moved out to block the Laian approach.

"*Harvester* has entered her missile range of the Militia force," Han announced. "...She has not fired."

"What is he playing at?" Piditel demanded.

"Terrans call it 'chicken'," Harriet told him. "He's waiting to see if we blink first. There's no question of who fired the first shots today, but...he might still be hoping we'll stand aside."

"That's not going to happen, is it?" the Rekiki asked. "Admiral Kurzman will make his range in just under sixty seconds."

"No," she replied. "No, if he doesn't turn his sixty-million-ton ship around in the next forty-five seconds, he's going to face a *world* of hurt."

"Our range in eighty seconds," Sier informed her from the bridge. "Any new orders?"

"No. As soon as you enter range, target *Harvester of Glory* with everything we've got. Deploy defensive drones now. His may be better, but at this point, we've got a *lot* more of them."

Twenty seconds to Kurzman's range. Kandak had already given up his best opportunity to pound the defenders with missiles. What was he playing at?

"Any communication from the Pincer?" she asked.

"No."

"Kurzman has fired!" Han's superior, Commander Kav Ikil snapped. A slight spray from the Indiri's always-wet red fur sprinkled across the junior officer, and Harriet made a mental check mark as Han ignored it in favor of updating the charts.

Cross-species interaction was always a minefield, and the Indiri looked like nothing so much as wide-eyed, red-furred frogs to human eyes. They were vaguely disturbing but had become one of humanity's fast allies.

"Kandak has returned fire," the junior Chinese-Russian officer reported. "There's too many missiles in space for detailed numbers, but both of them have their defense drones out."

Harriet checked the distances. Her range in ten seconds. *Harvester* continued to charge toward the defensive fleet, and,there was no way that Kurzman's people could avoid him now. He was going for beam range—and A!Tol Intelligence had no idea just what the war-dreadnoughts and assault cruisers mounted for shorter-ranged weapons.

They knew its range was enough shorter than the light-minute or so of interface-drive missiles that the missiles still made up a vast portion of the Laians' armament, but that was it. It seemed either no one had survived seeing the things deployed, or anyone who had was too terrified to sell that information on the black market.

"Range," Ikil stated calmly. "All units firing, impact is twenty seconds after Admiral Kurzman's salvo. Standing by for second salvo."

"Let's take the fight to them, people," Harriet ordered, coming to a decision. "Keep closing the range. Let's see if we can keep him too busy looking over his shoulder to plan what he's going to do to Pat!"

THE SALVOS SLAMMING into Pat's fleet were weaker than they had been the first time, and his people had had the time to make up their losses in drones and regenerate their shields. The damage to their armor and other systems that his super-battleships had taken wasn't so easily fixed, but it was also less important.

The Laian missiles died in their hundreds, a cascade of fire that was stopping well short of his ships this time. The same multilayered defense glittered in space, and Pat watched carefully for the switch in fire patterns that would risk his fleet.

So long as *Harvester* focused her fire on his super-battleships, the odds were in his favor. A few missiles leaked through, but the capital ships' shields easily absorbed them.

"This didn't work last time," he observed softly. "What does Kandak think he's going to do *this* time?"

"I'm not certain, sir," Chan replied. "But I'm guessing close to beam range."

Pat nodded slowly. They'd attempted a time-on-target salvo again, but this time, the Laians had been waiting for it. The drones had dodged backward when the missiles had swarmed them, giving them precious extra fractions of a second to defend themselves with.

"Order all ships to stand by proton beams and plasma lances," he ordered. Maximum effective range on any of his beams was five light-seconds—which meant the closing ships were still a full minute from that range.

"Tanaka's missiles are coming in from behind," Chan told him. "They're not having any more luck than we are."

Pat studied the hologram and wished for short-range FTL. If he and Tanaka could coordinate their salvos, they'd hammer down the Laians' defenses with sheer numbers of missiles, but...

The Imperial ships were almost two light-minutes away. There wasn't enough *time*.

"Plasma lance range in twenty seconds and closing."

"*Thunderstorms* are to focus on the secondary ships," Pat ordered, closing his eyes. "All other vessels will target *Harvester* with proton beams and give her everything we've got."

He *felt* as much as heard the change in the next moment, his flag deck suddenly going completely silent in shock. He reopened his eyes, staring at the hologram display as *Emperor of China* suddenly went into even crazier evasive maneuvers than normal.

President Washington was crippled. When he'd closed his eyes, the super-battleship had been moving in company with his own vessel, unleashing fire and thunder on the Laian war-dreadnought.

When he'd opened them, the front third of the seventeen-million-ton super-battleship was simply *gone* and the remainder was spinning out of control as her remaining crew tried to regain control.

As Pat watched, a massive ball of lightning-spewing plasma simply *appeared* next to *Emperor of China*, the evasive maneuvers having just *barely* maneuvered the super-battleship such that it appeared outside her shield.

More, smaller plasma packets began to appear around his cruisers. *Liberty* staggered as she ran headlong into one. Her shields held against that shot...and then three more sequenced plasma balls appeared *inside* her hull and vaporized Harold Rolfson's cruiser.

"Where the hell are they coming from?" Pat demanded, *Emperor of China* lurching under his feet as the incoming fire overwhelmed her shield.

"They're just *appearing*. The Laians are *teleporting* the damn things onto us!"

"WHAT IN DARKEST WATERS IS THAT?" Ikil demanded, staring at the sensor readings.

"That's what I was hoping you could answer," Harriet pointed out, watching as two of the *Stalwarts* she'd sent to reinforce Kurzman blew apart, their shields overwhelmed by impossible bursts of ball lightning appearing in deep space.

"I'm seeing energy spikes on the Laian ships, and then...that," the Indiri told her, gesturing at the hologram.

"Time delay is under point one seconds," Han added to his commander's comment. "Range appears to be about ten light-seconds with near-instantaneous delivery." The junior officer shook his head. "Time delay may be due to our distance from both of them, too. It could easily be instantaneous."

"My god," Harriet whispered. An instantaneous energy weapon. No wonder the Laians had phased out plasma lances in favor of...*whatever* the hell this was. The only thing saving Kurzman's fleet was the time it took the light from their ships to reach the Laians.

"Admiral Kurzman is closing with the enemy," Ikil reported. "They're turning to keep the range open, it looks like he'll bring them to lance range for his remaining *Thunderstorms*, but..."

As he spoke, the *Thunderstorm*-class heavy cruiser *Clarion Call* came apart, a burst of ball lightning and plasma materializing in the middle of the kilometer-long ship.

"Cut them off," Harriet ordered. "Take us in, maximum speed. All ships, stand by to engage the enemy as closely as possible."

"That may be suicide, Echelon Lord!" Sier objected from the bridge.

"If we abandoned Kurzman to face that on his own, that may as well be murder," she snapped back. "*Move,* people. I want that dreadnought *dead!*"

THE LAIANS WEREN'T GETTING EVERYTHING their own way. With two fleets pouring missiles into them, both *Harvester* and her escorts were taking hits. Shields were flickering across the Laian battle group, and even as more of the Imperial cruisers died, two of their Laian counterparts joined them.

Harriet's task force launched their charge directly toward the war-dreadnought, and Kurzman's came from the other side. As hammer rushed toward anvil, the weakness of Kandak's position became clear—he'd pushed to close to the range of his FTL energy projectors but in so doing had put his ships between the two fleets.

Harvester of Glory could avoid one of the Imperial fleets reaching proton-beam range but only by allowing the other one into it. Missiles continued to ravage his formation as the three fleets closed, but Kurzman's original defending fleet was being massacred in front of Harriet's eyes.

Somehow, *Emperor of China* was still intact. She'd taken several near-misses, but the super-battleship was still flying and firing as she continued to charge toward the Laian ship.

Duchess of Terra led her own consorts toward *Harvester* from the other side, long-range proton-beam fire already beginning to sparkle across the Laian warships' shields.

Harriet could run the numbers in her head. They weren't going to win this. Those energy projectors changed the entire equation at close range, but closing to proton-beam range was the only chance she had of doing real damage.

Their only hope was to inflict enough damage on *Harvester of Glory* that she'd be trapped in the system until Admiral Villeneuve and Fleet Lord Tan!Shallegh arrived.

That way, their almost-inevitable death would be worth it.

Her gaze was level as more Imperial cruisers died. The Laians were ignoring the destroyers, focusing their fire on the *Thunderstorm*s and *Stalwart*s—and *Harvester* herself was clearly focusing her projects on *Emperor of China*.

Then something changed.

One moment, the Laian formation was spread out, the cruisers expanding their formation to provide better missile defense and presumably clear lines of fire for the energy projectors.

The next, six of the remaining cruisers swarmed together in a desperate attempt to stop *something* Harriet couldn't see—and then blew apart as a swarm of starfighters the Imperial ships hadn't seen yet hammered into them on their way to *Harvester of Glory*.

CHAPTER THIRTY-SIX

For a moment, Pat Kurzman simply took relief in the fact that the Laians had stopped shooting at *his* ships, and then the reality of what he was seeing sunk in. A wave of over five hundred Wendira starfighters swept over *Harvester of Glory*'s escorts, shattering cruiser after cruiser with point-blank missile fire and devastatingly powerful plasma pulses.

One moment, he'd known his entire fleet was dead. The next, only *Harvester of Glory* remained of the attacking battle group, and hundreds of starfighters swarmed toward the war-dreadnought. There were seconds to make a decision, maybe less.

It was surprisingly easy. The Laians had killed his people. Threatened his civilians. Fought him, surprised him, condescended to him...

But Pincer of the Republic Kandak had at least *talked* to him.

The Wendira had done nothing of the sort. They'd simply shown up and started killing everyone.

"Redirect our missiles," he barked. "Target the Wendira."

"We're protecting *Harvester*?" Captain Fang demanded.

"No, we're killing the Wendira before they come for us," Pat replied. "Those starfighters are maneuverable as hell. Kill them now!"

Lightspeed delays meant they couldn't turn aside every missile, and with the cruisers gone and the plasma-cannon defense drones turned on the starfighters, dozens still slammed into *Harvester of Glory*. Her shields flickered under the combined pounding and missiles slipped through, cratering her massive armor and breaking off compressed-matter plating.

Then the next salvos leapt to the starfighters. The Imperial missiles weren't even much faster than the deadly little ships, but they were *enough* faster. Starfighters that had focused on the war-dreadnought, clearly the only thing they'd registered as a real threat, had missiles slam into them from behind at a relative five percent of lightspeed.

Dozens of starfighters died. Then hundreds.

Then *Tanaka's* fleet was there, slipping into proton-beam range of both *Harvester of Glory* and her attackers—and followed Pat's example.

The remaining starfighters split apart, their formation shattering into a scattered swarm of dancing fireflies that outpaced Imperial and Laian starships alike.

They left *Harvester of Glory* behind. Her shields were down. Her engines were damaged and she was gently spinning in space—and both Imperial Fleets were now in proton-beam range of her.

For a moment that seemed to last for eternity, Pat knew he could destroy Kandak's ship, end the Laian threat to the world he was protecting and avenge his people.

No one in the galaxy would blame him—but Tanaka was following his lead. If his ships fired, Tanaka's would follow. A *war* would follow...and the starfighter swarm meant that they'd missed a star hive arriving in system.

"Get me a channel to Pincer Kandak," he ordered with a sigh.

FOR THE FIRST TIME, there were no delays, no connection issues, and no attempt to ignore Pat Kurzman's transmission. They were close enough for a live video feed, and Kandak immediately opened one when *Emperor of China* reached out.

Harvester of Glory's bridge looked pristine. Untouched by the fire that had hammered the vessel...except that half of the screens behind Pincer of the Republic Kandak were black, and two large holograms that had been present in previous video of him were gone.

Kandak himself no longer stood as straight as he had. The mandibles around his mouth were retracted protectively and his upper clawed hands were held stiffly, as if he didn't trust them not to tremble.

"Pincer Kandak," Pat said flatly. "Your shields are disabled. Your interface drive is running at half efficiency. You are under our guns and have no chance of escaping proton-beam or plasma range of Imperial forces."

He let that sink in. Kandak straightened slightly, attempting to project some defiance, but the scarab beetle–like alien remained silent, refusing to dispute Pat's assessment of the situation.

"Too many of both of our people have died here today for this bloody stupidity," Pat continued. "We both know I have the power to destroy your ship, but that I'd lose ships doing it.

"The Imperium does not want a war with the Republic, and for that reason—and that reason *alone*, Pincer Kandak—I will let my dead lie unavenged.

"Get the fuck out of my star system."

It was a threat. A demand, backed by the certainty of deadly force...but it was also a mercy and a peace offering, and both he and Kandak knew it.

The Laian officer managed to return to his fully straightened height, a towering edifice of carapace and claws, and slammed his middle right claw into his chest in salute. The middle claws were the Laian limbs most commonly used for delicate manipulation—and much more vulnerable than the armored upper pincers.

"I thank you for the wisdom of your nest," Kandak said quietly. "I trust your honor, Vice Admiral Pat Kurzman, and I will repay your honor in kind.

"We will withdraw."

Several long seconds dragged on with the channel still open, and Pat wondered what the alien was thinking.

"We will also provide you with our full files on Wendira combat forces," Kandak said. "I do not know what strength they have brought here, Admiral, but I would rather that ship remain in your hands than ended in theirs."

The video cut off, but a flashing icon told Pat that the channel was still open.

"We are receiving a data stream," Chan announced. "Feeding it into a secure system air-gapped from the rest of the computers."

"Good." He was willing, however grudgingly, to let Kandak go. He wasn't willing to *trust* the big beetle.

"Is he moving?"

"Yes, sir," his scanner tech reported. "Heading in the opposite direction to those Wendira starfighters at point one five ccc. They kicked the *shit* out of *Harvester*, sir."

A video channel opened on Pat's command chair from the bridge.

"We could have taken him, sir," Captain Fang said.

"I know," Pat agreed. "We might have even done so without casualties...but we don't *want* a war with the Laian Republic. All we want is for them to go away, and that mission is done."

He scanned the displays around him.

"Right now, the Wendira may be the bigger threat," he concluded. "That fighter launch came from somewhere. Find me that star hive, people."

"GIVE ME *SOMETHING*," Harriet demanded. "Five hundred starfighters don't just appear from nowhere and disappear!"

"They came in ballistic at about five percent of lightspeed," Ikil told her grumpily. "They were probably heading for Kurzman's fleet originally but basically collided with the Laians."

"So, backtrack them and find me the star hive," she replied.

"We're running the files that Kandak sent Kurzman," Han said. "I..." The young human officer looked at his Indiri commander, who made a "go ahead" gesture.

"I don't think we're looking at a star hive yet, Echelon Lord," he concluded. "First thing I pulled was the starfighter capacity of one of them: it's listed as four Grand Wings."

"Which is?" Harriet asked gently.

"Sixteen wings of sixteen starfighters apiece," Han reeled off immediately. "A star hive carries over a thousand starfighters. We only saw five hundred."

"And between us and the Laians, we killed three hundred or so of those," Sier added, the Captain linked in from the bridge. "Not a bad ratio."

"Not an unusual ratio for starfighter strikes, either," Harriet told her flag captain. "There's a reason none of the other Core Powers use them. The Wendira can replace the pilots far more easily than anyone else can."

She turned back to Han.

"If it's not a star hive, what are we looking at?"

Ikil gestured for the human officer to take over the display, and a new ship appeared in the hologram. It was similar in design to the star hive, the same stacked concentric circles, but the display marked the scale as being significantly smaller.

"The name for this translates as 'star intruder'," Han explained. "The Laians think they're the largest stealth ship in the Wendira inventory, used as a mother ship for covert operations and stealth ground assaults."

"Well, that certainly fits with what we've been seeing," Harriet agreed. "And they have five hundred starfighters?"

"No. They each carry a single Grand Wing," the junior officer explained. "According to the Laians, they're basically unarmed themselves, but with over two hundred and fifty starfighters, they don't *need* guns."

He paused, mentally rewinding, and sighed.

"I'm reviewing the post-processed data run we did for stealth ships," he said quietly. "I think we have two star intruders in the system."

"Pass that on to the team," Ikil ordered immediately. "You and I need to see if we can follow the remaining fighters and let the Echelon Lord know if we can *find* the ships."

That was a good call in Harriet's opinion, too. Ilan had picked up the highest probability of what they were facing; his analysis was solid. The NCOs aboard could confirm his analysis with the brute-force data crunching. He and Ikil would be better suited to finding the enemy.

"We know there's at least one star hive out here, too," she reminded them. "The Laian files say they have no stealth fields?"

"There's something in their files about a hyperspatial anomaly cloak," Ikil replied, "but no normal space stealth fields."

Harriet remembered the strange flickering ghosts they'd seen in hyperspace.

"Shit. The star intruders are here...and the hive is nearby."

"In that case, Echelon Lord, what in darkest waters are they waiting for?" the Indiri officer snapped.

Harriet turned her gaze to the screen with Sier on it, her flag captain looking noticeably unhappy.

"We're not a threat in their minds," her flag captain pointed out. "So..."

"They were waiting for *Harvester* to leave," she concluded.

CHAPTER THIRTY-SEVEN

His ship was gone.

Harold stared at the orbital display in something close to shock. *Liberty* was gone, blown apart by a Laian mystery weapon they hadn't been able to see or dodge. Lyon was dead. Popovitch was dead. Saab had died before ever discovering if his time in command had been enough to earn him a ship of his own.

There was a horrible feeling to being a captain who'd outlived their ship.

His reverie was interrupted by Sommers clapping a hand on his shoulder.

"Rolfson, are you still with us?" he asked softly. "Hell of a day. Hell of a day."

Harold shook his head, trying to focus on the moment.

"Where are we at?" he replied.

"Your packages are in place," the Guard Captain told him. "Should I be telling anybody else just what we did?"

"Not yet. My call for now, at least until the Duchess gets here," Harold replied. On the display, *Harvester of Glory* continued to move away from the Imperial fleet. They were letting her go. Intellectually, he could understand that.

But he wanted the son of a bitch who'd killed his crew dead.

Sommers was eyeing him, and he suspected his face showed what he was thinking.

"You weren't on Earth when the A!Tol took over," Sommers reminded him. "I know what you're thinking."

"Do you?"

"I was Triple-S, Captain," the Guard officer said. "I had friends and brothers-in-arms on the ships that died. The A!Tol killed my best friend, my fiancée, and my oldest brother.

"I had a cousin in Russia. He died when our new overlords dropped rocks on the Russian surface-to-orbit missile sites. Another cousin only lived because the A!Tol decided to just stun the American last stand."

Sommers shook his head.

"A second cousin suicide-bombed the landing site in Delhi," he continued. "They had shielded tanks. His bomb vest didn't even scratch the paint.

"So, yes, Captain Rolfson, I know what it feels like to watch the people who killed your friends walk away without punishment because it's the right political decision," Sommers said grimly. "I *understand* why the Duchess made the call she did, and I can't argue that the Imperium's been bad for us, but I watched half a generation of my family die protecting Earth from them."

"And you're still in the Guard," Harold said, latching on to some-thing—*anything*—other than the knowledge that his ship was gone.

"Life goes on," Sommers told him flatly. "I chose a long damned time ago to put myself between the people and those who would endanger them. Only way to do that now is in the service of the Duchess and the A!Tol.

"So, I serve the sons of bitches who killed half my family. Indi-rectly, sure, but I serve them nonetheless.

"So, you, *sir*, can bloody well watch that ship fly away and live with yourself," he concluded. "Because you can't do anything else, and because the Imperium can't fight the Laians."

"No, we can't," Harold confirmed, shaking his head. He held out his hand to the Indian Ducal Guard officer and accepted the transmitter Sommers passed him.

"We'll soon discover if we can fight the Wendira," he continued. "And quite possibly the Mesharom. But this"—he tapped the transmitter—"means I can bloody well guarantee no one gets this ship but us."

CHAPTER THIRTY-EIGHT

The next few hours, to Harriet's surprise, passed without incident.

The remaining starfighters disappeared, presumably back aboard their cloaked carriers. Ikil and Han managed to confirm where the star intruders had picked up their broods, but not in time to allow the Imperial forces to do anything useful with the information.

Instead, Harriet moved her fleet into orbit of Hope, reclaiming Division Lord Torandus's surviving cruisers and the destroyers from the original picket.

Once all of the ships were in orbit, she sighed as she studied the neat formations.

The Duchy of Terra Militia contingent had been smashed. Vice Admiral Kurzman was technically senior to her, but Navy officers had priority, and with only a single super-battleship and two *Thunderstorms* left under his command...

"I'm going to contact Vice Admiral Kurzman from my office," she told Piditel. "Alert me if we have any sign of the Wendira—or anybody else, for that matter!"

"Yes, Echelon Lord."

Imperial design was quite fixed on where the office of a ship or formation commander should be: attached to their primary battle station. Harriet's office was just outside the flag deck, and fully linked into the super-battleship's communications system.

In the thirty seconds it took her to get to her seat and pour herself a cup of tea, Piditel had already set up the link to *Emperor of China*. She clicked CONNECT and then carefully hid her disquiet at Pat Kurzman's face when he came onto the screen.

She and the Militia Vice Admiral were almost exactly the same age, barely into their forties, but Kurzman looked like he'd aged decades since she'd last seen him, barely six months before.

Somehow, she knew most of that was in the last twenty-four hours.

"Pat," she said softly. "How are you holding up?"

He glanced around, revealing that he was in his own office. He'd clearly guessed that she wanted to have this conversation quietly.

"We lost more people at Second Sol," Kurzman finally replied, "but I wasn't in command then. We underestimated the Laians. And then...I let the bastard go."

"It was the right call," Harriet told him firmly. Technically, she could have overridden him. But it had been the right call.

"How long do you think we have before it all goes to hell?" he asked.

"We picked up at least two hyperspace anomaly signatures that were screwing with our long-range sensors when we arrived," she warned him. "I'd *like* to think those were the star intruders and they just managed to actually sneak in this time, but..."

"We have to assume they weren't," Kurzman agreed with a sigh. "We need to make sure there's no confusion on the chain of command, Harriet. The Imperial Navy has preeminence; we know the rules."

The rules were often ignored when Militia forces heavily outweighed the local Imperial force, as when Torandus had accepted

Kurzman's authority, but that was no longer the case in Alpha Centauri.

"Thank you," she said. "I assume command. We'll make sure everyone knows before it comes down to a fight."

"Time is on our side so far," he told her. "Villeneuve is only nine hours away, twelve at most. Seven more capital ships—including the new *Manticores*."

"I'm glad Kas!Val is being sensible," Harriet admitted. "She and I...did not get along when we last met."

And Kas!Val was senior to her, which meant she technically could be ordered to surrender command to the A!Tol when *A Dawning of Swords* arrived.

"She's a tentacled bitch," Kurzman replied, "but she's not *stupid*."

"The good news is that I think we took out enough starfighters than the star intruders aren't going to pick a fight until their bigger siblings get here," Harriet told him. "The bad news is, well, they've got at least one bigger sibling on the way.

"And I'm not sure our fleet can handle twelve hundred Wendira starfighters."

———

SOMEWHERE IN THE SYSTEM, two stealthed Wendira carriers lurked.

In Hope orbit, Harriet and Kurzman consolidated their fleet. Three super-battleships, all fully modernized with defensive systems. Four fast battleships, only half of them modernized. Two Terran *Thunderstorm*-class cruisers, with full modern defenses and plasma lances allowing them to punch well above their weight. Thirty-four remaining Imperial cruisers of various classes, twelve of which didn't have modern defenses.

A dozen destroyers, ten of them fully modern *Capital*-class ships, mostly Militia, and two un-upgraded *Descendants*.

Fifty-five warships, seven of them capital ships. It was a more powerful force in any sense than the one Earth had been conquered with five years earlier. It was certainly a more powerful force than Harriet had expected to command for several more years, even if a third of its most powerful ships were Militia.

It was also, she was grimly certain, nowhere near enough for the task ahead.

Kandak had given them the Laian Republic's full files on the Wendira space fleet, and they made for grim reading. The *Flying Sword of Fire*–class starfighter was capable of sustaining seventy percent of lightspeed for extended periods and carried two short-range point-eight-five-cee missiles, along with a plasma cannon vastly more powerful than the Imperium had dreamed could be mounted on such a small craft.

The star intruders, at least, had a noticeable weakness: to cram in an entire Grand Wing of starfighters, plus two battalion-equivalent assault transports, the ten-million-ton ships had no offensive weapons whatsoever.

A star hive, however, was ten times the intruders' size with only four times the starfighters. They carried an entire *division*, ten thousand strong, of Warrior and Drone landing troops. Plus massed batteries of point-eight-five cee missile launchers and proton beams.

Laian intelligence, at least, agreed with Imperial intelligence that the Wendira didn't have any secret superweapons. None of the faster-than-light weapons systems that they now knew both the Laians and the Mesharom had.

Just vast numbers of blisteringly fast, terrifyingly well-armed small parasite craft that the Imperial fleet had minimal defenses against.

"Echelon Lord?"

"Yes, Sier?" Harriet answered her flag captain before she realized that the Yin was standing in the door to her office. "Come in, sit down," she instructed.

"Any brilliant ideas?" he asked, settling into a chair and gesturing at the floating data display showing the star hive specifications.

"Hoping they arrive after Tan!Shallegh?" Harriet replied with a chuckle. "I'm not worried about the star intruders now," she continued. "We can handle two hundred starfighters, I think. But a hundred-million-ton carrier with a thousand starfighters?"

She shook her head.

"With Villeneuve here and our strength doubled, we can probably take her," she told him. "If they get here before the Militia, though, all I can see us managing is a holding action. We might be able to keep the fleet together through the first pass, but they'll just keep rearming the fighters and sending them at us."

"Until either they run out of starfighters or we're dead."

Her flag captain shook his head, his dark beak glinting in the light.

"Should we consider evacuating the colony?" he finally asked. "It's still relatively small..."

"If we packed our ships like sardines and risked the life support, we could evacuate about eighty thousand people," Harriet said quietly. She'd run the numbers. "That would leave, roughly, a hundred and thirty thousand behind.

"Plus, we'd be giving up that ship, and my orders are to do no such thing. If I could get everyone off that planet, I'd blow the damn thing from orbit and leave, but..."

"We could just destroy it," Sier suggested.

"Wendira psych profiles tell me that's a bad idea," Harriet replied. "The Royals, especially, are very...possessive. If they think something is theirs, they do not handle being denied very well. They'll negotiate if they think they've been beaten, but to simply have it denied..."

"Wonderful. I like them less by the moment."

"That's why the Laians hate them," she pointed out. "Laians look *just* enough like Wendira workers that, combined with the overthrow of the Ascendancy, the Wendira can't help but see them as workers that have forgotten their place.

"The fact that the Laians won't fall into line and obey like the Royals think they should…"

Harriet shrugged.

"Six wars," Sier said slowly. "I've seen estimates of over a trillion dead. Because the Wendira think the Laians should be their servants?"

"Hence why I don't think blowing up the ship is the best plan," Harriet replied dryly. "No, Captain. They're coming. We'll fight them, hold them until Villeneuve gets here.

"Then we'll kick their asses into next week and make Tan!Shallegh's entire trip out here unnecessary."

"Of course, Echelon Lord," Sier agreed with a confidence she doubted he felt.

That was fair. She wasn't nearly as confident as she pretended, either.

PAT KNEW HE SHOULD REST. Eat. Sleep. *Something.*

About all he was managing to do, however, was get off the flag deck so he wasn't pacing in public, adding to everyone else's tension.

President Washington had a crew of fifty-seven hundred. Each *Thunderstorm* had a crew of six hundred. Seventy-five hundred men and women had died under his command in the last few hours, and he wasn't certain what he could have done differently.

"Admiral, search and rescue is reporting in from *Washington*," Captain Fang's voice interjected into his pacing.

"Thank you, Captain," Pat replied gratefully. "How bad?"

"Better than we had any right to expect," Fang told him. The Captain sounded strained but not quite as heartbroken as Pat Kurzman felt. "When the Imperium designed these ships, they designed them well—our upgrades made them tougher, but the Imperium designed them to keep crew-sentients alive when they knew they could lose half the ship if something went wrong."

"And?" Pat said slowly.

"They're still chasing down escape pods, but the evacuation of the main hull fragments is proceeding," his flag captain replied. "Current estimate is we pulled three thousand, two hundred and forty from the wreck, and there's at least another twelve hundred we've either retrieved from pods or still in space."

Pat made sure his camera and microphone were off, turning away from his desk to rub his eyes, hard.

So, his losses weren't as bad as he thought. He still couldn't shake the feeling he'd screwed up somewhere.

"Thank you, Captain," he told the other man. He didn't know Fang well, but he suspected the Captain had known *exactly* what his Admiral was doing. "I appreciate the update."

"Part of the service, Vice Admiral."

Before the intercom channel could cut off, a shout echoed in the background behind Fang:

"*Hyper portal!* Multiple hyper portals! We have incoming."

Pat grimaced.

"I'll be on the flag deck immediately," he told Fang. "I'm guessing we have customers."

CHAPTER THIRTY-NINE

THERE WAS A CERTAIN ARROGANCE, PAT CONCLUDED, WHEN A stealth ship stopped bothering to hide. The two star intruders had been in Alpha Centauri for at least half a day, probably even longer, but they'd spent that entire time wrapped in the protective shroud of their stealth fields.

Now, however, both of them dropped their stealth fields. Each still had a wing of sixteen starfighters flying what humanity would have termed a combat air patrol around them as they headed to meet their big sisters, but they basically ignored any threat the Imperials could offer them.

Given those big sisters, however, Pat couldn't blame them. The image floating in the holographic display was a worse nightmare than he would have dared to allow himself to have. There wasn't one hundred-million-ton alien supercarrier.

There weren't even two.

There were *three* of the pyramid-like alien warships.

Three star hives. Each outmassing the entire defensive force. Accompanied, though it hardly mattered, by a dozen ten-million ton ships equivalent to an Imperial battleship. The Wendira name roughly translated as "star shield" but, unlike the two ships mothering starfighters, these did have equivalents in Imperial service.

Including the two intruders, four hundred and forty million tons of Core Power warships were now in the Alpha Centauri system. The star hives and their battleship escort were moving slowly for interface-drive warships, moving towards Hope at a mere ten percent of lightspeed while the two smaller ships headed to meet them.

"Well, Echelon Lord Tanaka," he greeted the Imperial officer with a cheer he didn't feel. "I'm glad you're in charge. What's the plan?"

Tanaka gave him a dirty look that he hoped no one else on either flag deck saw.

"Formation Foxtrot One," she said calmly. "No tricks or games for the moment. All escorts are to advance and cover the capital ships."

The Imperium had minimal anti-fighter doctrine, but the influence of Terran Captains—like Tanaka—who had insisted on using proton beams for missile defense meant that most of the ships in the fleet had both the software and the mobility to use the heavy beams as an anti-fighter weapon.

What they would shortly discover would be if the Sword and Buckler lasers were capable of hurting the fighter craft. Pat's bet was on "no", but they were going to have to try.

"The command is yours, Echelon Lord," he told Tanaka. "We'll do everything we can."

"For now, we hold position and we survive the first fighter strike," she replied on a direct channel. "Three thousand of them."

Pat hoped none of his crew saw his shiver of fear.

"The Imperium has never fought starfighters head on before," he said. "The modifications you convinced the Navy to make to their proton beams give us a better chance than we would have had four years ago.

"We don't know how effective they're going to be—but neither do the Wendira!"

THE COMMAND CENTER at the dig site was fully linked to the sensors of the fleet above them, which meant Harold Rolfson knew exactly how screwed they were. He and Indus both studied the fleet of massive ships bearing down on them, and then turned to each other.

"We need to dig in," she told him. "If we set up sufficient and dense enough fortifications, we can force them to fight us on the ground. They won't want to bombard the site from orbit; they'll risk losing what they came for."

Harold checked the screens for the local area. All of the civilians were long gone back to New Hope now, but there was the better part of five thousand Imperial and Terran soldiers around the dig site.

"You're right," he allowed. "But if we've lost the orbitals, all we're doing is bleeding them—and ourselves."

"What else can we do?" she demanded.

"What's our first responsibility, Battalion Commander?" Harold asked gently.

"The people," Indus responded instantly, then snapped her beak in a half-laugh, half-sigh.

"Fall back to New Hope City and dig in there," he told her. "Leave your automated systems in place with a token force; we'll use the STS missiles and automatic weapons to hold as long as we can— but if the fleet is gone, I'm more worried about our citizens than this damned ancient ship."

"Too many have already died for it," Indus said.

"I won't sacrifice two hundred thousand civilians for it," Harold replied. "It's your call, Battalion Commander."

As the senior officer of the garrison, the landed Marine forces would defer to her regardless of regular seniority.

"Sunstorms," she cursed, but there was no heat to it. "And where will you be, Captain?"

"Right here," he told her. "Handling the STS missiles and the automatic systems. Someone has to."

"But you would send the rest of us to safety?"

For a nonhuman, Indus could be *very* perceptive.

"What are you planning, Captain Rolfson?"

"What I must," he replied. "And yes, I would get everyone else to safety. Too many of our people have died for this wreck already. Get them out of here."

"Very well, Captain." Indus shook her head. Technically, he was senior to her, but rank differences didn't communicate well from space forces to ground forces, let alone from Militia to Imperial forces.

"We will withdraw to protect the city. But I warn you, I have no enthusiasm for explaining a heroic sacrifice to Dr. Wolastoq. Please stay alive, Captain."

"I have every intention of it," he said with a smile. "If I have my say, Battalion Commander, the only people who are going to die from here on out are Wendira."

"And what tools do you have to guarantee that?"

"None whatsoever," he admitted. "Just...hope."

Indus nodded, calmly, as if he hadn't just admitted he was likely to blow himself up with the ship.

"Sometimes, hope is the greatest weapon we have."

IT TOOK LONGER for the Wendira to consolidate their forces than Harriet had expected, though she was hardly going to complain about the extra minutes. The two lighter carriers joined the three star hives in the center of the formation, and the battleships jockeyed around, establishing a defensive perimeter around the motherships roughly three light-minutes away from Hope—well outside the Imperials' weapons range.

They drifted there for several more minutes while the star hives and star intruders spewed out starfighters in ever-increasing numbers. Harriet suspected they could launch faster if they needed to, but since they knew *she* wasn't going to attack them, they took the time to deploy their ships safely.

Over thirty-two hundred starfighters formed up around the Wendira fleet, and Harriet still wasn't entirely certain just what she was going to do about them. Six-thousand-plus missiles would be bad enough, though she was reasonably sure she'd have a fleet left after them.

She wasn't sure how *much* of a fleet, and the starfighters themselves would close on their missiles' heels. Whether or not Hope would have any defenders left after that was a question she wasn't going to make bets on.

"Start pre-deploying missiles," she ordered. "If they're going to give us lots of warning of where they're coming from, let's use it."

Pre-deployed missiles were usually a waste of time. They were hugely vulnerable, required more computer support than usual, and spent a disproportionate amount of their available flight time getting into position—when the flight time was under a minute, the fact that turning the drive off and back on again cost you eighteen seconds of flight time was important.

The fighters had to come to them and were almost as fast as the missiles themselves. The pre-placed missiles would have a third less range than her ship-launched weapons, but the starfighters' missiles had even less endurance.

Hundreds, then thousands, of missiles spilled out of her ships' launchers, moving delicately into shoal upon shoal of deadly fish.

"When do we stop pre-placing missiles?" Ikil asked after the second round went out. "If they wait long enough, we could end up with our entire warhead load sitting out in space."

"They won't wait that long," Harriet told him. "But...if they wait long enough, we'll hold at fifty thousand weapons."

That would take almost ten minutes to deploy and would be the point at which their computers actually started to have problems handling the telemetry links. She didn't expect the Wendira to give her that long.

The Wendira ships were almost invisible behind the glittering swarm of starfighter icons. Her analysts couldn't even *count* the tiny ships; they were simply too numerous and too far away.

One of those ships was *Wing's Nightmare*, under Hive Commandant Ashtahkah. One of the other two star hives, presumably, carried the Fleet Commandant actually in charge of this operation. Likely an experienced Warrior-caste, someone whose entire life had been dedicated to war.

Someone who had fought Core Power fleets. What would they make of her defenders, she wondered?

Would they overestimate her people or underestimate them?

The Wendira had the firepower to wipe her fleet from the face of the universe. Her only chance for survival was for them to make a mistake—and everything she saw suggested that being underestimated was all too possible.

"They're moving," Han said softly. "All the capital ships are holding position, just starfighters coming forward and... Sir, can you double-check this?"

Ikil was at the human officer's station before Han had finished asking, looking over Han's data.

Then he laid a wet, furred hand on his subordinate's shoulder and squeezed reassuringly before he turned his big eyes to Harriet.

"They're splitting their forces," he told her. "Holding at least four Grand Wings in a carrier defense formation over a thousand starfighters strong."

"Who the hell are they afraid of?" Han asked. "It's certainly not us!"

"If they're only sending two thousand fighters at us, they may change their mind on that tune," Harriet replied with a cold smile. "But you're right, Speaker Han. They're not afraid of us. They're worried about the Laians coming back or the Mesharom showing up.

"We're not a threat. We're barely an obstacle. They've underestimated us—so, let's all make damn certain they learn the error of their ways, shall we?"

"FORMATION NUMBERS ARE consistent with nine Grand Wings," Chan reported. "CIC is still resolving numbers, it's a *lot* of signatures to break down, but that would be almost exactly twenty-three hundred starfighters."

Pat nodded, watching as the swarm of red icons moved across the holographic display.

"Stand by for orders from the Imperial flag," he ordered. "But expect that we will open fire at twelve million kilometers with onboard launchers and pre-deployed missiles at eight million."

"Passing instructions on to the task force," Chan confirmed.

The silence on *Emperor of China*'s flag deck was thick. Thanks to the Laians' decision to try and screw over their traditional enemies, they now knew far more about the Wendira than they ever had before

That information wasn't going to be enough to save them, Pat suspected, but it would be enough for them to buy time. They now knew, for example, that the miniaturized point-eight-five-cee interface-drive missiles carried by Wendira starfighters only had ten seconds of endurance, a two-and-a-half-million-kilometer range.

The Wendira would fire their missiles at roughly the same time his two *Thunderstorms* tested how well their plasma lances worked on starfighters.

"Status of the antimissile net?" Pat asked.

"Back in triple-echelon formation; first screen of Bucklers is out six hundred thousand kilometers from the capital ships." Chan shook his head. "CIC isn't willing to make a guess on whether the Bucklers' lasers will have any impact on the starfighters."

"I thought the Laians said their drones did."

"*Laian* drones fire focused plasma bolts," his chief of staff replied.

"So do the half a dozen of old rainshower drones that *Tornado* still carries. *Our* drones use high-intensity ultraviolet lasers, and the energy transfer pattern is completely different."

"Anyone willing to put odds on it?" Pat asked with a chuckle, watching the timers tick down.

"Ha! No," Chan laughed. "The Laians gave us *everything*, but they've never fired a laser at a Wendira starfighter. So, we have no idea how they'll handle lasers."

"Well, then, I guess we get to experiment with something the Core Powers *don't* know," Pat said. "Any update from Tanaka?"

Chan checked his systems, reviewing the communication logs.

"Just got it," he confirmed. "Her orders are the same as yours: on-board launchers at twelve, pre-deployed at eight."

"We had the same teachers," Pat told him. Tanaka had been senior to him in UESF service and Pat had basically been a drafted civilian, but they'd both gone through the *very* abbreviated tactical course Annette Bond had assembled for interface-drive tactics.

Chan had gone through a more detailed A!Tol-designed training program after the desperate defense of Earth against the Kanzi. Sometimes, his superior envied him that; the learning-on-the-job aspect of *Tornado*'s exile had been one of its least pleasant aspects.

"Range in thirty seconds," Chan announced. "Task force tactical net is active and we are linked into the Imperial flag and our escorts."

Seconds ticked away in silence, and Pat took one last long glance at the display.

"Order our ships to target the center of each Grand Wing's formation," he said quietly. "Let's see just how arrogant the 'superior' Core Powers are."

CHAPTER FORTY

No OTHER POWER IN THE GALAXY HAD DEVELOPED A starfighter except the Wendira. The "acceptable losses" required to carry out a successful fighter strike were anathema to any race that didn't have an intelligent subspecies that was easily trained via genetic memory and grew to adulthood in four Terran years.

The Laian data revealed another downside Harriet hadn't guessed, too: the reason even the Core Powers didn't have starships running point-seven-cee drives was that the internal warping effects, unnoticeable except when transitioning to hyperspace at lower speeds, became far more dangerous.

The internal warping was part of why missiles only had limited lifespans, but there were ways to adjust for it. Those ways just weren't enough at point seven cee, which meant every time one of the Wendira Drones strapped on a starfighter, they were easily cutting months or years off their life expectancy.

She didn't think most of the races in the A!Tol Imperium could be convinced to sign on for that. *Some* humans, probably. Harriet had no illusions about what some people could be convinced to do, but she doubted they could get enough people to sign on to make it worth it.

The Wendira had an entire short-lived subspecies whose only hope for immortality was to be remembered. The Drones had produced many of the Wendira's great heroes, artists, and musicians from that drive to survive past their own deaths.

They'd also marched to those deaths in countless droves along the way, and that was what the fighter pilots in Alpha Centauri were doing.

"Initiating missile engagement," Ikil reported. Green icons marking the missile salvo speckled Harriet's display, and she watched in silence.

The main Wendira force was still hanging back, watching for someone they'd regard as an actual threat to appear. The starfighters continued their advance, ignoring the Imperial missiles as they swarmed out.

Harriet didn't expect them to be ignored forever. Her missiles might be obsolete by Core standards, but they were still more than deadly enough to wipe the starfighters from existence if they hit.

She watched the range counters drop, waiting for the response she knew had to come.

When the fighters finally responded, it was over in the blink of an eye. Their plasma cannons went live at two light-seconds, firing near-lightspeed packets of energized matter at the incoming missiles. By the time the packets and missiles intercepted, they were barely a light-second away from the fighters—and the starfighters were continuing to fire.

The entire exchange lasted two seconds from the moment the starfighters opened fire to the last handful of missiles missing their targets and flying off into deep space.

There were definite gaps in the Wendira formation, entire wings of starfighters obliterated as dozens of missiles had swept through... but they weren't large gaps.

"Ikil? Analysis?" she asked.

"We destroyed approximately one hundred and fifty fighters," the Indiri replied after a moment. "Second salvo impact in ten seconds." Ikil sighed wetly. "Their anti-missile doctrine is extremely effective, and the fighters themselves are maneuverable enough to require multiple missiles for a guaranteed kill."

"Keep hammering them," Harriet ordered. "And stand by the pre-deployed swarm. Make sure to coordinate it with our onboard launchers."

"Stand by, launching...now."

Harriet's fleet fired again, another two thousand missiles streaming into space. This time, however, the over *forty* thousand missiles they'd preplaced joined the salvo. Tens of thousands of missiles lunged in at their targets.

"That's strange," Ikil murmured.

"Commander?"

"Their defense against the second salvo was measurably less effective." He paused. "The Militia ships targeted the central forma-tion of each Grand Wing. It appears they succeeded in removing at least some of the strike leaders."

"Duplicate Kurzman's targeting orders," Harriet barked. "Hit the bastards with everything we've got."

"The preplaced missiles launched too late," the Indiri admitted slowly. "They'll launch their missiles simultaneously with that intercept."

"Damn," she said mildly. "Make sure everybody knows. We need to stay alive."

This time, the starfighters reacted. Forty thousand missiles required more than sheer arrogance as a defensive measure. The formations split, arcing wider and taller as they expanded, forcing the missile swarm to expand as well.

With over twenty missiles per starfighter, however, the missiles easily spread out to cover their prey. If there was any chance at all that Harriet's people were going to survive this, it was going to be in this single overwhelming strike.

Then the starfighters launched their own missiles, faster and deadlier than Harriet's fleet's weapons. There were still enough of them that almost four thousand missiles leapt at the defenders—a mere tenth of the salvo crashing down on the starfighters, but each missile carried twice as much force and was easily half again smarter.

The mass salvo smashed into the starfighters moments later, too late to prevent what Harriet knew was going to be at least the decimation of her fleet. Thousands of the Imperial missiles exploded as plasma bursts hammered into them.

Thousands more simply missed. The interface drive didn't require continuous vectors. Complex and random evasive maneuvers were easily done, the starfighters dancing around the deadly weapons trying to kill them.

Fifteen hundred starfighters died in a single moment of fiery glory. Another hundred evaded long enough to buy themselves fractions of a second more—but no more.

One second, two thousand starfighters swarmed towards the defending fleet.

The next, a mere four hundred charged.

And then it was the Imperium's turn. Two thousand missiles swept in at eighty-five percent of the speed of light. Buckler drones and Sword turrets sprang to life, but the weapons had been targeted with malicious foresight.

The starfighters hadn't been relying on the missiles to kill Harriet's fleet. They'd left that job for themselves. The missiles' role was to clear the path.

Buckler drones died first. Then destroyers. Then cruisers, as the missiles hammered a spike of fire through the triple-echelon defense network. Half of Harriet's destroyers were gone along with six of her Imperial cruisers—and the starfighters charged into the hole their missiles had torn.

They'd missed the two remaining *Thunderstorms*, though, and plasma lances lit up the gap. The lance might have been designed to kill capital ships, but the projected magnetic containment field latched on to half a dozen fighters at a time—and they had neither the shields nor the armor to survive the plasma strike.

"Target them with proton beams and Sword turrets," Harriet ordered. "Take them out!"

They came for her capital ships through the hole they'd blasted in her escorts. They ignored the fire from her remaining destroyers and cruisers, driving toward the seven capital ships at the heart of her fleet.

Somewhere along the way, whoever was left in charge of the fighter strike changed target priorities. They didn't have the strength left to punch out all seven Imperial and Terran capital ships—so they went for the weakest.

Barely three hundred starfighters reached the capital ships to clash with the proton beams and laser turrets of the heavy ships—and seventy of them hurled themselves onto each of the Imperial fast battleships.

It was over in seconds. The shattered wreck of the fighter strike, barely two hundred strong, passed Hope in a blur, leaving behind the battered defending fleet.

None of the four Imperial fast battleships survived to see them leave.

EMPEROR OF CHINA hadn't made it through unscratched, and Pat coughed against the acrid smoke as the ship's air circulators desperately tried to stabilize the burning odors on the flag deck. No one was injured—electrical backlash wasn't going to risk lives in the most protected areas of the ship—but multiple breakers and fuses had blown to create a terrible smell.

He sealed up his emergency helmet, taking a long breath of reserve oxygen, and then opened it again. His "uniform" contained hours of air, but it was better preserved for actual need—as opposed to avoiding the smell of burning wires.

"Anything critical, Captain Fang?" he asked his flag captain.

"Negative," the other man replied shortly. "We weren't their primary target; we were just a target of opportunity of what was left of the strike that took out *Oceanfang*. Our shields got overloaded and we took some hits along critical power infrastructure, hence the blackouts, but we're already back up on the secondaries."

"And how long for full primary function to be restored?" Pat asked carefully.

"Six minutes," the Captain said immediately. "Drones are out laying new wiring as we speak, and we have a team moving in several spare high-density power conduits. Some systems will be running on backup fuses for longer, but the primary power lines will be back in place in six minutes."

"Thank you, Captain."

He stood, crossing to the main hologram and studying it carefully. All six of the destroyers lost had been Militia ships. *His* ships, commanded by men and women he'd known for years. The seven Imperial cruisers and four fast battleships weren't unimportant, but he could name twenty people who'd died on those destroyers he would have considered friends.

And yet.

"We got off lucky," he said softly into his channel with Tanaka. "They came in fat, dumb and happy."

"Their Grand Wings' commanders were in the middle of their formation, easy targets," she agreed. "They didn't go for true dispersed defensive formations until we threw forty thousand missiles at them. They didn't think this was going to be a real fight."

"And they paid for it," Pat said, studying the loss figures. Nine Grand Wings had launched the assault, twenty-three hundred starfighters. Two hundred and six had survived to return to the star hives.

"So did we," Tanaka reminded him. "They won't be that arrogant again, which means even one star hive's wing will be enough next time."

"Overconfidence is a flimsy shield," he agreed. "One I'd love for them to rely on some more."

"They won't," she said flatly. "The Wendira keep fighting the Laians, and neither of them has actually managed anything more than a bloody draw yet. That's not the sign of a fleet that makes too many mistakes."

"Other than repeatedly fighting the same enemy, that is?" Pat asked.

"There's that. I don't suppose Admiral Villeneuve has magically called you to give you an update on his progress?"

"No," he admitted. "Three to five hours. That's our earliest relief. Tan!Shallegh?"

"Three cycles. Seventy hours, minimum," Tanaka replied. "We'll do what we can, Pat."

"We will. Any brilliant suggestions?"

"Let me know if you think of any," the Imperial officer told him. "I'm fresh out past 'die standing.'"

"I don't like that one much."

"Neither do I."

CHAPTER FORTY-ONE

"So, THAT'S WHAT IT'S *SUPPOSED* TO LOOK LIKE," PIOTR HAN SAID dryly as the Wendira started moving again. "Dispersed, rapidly rotating formations. We can't get a solid lock on numbers, and our missile targeting data is going to be trash."

"Not to mention what we can see suggests that at least a portion of the strike has sacrificed their missiles for electronic warfare and antimissile pods," Ikil added. "Seeing this, I am almost insulted at how poorly they estimated us."

"Given how badly they hurt us when they underestimated us, I'm not complaining," Harriet told the Indiri analyst. "What are we looking at?"

"They're still holding one Grand Wing back to protect the star hives," Han reported. "They're making up any shortfall by anchoring their attack with four of those battleships. It's going to hold back their fighters, but it also means they're more likely to survive to missile launch."

"And beyond," Harriet concluded. "Do we have a chance in hell of hurting those battleships? The Laians gave us data on them as well, right?"

Ikil blinked his heavy-lidded eyes and gestured. The tactical display shrank on the main hologram, allowing the fleet tactical officer to add a display of a shape that reminded Harriet of nothing so much as a dog turd, a double-ended series of circles growing to the largest at the middle.

"We're not sure of the class," he concluded. "But all of their ships share a similar range of defenses.

"They have heavy, single-piece, compressed-matter armor hulls with a higher compression ratio than ours. They are manufactured in place as a single shell, removing the vulnerability our vessels have along the join lines.

"The primary disadvantage to this is cost and time. It produces a superior defense but not *that* superior, so even the Wendira restrict it to their battleships," Ikil said. "The additional compression is a bigger problem; it provides significantly greater tensile strength and impact resistance. Their hulls are approximately six times as damage-resistant as *Duchess of Terra's*."

And that was despite the battleships being seven million tons smaller. This was going to be unpleasant.

"Their shields, in turn, are relatively inferior by Core Power standards, as are their active defenses."

"And what does that mean from our Arm Power standards?" Harriet asked dryly.

"Nothing good. Their shield generators are roughly fifty percent more powerful on a ton-for-ton basis. Depending on the class, they could be roughly equivalent to *Duchess's* or slightly superior. Active defenses are based around rapid-fire plasma cannon similar to those used by their fighters, roughly equivalent to modern Laian systems."

"So, three hundred or so years more advanced than ours," she concluded.

"Ours have proven more effective than we expected from the Core Powers' focus on plasma defenses," Ikil pointed out. "The Sword turrets on our capital ships were responsible for a large portion of their starfighter losses on the final pass.

"Apparently, our lasers are effective against their fighters."

"That's good to know," Harriet allowed. "I don't suppose we could just fling all of our Bucklers at them and have them destroy the starfighters?"

"The Bucklers would inevitably be localized and destroyed by long-range proton-beam fire," Han interjected. "Their effective range is far lower than traditional energy weapons."

"I know," Harriet said gently. "I'm looking for miracles, gentlemen. What have you got for me?"

Han and Ikil exchanged a long look.

"Ship for ship, those battleships are equal to *Duchess* and her consorts," Ikil said finally. "They've sent four ships. We have three. They have seven hundred and fifty starfighters. We have six destroyers and twenty-one cruisers."

"They have a three- to four-century technological advantage," Han added. "If they haven't chosen to send in more tonnage, they don't think they need it. They might still be underestimating us, but..."

"But they might not be," Harriet agreed. "No miracles, huh?"

"I suggest we focus fire on the battleships from the beginning," Ikil told her. "We can handle the starfighters' missile salvo easily enough; it's their gun pass that's going to hurt us. Killing one of the battleships is far more likely to make them pause and reconsider than even wiping the fighters out will."

"It's the best plan any of us have so far," she admitted. "Make it happen."

THE WENDIRA BATTLESHIPS opened fire from well beyond the defenders' range, showing the single advantage that Harriet's people had over the incoming aliens. The four battleships had as many launchers between them as her three super-battleships—but they still had the cruisers and remaining destroyers.

The attacker's launchers were enough better to make up much of the difference, but the Wendira still only had four hundred launchers to the defenders' thousand.

"We've reestablished the triple echelon," Ikil informed her. "We're basically out of Buckler drones, Echelon Lord. If we survive this, we'll be running low on ammunition, too."

"Kurzman brought colliers with him, didn't he?" Harriet asked, grateful for the distraction but still keeping one eye on the incoming missiles. "Check with his staff; see how many missiles and drones they still have aboard."

"The Wendira will need to give us time to get rearmed," the Indiri officer warned her. "That's...unlikely."

"We'll do what we have to. If we're still alive after this, maybe we'll have bought some respect from our enemies."

Duchess of Terra trembled under her feet as she spoke, the big ship's launchers returning fire as the Wendira capital ships entered her own range.

Moments later, the Wendira missiles hit her defensive perimeter and the Bucklers lit up. Her holograms drew in the invisible lasers as clean white lines, marking the deaths of missiles with sparks.

There weren't nearly as many missiles this time, but the battleship's weapons were just as fast and had more time to get the feel of the defenses as they approached. They also, unless Harriet missed her assessment, had better electronic warfare and brains in general.

The first salvo was targeted on the drones themselves, too. That appeared to be something the Imperium was going to have to incorporate into its doctrine, Harriet realized, as almost her entire outer layer of defensive drones was wiped out in the first few seconds.

"Captain Sier." She opened a channel to her flag captain. "Deploy our remaining drones and send them forward; pass off control to the escorts."

"Yes, Echelon Lord," the Yin confirmed immediately.

It wouldn't buy them much. The second salvo arrived before the new drones were in place, and this one hammered into the second layer of drones—the one interlaced with her escorts.

Several of the cruisers took hits, their shields shrugging them aside so far, but they lost even more drones.

"They're clearing a path for the starfighter missiles to take out our escorts," Harriet concluded aloud. They needed the defense in depth to survive the missile strikes, but it left their escorts vulnerable.

"Pull them back," she snapped, making a decision. "Formation Bravo-Three. Interlace the drone nets."

They'd regain some of what they lost in depth in redundancy—and in having the super-battleships' Sword turrets cover the escorts.

"We're out of replacement drones," Han reported. "Every Buckler we or the Militia brought has been deployed. Every one they kill now makes us more vulnerable."

Their own salvos were beginning to strike home, blasting through the Wendira drones and antimissile lasers with sheer numbers. They were losing over ninety percent of their missiles—but that still left the lead battleship taking a hundred missiles at a time.

Unfortunately, like *Duchess of Terra* herself, the Wendira ship could take that. For a time.

Potentially for long enough.

"Fighter-missile range in thirty seconds."

Harriet nodded. The capital-ship missile duel was a draw so far, but in this case, draws went to the Wendira. They were keeping her defenses focused on the incoming missiles, and they were about to add another two thousand missiles—a swarm she wasn't going to be able to stop.

"Order all ships to maneuver as needed for their own survival," she said quietly. "Our first objective must be to stay alive."

Even as she spoke, however, two of her cruisers' shields failed. They were the ones without the upgrades. No onboard antimissile defenses. No compressed-matter armor plates. Their shields failed and the missiles swarmed through—and the cruisers died in balls of fire as fusion and antimatter cores alike lost containment.

"Fighter launch in ten seconds," Han reported.

Everything she could do was done. Now all that was left was to see if her people could weather the storm.

And then the lead Wendira battleship, its shield strained but intact under the pounding of her fleet's missiles, lurched as if it had collided with something in space. Explosions glittered across her shields with no apparent source—and then her strained shields collapsed and missiles continued to appear out of nowhere, streaming into the gap and smashing her armor to pieces with the brilliant flash of warheads of some kind.

One moment, she was the lead incarnation of the death of Harriet's fleet.

The next, she was an expanding ball of vapor as multiple antimatter explosions obliterated her frontal armor and gutted her interior.

"*NANTEKOTTA I?!*" Harriet cursed. "Ikil! What am I seeing?"

"I am not certain," the Indiri replied. "We have no source for those missiles."

"They're emerging from hyperspace," Han reported. "The portals are brief and tiny, easy to miss, but when there's dozens of them..."

"Hyperspace missiles? From where?" Harriet demanded.

"Unknown," the junior officer said. "Their velocity is crap after emergence, maybe point one cee, but they're carrying twenty-*gigaton* antimatter warheads."

The Wendira battleships clearly had a defensive strategy for this situation. They were going *much* more evasive now, forcing the FTL missiles to make terminal approaches after emergence. They still only had fractions of a second, but those fractions were enough for the antimissile plasma cannon to do their work.

"They're not having much luck with the starfighters, though," Ikil said. "Their standard evasive pattern is too much. Whoever they are, they're pushing the battleships, but the fighters are almost untouched."

A second battleship's shields flickered under the pounding but came back up. The underlying armor absorbed a series of explosions that Harriet was quite certain would have destroyed *Duchess,* and the battleship continued to maneuver.

At least they were no longer firing at her fleet.

"There!" Han barked. "Two light-minutes away, sixty-six by one-forty-five by two-fifty."

The hologram shifted, lighting up with four new ships.

"I make it three Mesharom Frontier Fleet battlecruisers...and the Duchy of Terra ship *Tornado,*" Ikil added to his junior's report. "The Frontier Fleet vessels are the source of the hyper missiles."

"And the Wendira have seen them as well," Harriet said as she watched the fighter strike swarming towards her turn and head towards the new ships. "Why did no one see them?"

"They were running stealth fields up until the moment they fired," Ikil told her. "Even the Mesharom can't fire with a stealth field up, but it let them get within range of their hyper missiles."

"Gods. Hyperspace-capable missiles." Harriet shook her head. "Can we handle the remaining regular missiles heading our way?"

"I think so. It appears the Mesharom have now become the focus of our new friends' attention."

"Echelon Lord, incoming transmission from *Tornado,*" Piditel told her. "Broadband, addressed to you and Admiral Kurzman."

"Everyone is going to see it. On the main display."

The image of Annette Bond, managing to convey a cheerful pregnant glow despite looking utterly exhausted, appeared in the hologram.

"Echelon Lord Tanaka, Vice Admiral Kurzman. I hope at least one of you is still alive. Pull back to Hope and maintain a defensive perimeter. The Mesharom have promised to deal with the Wendira.

"The price was...obvious," she said softly. "But in the end, we find ourselves with little choice and I'd rather *sell* that damn ship than have it *taken*. *Tornado* will rendezvous with you in Hope orbit.

"The Frontier Fleet detachment will see what they can do about the Wendira and then meet us there as well."

Bond shook her head.

"I doubt I need to tell you this people, but you've done damned well and I only need one more thing from you today: stay alive until we get there!"

Cheers echoed around the flag deck, and even Harriet found herself grinning.

"Well, people, *that* is one order from a civilian I think we're all perfectly happy to obey!"

CHAPTER FORTY-TWO

In theory, the hyperfold communicator the Mesharom had given them should have been air-gapped from *Tornado*'s computers, rendered unable to communicate with the Terran warship's systems.

The ability to stay in live communication with her allies, however, had resulted in Annette overriding that entirely sensible precaution. She *needed* to know what the Mesharom were up to.

And it wasn't like the limited information on, say, BugWorks Two, aboard *Tornado* wasn't already limited to stand-alone computers with no wireless connection and no physical link to the main systems.

While she suspected that wasn't necessarily *enough* to protect it, that was also why there was almost nothing about BugWorks Two anywhere outside the actual project itself.

For now, she was prepared to risk the Mesharom learning a few of Terra's medium-priority secrets to be able to see what they saw as the battle for Alpha Centauri continued to unfold.

"We're getting better information from the system net than we are from the Mesharom," Amandine told her. "That's...interesting."

"We're getting *more detailed* information from our system sensor net than we are from them," Annette corrected. "They're providing real-time data within a thirty-light-second radius of their ships, which is *insane*.

"But we have this system heavily seeded with scanner platforms. I'd be shocked if we weren't getting more detailed data from that."

The Mesharom used some form of scanner that Annette understood to be basically the tachyon equivalent of active radar. Its range was limited, significantly less than the hyper missiles they were pounding the Wendira with.

That was part of what was allowing the Wendira to *survive*. If the Mesharom had real-time data on their targets, they'd be massacring their enemy.

With their data almost two minutes old, however, even their faster-than-light missiles had a massive potential radius for the enemy to be in at emergence. Annette had to admit she'd expected the weapons to be more effective than they were.

"Those battleships are falling back to the main formation," Commander Yeong Song, Amandine's Chinese tactical officer, announced. Like many of the massive Chinese contingent in the Duchy of Terra Militia, the tall, gaunt woman had been a member of the China Party's secret fleet. Instead of serving on one of the officially nonexistent battleships built to protect China from a rogue UESF, however, she now served on the military of Earth's externally imposed world government.

"And the fighters?" Annette asked.

"They're heading right for the Mesharom. Adamase's people are focusing their fire on them, but..."

"But those starfighters are almost impossible targets for hyper missiles," Annette finished for her. "I'm guessing that isn't an accident."

"The Wendira would have known more about the Mesharom's abilities than we would—and the Laians, for that matter."

They now had the data on the battle in this system, or at least enough of it to know that the Laians were clearly using hyperfold energy projectors as their main energy weapons.

The Mesharom hadn't given humanity specifications for those. They'd just given Bond the specifications for the communicator...and some very large hints as to how to transform an instantaneous communicator with a forty-light-year range into an instantaneous energy weapon over a much more limited distance.

"That's how they fought the Laians and won," Amandine said. "They designed a weapon that even FTL systems couldn't easily counteract."

"Watch for when they reach the range of the tachyon scanners," Annette suggested. "That will be the real test."

"We'll be joining Tanaka and Kurzman's formation before then," *Tornado*'s Captain replied. "Whatever happens next, Your Grace, you'll be as safe as we can make you."

"That's not always the main point, Captain," she said.

"No," he agreed. "That's why I agreed to your damn risky 'diplomatic mission,' Your Grace. But the mission is done; we've made a deal with the Mesharom. Now I'm going to get you behind as many super-battleships as I can find!"

Annette chuckled, shaking her head.

"All right, Captain. I won't argue that—but I'll be keeping a damned close eye on this fight." She glanced back over at the display, where three alien ships prepared to face off against a thousand starfighters.

What she wasn't going to tell Amandine was that the Mesharom had only expected *one* star hive.

THE THREE BATTLECRUISERS spread out as the starfighters closed. They were focusing their fire on the incoming fighter strike now, letting the Wendira capital ships retreat beyond their range.

Unfortunately, the Wendira starfighters had been designed to fight enemies with FTL weapons. The drone pilots took full advantage of every ounce of their vessels' incredible maneuverability, carving a massive probability cone in space where they might be once the missiles arrived.

Watching the Mesharom's much-vaunted hyper missiles in action, Annette couldn't help studying their weakness as much as their strengths. The biggest was simple: their emergence point from hyperspace was set at launch. There was no way around that, no way to detect their targets during their brief journey into hyper.

The battlecruisers' weapons had barely registered on the starfighter strike at all until the Wendira strike craft crossed the thirty-light-second mark. Suddenly, instead of having data that was as much as a minute old to target their weapons, the Mesharom data was real-time.

It still took the missiles a quarter-second to enter hyperspace and then fractions of a second to cross the distance at an equivalent of several hundred times lightspeed. But instead of their target locations being half a minute out of date, they were fractions of a second out of date.

Wendira starfighters began to die by entire squadrons. Single antimatter warheads obliterated three, even four ships—but there was only time for two salvos of hyper missiles as the strike craft closed.

The fighters launched their own missiles too, moments before the Mesharom demonstrated that, like the Laians, they had hyperfold energy projectors.

Mated with the tachyon scanners, their lethality was increased tenfold. The hyper missiles killed dozens of the strike craft once they had live data. The hyperfold projectors were firing at an energy level where they could cycle multiple times a second.

Starfighters died in the *hundreds*—and so did the missiles, the Mesharom using the same weapon system for missile defense as fighter defense.

The Wendira ships and missiles were dying so fast, Annette almost didn't realize they weren't dying fast *enough*. *Tornado*'s crew were staring at the fighter strike, a dying flower of fire and light reaching toward the Frontier Fleet ships, in awe.

Annette did the math in her head and realized that some were going to get through. Dozens of starfighters. *Hundreds* of missiles.

The missiles arrived first, smashing into the battlecruiser *Secrecy* in a deadly stream. The Mesharom ship's shields were more powerful than anything anyone else in the system had, but each missile hit with the force of over twenty gigatons of TNT.

Secrecy's shields survived the missile bombardment, but only barely—and then the remaining sixty or so starfighters swept over her, pounding her shields with close-range plasma cannon.

Her shields collapsed. Plasma burned into her hull, the active matrix moving compressed-matter plates around to absorb the energy —and then the fighters followed their plasma beams in, kamikazeing the white egg-like ship.

Something failed. It might have been the hull. It might have been something in the hyperdrive or the hyperfold projectors or some system the Mesharom hadn't admitted existed to any of the younger races.

The battlecruiser simply disappeared. It didn't implode. It didn't go into stealth. It didn't break or shatter. It just...no longer existed.

And thirty-six members of the oldest and most powerful species in the galaxy went with it.

Tornado's bridge was silent.

"We are joining the super-battleship formation," Amandine finally told Annette. "We are...as secure as we can be."

WHEN HE'D FIRST SEEN the A!Tol shatter the United Earth Space Force, Pat Kurzman had *known* he faced an unstoppable force, a juggernaut that no merely human endeavor could overcome.

They'd tried anyway, *Tornado's* exile a months-long endeavor to win an impossible war.

In the end, they'd compromised, and in so doing, discovered the people behind the juggernaut that had overcome their world. They had learned to live with the A!Tol and the other races of the Imperium and fought side-by-side with them against the Kanzi, forging the kind of bonds only built by shedding blood for each other.

And in doing so, they'd learned what their new nation feared: the Core Powers, the ancient and powerful races that ruled closer to the galactic core. And first and foremost among those Core Powers, the fickle if often friendly elders of galactic society, were the Mesharom.

Eldest and most powerful, terrifying, seemingly omniscient and omnipotent, the Mesharom were what the galaxy feared. Their quiet assistance had turned the tide when the Kanzi had attacked Sol.

As a race, they were the closest things to gods anyone had proof existed.

And they had just watched one of their warships die.

"What are the other two doing?" he finally asked as the shock began to wear off.

"Maneuvering between us and the Wendira for now," Chan reported. "Defensive position—I'm guessing they're trying to talk to the bugs."

"Good luck. The only Wendira who've even given us their names have been in chains on Hope," Pat said. "If we've got a Frontier Fleet shield, let's use it. Move the colliers up. Rearm everybody as best as we can and get every spare Buckler drone deployed."

"I can already tell you we don't have enough missiles for every-one," Chan warned him.

"Focus on the super-battleships," Pat decided instantly. "We can send the cruisers and destroyers running for it if we need to, but the super-BBs aren't getting out, no matter what happens."

"I'll pass it on."

A thick silence descended on *Emperor of China*'s flag bridge. The Mesharom had destroyed a single Wendira battleship when they'd arrived, so 'only' fourteen massive alien ships were staring down at Hope now.

Most of the Wendira starfighters were gone. The survivors from the first strike had returned to the star hives, coordinating with the single Grand Wing they'd kept behind when they'd launched the second wave.

Pat wouldn't be surprised to discover there were more fighters aboard the hives, but they'd gutted the capacity the Laians said the ships had.

But even without their fighters, the three star hives were hundred-million-ton warships that each carried as much weaponry as his entire fleet. Each of the nine remaining battleships, despite their smaller size, was more than an equal for each of the super-battleships among the defenders.

"What happens now?" his chief of staff asked softly.

"We find out if the Mesharom are as convincing as they are isolationist," Pat admitted. "And then, I suspect, we find out if the Mesharom technological edge is enough to overcome a twenty-to-one tonnage disadvantage."

"What if it's not?"

Pat winced.

"Then I'm afraid we may well be back to 'die standing' as a battle plan."

HAROLD WAS ALONE in the control center now; the entire dig site camp having emptied completely. A single shuttle waited for him, one that he would pilot himself when the time came.

Or so he'd understood, anyway.

"You do realize, Captain, that the transmitter is capable of activating the charges from orbit," Captain Naheed Sommers told him as he stepped into the center.

"I do," he agreed. "But it feels like someone should be here to watch the thing, regardless of what happens."

"Perhaps," Sommers agreed. "But I promise you, Captain, the

good archaeologist will be very, *very* pissed off if you blow yourself up."

"I wasn't planning on it," Harold told him. "It just feels weird to walk away after everything we've done to hold this place."

"I'll give you that," the Guard officer confirmed. He offered the Militia officer a flask. "Whisky?"

Harold took the flask and took a long swallow.

"Ah. Good scotch."

"Don't let the face fool you," Sommers told him with a grin, waving at his dark skin tone. "I grew up in Edinburgh. I know my scotch. And I know my idiot clansmen, be they Scot or Norse. You catch my drift, Captain?"

Harold chuckled.

"Yeah, I do. Habit, I guess. I lost my ship today and I wasn't even there to command her—and I'm not used to having anything else to live for."

"Dr. Wolastoq would strongly object to the idea that you have nothing to live for, I suspect," Captain Sommers replied. "As, I imagine, would our good Duchess, along with your military superiors.

"Besides, you may hold the trigger, but do you want to be the one who decides to push that button?"

"No," Harold admitted after another slug of whisky. "But this day just gets worse and worse. A Mesharom cruiser destroyed? I don't know what the consequences of that are going to be."

"The Wendira's problem, not ours," the other man said. "But I think you want to pass that trigger on to Her Grace. And then you and I, Captain Rolfson, should joined our men in New Hope City."

Sommers turned a bright white smile on him.

"Because, to be perfectly honest, you have about two minutes before I stun you and drag you onto that shuttle myself—and I, my dear Captain, am an *atrocious* pilot."

Rolfson chuckled again and passed the flask back.

"Go start the warmup," he ordered. "I'll call Her Grace. Let's get this hot potato to someone else."

He waited for Sommers to leave, studying the transmitter in front of him. Once he was alone again, he opened a channel to *Tornado*.

"This is Militia Captain Harold Rolfson. I need to speak to Duchess Bond, Alpha-One Priority."

"Hold one," the communications officer replied. "I'll get Her Grace into a privacy shell."

Harold waited impatiently, but it only took ten, maybe fifteen seconds to get Bond on the line.

"Rolfson. You're alive; good," the Duchess told him crisply. "I saw that *Liberty* was gone and wasn't sure. It's not been a good day for old friends."

"No," he agreed. "Ma'am, the ship is secure, but we've evacuated the area. We're relying on the orbital forces to keep any further landing forces from coming in."

"Everyone seems to have given up on subtle at this point, Captain. But... Evacuated? Why?"

"I don't know what deal we've cut with the Mesharom, but we wanted to make sure no one took the ship without our permission," Harold told her softly.

"What did you do?" Bond asked.

"We rigged six hundred-megaton antimatter demolition charges inside the hull," he said. "One word from you and the damn thing everyone's fighting over blows to vapor."

Bond was silent for a long moment.

"And where are *you*, Captain?" she asked.

"About to jump in a shuttle to get out of the blast radius," he told her. "I'm forwarding you the detonation codes over an encrypted side channel. It's your call what to do with them, and I'm perfectly glad to off-load the damn things on you."

"Get out of there, Captain," Bond ordered. "I promised the Mesharom the ship in exchange for technology and their help holding Centauri, so I'd rather not blow it to hell...but thank you.

"The option may open some doors we thought were closed."

CHAPTER FORTY-THREE

ADMIRAL JEAN VILLENEUVE WAS NOT A RELIGIOUS MAN. HE'D been raised in a household of traditional French secularists, with any form of the divine a distant afterthought at best. That Jean wasn't an outright atheist was mostly a matter of religion not being important enough in his life to even deny it.

At that particular moment, however, he was grateful to whatever divinity did exist. There was a huge variation in just how much the currents of hyperspace moved, and in his experience, they were always slower than hoped when needed.

This time, however, the current near to Sol and Alpha Centauri had gone from unusually uncooperative to unusually *cooperative*— and his fleet was arriving early.

Hopefully early enough.

"Hyper portal in ninety seconds. All hands to battle stations. All hands to battle stations."

The announcement echoed through *Empereur de France.*

Jean took one last check of the formation. It was a strange one: four super-battleships, three battleships, the four Imperial cruisers and eight Terran destroyers. Only a handful more escorts than capital ships.

Echelon Lord Kas!Val was being surprisingly cooperative, a much-appreciated concession on the part of an A!Tol who had made few friends in Sol. He dared to hope that the alien was as concerned over the state of affairs as he was.

"Standing by all sensors," Tidikat told him. With the surrender of his ships to the Republic, Jean had coopted the Laian Commodore as his new chief of staff. There was no one in the Militia with as solid an understanding of the enemies they faced.

"We'll have a complete sweep of the system as soon as we arrive, subject to lightspeed delays. It'll take us a few seconds to resolve the situation, but we should have you updated as quickly as possible."

"Thank you, Tidikat," Jean replied. Seconds ticked away.

"Emergence," Captain Ruan announced loudly over the intercom. "Brace for evasive maneuvers."

In theory, the warning was unnecessary. None of the superbattleship's maneuvers should impact the ship. But it was always possible something would go wrong.

Jean ignored the warning anyway, focusing on the holographic displays as his staff analyzed the incoming light. The planets were there immediately, the display updating with current information as they received it.

Ships followed. First the ones they'd expected, the joint Imperial-Militia fleet in Hope orbit. That fleet was much smaller than it should have been, and Jean swallowed a moment of bile. There should have been eight capital ships, but only three stood guard over humanity's colony.

Half the destroyers and cruisers were missing too. Hope's defenders had been badly handled—but one of the icons flagged as *Tornado* as he watched. Bond was there.

And so were the Mesharom. Two white battlecruisers appeared on the display, floating between Hope's defenders and...the enemy.

"*Mon dieu,*" he cursed softly. Over a dozen warships, the smallest of them the same mass as his *Manticore*-class battleships. The largest were Wendira star hives, a hundred million tons of death and war.

"Task force will move to Hope orbit," he ordered loudly. "We will rendezvous with Tanaka and Kurzman and check in with Her Grace."

Jean shook his head, sharing a surprisingly meaningful glance with the alien standing to his right.

"Hopefully, someone can explain just what the *hell* is going on," he murmured.

HARRIET BREATHED a massive sigh of relief as the unexpected hyper portal unleashed clearly Terran and Imperial ships. The Militia ships had emerged well out of range of any of the alien forces in the system and were now heading in the direction of Hope at flank speed.

"Scans make four super-battleships, three battleships, four cruisers and eight destroyers," Han reported. "Cruisers and one battleship are flying Imperial IFF codes."

"Echelon Lord, we are receiving a transmission for you from Echelon Lord Kas!Val," Piditel reported. The Rekiki paused. "For your attention only."

"Understood. Activating privacy shield," Harriet told them.

The screen that dropped around her wasn't perfect, but it was the best solution that didn't require her to leave the flag deck—and with the continuing standoff between the Mesharom and the Wendira, she wasn't going to do that.

The image of her A!Tol superior appeared on her chair screens, Kas!Val's skin dark green with determination.

"Echelon Lord Tanaka, the situation in this system is a mess," she said without preamble. "Brief me immediately. I will assume command once we reach orbit."

That was the entire message. Harriet sighed. She didn't even need to check—she knew Kas!Val had several long-cycles' seniority over her, though it was not generally considered acceptable to relieve the commander on the scene like this.

She couldn't *refuse*, however, and thankfully, Villeneuve still possessed the more powerful force. Unless the A!Tol was truly out of line, she would continue to defer to the Terran Admiral.

Hierarchy limited her options to one: obey.

"Echelon Lord," she greeted Kas!Val. "The situation in this system is complicated. We have been attacked by forces of both the Laian Republic and the Wendira Grand Swarm. Elements of the Mesharom Frontier Fleet are now assisting us after negotiations with Duchess Bond with regards to the ancient ship the colonists found.

"You will need to validate the exact details of the deal with Duchess Bond. She was charged by the Empress with handling the necessary affairs, but my understanding is that we are surrendering the ship to the Mesharom in exchange for their help defending this system and certain technological concessions.

"I strongly recommend that we remain in a purely defensive formation for the moment but assist the Mesharom if the Wendira do attack again."

Harriet paused the recording, considering if there was anything else she could add. "Please don't do anything arrogant and stupid" wasn't a politically wise addition, she supposed, so she swallowed her fear and sent the message.

Only time would tell now.

"THE MATH still isn't in our favor," Amandine pointed out.

"I know," Annette agreed. Villeneuve's force tripled the Imperial fleet presence, but she was under no illusion that the Imperial forces here were the deciding factor. The newly augmented combined Imperial Navy and Duchy of Terra Militia force could probably handle, oh, half of the battleships.

One of the three star hives might be doable. Maybe. Certainly not all three of them with battleship support.

Her best guess was that the two Mesharom battlecruisers were roughly equivalent in firepower now to the combined Imperial force. That added up to a roughly three-to-two advantage in firepower for the Wendira.

They were being hesitant to press that advantage, but she didn't expect that to last forever. The only reason they were hesitant at all, she suspected, was because they were used to only losing starfighters in most battles.

Wendira Drones, after all, were expendable in a way that their Warriors and Royals weren't.

"Your Grace, we have a private communication channel from Echelon Lord Kas!Val for you," Amandine told her.

"Put it through to the flag office. I'll take it there," she said. "If anything starts happening, let me know immediately."

It took her a few moments to reach the office, and Kas!Val's image was waiting for her. The Imperial ship was now close enough for only a few seconds' delay.

"Duchess Bond," Kas!Val greeted her. "I have been briefed by Tanaka, and I have to ask: what in darkest waters did you think you were doing?"

"Echelon Lord," Annette said flatly. "I believe I was doing my job, as charged by *our* Empress."

"Tanaka informs me that you have agreed to simply let the Mesharom *take* the ship?" the A!Tol asked.

"One way or another, the Mesharom were going to take it," she said slowly. She couldn't tell Kas!Val what Ki!Tana had told her. That was a secret that was supposed to have died with Empress A!Ana, after all.

"We can't stop Frontier Fleet from seizing it or destroying it at their will," Annette continued. "The only way to protect the colony was to surrender the ship—and the Mesharom agreed to provide protection and technological assistance in exchange for it."

"That ship is vastly more advanced than even the Mesharom," Kas!Val replied. "No technological assistance they could give us would be worth giving up that ship."

"Not losing two hundred thousand people was worth giving up that ship alone," the Duchess snapped. "Our oaths, Echelon Lord, are to guard the Imperium's people."

"Sometimes, sacrifices must be made. That ship is worth *everything*."

"The deal is already made, Kas!Val. Our Empress gave me the charge to negotiate here."

"She charged you to *defend the ship*," Kas!Val replied. "It is a strategic military asset of the Imperium. You have no authority to simply give it away, Duchess Bond. You are a *civilian* and the deal you made was outside your authority."

"That was not what Empress A!Shall told me," Annette said, a chill running down her spine. Just what did Kas!Val plan on doing?

"I will be taking command of all naval forces in this system," the Echelon Lord told her. "We will attempt to extend the tides until Fleet Lord Tan!Shallegh arrives, but let me be clear as summer waters, Duchess Bond: we will *not* surrender that ship.

"Not to the Wendira.

"Not to the Laian Republic.

"Not to the Mesharom—and not to a backwater Duchess with delusions of grand authority!"

THE CHANNEL CUT before Annette could even respond, and all she could do was sit at the empty desk, staring at the spot where the hologram of the tentacled *idiot* had been a moment before.

Kas!Val was about to betray the Imperium's word because *she* was convinced she knew better than anyone else.

The Mesharom wouldn't care about her reasons. They wouldn't

care about the internal politics, the tenuous position of the newborn Duchy of Terra inside the A!Tol Imperium.

They would only know that the A!Tol Imperium had broken its deal with them. The tenuous favor extended to the Imperium because of the blood Ki!Tana's past self had shed on their behalf would shatter in a moment.

And Hope would burn.

"Ki!Tana, can you come to the flag office, please?" Annette asked over the com. She brought up a display of the system as she continued to try and see a way out of this. The Militia ships had reached Hope orbit now, *Empereur de France* and her consorts sliding in around *Emperor of China* while *A Dawning of Swords* moved in between Tanaka's super-battleships.

The display didn't show her any answers. The horrendous technological and tonnage balance didn't change. The deal she'd cut with the Mesharom was the only thing that might save them, but Kas!Val was going to throw it away.

"What is it, Annette?" her first alien friend said, the door closing behind her as the massive A!Tol slid into the room.

"Kas!Val has decided the ship is of too great importance for a 'a backwater Duchess with delusions of grand authority' to be making the decision about its fate," Annette said woodenly. "She has declared it an Imperial strategic asset and will be taking command of all Imperial forces in the system, with no intent of surrendering the ship to anyone."

"*Blood tide.*"

"Given what I understand of Mesharom espionage technology, they likely already know this," Annette continued. "What are they going to *do*?"

Ki!Tana's skin had gone from blue (questioning or curious) to purple (sadness or stress) to black while Annette had spoken. Pure black, an inky fear-spawned black Annette had rarely seen on her friend before.

"If Adamase believes you will not keep your word, they will

destroy the ship," the A!Tol said flatly. "And anyone who tries to stop them. They will set their hyper missiles to emerge inside the planet and shatter the crust, breaking Hope into millions of pieces to make certain any fragments of the technology of Those Who Came Before are irretrievable."

The Mesharom feared the death of galactic civilization. The deaths of a few hundred thousand—demonstrably, even a few *billion* —were a small price to pay to protect those untold teeming trillions from the fate of Those Who Came Before.

"What do we do?" Annette asked hopelessly.

"Convince Kas!Val to honor the deal."

"She legitimately has command authority over every warship in this system. There is no one who can override her, no one who can relieve her, until Tan!Shallegh arrives."

"Which won't be for days," Ki!Tana agreed. "Annette...you *have* to stop her. At any cost."

"We can't arrest her. I could probably talk Jean into destroying *A Dawning of Swords*, but..."

"The Empress couldn't let that pass. Earth would face the full might of the Imperium again, and that's not a battle you can win."

Annette studied the hologram again, a blinking orange light on the planet marking the crashed ship...and a second icon attached to it, representing the codes Rolfson had sent her.

"There is one more option."

CHAPTER FORTY-FOUR

Once *Empereur de France* and *President de Gaulle* had moved into position to flank *Emperor of China*, Jean Villeneuve allowed himself a small moment of unadulterated relief. With every Duchy of Terra Militia capital ship in one place, they were about as safe as they were going to be.

The Mesharom battlecruisers halfway between them and the Wendira allowed another layer of safety and relief. He was aware of the odds even with the aliens' assistance, but their presence seemed to be making the Wendira hesitate.

And then the all-ships transmission came from *A Dawning of Swords*.

Kas!Val faced the camera directly, her skin the dark green of furious determination.

"All ships, this is Echelon Lord Kas!Val," she introduced herself, in case someone *didn't* know who she was. "As the senior Imperial Navy officer in this system, I am taking command of all Imperial forces and executing levy authority on the Duchy of Terra Militia.

"All Imperial and Militia ships are now under my authority. You will link to *A Dawning of Swords'* command net and provide full updates on your status, repairs and munitions supply.

"The defense of the Hope colony and the protection of the unimaginably valuable strategic asset discovered on the Corellian Plateau are our absolute priority," she continued. "Under no circumstances will we risk the colony or the Precursor ship.

"All non-Imperial vessels in the system are to be regarded as potentially hostile and not permitted within one light-minute of Hope. I will have further orders once I have reviewed the full status of our forces.

"Thank you."

Empereur de France's flag deck was silent.

"Sir," Tidikat said slowly. "Can she *do* that?"

"Yes, Commodore," Jean admitted to the Laian. "The Duchy Militias exist, at least theoretically, as a reserve for the Imperial Navy. She has the right as an Imperial flag officer to take command of our forces alongside her own.

"And as the senior officer, yes, she can take command precedence over Echelon Lord Tanaka."

Tidikat was silent again.

"Admiral?" Captain Ruan appeared on Jean's chair repeater screens. "What do we do?"

"What the Echelon Lord commands," he told his flag captain. "She has the legal authority."

"But I thought we had a deal with the Mesharom," Ruan said.

"We did," Jean confirmed grimly. "Unfortunately, it seems Echelon Lord Kas!Val didn't like the deal and, bluntly, we either follow her orders or go into rebellion against the Imperium."

The Laian bowed his carapaced head and stepped away, leaving Jean alone with his own thoughts and fears.

Without a word to his staff, he slammed the button that activated his privacy shield and began to issue commands. He might normally delegate to his staff, but he was perfectly capable of placing a ship-to-ship call on his own.

His call clearly surprised no one. *Tornado*'s communication staff didn't even speak to him before connecting him to Annette Bond.

"Jean," she greeted him.

"Your Grace," he said. "What do we do?"

"For now, we wait," his Duchess ordered. "We have a few irons we haven't mentioned to the Echelon Lord, but...she *has* the authority she's exerted."

"And the Mesharom?"

"I am confident that Tan!Shallegh and I have the same reading of A!Shall's instructions to me," Bond said. "Once he arrives, that situation will be resolved peacefully. We just need to make sure Kas!Val doesn't set off a galactic war before he does."

"She's arrogant and short-sighted," Jean admitted, "but I do not believe she is that stupid."

"And if the Wendira decide it's time to move?" she asked. "I don't know what Interpreter-Captain Adamase will do at that point. I am quite certain they're aware of Kas!Val's position on our agreement."

"Surely, they will still attempt to prevent the Wendira taking the ship."

"Yes. But they may choose to destroy the ship—and the planet it's on—as an easier solution," Bond said grimly. "Try and keep a leash on our Imperial friend, at least. We have even less influence on the bugs."

EVEN HAVING BEEN WARNED, it took Harriet a full minute to get past the shock of Kas!Val relieving her of command and so abruptly declaring everyone, including the Imperium's tentative allies, a threat.

Finally, though, Pat Kurzman raised her on a private channel.

"Can she do that?" he asked without preamble.

"You know she can command the Militia," she replied.

"I know that. I mean, can she actually just waltz in here and take over command of the system from you like that?"

"She's senior and she's A!Tol," Harriet admitted. "So, yes. Unfortunately."

"She's about to destroy everything."

"That's a distinct possibility," she agreed. "But for us to do anything else is mutiny. For *you* to do anything else is rebellion. The Militia may be a thousand times more powerful than the UESF was, but it's no more capable of fighting the Imperium."

"We have to do *something*, Harriet."

"There is nothing we can do," she said fatalistically. "She has the authority here, Pat. The Imperial Navy has no grounds under which I can relieve her. Once she issued those orders, my options are obedience or mutiny—and mutiny, Pat, dooms humanity one way or another."

"Damn it all," he cursed.

"Echelon Lord," Ikil interrupted via the one-way channel into the privacy shield. "The Wendira are moving." He paused. "So are the Mesharom."

She and Pat traded sharp nods of understanding, and she cut the channel.

"What is Adamase doing?" she asked.

"Moving aside," Speaker Han concluded. "They're not moving out of their range, but they're definitely staying out of everybody else's."

"I guess that answers if the Mesharom are eavesdropping on us, doesn't it?" Harriet asked rhetorically. "Stand by for orders from the flag, and keep an eye on all of them."

"Echelon Lord," Piditel spoke up. "We have a wide-band transmission coming from the center star hive. Everyone in the system is going to pick it up."

"Show me."

The image that appeared in the hologram sent a shiver down Harriet's spine. A Warrior-caste Wendira stood straight in the middle, their black and gold wings spread wide. The glittering color of what Harriet knew was a threat display almost overwhelmed the transmission as the extension made the gray-carapaced alien appear four or five times larger than it actually was.

"I am Fleet Commandant Vaiyah," the Wendira introduced themselves. "I am charged by the High Queens of the Grand Swarm to retrieve the ship of the Gods of Light on the world beneath you."

The immense wings beat once, glittering in the light of Vaiyah's command deck as the gesture lifted them momentarily into the air.

"You have fought bravely and my High Queens do not desire war with the Eldest Wyrm nor the Young Swimmers. Stand aside. We will retrieve the Gods of Light's ship and leave. There need be no more bloodshed."

"They are inbound at point five cee, battleships, star intruders and star hives alike," Ikil reported. "It's a full-court press, Echelon Lord. Four hundred million tons of warships."

Vaiyah stared levelly into the screen with both their main eyes and the secondary eyes on their extended eyestalks.

"If you do not stand aside, I will shower the world below with the wreckage of your ships and the blood of your flesh," she concluded matter-of-factly. "We will make what apologies we must to the leaders of the Eldest Wyrm, but that ship will be ours."

The transmission ended and Harriet managed not to audibly sigh. There were many potential responses to that, but she could guess Kas!Val's.

"Bring the Echelon tactical net to full density," she ordered. "Stand by to leave orbit."

Her flag staff looked at her in confusion for a moment, but then Kas!Val's orders began to arrive.

The Imperial force was to move out and confront the Wendira—while also staying between the Mesharom and Hope as much as possible. Several of her staff turned their species' equivalent of hopeful gazes on her, but Harriet simply nodded.

"Make sure everyone has the orders," she told her people. "Make sure the tactical nets are running clean and the divisional formations are in line. This is Echelon Lord Kas!Val's show now, but we can make sure our part goes off without a hitch."

Her people sprang into action. Somewhat delayed, yes, but nothing they would do now was essential. It would improve the survivability of her ships when they finally clashed with the Wendira, but their survivability was going to suck regardless.

"Echelon Lord," Ikil's voice murmured and she looked up to see that the Indiri had crossed the deck to stand right next to her. "*Tornado* hasn't moved. What do we do?"

"*Tornado* is the Duchess's personal transport," Harriet replied, eyeing the icon for Earth's oldest remaining warship. "She's the only ship in this system that isn't under Kas!Val's orders. We do nothing."

One cruiser, however powerful her mix-and-match technologies made her, wasn't going to change what happened here.

"Transmission incoming," Piditel reported. "Wait...that's weird."

"What's weird, Commander?" she asked her com officer.

"It's a tightbeam from the Mesharom to Kas!Val, but we're receiving a copy of the entire communication," the Rekiki told her. "And I'm not sure where it's coming from."

Harriet checked the time stamp. That was...impossible. She was receiving the communication less than a second after Kas!Val's responses were making it back to the Mesharom—and from the completely opposite direction of the Mesharom ships!

"Show me," she ordered.

Her repeater screens now showed two sides of a communication. One was Kas!Val, still looking utterly determined. The other was the four-meter-long caterpillar-like nightmare of a Mesharom.

"I am Interpreter Shialane," the Mesharom began. "You are Echelon Kas!Val. I must, on behalf of my commander, inquire as to your intentions.

"We reached a deal with Duchess Annette Bond, as a representative of your Empress, that the ship of Those Who Came Before would be turned over to us. We agreed to defend this system in exchange for that concession, and handed certain informational and technological gifts in payment.

"You have now ordered your ships to treat us as hostile." Shialane blinked, their legs twitching. They were clearly uncomfortable dealing with aliens, more so than in most video Harriet had seen of Interpreters.

They were also, if Harriet interpreted the brightly colored fuzzy hair covering most of their body correctly, significantly younger than most Interpreters she'd seen video of. At a guess, she was the backup Interpreter—and the main one had already spent too long talking to aliens to be able to continue doing so.

Kas!Val glared at the camera, her own inky black eyes unreadable to Harriet. The green determination of her skin didn't flicker. Whatever decision the A!Tol had made, she was going to see it through.

No matter how stupid it became.

"Duchess Bond had no authority to negotiate on behalf of the Imperium in this matter," she told the Mesharom. "That ship represents a strategic military asset. A civilian like the Duchess has no role in its fate."

Shialane's legs twitched again.

"That was not what our ambassador on A!To was told by your government," the Mesharom said calmly, and Harriet winced.

Of *course* the Mesharom had confirmed whether or not Bond could negotiate with the Empress's government. Kas!Val...wasn't going to believe them, though.

"I have no proof of that," Kas!Val replied, a momentary flash of blue uncertainty flashing across her skin before the solid green returned. "I must protect the assets of my Imperium."

"If the deal will not be honored, then we will not protect this system," Shialane said, their voice level despite their legs visibly spasming in stress. Harriet began to realize the alien's stress had nothing to do with inexperience and everything to do with what they were going to have to say.

"We must now destroy the ship of Those Who Came Before,"

Shialane continued. "Your fleet and the colony must also be destroyed to make certain no data from the ship or that we provided Duchess Bond is distributed.

"Your fate is your own choice, Echelon Lord Kas!Val. You have one fifth-cycle, as you count time, to change your mind."

"The Imperium will not be threatened or intimidated," the A!Tol snapped. "I do not need your time! Withdraw or be destroyed!"

Shialane's legs had stopped spasming and they had closed their eyes. Harriet had very little training in Mesharom body language, but she could recognize sorrow when she saw it.

"Then your choice is made and we will do what we must."

The flag deck aboard *Duchess of Terra* was deathly silent, and Harriet turned her gaze back to the main tactical display. The Mesharom were moving now. All three fleets were moving, converging on a single point in space where the Imperial fleet would die.

They'd take a good chunk of the Wendira with them. Then the Mesharom would finish off the survivors of both fleets and bombard Hope into debris.

"Piditel." Harriet coughed, clearing her throat, then turned to her com officer. "Piditel, can you tell if anyone else got that copy of the message?"

"I *think* we've located the relay that was sending it to us," the Rekiki replied. "But it was tightbeamed, and the relay is only about forty thousand kilometers away. There might be more relays, but I don't think that one was sending it to anyone else."

"What do we do, Echelon Lord?" Ikil asked. "Shall I get Captain Sier on the line?"

"No," Harriet decided. "*We*, Commander Ikil, do our duty and follow our orders. There will be no mutiny today."

She smiled.

"Commander Piditel, however, will forward that recording to *Tornado*. I have faith that Duchess Bond is not out of options yet!"

CHAPTER FORTY-FIVE

ANNETTE WATCHED THE RECORDING TWICE, TO MAKE absolutely certain she understood just what the *hell* was going on.

She'd known the Empress would back her. Apparently, the Mesharom had used their hyperfold communicators to confirm that before they'd listened to her. Kas!Val, however, didn't believe them.

As an A!Tol senior Imperial Navy officer, it was quite likely that Kas!Val was simply unable to believe that her Empress would trust a human that far. Or that any of the member races of the Imperium could see the situation better or more completely than she could.

And in her arrogance, Kas!Val was about to damn the first colony Annette's species had created unless Annette or her people did something.

"Permission to board *A Dawning of Swords* and educate the good Echelon Lord about the niceties of internal Imperium diplomacy?" Wellesley asked calmly from behind her.

"Please, James. I don't think forcefully boarding an Imperial flagship and shooting an Imperial flag officer is going to help Earth's position in the Imperium."

"I wasn't going to shoot her," the General objected.

"Beating her to a pulp would potentially help even less," Annette said dryly. "Time to weapons range?"

Wellesley shook his head.

"If I'm understanding everything right, the Mesharom are in range of the Wendira, but not of the Imperials, and neither the Wendira nor the Imperials are in range of anybody.

"We, of course, are hanging out back here, several million kilometers from anything."

"Hanging out back here with an FTL communicator," she concluded. "Amandine." She tapped a control. "Do we have a way to use the hyperfold communicator to reach the Wendira?"

The Captain coughed.

"We were only given the 'frequencies,' so to speak, for our Mesharom companions," he admitted.

"That wasn't the question," she said mildly.

Amandine chuckled.

"It may just happen that Ki!Tana and I were going over the same transmissions you were, and they, quite subtly, included the identifier for the relay drone the Mesharom used to send their message to Tanaka," he told her. "She believes she can order it to send a wideband transmission that the Imperial fleet will receive in real time."

"And the Wendira?"

"We've been studying the transmitter," Amandine said. "It has an equivalent of a radio's omnidirectional transmission. It's very short-range, relatively speaking, but everyone with a hyperfold transceiver within, oh, ten light-minutes will get the message."

"That would be both the Mesharom and the Wendira. Captain, how long until the fleets open fire?"

"That depends on how close everyone plans on getting," he admitted. "I'd guess about two minutes before the Wendira open fire, the Imperials about thirty seconds after that. Darkness alone knows what the Mesharom are planning."

"They've pushed a whole bunch of buttons that don't involve weapons, Captain, and they're waiting to see what explodes in response," Annette told him. "I'll be on the bridge in sixty. Get that relay and omnidirectional transmission set up."

"What are we telling them?"

"You'll see."

IT TOOK Annette less than the sixty seconds she'd promised Amandine to make it to the bridge, but she could already see things beginning to go downhill.

Tornado was far enough from the action to not have a clear idea of what was going on, but the pulses of active radar, lidar, and even more esoteric particles were clear as day on her scanners. No one was shooting yet, but all three fleets now had each other locked in as they closed toward the range to fire.

"Are we ready?" she asked Amandine as she stepped up beside the command chair.

"Coms are go," he confirmed. "You're on when you say go. What's the plan, Your Grace?"

Annette lifted up a small box with a single button on it, covered by a plastic shield. It was a standard Imperial remote detonator, linked in this case to the cruiser's main communications array.

"We have a chat with everyone," she said calmly. "Put me on."

She stepped in front of the Captain's chair and faced where she knew the main camera was, letting some of both her fear and her anger leak through onto her face as she looked directly at the people she needed to intimidate.

"Fleet Commandant Vaiyah. Interpreter-Captain Adamase. Echelon Lord Kas!Val. You all know who I am," she told them.

"You have all decided, for your own reasons, that the ship on this planet is worth fighting for. Killing for. Dying for.

"I remind you all—but *especially* Kas!Val—that this is *my* world. *My* Centauri Development Corporation owns that rock behind me.

We own that ship—and my Empress charged me to speak for her with regards to it.

"And now, despite everything, you are about to kill each other over it. You will blast each other apart, and whoever is left will take the damn ship and, depending on who it is, blow the colony or even the planet to pieces to cover your tracks.

"I can not permit this to happen."

She smiled.

"I made a deal that the ship would go to the Mesharom. But instead of *trusting* me, you have decided to take the word of an out-of-her-depth Naval officer over mine and decided that Hope must die.

"And Fleet Commandant Vaiyah—you are simply determined to break every law and principle of interstellar relations to get your claws on that ship."

She held the detonator up into camera view.

"I will not permit my people to suffer for your bullshit. The Corellian Plateau has been evacuated and six one-hundred-megaton antimatter charges placed inside the hull of the ship of Those Who Came Before.

"When I push this button, the whole reason for this conflict will be *vaporized*," she told them flatly. "So, this is *my* ultimatum, sentients:

"The instant *any* of you—and I do *not* exempt the Imperial forces from this!—opens fire, I will press the button.

"I'm not one hundred percent certain what that old singularity core will do when the ship is blown to pieces," Annette admitted, "but I will take that risk before I will let you harm my people.

"Stand down. All of you. Or I will blow the only reason we all have to fight to itty-bitty pieces."

TORNADO'S BRIDGE was silent as they waited to see just what the three battle fleets in the system did.

"Huh," the communications officer, a young dark-haired English-woman named Sarah Darcy, exclaimed. "The live feed from the Mesharom just reactivated. We're getting their scan data of the Wendira and Imperial fleets."

Annette considered that for a moment.

"They're more than thirty light-seconds away," she pointed out.

"I know, Your Grace. Tactical, can you confirm?" Darcy asked.

"I'm double-checking, but it looks like Sarah's right," Commander Song said a moment later. The Chinese tactical officer looked just as stunned. "Imperial Fleet is eighty light-seconds from the Mesharom, the Wendira are one hundred and three, so we're not getting live data."

"Any communications from anyone?"

"All fleets have stopped at their current positions," Song said. "No one is retreating, but no one is firing or advancing, either."

"That's progress, at least," Amandine noted. "So..."

"Incoming hyperfold transmission from the Wendira fleet!" Darcy interrupted.

"Show me," Annette ordered. "Can we link a live channel?"

"Yes, Your Grace!"

Fleet Commandant Vaiyah once again filled her screen. This time, Vaiyah's wings were furled, their black and gold blending smoothly into their dark gray carapace and uniform as the Warrior-caste Wendira studied Annette through the screen.

"Your Grace, Annette Bond, Duchess of Terra, Vassal of Empress A!Shall," Vaiyah greeted her smoothly, reeling off Annette's titles with a grace and calm that surprised her.

"It seems we have underestimated the hive wax of the Young Swimmers' latest acquisition. Are you truly prepared to risk the destruction of your colony rather than yield the ship to us?"

The tone was curious, quizzical, and Annette took a moment to check that the translation was occurring on her side. It was an easy-enough trick to force tone in a translation you were providing, but no.

Vaiyah was sending them her unaltered voice, and *Tornado's* computers were translating her tone and words.

"Try me," Annette said dryly. "Of course, even if I don't push the button, you'll have to go through the Imperials and the Mesharom."

"I can do that," Vaiyah stated flatly. "But I cannot, as you clearly understand, prevent you from destroying the ship with bombs. I warn you, child of Terra, that the destruction of the singularity core's containment may well destroy the planet."

"I'll take that risk over watching you 'higher powers' fight over my people," she replied.

Vaiyah's wings rustled, a strange chirping sound like grasshoppers on a spring evening.

"I have tested the wax of your hive, child of Terra," they said calmly. "I have fought your warriors and I look into the eyes of their leader, and I do not question your resolve."

The Wendira bowed slowly.

"I will not challenge the Eldest Wyrm for a prize I cannot attain," Vaiyah told Annette. "You are victorious, Vassal of the A!Tol. The Grand Swarm will withdraw. Today.

"Do not doubt there may well be consequences in the future," the alien warned, "but I have...faith in the strength of your hive, Duchess."

The transmission cut off.

Annette stared at the space where the winged alien had stood for several moments.

"Please tell me they're moving," she finally said.

"Hold on one, Your Grace," Song replied. "Checking the feeds from the Mesharom...yes, the Wendira are withdrawing at point three cee and recovering their starfighters. They are leaving."

Annette exhaled deeply.

"One down," she announced. "Get me a channel to Kas!Val. I suspect that conversation is going to be *much* less easy."

THERE WAS A REASON, apparently, that the A!Tol Echelon Lord hadn't already reached out to yell at Annette. *A Dawning of Swords'* communication team connected Annette instantly with the Imperial flag officer...but Kas!Val wasn't being particularly coherent.

She was bright orange with rage, a hue that Annette had *never* seen on an A!Tol before, and the spew of clicks and hisses she made at the screen for the few seconds was completely untranslatable. Either Kas!Val was speaking a dialect that hadn't been programmed into the translator—which was at least theoretically possible—or she wasn't actually *speaking* at all.

"You will be flayed alive for treason," she finally got out coherently in the middle of a stream of beak snaps. "We will rip your children from your body and feed them to worms. You will *suffer* for this betrayal!"

Annette's hands instinctively covered her stomach protectively, and the last of her willingness to play nice with the A!Tol officer vaporized in a single moment of incandescent rage.

"*I am a Duchess of the Imperium!*" she snapped, the force of her words finally bringing Kas!Val to silence. "To threaten me *is* treason. We can add that to list of reasons you are an incompetent fool.

"You have defied my instructions, broken the deal I brokered for peace, and betrayed your oaths to our Empress," Annette laid out flatly. "You have a choice, now, Echelon Lord Kas!Val.

"You can accept, as everyone else has done, that Empress A!Shall charged me to negotiate for the fate of the ship of Those Who Came Before and to do whatever I thought was necessary to protect the citizens of both Terra and Imperium.

"Or you can accept, if nothing else, that I am prepared to blow the artifact to *hell* rather than let you ruin the deal I made," Annette told her.

"In either case, your threats have crossed a tide that the Imperium *cannot* permit to be swum," she continued. "You can either surrender your command back to Echelon Lord Tanaka and place yourself under arrest in your quarters, or I will have my Guard board your ship and do so by force."

"I will do no such thing!" Kas!Val snapped. "You are the traitor here, you filthy primitive imitating your betters. You have no concept of the pride of Imperium, to surrender so easily. I will see you arrested, tortured, you will *suf*—"

"*Enough.*"

One of the advantages of the massive, barrel-like chests of an Anbrai male was just how much air they could suck in for a bellow. Even across the radio channel, Annette barely managed not to recoil as the senior of Kas!Val's two bodyguards, an Anbrai Imperial Marine that towered over his charge, cut her off.

The immense four-legged bodyguard wore commando power armor, augmenting his already-immense strength as he reached in and grabbed Kas!Val's bullet-shaped torso in two massive hands.

"Your words are treason," the bodyguard ground out. "The Duchess offered you mercy but you are blind. You are under arrest."

A Dawning of Swords' flag deck was now silent as the two Imperial Marines, towering over the two-meter-tall A!Tol, snapped chains onto her manipulator tentacles and bound her.

The image flickered and the channel shifted to *Dawning's* bridge. A second A!Tol, her skin purple and black with stress and fear, faced the camera levelly with her black eyes.

"I am Captain Ivash!," she told Annette. "We have transferred command authority back to *Duchess of Terra.*" Her tentacles fluttered uncertainly. "The Echelon Lord has the authority to do many things, but she is not permitted to threaten a Duchess.

"On behalf of the Imperial Navy, I offer our apologies. But..." Ivash!'s tentacles fluttered. "We would prefer if the ship were not to leave the system until Fleet Lord Tan!Shallegh arrives."

"Now, *that*, Captain Ivash!, is reasonable," Annette agreed. "I will speak with the Mesharom, but I think I can convince them to agree to that."

If nothing else, she still had the button.

THE TWO MESHAROM warships remained in position, floating inside their own range of the Imperial and Terran fleet but well outside the defenders' range of the battlecruisers. It was probably only Annette's imagination that their attention was focused on the withdrawing Wendira and the presence of the Imperial fleet was an afterthought.

The aliens were still forwarding *Tornado* live sensor data on every ship in the system, demonstrating the existence of stealth drones *nobody* was picking up as they kept real-time data on the rapidly retreating Wendira fleet.

"Star hives are opening a hyper portal," Song announced. "And... they're gone. There's just us and the Mesharom left."

"All right," Annette said with a sigh. "Get me a hyperfold link to the Mesharom. Interpreter-Captain Adamase, preferably."

She wasn't entirely certain that Adamase commanded the Mesharom force, though it seemed likely. What she was certain of was that the final-bearer was the senior Interpreter in the force and the most able to speak for their government.

They had to be an unusually strong-willed Mesharom, at that. Few Interpreters ever held command of a starship, as talking to aliens was a major emotional and physical drain for even the Mesharom insane enough—by their standards—to do it.

It took several moments, but she recognized Adamase when the Mesharom came onto the screen. It was hard to read body language across species, but Adamase looked shattered. Their eyes were half-closed and their limbs limp.

But nonetheless, Adamase was upright and facing her.

"Duchess Bond. We have allowed you time to resolve the situation to your satisfaction, and we are prepared to place our trust in your word. Will you be honoring the deal we made?"

"I doubt I need to explain, Interpreter-Captain, that I am furious with you right now," she said. "You threatened my people and a world under my protection, and immediately attempted to carry out that threat when you thought our deal was even challenged.

"Why should I trust that *you* will honor the deal now?"

"We had no reason to believe that Kas!Val did not have the authority to override you," Adamase replied. "We have learned not to rely on the statements of the younger races."

"And Ki!Tana's statements?" Annette asked softly. "Have you learned to ignore *her* promises?"

"Ki!Tana is a special case," the Mesharom agreed. "That is why we...tested the situation."

"Manipulated me, you mean," she snapped. "Forced us into a position where we had to challenge the Imperium, risked my planet's —*my species'*—safety."

"You know why."

"I do. And I think your entire race is mad," Annette said softly. "And I will not permit you to drag my species down with you."

Adamase bent forward, reducing their height almost in half as the alien seemed to slump.

"Will you then dishonor our deal?"

"You'd be almost as happy if I blew the damn ship up," she replied. "Wouldn't you?"

"The risk to the planet is not...insignificant if that happens," the Mesharom told her. "We gave you what we promised in payment. It would be better for everyone if we simply took the ship and left."

"Once Tan!Shallegh has arrived and confirmed my authority for those who are...uncertain," Annette said slowly. "Then. Then you will be permitted to take the ship.

"Can you wait that long?"

"Assuming average currents between Kimar and here, Fleet Lord Tan!Shallegh is four point three cycles away, as the A!Tol measure such things," Adamase told her. The alien paused, considering.

"This condition is acceptable, but be warned that the presence of Tan!Shallegh's fleet means any argument on his part would require...

extreme measures on ours to make certain the ship of Those Who Came Before is destroyed."

"You have my word, Interpreter-Captain, that the ship will either leave with you or be destroyed," Annette said firmly. "Is that sufficient for you?"

Adamase considered for several more seconds.

"Yes," they said. "Yes, Duchess Bond, you have proven your word worthy of weight."

CHAPTER FORTY-SIX

PORTAL AFTER PORTAL TORE OPEN THE SKIES ABOVE HOPE AND starship after starship emerged. First a handful. Then a dozen. Then hundreds.

Ten full squadrons of capital ships, a hundred and sixty behemoths of the void, led the way. Twenty squadrons of cruisers screened them, and another twenty squadrons of destroyers danced through the bigger ships and escorted the two hundred colliers and freighters the Imperium's newly designated Eleventh Fleet needed to keep those ships operational.

The very tip of the spear, the force that emerged half-expecting to have to fight for its life to cover the rest of the fleet from the Wendira or the Laians, was a solid echelon of forty-eight super-battleships that emerged in a single portal.

All forty-eight were *Majesty*-class or *Glorious*-class ships, fully upgraded at the new yards in Sol. They represented half of the *Majesties* in the Navy and the single most powerful three-squadron formation the A!Tol had.

They spread out, guarding the emergence point as the rest of the fleet returned to normal space and took up formations into a shield over a thousand ships strong.

This was how the Imperium kept its oaths. If Hope had fallen to the Wendira or the Laians or even the Mesharom, if an occupying force had laid its boot on the necks of Annette's people, *this* force would have been the answer.

"We have a channel request from Fleet Lord Tan!Shallegh for you, Your Grace," Darcy told Annette.

"I'll take it in the flag office," Annette replied. "Keep an eye on things for me, Cole," she told *Tornado*'s Captain. "Ki!Tana, you're with me."

ANNETTE BOND TOOK an exhausted seat in the office. Four days had passed since the Wendira had abandoned the system, leaving her alone with her people and the Mesharom. The galaxy's elders were waiting patiently, but she shuddered to think what might happen if they *stopped* being patient.

The image of Tan!Shallegh, small for his race but bearing the golden swords of his rank on his harness, appeared on the holographic display in the office. His skin was a whirling, chaotic mess of purple and black and blue—worries and questions, but a flush of red pleasure swept through as he saw the two waiting for him.

"Duchess Bond. Lady Ki!Tana," he greeted them, bowing his entire torso in respect to Annette's companion. This was as close as he would ever come to meeting a Ki!Tol—it was actively dangerous for all involved for a male A!Tol to be in the presence of one of the females who had passed through the birthing madness.

"I see that Hope is still here, but not without price," he concluded. "I have already received a long pre-recorded message from Echelon Lord Kas!Val and a much shorter report from Echelon Lord Tanaka.

"You have, as usual, created a tidal swell of trouble—and an attendant solution."

"I do what I must," Annette told him. "We made a deal with the Mesharom. The alternative was they blew up Hope."

"I...expected something along those lines, yes," he admitted. "What was the deal, Your Grace?"

"In exchange for defense against the Laians and Wendira until the ship could be removed, and certain technological data, we gave them the ship. Echelon Lord Kas!Val objected."

"I can see why she would," Tan!Shallegh said. "But I am aware of my mother's sister's instructions to you. The decision to yield the ship was well within your authority—and Harriet's report makes *very* clear how dark a tide Kas!Val rode."

"It was not my intent to challenge Imperial authority."

"And you did not," the Fleet Lord told her. "Kas!Val denied the authority the Empress granted you. *She* challenged Imperial authority, not you. I spoke with A!Shall before I left Kimar. I am quite certain of our Empress's desires in this matter, and I unhesitatingly support your deal."

He paused.

"What technology did they offer us?"

"Folded hyperspace communications," she told him. "What they've given us is an instantaneous communicator with a forty-light-year range. Combined with relays and the existing starcom network..."

"So, that is the answer to the communication mobility problem," Tan!Shallegh concluded. "We were swimming in the wrong ocean!"

"Exactly," Annette confirmed. "The device is not man-portable, but it is easily retrofitted into any existing ship. While the Mesharom refused to trade weapons technology, they *did* let us know several ways that the hyperfold *can't* be used as a weapon."

Tan!Shallegh flashed blue, an A!Tol nod.

"Currents to lead us down the right path," he replied.

"We have detailed sensor information on the Laians use of a

hyperfold-based beam weapon," she told him. "Combined with the Mesharom's hints, I think—"

The Fleet Lord held up a tentacle to interrupt her.

"That, Duchess Bond, is a conversation that I think you and I and...yes, both Tanaka and Villeneuve should have soon—but later. And in person.

"For now, please reach out to our new friends in the terrifying, powerful battlecruisers and tell them they can take their prize," he concluded. "I think everyone, including them, will be happier when both they and that ship are gone."

"Of course, Fleet Lord."

HAROLD ROLFSON STOOD on the observation deck of the super-battleship *Empereur de France*, watching a screen showing the cleared ground that had held the dig site around the strange alien ship.

Ramona Wolastoq stood next to him, her hand tucked into his as they watched the two Mesharom battlecruisers descend over the ship they'd spent so much effort finding and investigating. The massive white shapes hung motionless over the Corellian Plateau for several minutes, and then, with no apparent action on the battlecruisers' part, the Precursor ship rose off the ground.

The wedge-shaped vessel moved into the air to hang suspended between the two white ships. For a moment after that, nothing happened, then one of the Mesharom ships moved. A gap opened in its white hull, matching the ancient scout ship in size and then swallowing the artifact.

The Mesharom hull closed behind it and it was all over. The ship that had been the cause of so much bloodshed, so much violence, was gone.

The two battlecruisers lifted smoothly out of Hope's atmosphere, then blasted away from Hope at over half of lightspeed.

They vanished into hyperspace, and he felt Ramona sigh next to him.

"Not how I hoped for my first investigation into an ancient alien ship to end," she admitted.

"No," he agreed. He slipped his hand out of hers and wrapped his arm around her waist instead, guiding her close to him. "It wasn't all bad, though."

"No," she said, smiling up at him. Something buzzed and she pulled out her communicator, reading a message from the staff at New Hope City.

"Damn. I can't say I'm surprised, but damn them," she murmured.

"What happened?"

"Our databases and records of the whole dig have been wiped," Ramona explained. "Someone—only one guess who!—accessed our computer systems and deleted all of our files." She sighed. "Hashed, wiped, overwritten with garbage data, the works.

"Backups, too."

"What about the hull samples?" he asked. "And the second copy I asked you to hide?"

"Let me check."

She tapped a code onto the device then held it up to her ear.

"Yes, Karl. What happened to the hull samples?" She paused. "Well, go check!"

A minute or so passed and then she nodded.

"Damn them," she repeated, but there was no energy to her tone. "Thank you, Karl."

She closed the communicator and leaned into Harold, looking out over the world below.

"The containers were climate-controlled," she half-whispered. "They accessed the controls and raised the temperature to the point where the container self-destructed. The containers, the samples, and everything within about two meters is ashes and debris."

"Damn. They are *thorough*," Harold agreed. He pulled out his own communicator and tapped in a code.

"Commander Arwen," he greeted the woman who ran security for *Emperor of China*. "Can you check your black-box security for me? Is everything still intact?"

"It's a bloody sealed Faraday cage, Captain. What do you *expect*?" Arwen replied.

"When dealing with these players, Commander, I expect the impossible. Check the damn box."

She stepped away for several seconds, then returned.

"Chief Williamson is standing guard over it," she told him. "There have been no security breaches, physical or digital. I had him open the damn thing to be sure."

"And everything is intact?"

"Disks and your weird sample, yes. It's all there."

"Thank you, Commander. You've done the Imperium a bigger favor than you realize. Guard that box with your lives."

"Aye, sir."

Harold closed the communicator and turned a brilliant smile on his new lover.

"How do you feel about top-secret projects, my dear Ramona?" he asked. "While I don't think we'll be able to *admit* we saved anything..."

"You took another copy of everything," she accused.

"And a third sample of the hull. And locked them in a black box aboard *Emperor* before the Mesharom even arrived," he confirmed. "It's going to get locked at the bottom of a black hole somewhere, but we've got it all.

"So, if you're okay with not publishing anything..."

He didn't get any further before she shut him up with a deep kiss.

CHAPTER FORTY-SEVEN

Harriet Tanaka had expected to be escorted to Fleet Lord Tan!Shallegh's office aboard the super-battleship *Glory of Hearts*. She was surprised to instead be led through a series of security doors, deep into the heart of the capital ship.

She recognized a *Glorious*-class super-battleship's secure conference room from the outside, but *Glory of Hearts'* security went far beyond what *Duchess of Terra* had aboard. She had to surrender her communicator, and even her normal translator earbud was replaced with a specialty version with no wireless capability.

Unless she missed her guess, she'd now been led into the third of three nested Faraday cages. No electronic signal was going to make its way into or out of this room. The tiny conference room at the center of that multi-layered security was big enough for maybe ten humans or six A!Tol.

It currently held only Tan!Shallegh. He waved a tentacle, gesturing Harriet to a seat.

"I have reviewed everyone's reports of the Battle of Alpha Centauri," he told her. "Including Echelon Lord Kas!Val's."

"I see, sir," she said as levelly as she could.

"I should note that Kas!Val was quite complimentary to you," Tan!Shallegh continued. "Such things are, of course, relative to the rest of her ravings."

"What will happen to her?" Harriet asked.

"She will retire," he said firmly. "Her actions were not outside of her technical authority but were significantly outside of her given area of responsibility.

"Her Grace, Duchess Bond, has declined to enforce the penalties for Kas!Val's threats to her, but we cannot let her errors and...unwise statements stand. She had been given the option of resignation, a politically safe choice for us all."

"And she took it?"

"I made quite clear that the alternative was to drag out every action she had made, every threat she had uttered, and drown her family name in the mud of the deepest trenches," Tan!Shallegh said softly. "Her Grace may forgive Kas!Val's indiscretions. *I* do not.

"She had no right to take away command from you and no grounds to deny Duchess Bond's authority from the Empress. Allowing her to retire is more mercy than I would give her by choice," he concluded.

Harriet let that lie in the silence. It seemed harsh to her, but she wasn't one of the senior officers responsible for keeping the Imperial Navy functioning.

"As for you," he finally continued, "you did well. I know it isn't easy to think that after your losses, but you faced utterly over-whelming force, Echelon Lord. If you hadn't just been promoted, I'd be making you a Squadron Lord right now.

"As it is, you should expect new insignia before the long-cycle is up," he noted. "You have done *very* well. Which means, of course, I have a new task for you."

"That is the nature of things," she agreed. "What do you need of me?"

"We are waiting on two more," Tan!Shallegh told her. "This conversation shall be...fascinating."

ANNETTE AND VILLENEUVE made it through the layers of security aboard *Glory of Hearts* slowly, growing more and more hesitant as the briskly polite and respectful officers—all power-armored A!Tol aboard this ship—took away all of their electronics and gave them new translators.

Then they passed through a Faraday cage. And another. Until they finally entered the secured conference room at nearly the exact center of the immense warship, to find Fleet Lord Tan!Shallegh and Echelon Lord Tanaka waiting for them.

"Annette, Jean," Tan!Shallegh greeted them cheerfully. "Please, have a seat. There are refreshments in the side cupboard. We'll be serving ourselves, I'm afraid. For most official purposes, much of this meeting will never have happened."

Annette was taken aback but opened up the side board and poured fresh tea for all three humans.

"What's going on, Tan!Shallegh?" she asked.

"Secrets," he replied, still cheerful. "Problems. Solutions. Sit down and drink your tea, Your Grace. I have questions for you, first of all."

Annette obeyed, waiting to see what the being who'd once conquered Earth had in mind.

"The Duchy of Terra has proven a valuable member of the Imperium," he told them. "For all the trouble you've caused us, you've been more than worth it." Manipulator tentacles flickered at the warship around them.

"*Glory of Hearts* is vastly more survivable, having passed through your hands, for example. The influence of your world will likely turn the tide of the next war with the Kanzi—if the upgrades aren't simply intimidating enough to prevent any such war."

"But for all of that, you remain a quiet backwater. One that has drawn far too much attention...but I don't think that will repeat now."

"I hope not," Annette told him. "I'll be happy for Terra to be a quiet backwater out of everyone's sight."

"So will the Imperium. Tell me, Admiral Villeneuve, did you successfully keep copies of the research data from the scout ship?"

Annette glanced at her Admiral, who looked uncomfortable.

"Jean. I don't think this is the kind of meeting where we want to be keeping secrets," she told him gently. "I think this is an all-cards-on-the-table kind of game."

Villeneuve chuckled.

"*Oui*," he agreed slowly. "Yes, Fleet Lord, we did. Captain Rolfson arranged for a copy to be sealed inside *Emperor of China*'s black-box security, inside a Faraday cage and under armed guard.

"He also saved a sample of the nanomatrix hull material."

"Excellent!" Tan!Shallegh's skin flushed red. "That's even better than I'd hoped. And this...folded-hyperspace system the Mesharom gave you, Annette. It's a communication device, correct?"

"Yes. They also gave us some hints as to how to make it a weapon," she confirmed. "Mostly by pointing out likely false starts that wouldn't work."

"That sounds like them," Tan!Shallegh agreed. "I think we will want to roll out the *communications* side of it rapidly, across the Imperium. That's what the Mesharom will expect. The weapons side of it..."

"Should probably be researched at one of the Imperium's most carefully guarded research facilities," Annette said carefully.

"Indeed," the A!Tol said. "Tell me, Your Grace, how much sensor information did your people retrieve from this battle?"

"We have Alpha Centauri wired six ways to Sunday," she admitted. "We're busy surveying the system for extraction purposes, but those probes were piggybacked with military sensors being run from the AB2 outpost."

"So, you have detailed scan data on both the Laians' hyperfold projectors and the Mesharom hyper missiles?"

"And the Mesharom hyperfold projectors and tachyon scanners," she confirmed instantly. "Plus detailed scans of the star intruders' stealth fields and the starfighter interface drives."

"I presume you planned to hand a copy of all of that information over to BugWorks Two?" Tan!Shallegh asked.

Even intending to put all of her cards on the table, she found that the confirmation that the Imperium *knew* about the Duchy's absolute top-secret research facility was a shock.

"We did," she confirmed levelly.

"Is BugWorks still hidden in hyperspace?" the Fleet Lord asked.

"Not anymore," she told him unhesitatingly. "High atmosphere of Jupiter this time, protected by an extremely powerful energy shield that holds the pressure at bay. She's structured to be able to flip into hyperspace to protect herself, but it's a one-shot deal. She'd have to be towed away from Jupiter's gravity and taken through a portal generated by a starship to return to normal space."

"Clever," Tan!Shallegh agreed. "We knew it existed, but not where it was. You managed to hide it from *us*, Duchess Bond, and we knew you were building it.

"We see great value in that facility. We want to augment it," he told her.

"What are you thinking?" she asked carefully.

"We have samples of Core Power technology acquired over the years that we cannot publicly research. Even many of our secret facilities we are quite certain are compromised to one degree or another.

"But we can move researchers and samples and data to Sol relatively quietly. Deliver them to your secret base and build a research program the galaxy knows nothing about. One that will create an entire new generation of Imperial starship.

"One that can go blade-to-blade with the Core Powers."

"We would have to surrender control of BugWorks, I presume," Annette said quietly.

"It will be a joint project, I think," he replied. "The initial samples worked up as Militia units. No one pays that much attention to Militia, not without a reason—and even the Laians really no longer have a reason to be watching you.

"No, Your Grace, I think the Duchy of Terra and the Imperium will work together on this project."

"We'll need to change the name," Villeneuve mused aloud. "Bug-Works Two won't work for such a completely different scale of project."

"Harriet? Any suggestions?" Tan!Shallegh asked, clearly taking the Admiral's comment as agreement.

"Why ask me?" she replied.

"Because you are going to be responsible for this new project's physical security," he told her. "You will command the guard detachment we're going to hide in Jupiter, and run the convoy escorts that will make certain everything arrives safely.

"The Imperium, after all, must have its tentacles deep in these waters for this plan to work."

"I see."

Tanaka looked around the room, meeting Annette's gaze and sharing a nod.

"We will make our Duchy and our Imperium great, I see," she said softly. "For us. For our children."

Tanaka was a mother, with two children left behind on Earth with her husband. A posting to defend the research facility would let her actually spend time with them—and her words sent Annette's hands to her own stomach. Soon, she would have heirs—and protecting the Duchy's future had never seemed so important.

"I think there's only one name left we can use without it seeming unworthy of the cause," Tanaka continued. "I suggest we call this new project DragonWorks."

The story of the A!Tol Imperium and the Duchy of Terra will continue in the Darkness Beyond *trilogy, starting in 2018*

ABOUT THE AUTHOR

Glynn Stewart is the author of *Starship's Mage*, a bestselling science fiction and fantasy series where faster-than-light travel is possible but only because of magic. His other works include science fiction series *Duchy of Terra, Castle Federation* and *Vigilante,* as well as the urban fantasy series *ONSET* and *Changeling Blood.*

Writing managed to liberate Glynn from a bleak future as an accountant. With his personality and hope for a high-tech future intact, he lives in Kitchener, Ontario with his wife, their cats, and an unstoppable writing habit.

facebook.com/glynnstewartauthor

twitter.com/glynnstewart

OTHER BOOKS BY GLYNN STEWART

For release announcements join the mailing list or visit GlynnStewart.com

Duchy of Terra

The Terran Privateer

Duchess of Terra

Terra and Imperium

Light of Terra: A Duchy of Terra series

Darkness Beyond (upcoming)

Starship's Mage

Starship's Mage

Hand of Mars

Voice of Mars

Alien Arcana

Judgment of Mars

UnArcana Stars (upcoming)

Starship's Mage: Red Falcon

Interstellar Mage

Mage-Provocateur

Agents of Mars

Castle Federation

Noble's Honor (upcoming)

Fantasy Stand Alone Novels
Children of Prophecy
City in the Sky